FIRST WATCH OF NIGHT

FIRST WATCH OF NIGHT

ICARUS CODE BOOK TWO

RYSA WALKER

STARRY NIGHT BOOKS

For Griffin, who has been with me in the study for nearly every keystroke. Here's hoping for many more happy years with my writing buddy.

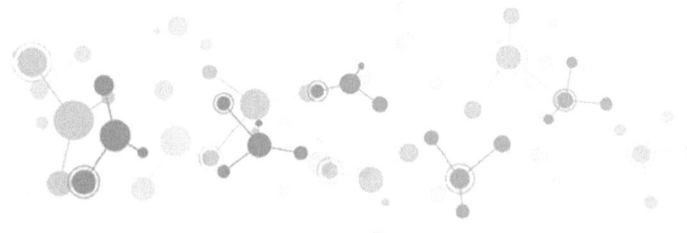

There is no light in earth or heaven
But the cold light of stars;
And the first watch of night is given
To the red planet Mars.

~ Henry Wadsworth Longfellow, "The Light of Stars" (1843)

———

All the suns—are these but symbols of innumerable man,
Man or Mind that sees a shadow of the planner or the plan?
Is there evil but on earth? or pain in every peopled sphere?
Well, be grateful for the sounding watchword Evolution here,
Evolution ever climbing after some ideal good,
And Reversion ever dragging evolution in the mud.
What are men that He should heed us? cried the king of sacred song;
Insects of an hour, that hourly work their brother insect wrong,
While the silent heavens roll, and suns along their fiery way,
All their planets whirling round them, flash a million miles a day.

~ *Alfred, Lord Tennyson, "Locksley Hall Sixty Years After" (1886)*

CONTENTS

PART II

PART I

FROM THE JOURNAL
OF EBERIN DAS

07.13.508

THE OTHERS WILL CLAIM that they saw this coming. They will shake their heads at the next gathering, assuming there's still time for one, and tell each other that I've always been odd. A bit off-center. Always had that morbid streak, that bizarre obsession with the terminals. [*Direct translation: time limited.*]

It's a fair point, I suppose. Among our cohort, I was the only one who sought out people on the verge of death during training. It was for a research project, but I was the one who selected the topic. And my interest in terminality continued well after the project ended.

Still, I would assert that it was the Academy that started me on that path. In all of my [*ages? iterations?*] before I volunteered for this assignment, I had never been especially intrigued by terminals. My interest in them was piqued by what I believed—by what I still believe—to be a serious gap in our preparation for this job.

For my project at the Academy, I spoke with fourteen people in total who were on the verge of death. Ten were voluntary terminals preparing to die, as I will, by their own hand. I kept tabs on them during my last year at the Academy, and six had died by the time I left.

To be honest, I barely remember anything about the individuals in that group. They were the easiest to locate and quite willing to talk, but they weren't as relevant to the questions I wanted to answer. Death was a choice, not something that had been forced upon them. I was far more interested in those who had *no* choice, since I would be living and working among them here, which is probably why my clearest memories are of the four remaining terminals in my study. One of those interviews was rather short because the man was in considerable pain when we spoke. He was one of three in my study who had suffered a serious injury and then discovered that they were part of the small, unfortunate group whose bodies reject regenerated organs.

The final, and for my purposes the most interesting subject was a member of the even smaller group whose bodies reject [*from context: perhaps a drug or medical procedure?*]. After her diagnosis, she chose to join a community with five other terminals. All but one of them had died by the time I interviewed her, but three others who had joined were still healthy.

I interviewed those other members, too, even though they weren't on the verge of death and therefore didn't fit the parameters of my project. Their experience was, however, closest to that of the people among whom I would eventually be living. Not identical, since they did not learn of their limited existence until adulthood, while here everyone knows from childhood on that they, like all the generations before them, will grow old, weaken, and eventually die.

All these [*ages? iterations?*] later, I can still picture the reaction of my instructor when she realized I had not only interviewed all of these people but had done so in person. That look of distaste. That small step backward, as if I might have somehow contracted the ill-fortune I'd witnessed, might be passing it along to her at that very moment. It was a brief and oddly feral look, quickly masked by the admonition that I should have restricted my research to the official archives of final statements, and the observation that I had most likely violated the Academy's strict rules on privacy.

I assured her that my subjects had been willing participants. And since there were signed statements to that effect in the report, the matter was dropped without further action. It was clear from their statements that none of my subjects, even the one who was in pain, viewed our discussion as an intrusion. They had been more than simply willing to talk. They had been eager. Unlike my instructor and those who designed our curriculum, they understood why I believed their stories were vital to my training.

If you are going to live among people who have not yet conquered death, you need to understand it. You need some comprehension of how their lives are shaped by the knowledge that death waits not just for them but for those they love. The vast majority of my people can no longer comprehend the role that death—the fear of it, the inevitability of it, the universality of it—plays in a terminal culture because we have excised death from our own lives.

Except, of course, for those of us who are tasked with delivering it.

(Confidence interval: 87.2%)

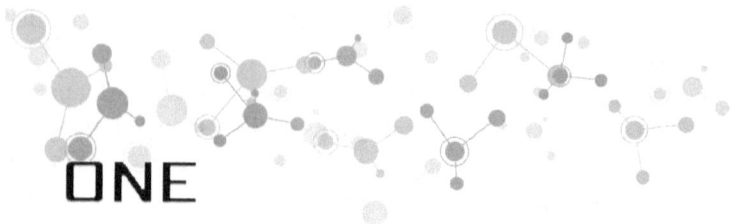

ONE

CLAIRE OPENED the weekend bag and stashed her daypack inside, hoping to minimize the number of things she'd have to keep up with on the train. It was a tight fit, but she managed to get it zipped again and was just about to head downstairs when the drone detector vibrated inside her pocket. At almost the same instant, her phone sounded the alarm.

Another one.

If the thing had shown up ten minutes later, her car would have already arrived, and she'd be on her way to the station. Twenty minutes later, and she would have been on the hyperloop heading north.

Claire sighed, flipping the still-buzzing device to jamming mode. She then stretched her phone screen out to its max and pulled up a view of her front lawn. Quickly scanning, she spotted the thing hovering about a meter above and just to the right of the trash cans she dragged out to the curb the previous night.

She zoomed in. It was a little larger than the last one—about the size of a cicada—but still well under the legal limit.

After Tobias Shepherd's close call with an insect-like nanodrone onboard the *Ares Prime* and being tailed by a similar bugbot in Daedalus City, Claire hadn't been inclined to take chances when she got back from Mars. She'd snapped up three top-of-the-line, perfectly legal (but easily modified) drone blockers from her security service. The first two, one for her and the other for her housemate Rowan, had been thoroughly tweaked by Wyatt's friend Kes. The souped-up version still repelled the bugbots. But, a quick triple-press of the silence button sent a kill signal, dropping the drone to the ground and some-times, if she was lucky, frying it entirely.

The kill signal was technically illegal. While Maryland law allowed you to block drones from trespassing on property you owned or leased, or from coming within one meter of your phys-ical person, you weren't supposed to disable or destroy them. The law was generally ignored, however, if the drone crossed onto your turf. That went double if it was unlicensed.

Only one unlicensed drone ventured onto Claire's property in the first few months after her return from Mars, and the package it carried wouldn't have been lethal unless the recipient had danger-ously clogged arteries. Fortunately, there were no worries that the fast-food joint might complain about her security system bringing it down. Any company that cut corners by using secondhand, unregistered delivery drones *and* flying them too low over private property wasn't going to risk filing a report, especially when older models crashed so often on their own. Claire made a note to ask Kes to adjust the size parameters on the system to prevent a repeat occurrence, then she dragged out a ladder to clear the wreckage from the roof. Ten minutes spent scooping French fries out of her gutters almost convinced her that Ro was right—maybe her security precautions *were* a bit over the top.

Then, a little over a week earlier, everything changed. The FBI field office in Baltimore called Claire to come in and give a more detailed accounting of the attack at Icarus Camp that killed two members of the Martian research team she was on and very nearly killed Claire herself. She had given the agent a brief statement about the bombing, orchestrated by the Earth Watch Alliance – better known as the Flock – shortly after her return. Now, several months later, it appeared they had finally decided the attack merited an official investigation instead of being swept under the rug.

The Flock certainly didn't have the sort of political connections to make the government ignore the case, but their interests lined up nicely with those of people who *did* have that sort of influence.

Anyone with investments on Mars had a strong incentive to make the entire thing disappear. Claire placed Anton Kolya first and foremost in that group since Stasia Ljubic, one of Kolya Terraforming's top executives, and two other KTI employees had been implicated in the attacks.

Learning that his ex-wife was now going under the name Corbin Drexel and that she was the new leader of the Flock would have made Kolya even more eager to have the entire thing forgotten as quickly as possible. Negative publicity like that wasn't good for tourism or investment, and Kolya was counting on both of those increasing exponentially after the current planetwide lockdown for stage six of the terraforming project ended in a few months. He'd given one interview in which he renounced Drexel firmly, saying that they had parted on friendly terms and that, while he had no cause to doubt the preliminary findings that the Flock was behind the attack, he found it hard to reconcile the kind-hearted woman he'd married to the sort of person who would condone, let alone order, such a heinous act.

When Claire asked Andrew West, the agent who interviewed her, about the delay in investigating the bombing, he'd waved a dismissive hand and blamed it on the bureaucracy, claiming it had taken a while for the authorities to sort out who had jurisdiction to launch the investigation. And then they had to determine which office would be heading it up. Not only had the attacks taken place on a planet that was in the process of setting up its own government, but the deceased were from four different countries on Earth and three different states within the US. In addition, aside from Claire, all of the injured survivors were still on Mars, working for mining companies connected to KTI—or rather, waiting out the lockdown so that they could continue their work. If the fine print in their contracts didn't outright prohibit them from suing, it at least highly discouraged it.

She didn't doubt that it was a bureaucratic quagmire, and the delay might have seemed plausible if not for the timing. It just didn't feel like coincidence that the FBI insisted that she come into their office in Baltimore ASAP to give a full statement a mere two days after a story on the Flock appeared under Wyatt Garcia's byline in the *Atlantic Post.*

The article that jump-started the FBI's newfound investigative fervor included several new images showing Drexel with Stasia and her two co-conspirators in the Mars bombings. Those pictures were taken both at the Culpeper compound near DC and, much more recently, at a compound in rural Ohio. Wyatt had held off publication until he had at least a few bits of information that weren't gathered in Culpeper since that was where his whistle-blower worked. Devin (last name Shepherd, like all of the Flock) was still Wyatt's only source inside the organization, so he'd been reluctant to publish until he could provide the guy with some cover.

Wyatt had almost certainly obtained the Ohio images with an illegal nanodrone very much like the one currently buzzing around in Claire's cul-de-sac. She didn't know for certain, because he'd been working out of town on another investigation since the story dropped, and they'd had no time to discuss anything face-to-face. That was one reason she was staying overnight in New York rather than going straight to Boston, where she was meeting with her brother and his research partner Beck for a long-deferred discussion about what they were going to do with the manuscript they'd found encoded in the samples she brought back from Mars.

Any doubts Claire might have had about the need for height-ened home security had vanished as soon as she returned from the FBI field office. A drone set off the perimeter alert before she'd even gotten her shoes off, and six more had popped in for a visit over the next twenty-four hours. She managed to take down three of them with the blocker that Kes had turned into a bugbot zapper, but the Flock had kept them coming every day since, varying the schedule for maximum harassment. Some days, her perimeter alert went off every few hours. Other days, just once or twice. A drone would zoom inside the property line long enough to set off the detector, then zip back into the cul-de-sac, hovering just out of legal range.

Apex Security, a company Claire paid well enough that they weren't inclined to question the number of drones that had "accidentally crashed" on her lawn in the past ten days, had examined each of them and assured her that they weren't carrying neurotoxins. They also claimed that the devices couldn't collect any information from her communications or from conversations inside the house, thanks to the scramblers she'd had them set up on the exterior of the building. And as long as she kept the window shades drawn, the only visual intel they were getting was when people left and entered the house. The company's security report also included a gentle reminder that while they would, of course, continue to collect any devices that "accidentally crashed" on her lawn in the future, they would be unable to retrieve any that crashed in the cul-de-sac.

When Claire reported the situation to Agent West at the FBI, he said that unless she had proof that the drones were connected to the Flock, it was a matter for local law enforcement. It could just be kids pranking her, especially given the initial flurry of media attention surrounding the discovery of the buried chambers, the bombing, and the bugbots that had been used to knock out some of the security guards both at Icarus Camp and at Daedalus Station.

When she followed West's advice and contacted the local police, they had agreed that it might be a prank, and said they'd keep an eye out. If it was in any way connected to what had happened on Mars, however, they said that was something she should report to the FBI.

She hadn't even bothered contacting the police again after that. There might have been a few more cruisers in the area for the next day or two, but that seemed to be the extent of their activity. And maybe it was just as well. The local police were underfunded and overextended, and her private security system could offer far more protection than they could. Plus, she really didn't want to risk them finding out about the illegal bug zappers.

Kes, who was now on permanent retainer as a second opinion for all security matters, especially those that skirted the law, said it certainly wasn't kids. The drones were too expensive for that. His theory was that the Flock was just taunting her. The group was more than willing to harass anyone involved in advancing science, but Claire offered them the perfect target. She was still very much the junior science reporter at the *Atlantic Post*, but she'd gotten a major boost in subscribers to her *Simple Science* series thanks to the two Mars exclusives—unveiling the chambers buried at Icarus Camp and giving the public a limited sneak peek at stage six of KTI's terraforming project. On top of that, she was connected to a second bombshell story that had broken in the past few months thanks to her family ties to Jonas Labs, which was being bombarded with protests surrounding the rollout of their new anti-aging drug, Rejuvesce. And then there was the fact that she was romantically involved with Wyatt Garcia, who had written the exposé on the Flock's role in the Martian attacks.

Wyatt had freaked out a bit when the attacks began, but eventually agreed with Kes after it was clear that the drones weren't weaponized. "They're pissed off about the article," he'd said after a check of the security feed at his apartment turned up several bugbots hovering near his balcony, as well. "I just hate that they're taking it out on you. It will probably taper off soon, but if they keep setting off the alarm and retreating, just zap the damn things in the cul-de-sac and move the carcasses onto the lawn for Kes or the security people to collect. Or toss them into the trash. It's not like the Flock is going to press charges. And if one of your neighbors spots you in the act and is nosey enough to turn you into the local cops, it's not a felony. You can afford the fine. The real cost is the toll it's taking on your nerves."

He wasn't wrong. That toll was why the detector was now linked to Claire's phone, rather than sounding over the house security system as it had in the beginning. It was also the reason that Ro and Jemma were in Vancouver. Jemma, who had recently turned five, was aware of their issues with what she called *bitey bugs* but they had been trying to shield her as much as possible. After an unprecedented nine drone alerts on Saturday, Ro had decided to schedule her vacation early and visit her mom.

"I've been wanting to go for a while now," Ro said after making the flight reservations, apparently forgetting that she'd once told Claire that a visit with her mother was roughly equivalent to visiting the ninth circle of hell. It had been one of their first long conversations, over a bottle of Cabernet, shortly after they met at the apartment building where they'd both lived before Claire bought the house in Kings Contrivance. Wyatt had once joked that they bonded over their mommy issues, and he wasn't entirely wrong.

"Jemma barely knows her," Ro continued. "And my mom is okay with *little* kids. It's just once they get older and start having minds of their own. It's nice there in the summer, too. I have two weeks of vacation time, and I really *do* need a break from work."

When she realized Claire wasn't buying it, Ro finally admitted it was also because of the drones. "Although, if I'm being honest, I'm more worried about your *reaction* to them. Jemma is with you half the day and she picks up on your mood. Given what happened on Mars, I completely understand why this has you on edge. But since that's almost certainly the Flock's goal … can I make a suggestion? Kes and the guy from Apex Security both said that *none* of the drones you've zapped have been weaponized. Maybe this is a case where if you ignore them for a few weeks, they'll just go away?"

Claire wasn't at all sure about that last part, but she knew Ro was right about Jemma. The girl seemed to gravitate toward the scarier variety of children's stories—witches and giants and so forth—but she'd had several nightmares about bug-monsters just before Claire's trip to Mars, thanks to a movie she'd watched at her dad's house. After months of no bug dreams, she'd had three in the past week, so Claire had no doubt that the drone attacks were responsible.

If this kept up, they'd have to look at moving Rowan and Jemma to another house. Which would upset Jemma further and, worst of all, was no guarantee that it would solve the problem. If the Flock's goal was keeping Claire on edge, threatening the people she cared about would still be their top priority, regardless of whether they lived under the same roof.

She really *should* ignore the drone, which was now perched atop her mailbox. She'd ignored three of them yesterday, thinking that even if it didn't work, she would at least be able to tell Ro that she'd tried. But her car was due to arrive soon. That thing could easily follow her or even hitch a ride on top of the car. Whoever was controlling it would then know that she was headed out of town. They could make an educated guess as to where she was going, too, if they consulted the hyperloop departure times. For that matter, the drone was small enough that it could zip inside one of the baggage compartments and come along for the ride.

All of which meant that she was about to commit another misdemeanor by bringing the drone down in the cul-de-sac. Maybe two misdemeanors, because if her zapper didn't destroy the thing, she fully intended to whack it with a shovel until it was nothing but a twisted pile of bugbot rubble.

Slinging the daypack over her shoulder, Claire hurried downstairs to the breakfast nook with the zapper in hand. The bay window was the one spot in the house where the drone would be fully in range. Sigrid, Jemma's tortoiseshell cat, yowled and scurried out of the patch of morning sunlight in which she'd been lounging. Between that indignity and the fact that she was about to wrestle the cat into a carrier and drop her at the kitty hotel, she was going to be in Siggy's bad graces for weeks.

Claire scanned the street. No one was out, aside from the garbage truck a few doors down. Did those things have cameras?

Probably, but Wyatt was right. If anyone reported her, she could afford the fine.

Three quick clicks of the button, and the bugbot tumbled off the mailbox onto the asphalt. But she could still see the wings twitching, even from inside the house.

With seven minutes until the car was due to arrive, she stashed the jammer back into her pocket and grabbed the shovel from the utility room, along with the gas mask she'd bought in case any of them were actually equipped with anything toxic. Then, certain that she looked completely ridiculous, she went outside to see if another blast from the zapper would result in a clean kill.

No such luck. The amber eyes of the chubby cicada drone continued their steady blinking pattern.

Claire raised the shovel as she approached and was about to smack it, but she stopped in mid-swing. Most of the time, the bugbots chirped softly after they were downed, unless you were lucky enough to completely disable them. This one, however, was talking. She had to strain to make out what it was saying over the whirr and crash of the garbage truck, but they were definitely words.

"… shalt surely die."

Claire took an automatic step back. The voice was female and disturbingly high pitched, almost like that of a child.

"Of every tree in the garden thou mayest eat freely. But from the tree of knowledge, thou shalt not eat. For in the day that thou eatest thereof thou shalt surely die. Of every tree in the garden…"

Great. The Flock had always been insufferable, thinking that they alone could save the planet from the dreaded demon Science. Now they were adding bible verses to the mix?

She pulled out her phone, waited until the sound looped back around to the beginning, and hit the button to record. As soon as she had the full spiel, she dictated a quick message and sent the video to Wyatt and Kes. She came close to sending it to Ro, as well, but the whole purpose for the Vancouver trip had been to get away from all of this. Yes, Claire would have to fill Ro in before she and Jemma headed home, but at least she could give her friend a week or so of blissful ignorance.

The eerie message continued to play. Claire folded the phone into her pocket, then raised the shovel over her head and brought it down hard. The bugbot's wings snapped off, ending the screechy voice in mid-verse. Another whack, and its amber eyes flickered out, as well.

It was definitely dead, but she whacked it once more just for the sheer pleasure of it. Then she scooped the fragments up with the shovel and dumped it into the trash.

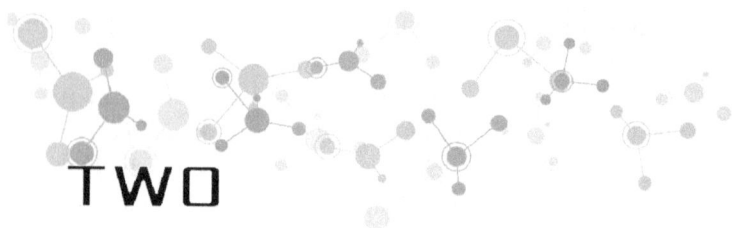

TWO

CLAIRE HAD HOPED to be in New York an hour early, so that she'd have plenty of time to leave her bag at the hotel and maybe relax a bit before heading over to her meeting at Columbia. But the incident with the bugbot and the fun adventure of getting Siggy into her cat carrier had taken longer than she'd thought, which meant that she missed the earlier train and was now scurrying to make her appointment with Ben Pelzer.

Technically, Siggy had lost the battle, given that she was now at the kennel. But she'd put up a valiant fight that caused Claire to have to hunt down a box of bandages and change her shirt. So, everything considered, it might be more accurate to call this one a draw.

A quick glance at the dash display showed that she still had fifteen minutes to get a bit of work in before the car arrived at the coffee shop. Pelzer, the geologist on the team she'd traveled with to Mars, had managed a feat Claire had started to believe impossible—arranging a face-to-face meeting between Claire and Holly Leffler, the head of Columbia's Computational Archeolinguistic Working Group. She'd started lobbying for an in-person interview with the woman about a month back, as soon as it became clear that Leffler's interest in translating the messages engraved on the walls of the Martian chambers had cooled considerably.

Dr. Leffler had said that Claire should just send a list of any specific questions she wanted answered. Classes were starting soon, she'd explained, and since she was already planning to record a supplemental lecture about the Martian discovery for her undergraduate classes, this would allow her to kill two birds with one stone. Leffler would then have a full lecture for her own use and Claire could just pull any excerpts she needed for the *Simple Science* episode.

Claire had agreed—what choice did she have?—and then contacted Leffler a day or so after receiving the recorded lecture, claiming that she had a few follow-up questions. And since the episode was going live the next week, maybe she could just stop by New York on her way up to Boston and record her answers?

Leffler's initial response had been *no, so sorry, much too busy.* That was the point at which Claire had contacted Ben Pelzer to see if he could help arrange a meeting.

To be fair, Claire's follow-up questions were entirely a ruse to get her foot in the door, because begging (and, if necessary, bribing) the professor to keep working on the project were the kind of things that really should be done in person. And if begging and bribing didn't work, she wasn't above playing the guilt card. Pelzer had told her that Laura Brodnik and Holly Leffler were friends. Surely the woman would want to help fulfill Laura's dying wish?

Calling it a *dying wish* was an exaggeration, but not by much. Laura's last words had been *Those symbols are important. Make sure the world sees them.* But one could argue that seeing the symbols and translating them were two very different things—and the world had already seen them. The discovery of the chambers and the bombing that followed that discovery had been major news in every country.

And Claire would most likely have been willing to leave it at that if not for the far longer message they'd found encoded in the samples she'd brought back from Mars. Someone had gone to a great deal of trouble to make sure that message survived the destruction of the planet. She couldn't shake the fear that it was a warning of some sort. Joe wasn't entirely convinced. Beck's position was closer to Claire's—it *might* be a warning, but even if it wasn't, it contained vital information. That was the main reason she was heading to Boston the next morning and the main reason she wanted to talk to Holly Leffler in person before she left New York. In what little spare time Beck had these days, he had managed to extract the code from the sample into standard image files, enlarging and enhancing them so that they could be read without a microscope. Since they were now at the point where the information conceivably *could* be shared, Joe had finally agreed to take at least part of the day off so that the three of them could discuss how to go about releasing it to others.

Joe wanted to just hand it over to a university and leave it at that, but Claire was hesitant to release the manuscript until they had some idea of what it was. Beck had agreed, suggesting that they pull in another expert. Leffler was the obvious choice, since she was the one that Columbia University had tasked with looking at the script found etched into the chamber walls. But Claire wanted to get a feel for whether the woman could be trusted with this far larger trove of data without running straight to media outlets, which wasn't the sort of judgment she felt comfortable making based on email and phone conversations alone.

She had originally planned to go back over Dr. Leffler's video to find a few plausible follow-up questions during her trip from DC, but her encounter with the bugbot in the cul-de-sac had left her jumping at every stray sound or movement on the crowded train. It had, in fact, creeped her out almost to the point of trying to book a private AeroLyft for the day. While she did appreciate the irony of the Flock's harassment pushing her toward the very sort of environmental excess they preached against, getting a long-distance reservation on such short notice would have been almost impossible.

The main thing that kept her from even trying to book private transport, however, was imagining Ro's reaction. The look of concern. The subtle arch of her eyebrow. And worst of all, the unspoken word that would hang in the air.

But was it really *paranoia*? Even Ro would have to interpret *thou shalt surely die* as a threat.

It was also yet another deviation from the Flock's typical patterns of behavior. The Flock, at least under Shepherd, had been resolutely nonviolent, low-tech, and secular although Shepherd had used vaguely godlike terms in reference to the beings he called the Sentinels. Apparently, Earth was doomed, but these Sentinels—a group of highly intelligent aliens—were coming to rescue all members of the Earth Watch Alliance who fought the enemy by working on communal farms and, of course, harassing the scientists whose discoveries Shepherd believed to be responsible for the planet's imminent demise.

In the past, however, the Flock had restricted that harassment to picketing, defacing property and hurling debris at employees, along with occasional stunts like releasing rats in the lobby of Jonas Labs. They'd never incorporated religious teachings. Claire had always thought that was a financial decision, since linking up with any one religion might have discouraged those of other faiths from joining and handing over all of their worldly possessions to Shepherd.

She dragged her attention back to the task at hand, rewinding the video to the five minute mark. Leffler, a rail-thin woman in her eighties with a mass of wild gray curls that made her head seem almost comically out of proportion to her body, stepped to one side of the display and gestured with the tip of a laser pointer.

"Okay, so here on the left, we have three images—no doubt familiar to anyone who has been paying attention to the news—of the engravings found inside the upper chamber excavated at the Icarus mining camp on Mars. Most of you have also seen or at least heard of *this* item as well." Leffler clicked to isolate the image on the far right. "The Rosetta stone is an ancient Egyptian stele or monument that was unearthed in 1799 and translated over the next few decades. Its discovery was important mostly because it included the *same* decree written in three different scripts—ancient hieroglyphs, an Egyptian cursive script called demotic, and ancient Greek. Sections are missing, as you can see from the image, but it was intact enough for scholars to realize these were three different versions of the same text. After several years of work, they also were able to conclude that it was logophonetic rather than strictly logographic. With these discoveries—"

Claire stopped the recording and jotted down the timestamp along with the words *logographic* and *logophonetic* as a third question to ask Dr. Leffler, although she was reaching at this point. She could very easily look up those meanings and even post definitions on the screen if she decided to use that bit of video. And she certainly couldn't claim that she needed additional footage. Dr. Leffler had provided far more content than she could squeeze into a twenty-minute *Simple Science* episode.

But the follow-up questions didn't really need to stand up to serious scrutiny. They just needed to exist. Unless Leffler was incredibly dim, she would quickly figure out that they were a cover. She'd probably done so already.

Claire started the video again.

"—they finally had a tiny glimmer of light that allowed them to begin decoding the ancient script. That is why the term *Rosetta stone* has come to mean a key breakthrough or a vital initial clue to a puzzle that previously seemed unsolvable. Would we have been able to unravel the mystery of Egyptian hieroglyphs without the Rosetta stone? Probably, because while this was the *first* stele of this nature that was found, it's not unique. Other stones with multilingual markings have been unearthed over the past two centuries. Translating the script would, however, have been exceptionally difficult, if not impossible, without a multilingual key of some sort. Many archeological finds have text that has never been deciphered, or at least, there's no *definitive* translation. For example..." She clicked the pointer. "This artifact is called the Phaistos Disc. It was found in 1908 during the excavation of a Minoan palace—"

Claire skipped past Leffler's seven-minute side lecture on ancient Minoan and Mycenaean artifacts, hitting play again when she saw the professor zoom in on the top of the Rosetta stone, the section that contained the hieroglyphs.

"—can at least hypothesize about the meaning of some symbols because, despite the vast differences in our cultures, there are constants both in humans and in the physical world in which we exist that persist across time. For example, there are depictions of humans and animals among these symbols." Leffler clicked again. "We can all recognize the glyph on the left, for example, as a human eye. While the eye held numerous symbolic meanings for ancient Egyptians, many connected to their religion, its logographic meaning is *sight* or *watchfulness*. And here on the right we see that same eye with three lines extending from the bottom. Even young children would probably recognize that as a crying eye and associate it with sadness or grief, because tears seem to be another constant between human civilizations."

Another click. Now the display showed a montage of non-human eyes from science fiction movies and drawings, ranging from glassy black orbs to red dots on the tip of antennae.

"We cannot, however, make a similar assumption about symbols from a non-human culture. At this time, there's no way for us to know what sort of eyes ancient Martians had. Even the assumption that they *had* eyes requires a leap of faith, given that the only writing we have from their civilization was etched, rather than printed on a smooth surface. Some species of bats here on Earth can detect minute differences in texture through echolocation. Likewise, ancient Martians might have read these symbols by hearing or touching them, so we cannot know for certain that they had a symbol or word for *sight*. And this is but *one* of countless unknowns. All that I'd be willing to venture about this script is that it seems to be an alphabetic language rather than logographic, given the relative simplicity of the symbols. One large symbol on the inner chamber looks like an H2O molecule, which would be a logograph, but that could be coincidence. I would also agree with Dr. Brodnik that this *appears* to be a burial chamber, even though no trace of a body was found, so perhaps this is a eulogy or a memorial of some sort.

"But beyond that...?" Leffler shrugged her thin shoulders.

"There's just not enough information, and machine translation models can't overcome that problem. They require a massive amount of accurately translated text as training data to learn patterns and meanings. We have a *miniscule* amount of data and *no* translation at all. This is the only document we have from a civilization that might be—I would even say *must* by necessity be —very, very different from our own. I suppose you could still perform frequency analysis to determine the most commonly used words. If these symbols were from a human civilization here on Earth, that might enable us to make some guesses. But they would be very *wild* guesses given the sample size. And this is an *alien* civilization about which we know nothing. It's like trying to solve a jigsaw puzzle with the blank side up—except there are no edges or corners and every piece fits into dozens of different spots. You might *appear* to have solved it, but the odds would be strongly against your solution being the *correct* answer when you flipped the puzzle over to check. Only in this case, there's no image on the other side to check it against. You could have hundreds of wildly different translations and no way to tell which one is correct. Which is why, in the absence of additional data, any attempt to decipher these symbols is an exercise in futility."

THREE

THE CAR CHIMED SOFTLY as it pulled up to the curb across from Columbia University. Claire reached for the door handle, then hesitated, taking a moment to scan the street outside. It wasn't merely the scripture-spouting cicada outside her house that had her jumpy. The last time she was on this street, she'd quite literally bumped into a woman she'd later learned was the Flock's new leader. Corbin Drexel had taken that opportunity to attach a listening device to Claire's messenger bag ... a device sophisticated enough that it had gotten past the security gate at Jonas Labs and was very nearly missed when Kes did a complete security sweep of her house.

Unfortunately, the sidewalk along Broadway was far too crowded for Claire to pinpoint anyone or anything that might be following her. She'd just have to merge with the crowd and trust the drone blocker.

The car chimed again, followed by a recorded reminder that all passengers should exit quickly as a courtesy to others waiting for a ride. So, Claire grabbed her bag from the floorboard and stepped out into the hot dank embrace of an urban heatwave.

As much as she loved New York, Wyatt was right. Anyone who visited this city in the heat of summer was crazy. But it was the one time they'd been able to sync up their schedules, and she only planned to be here one night. The weather probably wouldn't be much better in Boston, but she'd be inside most of the weekend, or in the Jonas Labs biodome where a person could enjoy nature without risking heatstroke.

Claire rounded the corner to find several dozen people congregating around the door of the coffee shop. The place was right across from campus, so it had seemed like a good choice when she suggested it. But apparently not.

Her phone vibrated as she approached the shop, and she thought it might be Pelzer. But it was just a drone alert from the security app. Either the Flock was sending the things out on a prearranged schedule, or they didn't realize she'd left town.

She started a text to ask if they should meet somewhere else, but then she heard someone calling her name. Pelzer was tucked away in the shadows of the awning, all but his head hidden behind the line of people waiting to enter. As he approached, she could see that he was holding two iced coffees.

"I should have warned you that this was a bad location," he said. "The fall semester starts on Tuesday, and we usually get a flood of early arrivals. Which means there are no tables this morning and it's way too noisy to talk. I got these from a place a few blocks over, but if you want something from here, we can..."

"Oh, no, no. This is perfect. Thank you." Claire took the drink he held out toward her. The cup was already slick with condensation.

"Maybe we could take it over to the steps near the sundial? Or we could go back to my office, but to be honest, it won't be much cooler up there. It's an old building and climate control is struggling to keep up."

"The sundial is fine. But weren't we supposed to meet Dr. Leffler here?"

He shook his head. "She had a meeting this morning and was worried it might run late. You can message her from the lobby, and she'll come down to sign you in. So ... does this interview mean she's made some progress?"

"No. More like the exact opposite. I received a very long video earlier this week explaining why the task is utterly impossible. I'm just here with follow-up questions. And maybe to beg a little." She decided not to mention the potential bribing and guilting.

"Are you absolutely *sure* Dr. Leffler is the person Laura would have chosen?"

Brodnik hadn't mentioned any specific names before she died, but Pelzer and the other surviving member of the team, Chelsea Friesen, had both insisted that she would have turned to Leffler.

"Absolutely," Pelzer said. "Holly is a little quirky. But she's the best in her field. If she tells you it can't be translated, she's almost certainly right. And…" He made a reluctant face. "I *know* you don't want to hear this, but I've never thought the odds were good. We have no common frame of reference with whoever left those symbols. We can't even be certain that they're humanoid."

"I know, but—"

"But it was Laura's last wish," Pelzer said. "Which means you have to at least try. That's also why I was willing to hound Leffler into meeting with you." He nodded down at Claire's leg as she stepped onto the sidewalk on the other side of Broadway, pulling her bag behind her. "At least you're getting around a lot better than you were on the trip home. When did they remove the boot?"

"Three, maybe four weeks after we got back. Luckily, it came off before this heatwave hit or it would have driven me crazy."

"Any word on the investigation?" he asked.

"Not since I went in for questioning," she said. "I'm guessing they talked to you as well?"

"Yeah. Showed up at my door a little over a week ago. Took them long enough."

"Amen to that. I'm glad that they're finally digging into it, but it's also stirred the pot. The Flock has been harassing me with fly-by drones and I can't get anyone in authority to take it seriously. Have you had any issues with them?"

"No. They haven't been on campus as far as I'm aware, but then I wasn't around much over the summer. Spent a week at the beach with the family. Did a bit of writing. But I did manage to get on campus for some lab time in order to run the metal samples from the chambers."

"Any surprises?"

"Not really. For the most part, it just confirmed the data from the portable spectrometer I had with me on Mars. As I suspected, that alloy isn't anything we've encountered before."

They emerged from the shaded walk between the buildings into the large open area of South Lawn. During Claire's previous trips to the Columbia campus, the quad had been teeming with activity. Now, the heat seemed to have driven everyone indoors. There were still a good many people on the paths, but only a smattering who lingered on the benches or stairs.

Pelzer picked a spot near one of the buildings where the shadows provided a bit of relief from the late-morning sun. "The one odd thing about the sample," he continued, "is that it contains a couple of elements we hadn't previously found on Mars, only in meteors that landed here on Earth. Presolar grains, too—tiny bits that formed before our sun. Which they could have gotten from meteors that landed there, I guess, although probably not in this quantity. Or maybe they had the ability to grow something of that nature in a lab."

Claire grinned at him. "Any chance I can coerce you into talking about that for *Simple Science*?"

"I'll let you know when I get everything written up," he said with a chuckle. "I may be asking you to return the favor of an interview. I'm … kind of writing a book."

"Really? On what you've discovered about the chambers?"

"That would be part of it, but it's more about the trip as a whole. I may be biting off more than I can chew here, so we'll see how it goes. I've published a few dozen technical papers and co-authored a textbook, but this sort of writing is a departure for me. Still, that was almost certainly my last Mars trip, and it was by *far* the most eventful. Might as well memorialize it."

"Why do you think it will be your last trip?"

He shrugged. "Funding, for one thing. NASA shifted most of their money away from our program after the incident with Kimura. Even though we now know he was right that something was odd with the samples, he was an idiot to point fingers in a public forum. And our biggest source of *civilian* funding is KTI. Once they open up again after the stage six lockdown, Kolya probably isn't going to make much space on his transports for academics. Plus, the university would have to basically recreate the team. Between losing Laura and Kim, and Chelsea heading off on her postdoc, it's just me." He sighed, looking out over the broad lawn. "It feels weird even being on campus without Laura around. Deirdre always called her my work wife. She said it was good to know that Laura was around to keep an eye out for me when we were off planet."

"Maybe Chelsea will come back when her fellowship is over?"

"Not likely. It does happen, but departmental dynamics get a little weird when you hire people who used to be grad students. She'll be better off getting a fresh start somewhere else. And that goes double with Kimura's shadow hanging over her."

"But Chelsea found evidence that Kim was right. Someone *did* tamper with those samples. And they were friends. Wouldn't she want to vindicate him?"

"She *wants* to, sure. But her advisor cautioned against it. So did I. On the trip home, I told her that if I were in her shoes, I would put as much distance as possible between my career and that of Daichi Kimura. His ... well, I was going to say his paranoia, but that doesn't really fit given that he was right. So let's just say his *obsession* with the Martian samples, with being the one to pinpoint who tampered with them, ended up causing three deaths—very nearly four, since you were touch and go for a few days."

"Chelsea strikes me as the inquisitive type, though. Are you sure she didn't sneak out a sample for her own use?"

He snorted. "Seriously? You saw the hoops we had to jump through in order to get those samples back to Earth."

"True," Claire admitted. "But I'd think it would be pretty easy to *hide* a sample of something so infinitesimally small."

"I suppose it's possible. But Chelsea wouldn't have much

incentive to do it aside from satisfying her own curiosity. If she wanted to use the sample in academic research, she'd have to show chain of custody." A flash of suspicion crossed Pelzer's usually open face. "I seem to recall that you came back with samples of your own. Did you discover something interesting? Are you now regretting that you signed an agreement not to publish your findings?"

Claire laughed. "The samples were for my *brother*. I wouldn't have any idea what to do with them. Unfortunately, Joe is too busy with his own research to pay them much attention right now. And I only promised not to publish in *academic* circles. If he finds anything interesting, I will definitely be doing a *Simple Science* segment on it. I was just curious. Because, in her shoes, I might have been tempted."

It was mostly true, but she was also a bit possessive of the manuscript they'd uncovered in the *Deinococcus aganippe* sample. Claire wanted the mystery solved, first and foremost, but she also wanted to be part of solving it. She'd very nearly died getting that sample. And while Chelsea had softened a bit by the end of the trip, she'd been abrasive enough at the beginning that Claire didn't much care for the idea that she might also have found the manuscript and might at this moment be over on the West Coast assembling a team to decrypt it.

"Maybe Chelsea learned a lesson from Kimura's death," Pelzer said. "Curiosity can get you killed. If he hadn't been so desperate to get his hands on your samples, he might still be alive. Laura, too."

Claire felt herself flush. It was almost as if Pelzer had read her mind. "Yeah, maybe. Although they never determined whether the bomb was motion-activated. Kim taking it behind the chamber wall could be the reason that *only* three people were killed. But I do get your point. Chelsea has good reasons to let the whole thing go."

"Yes. We all do, to be honest. The sooner everyone forgets about all this, the sooner Columbia will be back in the running for grant money from NASA. So I doubt the biology department or the university's Science Advisory Board are going to approve anyone picking up Kim's research agenda."

"Did you know Anton Kolya's on that board?"

"I do indeed know that," Pelzer said. "And given that KTI was Kim's prime suspect for the tampering, Kolya would be one *guaranteed* vote to shelve those samples indefinitely. And I'm guessing the entire board will concur."

Claire couldn't argue the point about Kolya. During their last conversation in her hospital room at Daedalus City, he'd told her that he felt sure someone would try to pin the blame for altering those samples on KTI, even though the second chamber, the one that was still embedded in the cliff at Icarus Camp, had been sealed tight.

Except that wasn't exactly true. The samples she'd obtained were from liquid they'd found oozing out of a crack in the wall. She couldn't figure out what motive Anton Kolya would have for encoding a document inside those samples, but even if he wasn't the one who had tampered with them, she had no doubt that he'd push for the entire thing to be ignored. His only interest was the terraforming project moving forward on schedule.

But Pelzer was wrong that any decision by the board would be unanimous. If the matter ever came to a vote, Kolya would have at least one member on the other side. Kai Jonas didn't know they'd found anything unusual inside the samples. Claire had explicitly told Joe that she didn't want their mother involved. But there was no way Kai would support Anton Kolya on *any* issue.

FROM THE ATLANTIC POST

(AUGUST 27, 2084)

ZIMMER AWARD SHORTLIST UNVEILED

~ BRYCE AVERY

(Washington, DC) The International Association of Science Journalists today released its finalists for the annual Zimmer Award, honoring key advancements in science. This year's shortlist includes the following five candidates, each of whom has pushed the boundaries of human understanding and innovation.

Averotech (Hiroshi Tanaka): Mind-Computer Interface (MCI) Advancements

> Tanaka's groundbreaking research has led to the development of highly sophisticated MCIs that allow individuals to control computers and devices with their thoughts alone. This work has massive implications for individuals with disabilities, and many potential applications in neuroscience, artificial intelligence, and beyond.

Jonas Labs (Kai Jonas, Joseph Echols, and John Beckett): Rejuvesce

Following in the wake of its success with the anticancer medication, Arvectin, Jonas Labs has developed a new drug with the potential to extend human lifespans by an astounding twenty-five years, targeting cellular aging and promoting regeneration. The implications are profound, potentially revolutionizing healthcare, economics, and society.

Kolya Terraforming International (Anton Kolya and Davina Monroe): Martian Terraforming Stage Six

Kolya Terraforming International (KTI) has achieved a significant milestone in the quest to make the Red Planet habitable. Utilizing a two-step approach, a modified version of *Azospira oryzae* was released to rid the soil of perchlorates, followed by the introduction of AE (accelerated evolution) biobots to create a unique microbiome, potentially opening the door for the transformation of other planets within our solar system and beyond.

Massachusetts Institute of Technology (Poul Sylva and Elina Ramirez): Biomimetic Carbon Sequestration

Addressing the pressing issue of climate change, SylvaTech's innovative technology takes inspiration from nature. Sylva, Ramirez, and their team have developed an efficient carbon capture solution, potentially mitigating the effects of climate change by dramatically reducing atmospheric carbon dioxide levels.

SolarReserve (Sava Patel): Quantum Dot Solar Panels.

SolarReserve has unveiled a groundbreaking innovation in solar technology—quantum dot panels. Patel's work promises to enhance the efficiency and affordability of renewable energy generation, offering a glimpse of a more sustainable energy future.

In a normal year, any one of these breakthroughs would be a strong contender for the prize. This year, however, Jonas Labs and KTI are the clear frontrunners, marking major advancements that have the potential to dramatically alter life on this planet and beyond.

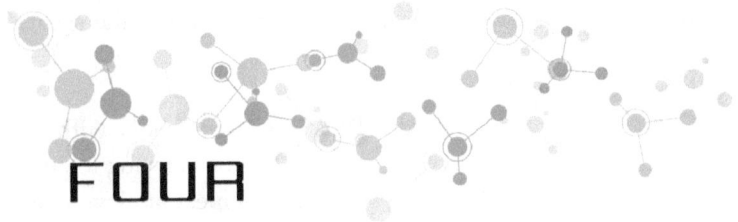

FOUR

WHEN THE COFFEE was gone and they'd exhausted all obvious topics of conversation, Pelzer took Claire's empty cup for recycling and pointed her toward a tall boxy structure several buildings over that housed the Data Sciences Institute. They said their goodbyes and she headed in that direction, looking forward to getting out of the heat and away from the noise. Walking through the Columbia campus reminded her of being in a city park—no cars in sight, but you could never quite escape from the horns and sirens blaring on nearby streets.

It was still a few minutes before eleven when she reached the lobby, a multistory cube with glass walls that looked out on the plaza below. There was no response when she rang Dr. Leffler's office, which wasn't too surprising given that she was early. She found a leather bench in a corner that was out of the foot traffic and pulled up the Apex Security app on her phone. It had buzzed twice while she was talking to Pelzer, so she switched it to digest mode where it would just send her a list of drone incursions instead of notifying her each time. Then she played sudoku for a bit and tried Leffler's office again at eleven.

Still no response. This time, she left a message before returning to her game.

When she hadn't heard back by five after, she searched the directory and found a number for Computational Archeolinguistics ... only to discover that it redirected to Leffler's office. After another five minutes or so of frustrated pacing, she sorted the directory by department and found three other people in that group. The first person on the list didn't answer, but the second one did.

"Hardt speaking."

"Good morning, Dr. Hardt. This is Claire Echols with the *Atlantic Post*. I'm sorry to bother you, but I've been trying to get in touch with Dr. Leffler. We were supposed to meet at eleven, and I'm only in town for the day, so—"

"Yeah. She said she was going across the street to CVS after our team meeting ended, but that was nearly half an hour ago." There was a pause, and Claire was about to ask if he had a personal number for Leffler, but then the guy heaved a disgruntled sigh, and she heard the squeak of an office chair. "Hold on. Maybe Alice knows where she is."

Alice Dobroski was the third name in the directory, so Claire waited, expecting the call to be transferred. It wasn't. When the man came back on the line a few minutes later, he said that Alice hadn't heard from her, either. "I'm guessing she got tired of the heat and decided to work from home for the rest of the day."

And then he hung up.

Claire stared down at the screen for a moment, debating whether to ring him again to ask for another contact number. But he probably wouldn't give it out. And it seemed increasingly clear that Holly Leffler had ghosted her.

Pelzer said earlier that Leffler was a bit odd. Still, she was a professional, right? You'd think she'd at least have messaged. Claire pulled out her phone and started a text to let Pelzer know what was going on and see if maybe *he* had Leffler's personal number. Then she deleted it. It would sound like a complaint, and this certainly wasn't his fault.

And, to be fair … what if Leffler had realized Claire's main reason for coming to New York was to beg or bribe her into continuing work on a project the woman thought was impossible? A project that she might already feel guilty about abandoning since she was friends with Brodnik? Maybe she was just conflict averse.

Claire was halfway through the door when she heard someone calling her name. A young woman was hurrying over, her low heels tapping against the marble tiles. She was short and very curvy, with dark curls and orange-framed glasses that made her eyes look enormous. When she reached Claire, she stopped and put a hand on her shoulder as she tried to catch her breath.

"Apologies! Josh—Dr. Hardt, that is—didn't tell me who was looking for Holly. I realized after he walked out that it was probably you, but he was on another call when I got to his office, and I don't have your number. So I had to run like mad to catch you. Holly should have been back *ages* ago."

She tapped the inside of her left forearm. A clear panel lit up. "Call Holly." Then she extended her hand to Claire. "Alice Dobroski. I've been sort of … lurking, I guess? … while Holly examined the Martian glyphs. And I've watched your videos of course. You must have been *so* psyched to be the first person inside that chamber, to actually see and touch a message from an alien civilization…" She paled. "The *outer* chamber, I mean. The one under the dome at Daedalus. Being inside that second one had to have been an absolute nightmare. I didn't really know Dr. Brodnik, but—"

"It's okay," Claire said. "I knew what you meant. And you're right that—"

Dobroski held up a hand, frowning slightly as she listened to something. Claire couldn't hear anything, not even the faint hum you usually pick up with the speakers embedded into glasses, so the woman must have ear implants like Wyatt's. He loved them and they definitely seemed convenient, but Claire couldn't quite get past the squick factor of someone operating on her ears.

"I'm trying to reach Dr. Holly Leffler," Dobroski said. "Who is this? Why do you have her phone?"

Another silence and then a sharp intake of breath.

"Oh. Yes, yes, of course. Alice Dobroski. 322-D West 113th. … We're more *colleagues*, really, but yes. … No. I don't have that information. I'm sorry. … Yes, yes. Is she okay? … Sure. Morningside. I'm on campus, so ten minutes at the most." She ended the call and pushed the door open, calling to Claire over her shoulder. "Can you walk with me? It's only a few blocks."

"Okay." Claire picked up her bag and followed Dobroski across the plaza toward the stairs that would take them down to street level. "What happened?"

"Holly is at the emergency room a few blocks down. They think it's heatstroke. Someone needs to contact her family." She tapped her arm panel again. "Call Josh."

"Maybe I should just reschedule," Claire said.

"Let's ask her when we get there. And … this will give us a chance to talk without her around."

Claire wasn't sure how to respond to that, so she just increased her pace to keep up.

"Damn. He's not answering." Another tap. "Call faculty services."

That number answered. Claire followed along, listening to one side of the conversation as Dobroski relayed the news about Leffler and asked them to contact the professor's family.

When the call ended, the woman took a deep breath. "Okay. Don't get me wrong. Holly's great. She's the chair of the department and one of the top names in computational archeolinguistics. But…" She pulled a hesitant face. "Let's just say she's more the *linguistics* side of the equation."

"And you're more the computational side?"

"Exactly. I've seen the video she sent you, and she's absolutely right. This would be so much easier if we had a multilingual key and more data and if we knew we were dealing with a humanoid species and … all of that. What I can't fathom is why she won't even take a stab at it. If she tried, I'm sure she could get the team at Berkeley to work with us. They've got a group that's trying to construct a unified theory of language. Building on Chomsky's work from ages and ages ago. It's nowhere near the publication stage, but I'm sure they'd love the chance to plug the text we have into their model, which would compare it to all known human languages. It would be great publicity for their program, too. But when I suggested it, Holly just said that the model would spit out a ton of different possibilities. Every single one of them might be horribly off base and we'd have no way to know for sure. And she's right. *Of course*, she's right. But ... it just boggles my mind. How can you have information like this and not even *try* to see what kind of patterns you find in it?"

Claire completely agreed, but felt that she should defend Leffler a bit, if only because the woman was currently in a hospital emergency room. "Maybe she's worried about the *being wrong* part? You said she was one of the top names in the field. She might not want to tarnish that reputation by having it attached to something so ... subjective."

Dobroski canted her head to the side, halfway between a nod and a shake. "Maybe? She seemed excited when Laura first spoke to her about it back in March, right after they returned from that first trip. And she was even more psyched after she got the full images. Did you see the interview in the *Spec*? Oh ... probably not. That's the university paper. Anyway, they interviewed her right after we got the data. But when we met again just before summer break, she said it was a lot of time for the group to put into something that would never yield any publishable results." She gave a wry chuckle. "Which should be *my line*, since I'm still a probationary hire whose curriculum vita could use some added heft. But yeah. She's planning to retire next year so maybe you're right. Maybe she doesn't want to end her career working on something she thinks is destined to fail. Holy hell, though ... I hope I never reach a point in my life where my *curiosity* dies. You know?"

Claire nodded. They walked in silence for a couple of minutes, both a bit winded from the heat and the quick pace. When the sign for the emergency room at Mount Sinai Morningside came into view, Dobroski stopped and turned to face her.

"You're not going to convince her to change her mind. Believe me, I already tried. Holly *is* going to shut you down. I, on the other hand, am too insanely curious to let this go and more than happy to devote my spare time to it." She pulled a card from her pocket and handed it to Claire. "The sticker on the back has my private contact info. I'm already working with the data we have. If you have any ideas or other information, please, please let me know. But ... Holly is the head of the department. And as I said, I'm still in my probationary period, so you have to *promise* to keep this conversation between the two of us."

"*What* conversation?" Claire gave her a conspiratorial grin as she waved her phone over the sticker. A new contact popped up with a number, several social media addresses, and two links that she didn't recognize. The bottom link was circled.

"Thanks. Use that last contact first. You may need to grab the app if you don't have it, but it's really the safest method if you want a private conversation." She chuckled darkly. "For now, at least. I move to a new service every six months or so. And yes, I've been called paranoid for that, but usually only by people who have no idea what they're talking about."

Claire felt a rush of kinship. *Paranoiacs of the world unite.*

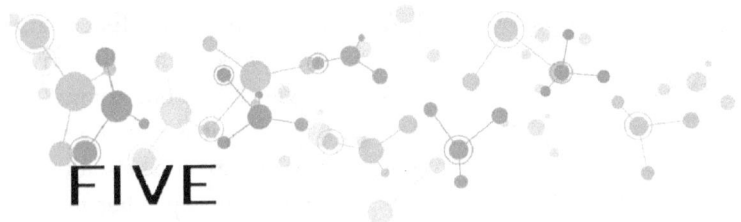

FIVE

A COLD SHIVER ran down Claire's spine as she stepped through the security screen and into the waiting room. It was at least twenty degrees cooler inside than it had been out on the sidewalk, where it had to be approaching triple digits. But it was only partly the temperature change. Mostly it was the general atmosphere of the place—the smells, the faint beep and whirr of machinery, the sound of rapid footsteps in the distance, and the general miasma of dread hanging over the room.

"You okay?" Alice asked.

Claire nodded. "I'm just not good with hospitals."

By the time they were cleared to go back, Leffler was barely conscious. She was also barely recognizable as the woman Claire had seen in the video lecture. Leffler's wild gray curls, by far her most distinctive feature, were now pulled up into a knot. She was also ghostly pale, aside from a scraped forehead and a vivid pink splotch on her neck. The pink patch was roughly circular, with a small cut near the center.

As Alice was telling the nurse that the university was contacting her family, Leffler began to convulse. The nurse, who seemed on the verge of collapse herself, shooed them out of the cubicle and tapped a button on the side of the bed.

Claire started to leave but stopped with one hand on the curtain and turned to look back at that odd mark on the professor's neck.

She *could* be wrong. In fact, she thought the odds of that were quite high.

But Leffler was still alive. And on the off chance that Claire *wasn't* wrong, this might be the only chance to keep her that way.

"Nurse? Could you ask the doctor to check for neurotoxins?"

The nurse didn't exactly roll her eyes, but it was a close call. "Convulsions are very common with heatstroke. She's already convulsed once, on the sidewalk before they brought her in. The doctor will—"

"What about the red patch on her neck? The scratch? Are those also common with heatstroke? Tell the doctor to check for *neurotoxins*."

That pissed the nurse off big time. She pointed toward the hallway beyond the curtain, her hand trembling with barely suppressed rage. "Waiting room. Right now. Or I *will* call security."

"Call them. I don't care. Maybe they'll have the good sense to listen to what I'm saying." Claire held the nurse's gaze for a second, hoping her words would sink in. They didn't. And the nurse was now on the verge of what looked like a panic attack, so Claire stepped out and pressed her back against the wall to wait for a doctor.

"What's going on?"

Claire jumped at the sound of Alice's voice behind her. "God. I thought you'd *left* already. You should go. No need for both of us to be dragged out by hospital security."

A man and a woman, both in scrubs, rounded the corner. Grabbing the arm closest to her, Claire tried again. "*Please*. Could you check the patient for neurotoxins? I asked the nurse, but..."

The man yanked his arm out of her grasp, shaking his head in annoyance. And, from inside the room, she heard the nurse saying, "Security to nine! Stat."

Claire muttered a curse under her breath, reminding herself that she was probably wrong. It almost certainly *was* heatstroke, and she was just overreacting.

"Come on." Alice began dragging her down the hall. "You *told* them. There's nothing more you can do. Either they listen or they don't."

There were no chairs available when they reached the waiting room. They checked the adjoining areas and eventually found a narrow bench built into one of the recessed windows. As she sat down, Claire caught a glimpse of a security guard entering the lobby and quickly averted her eyes.

Alice dropped down next to her. "Okay. You don't think it's heatstroke. Why?"

"A similar attack…" Claire stopped just shy of telling her that a similar attack had happened to Tobias Shepherd onboard the *Ares Prime*, remembering at the last second the NDA she'd signed. She'd told the FBI, of course, but she probably needed to be cautious with how much she told Alice. It wasn't that she'd gotten bad vibes from the woman. Quite the opposite, in fact. But she hadn't gotten bad vibes from Stasia Ljubic either, and Stasia had been behind the attacks that killed multiple people on Mars. Given her recent track record, it might be best to keep things vague for now.

On the other hand, if that was a Flock drone, it seemed likely that Leffler was being targeted for her connection to the Mars chambers. Claire had made certain the cicadabot couldn't follow her, but they seemed to have an entire brigade of nasty critters. If Alice was thinking about taking over the project, even unofficially, she needed to caution her that it might be risky. And the fact that similar drones had been used on Mars had already been widely reported. She could hardly be expected to avoid talking about that.

Claire cleared her throat and started again. "A similar attack was used by the Flock against some security personnel on Mars. And the group's new leadership has ramped up the level of violence, so I wouldn't be surprised if they're using nerve agents here, too. Has Dr. Leffler ever clashed with them?"

Alice shook her head. "Not that I know of. And I'm not sure *why* she'd have trouble with them. Archeologists aren't the sort of scientists the Flock usually targets, and that probably goes double for archeolinguists. I mean, we're focused on unraveling the lost history of the planet, not making the sort of advances that they claim could destroy it."

It was a fair point. The Flock usually went after cutting-edge tech companies or pharmaceutical firms like Jonas Labs. They did picket universities from time to time, but they usually focused on university hospitals connected to drug trials. KTI had, of course, been a prime target as well, even before the bombings, but that made sense. As the most highly publicized scientific effort of the era, even their failed attempt at stopping or postponing the terraforming had garnered more media attention than the group had gotten from dozens of smaller attacks on Earth.

The one thing that struck her as odd, however, was that the Flock had never officially claimed responsibility for the bombings on Mars. That alone was a major change from their mode of operations under Tobias Shepherd, which was to cause as much trouble as possible, claim credit, and then use that attention to spread their message that science was killing the planet. They'd even claimed responsibility for actions that were later discovered to be the work of other groups. But under Shepherd's leadership, none of the attacks had resulted in death or serious injury. That was the sort of thing that made the authorities move a group out of the nuisance file and onto the most wanted list, so maybe Drexel had decided it was wiser to embrace anonymity.

"True," Claire admitted. "Leffler wouldn't be their typical target. But the Flock's new leader seems to be a little fixated on the Mars story. After I testified to the FBI about the attacks at Icarus Camp, the Flock started bombarding my house with bugbots. Nothing toxic so far, as best we can tell, but it's very unsettling. The one this morning was even spouting bible verses. So ... if this actually *was* an attack and not just paranoia on my part, you might want to take some precautions. Keep any work you're doing on the translation project on the down-low. And maybe invest in a drone blocker. You can pick up a decent one for a hundred bucks or so. A little more if you want top of the line."

Alice tapped the transparent panel on her arm, then pulled upward on the edge to expand the screen. She began scrolling when the display lit up, stopping on the third frame. The icon at the center left was a spray can marked with a skull and crossbones. Next to it on the right was an ear icon marked with a red X.

"So … is that spray can icon supposed to be *insect repellent* or *insecticide*?" Claire asked.

She smiled grimly. "No comment. But I am *very* vigilant about my personal space. My privacy, too. If there are any recording devices nearby, they're picking up nothing but white noise from this corner."

Claire thought there was probably a story behind that. But it was not likely to be a story that Alice would be comfortable sharing on short acquaintance, so she didn't press the subject.

They were about to have company, anyway. The security guard who'd been scanning the lobby when they first sat down was now talking to the doctor Claire had asked to check Leffler for neurotoxins. And judging from the doctor's expression, he wasn't bringing good news.

FROM NEXUSCHAT/MARS

(AUGUST 29, 2084)

Avi3524: Yeah, but what if this chamber is a warning? Maybe there's a bigger message here? We all know the plot of this movie —ancient alien warnings and humanity pushing too far only to face consequences. Classic case of FAFO. I'm just saying...

Wes2256: God. You sound like the Flock. Are you sure *you* didn't set those bombs? Or maybe your real name is Tobias Shepard?

Avi3524: Pretty sure *Shepherd* is dead. Someone named Drexel is running the show now. She's a lot hotter than Toby. Click for pix.

Wes2256: Nice try, Avi. Not falling for that old trick. That's Kolya's ex, btw. Used to go by the name of Jenelle Tuller. And Toby's not dead. He's on Mars with a smaller flock. Don't you keep up with the news?

Avi3524: Depends on what you call news. I have my own sources. But if Toby's really on Mars, maybe he set the bomb??

Avi3524: Chamber bomb was small fries, guys. BiL is a contract laborer at Millex mining camp on Mars. Told my sis an entire barracks blew up a few weeks back, but BiL thinks its cover for something way worse.

SIX

CLAIRE GLANCED up at the clock again. It was an analog model, round with a silver rim, white face, and black hands, which currently indicated that it was five thirty-seven. Judging from the faint patina of grime and dust on the glass, and the spatters of different colors of paint around the rim, the clock had probably been up there since World War II. It was only a few minutes off, though. She'd checked it against her phone shortly after the NYPD detective left the room, promising that he'd be right back, and that Claire would be free to go at that point.

That had been nearly half an hour ago. If they didn't let her out soon, she was going to be late for dinner with Wyatt.

Her stomach rumbled at the thought of food. Aside from the iced coffee and a bottle of water, she'd had nothing since leaving the house. As it was, she'd have to go straight to the restaurant rather than checking into her hotel for a shower and change of clothes—both of which she desperately needed after nearly five hours of questioning.

Or, more accurately, nearly one hour of questioning, and another four hours of waiting to be questioned, first by hospital security and then by the NYPD. They didn't seem to think she'd had anything to do with the attack on Leffler, but she was the only one who had any information about a possible motive. At least she'd had company at the hospital, but the NYPD had no reason to question Alice further, so they'd let her go before transporting Claire to the local precinct office.

She stared at the door, willing it to open. When it stubbornly refused to budge, she called the restaurant to ask about changing the reservation. They said the very best they could do was hold the table for half an hour, so she messaged Wyatt to change the time. She was about to add an explanation, but that was when the door finally opened.

It wasn't the officer she'd been talking to—mid-fifties and bald —but a tall woman in her thirties, dressed in a dark blouse and khakis, with long reddish blonde hair and the choppy ultrashort bangs that had been a very brief fashion trend when Claire was in college.

"Agent Emily Wheeler." She flashed an FBI badge and took the chair on the other side of the small table. "I'm sorry to have kept you waiting, Ms. Echols, but we received a call from our office in Baltimore. The agent down there has a few questions and … well, I suspect the attack on Dr. Leffler may fall into our hands anyway. So … can you tell me what brings you to New York today?"

Claire sighed. "As I explained to the security officer at Mount Sinai and, more recently, to Officer Daniello, I'm heading up to Boston for the holiday weekend. I stopped over in New York for the day to do a follow-up interview with Professor Leffler for one of my *Simple Science* segments in the *Atlantic Post*. I'm also meeting a friend for dinner across town. *At seven.*"

Wheeler gave her a thin smile. "We'll get you out of here as soon as possible, Ms. Echols. I already have the statement that you gave to Sergeant Daniello, so I don't think we need to rehash the events at the hospital. But could you tell me a bit more about your connections to the Earth Watch Alliance?"

"My connections? You mean *aside* from the group trying to kill me on Mars and harassing me since my return?"

"Any connections you think are relevant, Ms. Echols."

"Okay. I've been aware of the EWA most of my life. My family founded Jonas Labs, and we seem to have been a special target for the group since their beginning a few decades back. There are numerous videos online of their protests outside the Jonas Labs campus and quite a few of the one memorable occasion when they made it inside and released a bunch of rats in the lobby.

There's also one of me getting smacked by one of their blood bombs when I—"

"Blood bombs?"

"Sorry. That's what my brother calls them. They're balloons—the ecofriendly kind, or so they claim—filled with some red gunk that they swear isn't blood. It still smells like blood, though. The Flock continues to insist that Jonas Labs engages in animal testing, but the labs scrapped animal testing in favor of *in silico* trials—computer models, that is—decades ago. Anyway, I was visiting my brother about … five years ago, I think? … and a member of the Flock pegged me with one of their stupid balloons. Someone got video of me screaming at the guy, which they tagged with my mother's name when they posted it. It was blurry enough that it was hard to tell it wasn't her. Let's just say she wasn't happy."

"I can imagine."

"Aside from that, I'm a science reporter. I've written a few articles that mentioned the Flock, but I didn't have any other direct contacts until this year. The last time I was in New York, Corbin Drexel arranged a bump-and-grab on the sidewalk outside Columbia, only instead of snatching my bag she attached a listening device. Then, on the evening before I left for my recent trip to Mars, I filled in for one of my colleagues, Bryce Avery. He'd called in sick and a source of his within the EWA showed up at the office wanting to speak to him. The source wasn't willing to talk to me and stormed out."

"Do you know the individual's name?"

"I know the last name is Shepherd."

Agent Wheeler responded with an unamused chuckle. "That part I could fill in on my own. What about a first name?"

Claire shook her head. "I'm sorry." What she really meant was that she was sorry she couldn't divulge that information, but she decided it was probably best to keep it vague. She definitely remembered Devin Shepherd's name, but he was now Wyatt's source—his only source—inside the Flock. And even if he'd still been Bryce Avery's source, she wouldn't have given up his name or anything else that could put the guy at risk. "A couple of hours after my encounter with Mr. Shepherd," she continued, "I spotted an illegal drone following me through a park in downtown DC—"

"How did you know it was an *illegal* drone?"

"Too small to be legal for personal use. Not much bigger than the tip of your pinky. Wrong color, too. It had a green light, with a distinctive blinking pattern. Metro police drones are bigger with a solid blue light. At any rate, it kind of spooked me. I increased security on my house, since my housemate and her daughter would be there alone while I was off planet. But I didn't really think much more about it until I saw that same pattern just moments before Tobias Shepherd was nearly killed during a public event onboard the *Ares Prime*. And another one followed me when I was in the dome at Daedalus City. That's all in the statement that I gave to the Baltimore office."

"You told Officer Daniello that those drones were different from the one that attacked Dr. Leffler, right?"

"Not exactly. I said that I didn't think they were the same, based on the security videos the NYPD showed me. But I couldn't tell for sure. The video taken outside the CVS was from a bad angle and the one across the street was too far away. I'd actually be surprised if the Flock is using the same model, though, given that the drones that followed me and the drone that attacked Shepherd were stolen from Kolya Terraforming."

"You're saying that KTI uses illegal drones?"

"They were stolen on Mars. And as a friend of mine is fond of saying, Mars is the wild freakin' West. Given the wide array of bugbots that have been around my house in the past ten days or so, I think it's safe to say that the Flock has diversified its fleet."

"Okay, then. Could you tell me a bit more about the drones that have been targeting your house? I'm especially interested in why you thought it was a good idea to *destroy* the one you encountered this morning."

Claire had decided earlier that the only viable course of action was to come clean about killing the cicadabot. Most of her neighbors had doorbell cams. For that matter, there would be damning footage on her own security cameras of her raising the shovel over her head and bashing something on the pavement just a few seconds after she sent the video to Wyatt and Kes. After all, as Wyatt had noted, whacking the things wasn't a felony, and it wasn't like the NYPD was going to hold her for a misdemeanor committed in Maryland.

Of course, that was before Leffler was killed. Now the drone wasn't just a nuisance that she had disposed of, but a possible link connecting the Flock to the crime. She was beginning to regret not calling an attorney.

"The drones started showing up the same day I gave my statement to Agent West. I reported this to him, but he said it was a matter for local law enforcement unless I could tie the things directly to the Flock. They seem to be very poorly made, because several of them have crashed on my lawn. My security company has been collecting them, but I was heading out of town and ... yes, I'm tired of dealing with the harassment. The alarms go off multiple times a day. It's reached the point where my housemate and her five-year-old daughter had to take an unplanned vacation just to get away."

"I can see how that would be upsetting, especially for the child." A flicker of genuine sympathy crossed the agent's face for the first time. "But ... that drone could have been evidence."

"Then maybe someone should have taken me seriously when I complained about them. You have the video. You can check with Apex Security to see if they kept any of the other drones. Better yet, I've gotten multiple alerts since I left home, which means the Flock is still sending them. Tell the Baltimore office they're welcome to come grab a few. As for the one this morning, I sincerely doubt that the Flock is going to contact you to complain that I damaged their property, but if they do, I'll happily reimburse them."

"Understood. I don't think anyone is planning to press charges on that front. How well do you know Tobias Shepherd?"

It seemed like a rather abrupt shift in topic, since Shepherd was no longer in charge of the Flock, but again, Claire figured she had nothing to hide. "I barely know him at all. We've spoken on three occasions. Once was just prior to the debate that I moderated between him and Anton Kolya onboard the *Ares Prime*. We interacted during the debate, as well, but only in the sense that I introduced him and informed him and Kolya when their time was up. We also had a brief conversation while on Mars."

"And what was that conversation about, Ms. Echols?"

"He thanked me for my quick action in telling Kolya that they should check for neurotoxins."

"Which I believe was the same thing you asked the nurse to do today. You told Officer Daniello..." She paused and pulled up something on her device. "You said that the attack on Shepherd was what made you think Leffler wasn't suffering from heatstroke. So ... exactly what made you think *Shepherd* had been hit by a chemical weapon when he collapsed at the debate?"

Claire frowned. "Shepherd slapped his neck and fell to the ground in convulsions. Something skittered under the chair next to me at almost the same instant. It was a drone. I think the idea that it might have been weaponized was a fairly logical conclusion under the circumstances, Agent Wheeler."

"Oh, absolutely. I'm just surprised that *you* were the only person who noticed it. It was a public event, right? There were dozens of people in the room?"

There was a sly look in the agent's eyes. And her tone of voice was almost ... anticipatory. Like she wasn't asking questions so much as she was trying to lead Claire toward some sort of admission. Again, she was tempted to stop and call an attorney. But the only thing she'd done wrong was destroying the drone. Okay, it would be *drones* if they bothered to go back through her security footage over the past few weeks, but she'd never come right out and said that was the only time she'd disposed of one. And Wheeler already said they weren't interested in pressing charges about that.

"Yes," she said. "There were probably close to eighty people in attendance, given that most of the crew was also there. But I wasn't the only one who saw something. One of the other members of the team I traveled with was in the audience and she saw the same thing I did."

"And who would that be?"

"Chelsea Friesen."

"Do you have her contact information?"

"No. She was a grad student at Columbia, but she's currently doing a post-doctoral fellowship on the West Coast. I'm not sure what university that's with, but she should be fairly easy to find. KTI security told her the same thing they told me—to keep her suspicions to herself. They were worried about starting a panic among the passengers. If Chelsea saw it, though, I imagine there were others, too. I was merely close enough to look under the chair and make a positive identification. Close enough to Anton Kolya that I could point it out to him, and he could pass the word along to the medical team. I also had an advantage because I noticed the blinking light in the audience a few seconds before that, and I remembered it from the drone that followed me through Franklin Park the night before I left for Mars. I'd just had the thought that it was the same pattern when it attacked Shepherd. "

"Okay. I suppose that makes sense." She entered something into her device, taking her time.

When the agent looked up again, Claire glanced pointedly at the clock, which now read five fifty-five.

Wheeler followed her gaze. "I just have a couple more questions, Ms. Echols. Did you and Dr. Shepherd talk about anything else when you saw him at … I believe you said it was at…" She looked down at her device again. "At Ehden?"

Claire kept her face neutral, but something was definitely off. She was certain that she hadn't mentioned Shepherd's location on Mars. Not to hospital security, not to the NYPD, not even to the agent she'd spoken with in Baltimore. She might not have been

Tobias Shepherd's biggest fan, but the same people who tried to kill her had tried to kill him, and she suspected that the Flock might decide to have a second go at the man once the current terraforming lockdown was lifted and they could get their people back on the planet. The FBI might have gotten his location from someone at KTI, but they certainly hadn't gotten it from her. They hadn't asked, and she hadn't offered.

"I told him that I'd seen a drone like that before and asked if the one that attacked him was similar to ones used by the Flock. He said that the group had never used drones at all while he was in charge. And then he said he needed to get back to the meeting he was having with Kolya."

"That was all?"

"Yes."

"And Shepherd didn't *give* you anything?"

"What? No. We just talked."

"He didn't pass anything off to you? A microdrive, perhaps?"

"No. Why would you even think that?"

"Just following up on some information we received."

"From whom?"

Wheeler raised her eyebrows slightly. "I obviously can't tell you that. Just as you weren't willing to tell me the name of your colleague's source. Was that everything that you and Dr. Shepherd discussed?"

"I think … I think I also asked him about the fact that some of his followers were joining him, but that's when he said he needed to get back to his discussion with Kolya. And that was our entire conversation."

"Very well, Ms. Echols." The agent flashed a tight smile and stood up. "I believe I have everything I need. Thank you for your time."

She was almost to the door when Claire realized something she'd forgotten. "Wait. He didn't *give* me anything, but he did return a scrunchie that I'd dropped in the restroom while I was changing out of my pressure suit."

Wheeler walked back toward the table. "A what?"

"A cloth hairband. A scrunchie. I think it was pink."

To her surprise, the agent stopped and typed this into her device. "And where would that hair band be now?"

Claire couldn't help but laugh. "I have no idea. Most likely at my house, I guess? I probably have a dozen of the things. But given that it was inside the bag that was in the cave with me when the bomb went off, it could just as easily still be on Mars. It might have been blown to bits for all I know. Why does it matter?"

"Oh, I'm sure it doesn't." Wheeler jammed the device back into her pocket. "Just making sure to dot every *I* and cross every *T* before I submit my report. Have a good evening, Ms. Echols."

SEVEN

FOR QUITE POSSIBLY THE first time ever, Wyatt was the one waiting for Claire to arrive. She found him in a curved booth near one of the three clear aquarium pillars at the center of the restaurant. He'd even dressed for the occasion, trading his usual jeans for a pair of slim black chinos and a dark green shirt.

As she'd expected, there was no time to stop by the hotel to shower and change. No big deal. Wyatt had seen her looking worse and she was in dire need of food and a drink, both of which —bless him—he had waiting at the table. She grabbed a spring roll from the plate and sank her teeth into it as she slid into the booth next to him.

He grinned. "You keep me waiting for nearly thirty minutes and this is the treatment I get? No kiss, no hello. You just go straight for the appetizers."

"Do *not* tease me, Wyatt Garcia. The last solid food that entered my mouth was half a bagel a little before seven this morning. It's been a truly horrible day."

"I can see that." He ran one finger over the twin bandages on her upper arm. "What happened?"

She glanced down, confused for a moment. "Oh. I'd completely forgotten about that. Ro and Jemma also left town, so Siggy needed to go to the kennel. But your dearest darling refused to get into the cat carrier. And yes, I tried bribing her. She just twitched her tail and glared at me. I was tempted to set out the auto-feeder and leave her grumpy little ass home alone. But then I remembered what happened the last time, and that wasn't even a full day. Siggy would probably find a way to torch the place if left on her own for three entire days."

When Claire was on her way back from Mars, Ro had worked an unplanned double shift on one of the rare nights that Jemma was at her dad's place. Ro had arrived home to find spice jars all over the kitchen. Toilet paper was in shredded mounds on the floor of all three bathrooms, and one of Claire's piano books hadn't fared much better. The cushions of the chairs where Ro and Claire sat at the table had to be replaced because they smelled of cat urine, while the guest chair (which Wyatt occasionally occupied) and Jemma's chair remained unspoiled. Siggy's message was clear. The fact that she had been left alone for nearly twenty hours was the fault of the *spare* humans.

"Yeah," Wyatt said. "Ro sent me pictures. Along with an all-caps message to come get my hell beast. But by the time I made it back into town, she'd calmed down. A bit."

"More likely she'd realized Jemma would never forgive her if she gave the cat back."

He grinned. "Or that. So … if battle scars are the part of the day that you'd almost forgotten, I'm guessing you had no luck with the professor. I may be able to cheer you up a bit on that … front." He paused, gauging Claire's expression. "Wait. *Is* this about the meeting with the professor? Or is it connected to the video you sent me this morning?"

"Both," she said after swallowing the last bite of the spring roll. "Dr. Leffler was attacked by a nanodrone just outside the CVS across the street from the university, around eleven this morning. Only this one was armed with a V-class nerve agent."

Wyatt's eyes went wide. "What the hell?"

"Yeah. She didn't make it. I was there when Alice Dobroski—Leffler's colleague from the university—got the news that she'd been taken to the emergency room. The doctors assumed it was heatstroke. Some of the symptoms are similar, I guess. And they've been seeing a lot of heatstroke patients this summer, so it was the more obvious diagnosis. Leffler died about ten minutes after we arrived. Maybe five minutes after I told the doctors that they should check her for neurotoxins."

"Now I'm wondering…" He stopped, shaking his head.

"Wondering what?"

"Just a lead that came in this morning. I hadn't given it much thought. Mostly because it was anonymous, and you know how rarely those pan out. But … now I'm thinking I may need to reassess. What made you think that it *wasn't* heatstroke with Leffler?"

"I'm not entirely sure. It was more of a hunch. Maybe the drones were just on my mind after seeing that freaky cicadabot outside my house this morning … I don't know. I just noticed she had this scratch on her neck, surrounded by a reddish patch. Later at the police station, when they showed me the security footage taken outside the drugstore, I realized the mark was from when she slapped the drone. The doctor said she'd likely have died within minutes, but it got tangled in her hair and didn't get a clean shot. When they brought her in, the nurse noticed a fragment of the rotor in her hair and pulled it out, thinking it was a broken hair clip. The edge pricked the finger of her glove, so she was exposed too, but they delivered the antidote in time to save her. If she'd listened to me when I first told her about the nerve agent, they might have been able to save Leffler, too, but … maybe not. As I told the police, the nurse seemed a little disoriented when I was talking to her so the nerve agent may have already been screwing with her head."

"So that's why you were late?"

She nodded. "I was grilled first by hospital security, then the NYPD, and then the FBI."

"Well, that's a fun little trifecta. They don't believe you had anything to do with it, do they?"

"I don't think so. Once I explained about seeing a similar drone attack Shepherd on the *Ares Prime* and the fact that I've been swarmed by the damn things recently, they seemed to understand why I suspected it was a drone attack. And maybe there's a silver lining. Maybe the field office in Baltimore will take my complaints about the drones a bit more seriously now that one of the things is connected to a murder here on Earth."

"So you told them about the one outside your house this morning?"

"Yeah. I sent the video to the agent in Baltimore, along with a message about the attack on Leffler. I didn't think I had much choice since I'd already sent it to you and to Kes. I'm sure they could track those messages if they wanted to. Plus, I was probably in full view of half a dozen doorbell cams when I beat the thing to a pulp. But that is no doubt why they kept me waiting an extra hour until an agent from the local FBI office could question me. Which ... was kind of weird, to be honest. She seemed more interested in what I knew about Tobias Shepherd than she was in what happened to Leffler."

He ran a hand through his hair. "If something like this happens again, do not say *anything* to the police without pulling in one of the *Post's* attorneys. That's why they keep them on contract. You give the cops your name and The Speech. That's it. They do teach science reporters The Speech, right?"

She narrowed her eyes at him. Teasing her after the day she'd had was venturing onto very thin ice. Even lowly science reporters had to recite The Speech when they were hired. Not that she'd ever had to use it.

"No," she said, her voice laced with sarcasm. "I failed Journalism 101 and still, somehow, managed to graduate. Please enlighten me, oh wise one."

"Okay," he said with a sheepish look. "I deserved that."

"You did. They didn't even *ask* for my phone, Wyatt. My bag had to go through a scanner a couple of times, but they didn't search it. I wasn't under suspicion."

"Yeah, but you're never under suspicion until suddenly you are. All I'm saying is that you should be careful. I'll just pass along the advice that Jamaal—by far the best attorney on contract with the *Post*—gave me. After you provide your name and your press credentials, you ask *them* a question—am I being detained or am I free to go? That's it. If they answer that you are free to go, then you go and you call your attorney. If they say anything else, the only thing they get is The Speech until your attorney is conferenced into the discussion."

"Duly noted." It actually seemed overly suspicious to Claire, and also a bit like a plan concocted by attorneys to guarantee the maximum number of billable hours. But it *had* kept Wyatt out of serious trouble, and he was in an area of journalism that often skirted the edges of legality. Anyway, she really wasn't in the mood to argue.

"So … do you think the drone at your house was weaponized, too?" Wyatt asked.

"Probably not? The only thing that was different from all of the others that have barraged the place this week was the recording. And even if it was weaponized, I didn't touch the thing. I wore the gas mask, whacked it with a shovel, and tossed it into the trash."

"What exactly was on the recording? I gathered from your text that there was a message of some sort, but I could only make out a few words above that screeching noise in the background. It was saying something about a tree, right?"

Claire frowned, trying to remember what noise he meant. "Oh. You mean the garbage truck. Sorry. The drone was playing a bible verse, believe it or not. I'm paraphrasing a bit here, but it's the one warning that if you eat from the tree of knowledge, you will surely die. Have you heard any other reports of the Flock going biblical?"

"No. They've always been strictly secular. Although, they may be finding new allies within some religious circles. I don't know how much time you've spent on social media lately—"

"As little as possible."

"Smart move. But you know how the past few months have shaken things up. I would have thought it impossible for this many different religious leaders to agree on anything, but a whole bunch of them seem to think your brother's work is … heresy? Or would it be blasphemy?"

"I've seen people claiming both. Luckily, Joe and Beck have gotten pretty good at ignoring the chaos."

"Good for them. It's such complete hypocrisy. Ninety-nine-point-nine percent of the people currently blasting them for playing god are going to end up taking the drug as soon as it's available to them. Some of them are probably already trying to bribe their way into higher placement in the lottery."

Rejuvesce was set to be released beginning in October in the US, the Northern European Union, and six other nations that had been chosen at random—one from each of the six regional divisions of the World Health Organization. Additional countries were scheduled to be added over the next few years. There was considerable grumbling over the US and Northern European Union being automatically placed in Tier One, but Jonas Labs had received grants from the national health services of both governments and those contracts mandated priority access.

The drug would be distributed through the normal public health channels in each country, and through the WHO in those that lacked the necessary infrastructure. Since demand would greatly outpace supply at the beginning, everyone in these countries between the ages of fifty and sixty-five had been entered into a lottery to determine when they would be allowed to begin the treatment.

Protests had started within hours after the results of the lottery were published. The media quickly dubbed these demonstrations the *Gray Riots*, which was fairly accurate. Some of the protestors were angry that they'd landed in a higher tier of the lottery, and the US Department of Health was accused of racial, gender, and economic bias from members of pretty much every demographic. But the angriest group by far was made up of individuals over the cutoff age of seventy. The drug *did* help patients above that age, but it had a much higher rate of failure, and the benefits were far more limited. There were plans to increase the age limit over the next decade, but as these older individuals often noted, they didn't really *have* the time to wait. In their case, access delayed could well be equivalent to access denied.

Most of the protestors aimed their anger (and in some cases, their lawsuits) at Jonas Labs and the government distribution centers. But with tensions running high, there had also been a number of clashes between the anti-Rejuvesce crowd and the ones demanding quicker access. One video that made the rounds showed an elderly man at a rally outside a distribution center in Denver whacking a younger anti-Rejuvesce guy from the local Gates of Destiny Cathedral over the head with his protest sign.

"Just wait and see," Wyatt continued. "The religious objectors will lie and say they're not taking it. But I bet they won't cough up medical records to prove it. Almost all of them are going to delay their trip to heaven in exchange for a few extra decades down here with all of us heathens."

Claire chuckled. Wyatt had little patience with organized religion of any stripe, and even less with the fundamentalist variety. That seemed to be an occupational hazard for those who covered terrorist groups, given that they got a close-up look at the bloodshed that all too often resulted from the toxic mix of religion and politics. But she suspected he was right that many of those currently claiming they had no plans to take Rejuvesce would be singing a very different tune as soon as they were notified that they were finally eligible for a prescription.

"I'm definitely not taking their side," she said, "but you have to admit it's been a rough couple of months for people with a traditionalist worldview. Rejuvesce would have shaken things up enough on its own, but with the Mars story coming out right on its heels some of them seem to feel doubly threatened."

As angry as Claire had been at Kolya over the way that KTI had chosen to release the news about the chambers, she now realized that he had been right about one thing—it was probably the only way to be sure that the story wasn't buried. Unfortunately, it had also poured fuel onto the inevitable fire of conspiracy theories. It wasn't just religious groups and the usual truther crowds, either. Several governments had expressed skepticism about the authenticity of the discovery, including a few US politicians.

"But rejecting the Mars discovery makes sense," Wyatt said. "At least, from their perspective. I mean, I'm not aware of any religious texts that talk about how God did a trial run on another planet first and then trashed the whole enterprise. Although maybe they could say it was a Noah's ark kind of thing. But I think they'll eventually come to terms with Rejuvesce...both because they really *do* want an extra decade or two of life and because they can dredge up a biblical precedent for people having really, really long lives. Jonas Labs's marketing department missed the ball when they picked the name. If they had packaged the drug as Methuselah, they could have avoided a lot of these protests."

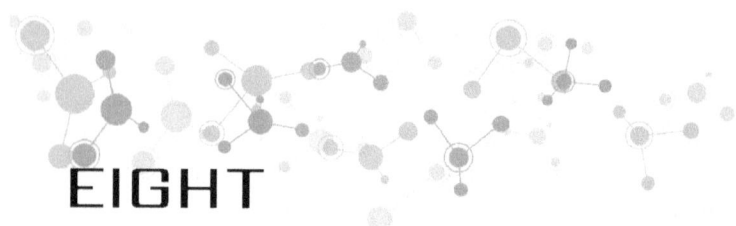

EIGHT

WYATT WAS SILENT FOR A MOMENT, swirling the whiskey around in his glass. "You need to start carrying your gun. It doesn't do you any good if you leave it in the closet. And maybe you should hire a full-time security guard until all of this is over. I know Ro will hate it, but I don't like the idea of the three of you there alone. Or the *two* of *them*, depending on how long you'll be in Boston."

"You may be right about the security guard," she said, ignoring the part about the gun. They'd been over that territory plenty of times already and he'd heard all of the reasons she hated carrying it. "But I'll be back *before* Ro and Jemma. Like I said before, they're out of town. She decided to take Jemma and visit her mom in Vancouver for a few weeks."

Wyatt made a sick face. "You mean the mom she calls Nina the Narcissist?"

"That's the one. And … I don't know. Maybe Ro was right to clear out for a while. It's been a pretty steady bombardment for the past week. Jemma's having nightmares again, and Ro thinks it's due to the drones. Or to be more precise, due to my reaction to the drones. And again, she's probably right."

"I'm sorry, babe. I really kicked the hornet's nest with that last article."

"What else could you do? The Flock killed seven people on Mars and now Leffler. And those are just the ones that we *know* of. Someone has to make sure that the justice system holds them to account."

"But why Leffler?" Wyatt mused. "I feel like we're missing

something here. The Flock targeting me makes sense. I'm investigating them, after all. Targeting the surviving members of the team who were at Icarus ..." He paused. "You *did* let the others on the team know what happened to Leffler, right?"

Claire nodded. "I messaged Ben Pelzer and asked him to contact Chelsea, who is in California on a fellowship of some sort. I didn't go into a lot of detail, since I was in the NYPD precinct office at the time, but Ben's smart enough to put the pieces together."

"Good. Because, as I was about to say, targeting the three of you makes sense, as well, given that you all may be called to testify if this ever makes it to trial. And in your case, they've got *two* reasons because of Rejuvesce. Three, if I'm being honest, because I'm sure they know about us. It's not like we've kept our relationship a secret. But none of that applies to Leffler. From what you've told me she wasn't even particularly interested in translating the inscriptions."

"I think it's more that she didn't believe it was *possible* to translate them. But yeah ... given the timing? It almost feels like they were trying to send me a message to back off. Or maybe it's a message to both of us. If they're monitoring my travel, they probably know you're in New York, too. What I don't get is why they wouldn't just come after us directly. Sure, we've taken precautions with the drone zappers, but that can't be the only weapon at their disposal. Drexel has dozens of devoted sheep who would be happy to pick people off with a sniper rifle. Or plant a bomb, for that matter. They even have a few mad bombers with experience now. And the risk of getting caught won't be much of a deterrent for them. Fanatics tend to be a lot less worried than others about getting away alive or avoiding..."

She trailed off as the screens in the center of their table lit up, reminding them that they still needed to order. A young woman who was far too perfect not to be an avatar smiled broadly from the center screen and spread her hands in greeting. "Welcome to Ăn Ngon Miệng. Tonight's specials are chả cá lã vọng—a house-grown halibut pan-fried with fresh herbs—and bún thịt nướng, which contains cultured pork, grilled and tossed with rice noodles and a medley of vegetables. Once you've browsed through the menu screens and made your selection, tap the button to the right to bring up the kitchen, where you can watch as Chef Quang prepares your dinner."

When Claire finished ordering, Wyatt was still staring blankly at the first page of the menu screen. That wasn't like him at all. She had often joked that they should stick to restaurants with short and simple menus because he was notoriously bad at reaching a decision, and would waver back and forth, debating aloud the merits of half a dozen different entrees. She suspected that his mind was still on their conversation about the Flock. He'd already been feeling bad about the story stirring up trouble and learning about Leffler had no doubt made it worse. And it probably hadn't helped that she went off on her rant about all of the other ways the Flock could pick them off if they were so inclined.

She waved a hand in front of him. "Earth to Wyatt."

"Oh. Sorry." He tapped one of the specials on the first screen without even glancing at it.

"Do you want to watch the chef?" she asked.

"I'll pass. The food is good here, but that part feels a little gimmicky."

"Yeah. I don't even think it's a live feed. One reviewer said she ordered her meal without mushrooms, and it *arrived* exactly as she ordered it, sans mushrooms, even though she clearly saw the chef tossing mushrooms into the pan with the other ingredients. They probably record one video for each dish on the menu and play it for everyone who orders it."

Claire switched off the screen, then leaned over to give him a kiss. "I'm sorry I came in all grumpy. And grungy, for that matter." She nudged the daypack on the floor with her foot. "I really *did* pack my blue dress but … between being interrogated by the doctors and then by the police, there was no time to change."

The blue dress was something of a shared joke, one of their signals for navigating a relationship that had moved from friends to lovers and back again more times than Claire could remember. She rarely *wore* the dress and hadn't actually planned to tonight. But it was a handy, if somewhat cliché method for broaching the subject of whether the dinner, the weekend, or whatever other plans they were making would be as friends or as something more. There had been many, many dinners when one or the other of them was dating someone else and they'd even taken a three-day trip Claire had booked before discovering that the guy she was dating hadn't been entirely honest about his interest in skiing. She and Wyatt were perfectly capable of keeping things platonic.

But this was *supposed* to be a blue dress evening. They'd established that when she messaged him last night. Which meant that Wyatt should have responded with some bit of innuendo … perhaps a suggestion that she could always model the dress for him back at the hotel. Or a cheeky observation that it would have wound up on the floor anyway.

He didn't. Instead, a silence settled over the table.

That was rare—they usually had plenty to talk about. But even when they didn't, she never felt the need to force conversation. This silence felt different, though, and it unnerved Claire enough that she tried to think of something unrelated to Leffler's death that might fill the void.

Which, of course, meant that the only thing that popped into her head was something that *was* related, at least tangentially. But it was also something that Wyatt had mentioned before she told him about Leffler, and she was curious.

"What did you mean earlier? You said you had some news that might help … did you mean with the translation?"

"Oh, that's right!" Wyatt perked up, clearly grateful for the conversational lifeline. "Can't believe I forgot. And I don't know if it will actually *help*, but it's definitely connected. Weird, too. You need to keep it confidential, though. At least until it hits the bookstores in…" He stopped and made a mental calculation. "Six days."

Claire made a lip-zipping motion.

"The copy Devin gave me is an earlier version, though. I don't even think it's been edited. At least, I hope not. Talk about purple prose…"

"Are you saying Devin wrote a book?"

"What?" He snorted. "*No.* Devin is my source, but the book was written by Tobias Shepherd. A memoir, supposedly, but some sections of it seem pretty damn fictional to me. He's now saying he actually *knew* one of these Sentinels he's always talking about, back when he was a kid."

Claire gave him a skeptical look. "That seems like the kind of thing any aspiring cult leader would include in the recruitment literature from day one."

"Exactly. I wondered if it was something that he had shared with members only after they turned over the contents of their bank accounts, but Devin says it was never mentioned in meetings. All Shepherd ever told them was that he'd been chosen as the Sentinels' messenger, so they probably thought it was an Elijah and the burning bush sort of thing."

"Pretty sure the burning bush was Moses."

He shrugged. "One of those guys. *Anyway,* I just skimmed the early chapters, since the stuff I'm planning to use is about the group's organizational structure and some of Shepherd's claims about Corbin Drexel."

"Does he explain her name change? Because I have to admit that it sticks in my mind. The name sort of evokes … I don't know. A comic book villain, I guess? I'd been picturing someone who looked like Lex Luther before you showed me that video."

"He doesn't explain it. I'm thinking it's a messianic sort of thing. I'll send you a transcript from a recording that Devin made of her speaking to the Flock at Culpeper right after the takeover and you can judge for yourself. Anyway, one of the photographs in the first half of the book caught my eye. I'll transfer the full manuscript to your box at the *Post* along with the Drexel transcripts, but this will give you an idea of what I'm talking about." He took out his phone, searched for a few seconds, and expanded the screen before turning it around to face her. "I don't know about you, but I'm almost certain that I've seen those symbols before."

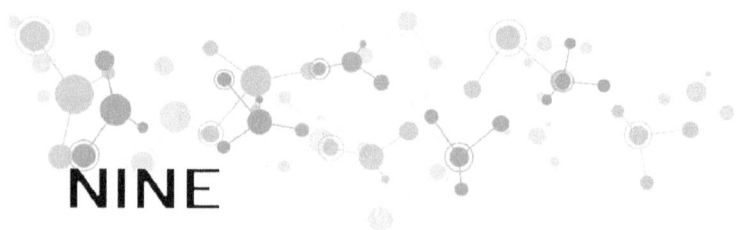

NINE

CLAIRE TOOK Wyatt's phone and stared down at the book in the photograph. A children's book, judging from the colorful, cartoonish drawing on the cover. At the center of the picture was an animal of some sort, with blue fur, walking through a surreal forest that reminded Claire of the plant life she'd seen on Mars, during the drive from the Red Dahlia to Dome Three just outside Daedalus City. It wasn't that the plants themselves were similar—they weren't anything alike—but more that they had the same otherworldly feel.

She couldn't read the words above and below the picture, but Wyatt was right. The symbols were very familiar indeed.

"See the one here that's kind of like a bullseye?" He pointed toward the top of the screen. "And that one at the end. Sort of a squashed *S* or maybe a reversed number two?"

"Yeah. The little staircase, too. I recognize all three of those from the chambers and from…"

Claire stopped just shy of mentioning the manuscript encoded in the *Deinococcus* sample in Joe's lab. It wasn't that she didn't trust Wyatt. She knew he'd keep it secret, just as he knew he could trust her with Shepherd's memoir. In fact, she'd probably be giving him the full story the next time she saw him. But Beck had been adamant that they tell no one until they had time, at a minimum, to hash out the ramifications of going public with the find. She didn't want to break that promise.

"And from the message in the lower chamber, too," she continued. "All of the symbols seem a bit more rounded here and there are some other minor differences, but yeah … it's much too close to be a coincidence." She gave a rueful laugh. "I'd actually gained a tiny bit of respect for the man after talking to him at Ehden and then he pulls a scam like this, tying his stupid Sentinel mythology into the Mars discovery in order to sell more books."

"That was my first thought, too. But Devin says Shepherd sent the entire book—photographs and all—to the publisher a week or so before he was forced out as head of the Flock. He has a two-book deal with some small press in Virginia. One of the other … dissidents, I guess? … worked with Shepherd to get both manuscripts ready before he left."

"Then maybe the publisher did it? Because it would be really easy to fake that cover based on the pictures and video we brought back."

"Except this is the draft version that Shepherd sent to the publisher *before* he left for Mars. Or at least that's what Devin claims. And given that he's my only source inside the Flock, I really hope he's not lying. But yeah. Erica thinks the entire manuscript is a fake."

Erica Roth was Wyatt's long-suffering editor at the *Post*. Claire suspected that at least half of her job was making sure that his stories didn't get the paper sued or, worse yet, given the violent nature of the groups he usually wrote about, blown to bits.

"Well, you clearly don't think Devin capable of perpetuating this kind of fraud, so … do you think the Flock's new leadership planted it?"

Wyatt shook his head. "I just don't buy it. The depiction of Drexel seems too unflattering for her to want this published. But there were several other people vying for control of the Flock after she pushed Shepherd out, mostly people who weren't happy that she kind of came out of nowhere. I don't think she'd ever had any dealings with the group until around the beginning of this year. Devin said the guy in charge of the Culpeper compound tried to oppose her at first, but they apparently worked out their differences. Could be that one of the other leaders wrote this to try and discredit her. Maybe to discredit Shepherd, too, given that a lot of the book seems pretty ... out there. Although I doubt that anyone who would bother reading Shepherd's memoir is going to be too surprised that the guy claims he befriended an alien as a kid. Either way, though, Erica says if I'm going to rely on this information, I need to confirm that it's the real deal." He gave her a hopeful smile. "Any chance that you'd be willing to lend a hand with that?"

"Sure," Claire said, a little confused. "I can take a look at it on my way up to Boston. But I only had a couple of conversations with the man, so I don't have any confidence at all that I'd be able to tell if this was written by him. And there are much better ways to figure that out. This is far from the first thing that Shepherd has published. There must be at least half a dozen books and a ton of articles. Why don't you get someone at work to run a similarity analysis?"

"Already did. It's actually well over a dozen books and the memoir seems consistent with the stuff he's published previously. The fact that there *are* so many of his works out there is more of a curse than a blessing, though, because it makes his writing style really easy for AI to imitate. Which is precisely why Erica insists that I confirm Shepherd actually wrote this if I want to include any of the allegations from the book in my follow-up piece on the Flock."

"Why not just ask him? He's in the dome at Ehden. Communications are a little dodgy so it may take a few tries, but you should be able to get a message to him."

"Tried that, too. I've messaged four or five times over the past week with no luck. So ... do you think maybe you could ask Kolya to put you in contact with him? From what you said before, Ehden is operating as a KTI protectorate. Which means Kolya would have a better shot at getting him to respond than anyone, right? And he does kind of owe you since it was KTI employees who nearly got you killed."

Claire rubbed her temples and grimaced. This wasn't exactly how she'd planned to tell Wyatt about her almost-fling with

Kolya. After the dozens of snide comments she'd made about the man over the years, Wyatt was almost certainly going to laugh and ask her what in God's name she'd been thinking. On the other hand, he was less likely to do that in public. And she was getting very tired of keeping secrets.

"Contacting Kolya would be awkward." She took a long slow sip of her drink, then sighed. Might as well get it over with. "I won't bore you with the details, but Kolya and I engaged in a … well, I guess you'd call it a mutual flirtation. Nothing happened, in part because I found out that he'd had an affair with my mother. For several years, in fact. *While* my father was alive."

If nothing else, she managed to render Wyatt speechless for several seconds.

"And no," she added quickly before he could find his voice, "I really *don't* want to talk about it."

"Good," he said after another long silence. "Because I have no idea what I could say that wouldn't get me into some sort of trouble. Does Joe know?"

"No. Or at least, if he knows, it's not because I told him. And I don't think I should. But that question qualifies as *talking about it*, which I'm pretty sure I just said I didn't want to do."

"Sorry. Are you okay? I mean, I know you and Kai aren't exactly…" He raised his hands. "Which … would also be talking about it."

"Yes. But I'm *fine*. And leaving all of this aside, I don't have Kolya's personal number." That was true, although she had no doubt that she could get someone at KTI to patch her through. "What I *do* have, however, is contact info for Paul Caruso. Assuming Kolya had the good sense to move him up to Stasia's position, he should be able to put me in touch with Shepherd himself. If not, I'm sure he'd pass a message on." Claire pulled out her phone to find Paul's info. "Or better yet, why don't I put you and Paul in touch so that he can connect you directly to Shepherd? That way if you have any additional questions, you can just—"

"That would be a *bad* idea."

She stopped and looked up from the screen. "Okay. What aren't you telling me?"

"Pretty sure that I'm *persona non grata* with the KTI press relations office. Which probably means that your friend Caruso already knows my name. Let's just say they know I'm working on a story that Kolya is not going to like."

"I doubt that he was particularly fond of your *last* story, either." The server was approaching, so she waited until their plates were in front of them, the wine was poured, and they were once again alone before continuing. "Is this the follow-up piece on the bombings?"

"No. It's based on something from my source in the MFL. She has some new information about the accident at Millex."

His mention of the MFL took Claire back to the mezzanine of the Red Dahlia's executive pavilion, her fingers idly wandering over the keys of the red baby grand as she waited for Kolya to emerge from the dark cube of the conference room where he was mediating a dispute between mine owners and representatives of the newly formed Mars Federation of Labor. The mine owners had balked at having to pay bonuses during the lockdown, which was projected to last six months. Bonuses were a substantial part of the pay structure, however, and almost all of the workers were limited to a two-year contract in order to minimize health complications from the lower gravity on Mars. For many of the workers, losing the bonuses would have meant forfeiting about a quarter of the income they'd been expecting from their time on the planet, so they weren't inclined to back down. That was the key issue that led to them forming a union and, eventually, threatening a strike. Kolya later said that they'd been on the verge of an agreement when negotiations were halted due to the news that several workers had been killed in an explosion at a tridymite mine in Cerberus Fossae—an explosion that they'd eventually determined was orchestrated by Stasia Ljubic and the other two Flock members a few days before they set the bombs at Icarus Camp.

"Okay," she said, "but I wouldn't exactly call what happened at Millex an accident. I mean, they confirmed that the Flock was behind it, right?"

"Probably, although there are some who think it was a grudge with another mining company. But I don't mean the bombing. I'm talking about a containment breach. There's a couple of different versions of the story. One version says the owners had a change of heart about adhering to protocol a few weeks into the lockdown. The other says it was a manager from another company that some of the workers were subcontracted out to. Anyway, whether it was the Miller brothers or one of their managers, *somebody* got the bright idea of getting a jump on the competition by resuming operations a few months early. Rumors started circulating that they were looking for people interested in earning the *full* bonus instead of the three-quarters compromise agreed upon in the labor talks at Daedalus City. They assured them that between the biohazard suits and the camp's new, upgraded decontamination process, it would be absolutely safe. And it absolutely wasn't."

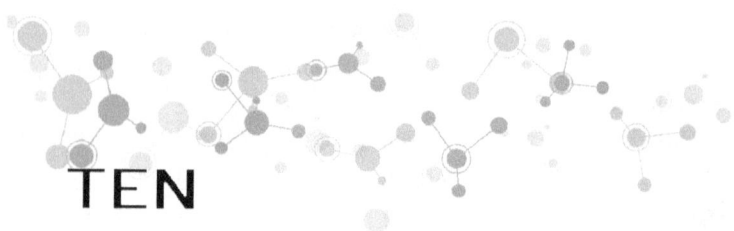

TEN

"THE CONTAMINATION SPREAD through one of their barracks along the outer edge of the dome overnight," Wyatt said. "At breakfast the next morning, one of the managers noticed that the transport that brought them in for meals hadn't arrived. Forty, maybe fifty workers, in total."

"And the containment breach killed *all* of them?"

"Probably? It's hard to really pin down a cause of death, though, since maybe five minutes after that manager reported the absences, their barracks collapsed and caught fire. Or exploded, depending on who you ask."

"Let me guess ... they're claiming that was a coincidence?"

"Ding, ding, ding. Give the lady a prize. The owners issued a press release stating that the barracks had unfortunately been built over an undetected sinkhole, which they believed had caused the collapse. They kept back a small work crew and temporarily relocated the rest of the miners—including my source —to another dome nearby for about a week, claiming they were worried about hazardous emissions from the sinkhole or the fire or something like that. By the time the workers returned, there was no sign of the barracks or the purported sinkhole. Just a big pile of rocks where the building had been. The company said all of the residents died in the collapse. My source tried poking around a bit, asking the work crew that stayed behind what they saw. She found four or five people who were willing to talk before word got out that she was asking too many questions, and the owners convinced her to stop."

"Convinced her *how*? Is she okay?"

"Yeah. She told them she was just upset because she lost several friends in the collapse and that she was trying to make the whole situation make sense. And she *had* lost some friends, so I think they bought it. Mostly they just waved her contract in her face and said she'd be sent back to Earth, without her bonus, as soon as the lockdown was over if they heard that she was causing any more trouble."

"And you've already asked KTI about the accident?"

"Of course. I contacted them for a comment nearly three weeks ago, since Millex is one of their contractors. They're fully backing the owners' version of events, which was pretty much what I expected, but ... I had to give them the opportunity. When I mentioned that there were rumors of a containment failure, one of Kolya's lackeys accused me of rumormongering and threatened a lawsuit."

"Yeah ... that seems to be their default response to any press they don't like. How sure are you about your source?"

"She has *four* different witnesses to what actually happened that night. Says she also has photographic evidence. Millex and KTI have a pretty tight lock on communications, though. We've got a code worked out for getting information back and forth, but that doesn't work for images. She'll have to send those the old-fashioned way."

"Which is?"

"Get someone to sneak it out on a data drive when a ship leaves Ares Station, which unfortunately means it will be a few months after the lockdown ends before it reaches me. I may have to sit on this story for a while. But yeah, I'm convinced Millex is lying. They sent a team out. May not have been a full crew. May have been just a few people as a test. But someone who came back either had a tear in their suit or the decontamination units for entering the camp were garbage. Maybe both. Several people in the other barracks got messages from friends that night saying they'd contracted some kind of flu, and then later, they sent reports that what they were coughing up was green. And not phlegmy greenish-brown gunk like you might expect with a flu or whatever, but *dayglo* green. The same color as whatever they call that crap that covered the surface of the planet at the beginning of stage six. *Azo* ... something."

"*Azospira oryzae*," Claire said. "Although KTI may have given it another name, since it's an amped-up proprietary version that spreads much more rapidly. Davina Monroe said it was hazardous ... that it could form a biofilm in the respiratory tract. On your mucous membranes, too."

"I'm glad you didn't nick your suit when you recorded that demonstration video."

"I actually *did*. But we used a glove unit to make sure the bacteria were released inside the dome and the fabric on my suit was self-healing. Good thing, too, since I did a whole lot more than nick the suit when that bomb went off at Icarus. Although ... thinking back, most of the miners at Icarus were issued the older, bulky units they call puffsuits. It was probably the same at Millex. I doubt those suits offer the same level of protection." Claire frowned. "I'm actually kind of surprised that KTI is covering up for Millex. This sort of danger is the reason Kolya insisted on the lockdown and even covered some of the costs for the smaller companies. If what your source says is true, the mining company is the one at fault here."

"Does it matter? Kolya is the public face of the terraforming project. And the bacterial slime that colonized the lungs of those miners was modified in KTI labs. That's not a good look, even if he did insist on the lockdown. Of course he'd want to cover it up. Anyway, that's why no one at KTI is going to give *me* the time of day." Wyatt tossed back the last of his drink. "Pretty sure they're also the reason my press credentials were denied by the UN yesterday."

"You're kidding?"

"Nope. I thought I'd do an end-run around their little informa-tion blockade and corner Kolya to ask him about the accident when he's at the UN this coming Tuesday for the Ares Consortium meeting. So I put in what I assumed was a routine request for a press pass, given how many times I've covered protests there. But I was informed that they're restricting attendance to—and I quote—*select reporters only*."

Claire couldn't resist a smirk. "Well, to be fair, they know you wouldn't be asking to attend unless you have an indication that there will be trouble or are planning to stir some up yourself. I mean, when was the last time you covered a science conference? Never, right? They probably have the bomb-sniffing bots combing the entire area, thinking there must be a threat or you wouldn't be interested."

"You may have a point."

"I can *probably* get in, though. I'll just say I want to do a follow up on the terraforming series for *Simple Science*. The only catch is that we rarely cover anything like that in person, since the major sessions are all recorded. And I'm not exactly back in Bernard's good graces, so getting him to okay it isn't a given."

"Bernard is an ungrateful troll. You bring in the biggest story of his editorial career and all he can do is complain."

It was true, but Claire knew her editor had good reason to grumble about the way that KTI had manipulated the release of information about the chambers. He'd put in sixteen hour days for a week or more in order to deal with the backlash from government and international agencies. The fact that the story had gone to the most junior of his three science reporters had also resulted in a rather tense situation in their department. Bryce Avery, the senior reporter, had threatened to quit almost daily for over a month. When those threats stopped abruptly, Claire's other colleague took that as an indication that Bryce had gotten a big fat raise, and decided that she should start complaining, too. Claire had considered telling Bernard to slash her salary and split it between the others. She didn't need the money. But it seemed wrong to reward that kind of pettiness, especially when they both earned more than she did already. And Bernard would probably just grumble about the paperwork involved in her working pro bono, if that was even a thing that the *Post* allowed its reporters to do.

"He *might* okay it if I tell him it's connected to the translation project," she said, thinking aloud. "Especially if I say that I won't file an expense report. I seriously doubt Kolya will answer questions about Millex, even if I decide I want to talk to him. But Paul will probably be there, so I can ask him if I don't catch up with him beforehand. And I can keep an ear out for chatter among the attendees. Because if you've heard the rumors, I'd be shocked if most of the Consortium members haven't heard them, too."

Wyatt considered it for a moment, then shook his head. "I don't know, Claire. If not for everything that happened today, I'd have said that was a good idea. But after the drones at your place and now this attack on Leffler ... maybe you should keep a low profile? In fact, I'm thinking maybe we should leave separately and take a rain check on the rest of the evening. I've got to meet with someone tomorrow morning, so I'd have to head out super early anyway."

He studiously avoided Claire's eyes and focused on his food, pushing a piece of bell pepper to the side. His hatred for any pepper that wasn't spicy ran deep, confirming her suspicion that he hadn't even glanced at the menu when he ordered.

She took a few bites herself, weighing her words before responding. "Is this because of what I told you about Kolya?"

"What? No. Come on. You know better than that. I just don't want you taking any risks you don't have to."

"Okay, then. But ... you do realize that this is *my* story, too, right? I am every bit as invested as you are in finding out whether that's actually Shepherd's memoir."

"Claire—"

"Stop. And work aside, it's also my *life*. I am equally, if not more, invested in seeing Corbin Drexel and her followers pay for killing Brodnik and the others, and for nearly killing me. Do you *really* expect me to hide in a safe room until this is over?"

As Claire watched his reaction to her words, she realized that he might not *expect* her to do that, but it was definitely what he wanted. He wanted her *safe*. Which was understandable. She wanted the same for him. But he'd chosen a job that constantly put him at risk. She couldn't expect him to play it safe and still do his job effectively, so she'd resigned herself to a certain degree of worry, because the only other choice was to distance herself from him.

Which, it now occurred to her, was almost certainly what Wyatt had been doing. How many times had he seemed right on the verge of wanting something more from their relationship, only to suddenly claim he'd met someone absolutely perfect wherever the job had just taken him? The new Miss Absolutely-Perfect rarely lasted more than a month. And while Claire couldn't pull up precise dates for all of them, she was fairly certain that one was right around the time of the Hsinchu City uprising. Another was just after the Southern Sons bomb threats. The last one, Steph, was just after he finished the exposé on the Boise Bois militia in Idaho. How much of Wyatt's behavior over the past few years was due to a fear of commitment, as she'd assumed, and how much was an attempt to shield her from the consequences of his job?

And did it even matter? She didn't like the idea of him constantly thinking that he needed to protect her, and he wasn't going to give up his work. Nor would she want him to.

"You know that's not what I meant," he said. "You even admitted a few minutes ago that Ro and Jemma—"

"Oh no, no, no. Don't you dare use them to manipulate me."

He extracted another chunk of bell pepper and placed it on the empty spring roll plate. "You're right," he said, looking miserable. "That wasn't fair."

"It wasn't. But … I *get* it, okay? You're worried. I am, too. You feel responsible. *So do I.* In case you've forgotten, I was involved in all of this before you were, as soon as I decided to take the assignment on Mars. If anyone is to blame for all of us being in danger, it's me. The FBI would have gotten around to investigating the bombing eventually, even without the story you wrote.

The Flock knows my family connections, too, so it could just as easily be the Rejuvesce launch that set them off. Or something else … entirely."

She had mostly been casting about for any conceivable argument to convince Wyatt that the timing could have been a coincidence. And even now, she was still reasonably sure that the article he'd written really was what had ignited the fire under the FBI to start the investigation in earnest.

But was the FBI investigation actually what caused the Flock to launch their bugbot offensive? She'd gotten the call from the FBI around ten a.m. on one of her rare in-office days. Less than half an hour before that, she'd told Bernard that she was taking a few days off to visit family in Boston, but she was planning to stop in New York on the way up to get a bit more info from Leffler for what she'd been calling the Rosetta stone episode. Bernard had grumbled about needing to clear hotel expenses, as he always did, then brightened when she lied that she'd be staying at her family's apartment. He added that it would be really great if she could also bring back an interview with her brother, even though she'd already told him multiple times that, as someone with stock in Jonas Labs, she wasn't doing any stories about the company. Was legally prevented from doing them, in fact, given the agreement her mother made her sign. After that, she'd returned to her desk and called Ben Pelzer to see if he'd managed to set up the meeting with Leffler, messaged Wyatt to see if he could meet her in New York, reserved the hotel, and messaged Beck to see if he could start twisting Joe's arm to take the day off so that they could discuss next steps.

All of those calls were made at the office. On her personal phone, sitting at her little cube, but she was *at* the office. And the drone attacks started about four hours later.

Now Leffler was dead.

Targeting a linguistics professor might not make sense if the only thing you were worried about was someone translating a fairly short message carved into the walls of what was almost certainly a burial chamber. Claire wouldn't even have been hounding Leffler to continue the project if that were the only thing at stake. She'd only come in person in order to determine whether to trust Leffler with the much longer manuscript waiting in Joe's lab.

Stasia Ljubic knew that Claire was collecting samples to bring back to Joe. Which begged the question—was the Flock aware that something was hidden inside those samples, something important enough that they were willing to kill to keep it secret?

Wyatt was saying her name, and judging from his expression, not for the first time.

"What? Sorry. I was thinking."

He chuckled. "Well, I could see that. Which is why I just asked *what are you thinking*?"

"I was putting together a couple of things I know. One of which I can't share with you right now except to say that it makes me even more convinced that Leffler was targeted because she was publicly connected to the translation effort." She hesitated for a moment. "And ... I was thinking that you're probably right."

"I'm right that you should lay low for a while?" There was a wary note to his voice. He clearly sensed a trap.

"No. That part's not an option. I *will* be at the Ares Consortium meeting on Tuesday, whether Bernard approves it or not. I'll talk to Paul about putting you in contact with Shepherd, either at the conference or, hopefully, before. If I talk to Kolya, I may poke around a bit to see if he knows anything about the accident at Millex. What I think you're right about is the rain check. I'm going to skip the hotel and head on up to Boston. Oh ... and I need you to send that file to my *private* box. The one that Kes set up."

"Okay. But ... why not through the *Post*?"

"A hunch. It might be nothing, but I'm thinking I should avoid using the work portal for anything dealing with all of this. Maybe you should, too." She grabbed her bag from under the table, then leaned over and kissed the side of his mouth. "Stay safe, okay? Or at least, stay as safe as you can."

FROM THE ATLANTIC POST

(AUGUST 31, 2084)

RIOTS SPREAD IN TIER ONE NATIONS

~ STAFF

(*Ciudad de México*) The release of Rejuvesce, a groundbreaking drug that promises to extend the human lifespan by up to a quarter-century, has sparked global anticipation and domestic turmoil. The World Health Organization (WHO), in collaboration with member governments, has devised a tiered system to distribute the medication. However, the system faces fierce opposition as Tier One nations prepare to begin distribution on November 1st.

The limited supply of Rejuvesce means that not everyone can be treated immediately, prompting the decision to limit the drug's availability not only to certain nations at the beginning, but also to individuals between 50 and 69 years of age. The rationale is that the drug's efficacy diminishes with age, but this does not sit well with those over 70 who argue that they have a more pressing need for the drug, given that they are statistically closer to the end of their lifespan. "Who cares if the drug is *less* effective for us?" argued Stefano Pareja, a 74-year-old protestor wearing a hand-lettered *Alborotadores Grises* shirt. "If it's effective at all, we deserve a chance."

Critics argue that the random tier system, while designed to prevent wealth and influence from dictating access, inadvertently creates a different kind of inequality. Proponents counter that the only alternative to a tiered lottery system would have been to wait until there was an adequate global supply to begin distribution, which was estimated at five to seven years—during which time no one would have had access.

A beleaguered WHO administrator in Mexico, whose identity is being withheld for security reasons, has been at the center of the whirlwind as they begin preparations for the first round of distribution. "We understand the concerns, but our hands are tied by the global agreement," the administrator said. "We're working day and night to ensure the fairest distribution possible within the agreed framework, but there is no solution that will satisfy everyone."

The administrator's challenges are compounded by the escalating tensions, which have seen older citizens who are seeking access and those who oppose the drug on religious or environmental grounds clashing both with each other and with security personnel outside distribution centers and manufacturing facilities.

An employee at the Lomas Verdes factory, one of many locations worldwide where Rejuvesce is produced, shared her distress over the daily confrontations. "I believe in what we're doing here," she said, requesting anonymity due to the ongoing security concerns. "I took this job because I want to help people. But each day lately, I must fight my way through rioters and fanatics who are calling us heretics for tampering with God's plan. It is very frustrating."

After the initial publicity surrounding the release of the drug, Jonas Labs has fallen largely silent on the issue, stressing that they are not directly involved in distribution. In one of her rare statements over the past few months, Jonas Labs CEO Kai Jonas stressed that the company's agreement to relax their patent and to allow biosimilar production after two years will help to increase global access. "That is a significant concession given the vast amount of resources and the years of research that Jonas Labs has invested in Rejuvesce. The company also yielded to the WHO's request for sliding-scale pricing for less affluent nations in order to ensure greater equity, something that did not make me especially popular with our shareholders, I might add. All other decisions are now out of our hands."

The WHO has called for calm and continued dialogue but acknowledges that there are challenges ahead. "We're in uncharted territory," one administrator said. "Our priority is to save lives, but we must also maintain order and adhere to our principles of equitable distribution. We are on the precipice of the biggest health advancement in human history, but progress doesn't happen overnight. And I would suggest that those who are unhappy with the current system step back for a moment to view this in historical context. Only five or six decades ago, this drug would have been sold to the highest bidders in the wealthiest countries."

ELEVEN

CLAIRE ARRIVED at the turnoff to her old neighborhood just north of Wenham a little after eleven. Everly Estates was a small, semicircular enclave, with six houses that backed to several acres of woods. All of the houses were the huge generic-looking neocolonials that were popular among the wealthier class around the turn of the twenty-first century, with long lighted driveways, three or four car garages, and meticulously landscaped lawns. Her dad had sometimes called this type of home a McMansion, although never within earshot of his mother, who had picked out the house herself a few years before he was born. Grandma Echols had only lived there during the summers when Claire was growing up, preferring to spend the winters with her sister at a house on the Georgia coast. But it made her happy to see another generation of Echols children growing up there and she had sulked on the few occasions when Claire's dad or Kai tentatively broached the subject of building something more modern and closer to the new campus.

As the car approached the gate, which had always been automated, Claire was surprised to find a manned kiosk. At first, she wondered why Joe had sent her an updated entry token, but then she hadn't been certain what time she would arrive when she spoke to him. Maybe the guard was only part-time?

She lowered the window and showed her identification. After a quick glance at her ID, the woman returned it and stepped back. That's when Claire saw that her badge read *Jonas Labs Security* at the top.

"Thank you, Ms. Echols. Enjoy the rest of your evening."

The second odd thing Claire noticed was how dark the neighborhood was. While the security gate had been well-lit, the street itself was not. It seemed a bit too early for *all* of the neighbors to be asleep, even on a weeknight, and yet the other five houses were completely dark. They were set back from the street a bit, but she should have been able to see glimmers of light from their windows. Even if they had all turned in early for some reason, or if they'd all decided to head out for the holiday weekend a day or two in advance, their external lights should be on. It couldn't be a problem with the power grid, either. The neighborhood had solar backup. And the sixth house, the one in which Claire had grown up, was fully lit.

It was also behind a separate gate now … a gate that actually looked a lot like the one that had previously been at the main entrance. At least that explained why Joe had sent her the entry token.

She made a mental note to ask Joe about the changes in the neighborhood as she pointed her phone at the sensor on the gate. But when she got inside the house, she found him collapsed on the sofa in the family room, snoring gently. Knowing Joe, it was the first time he'd been home in a week. Given how completely out he was, you'd think it was the first time he'd *slept* in a week. With his long dark hair over his face, he reminded her of a hibernating bear, and she knew from past experience that his temperament would be similar if he was awakened too soon. She grabbed a blanket from one of the downstairs closets and tossed it over him. Then, in the highly unlikely event that he woke before she did, she scribbled a note telling him she'd arrived safely before heading up to bed.

On the two occasions each year when Kai and Claire grudgingly agreed to meet—Christmas and Joe's birthday—they gathered at the apartment Kai kept in New York. Claire hadn't been inside this house in more than six years, and as she climbed the stairs, she had the odd sense of slipping back in time. Things might be different in the neighborhood, but nothing, absolutely *nothing*, had changed inside the house.

Her bedroom was a time capsule. The same quilt and pillows on the bed. A selection of toiletries she'd been partial to in college were still in the adjoining bath. She'd taken most of her clothes with her when she moved out, but there were still a few items in the closet, including two expensive prom dresses that should really be donated to charity before they were so out of fashion that no one would want them. The dresser held a motley assortment of items, including several bathing suits, which was a good thing since she'd forgotten to pack one. The same books were on the shelf, almost certainly in the exact same order, and when she flicked on the wall screen opposite her bed, it defaulted to her list of favorites. Or rather, it defaulted to what *had* been her list of favorites the last time she slept in this bed.

The fact that her room was exactly as she'd left it wasn't due to any sentimentality on her mother's part. Kai probably hadn't even stepped foot in the room. If she had needed this space for some reason, she'd have hired someone to box up Claire's things and stash them in the attic. Or, more likely, she'd have told them to toss everything out. But with six bedrooms, the house was obscenely large for two people, especially when those two spent the vast majority of their time in the lab (Joe) or traveling (Kai). The cleaning crew that came in weekly undoubtedly viewed this house as one cushy assignment.

The other thing that hadn't changed was the ghosts. They were everywhere. A ghost of Martin Echols had been in the foyer when she pressed her thumb to the lock—his arms crossed and an unconvincing scowl on his face because she was fifteen minutes past curfew. She'd encountered him again at the hall closet as she slipped off her shoes and felt her heart wrench at the absence of the tartan jacket that had always hung on the last peg. He'd been sitting on the couch opposite Joe when she entered the family room, in the same place he'd sat most evenings while reading or sketching designs on his tablet, and she'd spotted him again in the formal living room near the piano where they'd always put up the Christmas tree together.

Her father's ghost was a welcome presence. Each glimpse brought with it memories of a childhood that had been a happy time because so much of it was spent with him.

But being in this place where everything reminded Claire of her father also brought back how completely everything had changed when he died. And that ushered in a far less welcome ghost—her teenage self. Adolescent Claire was a very *angry* spirit. How many times had she slammed the door to this bedroom in the two years between the death of her father and her escape to college? Yes, she was still angry at her mother, especially after learning about her affair with Kolya. But that anger was now more of a simmering resentment, while the Claire who had lived in this room had very nearly been consumed by it.

Before her father died, she'd gotten along fairly well with her mother, mostly because Kai had left her upbringing to Martin. Her sporadic attempts at parenting usually involved pushing her daughter to strive harder, to achieve, to be the absolute best. She had pushed Joe even harder. But Joe thrived on competition, not so much against others as against all the things in the universe that had yet to be explained to his satisfaction. Joe finished his PhD program when most people were still undergrads, and he'd barely stopped for breath in the years since. Her brother simply wasn't happy unless he was working toward a goal, preferably one that others had written off as impossible.

Claire was pretty sure Joe would have accomplished every bit as much without their mother nagging him. Kai, however, viewed her son's achievements as a testament to her parenting approach, and she seemed baffled and frustrated that she couldn't replicate this astounding success with her second child.

Claire had tried at first, but Kai's expectations were exhausting. Martin understood that his daughter's nature was much more like his own. She needed time to simply *be*. And when he died, Claire discovered exactly how much of a buffer he had been between her and Kai. Within days of the funeral, Kai swooped in to take charge of her daughter's future. She decided that the public school Claire was attending—where she had an almost perfect GPA—was not challenging enough and transferred her to a local prep school that specialized in the sciences. A tutor was brought in for the advanced classes that she insisted Claire take. Later that year, she messaged Claire with the names of the five colleges she had deemed acceptable and informed her that if she couldn't meet the average scores for acceptance into at least one of them by the application deadline, she'd have to do a "post-grad-uate year" of high school before applying. That would have meant an additional year in the house with Kai, which was incentive enough for Claire to study non-stop for the last half of her junior year. She got into three of the four schools without the threatened extra year and picked Stanford for the simple reason that it was three thousand miles away from Kai.

Once Claire was in college, she latched onto any and every excuse to avoid coming home over the holidays or in the summer. An internship in London. A ski holiday with friends. The last time she was at the house would have been spring break of her senior year, when she finally informed her mother that she had not been accepted to any of the five biology PhD programs that Kai had approved the previous year. Could not, in fact, have been accepted because she never applied. The degree she was receiving in the spring would be summa cum laude, but it was in journal-ism, with a biology minor, and she would be entering the master's in journalism program at George Washington University in the fall.

Kai had been furious, as Claire had known she would be. But she was also powerless, because Claire no longer needed her money. She'd inherited one-quarter of her father's shares in Jonas Labs and over a hundred million dollars held in trust when she turned twenty-one.

Claire's only regret in all of this was that the conflict with Kai meant she didn't see Joe as much as she'd like. He'd been trying to get her to come "home" for a visit for several years now. She and Beck had both been trying for several *months* to get Joe to carve out some time to discuss how to handle the Martian manuscript. Two weeks back, those two efforts had converged. Joe messaged her that Kai would be at the lab in Lomas Verdes until the Wednesday or Thursday after Labor Day, and pointed out that the pool would be a great way to escape the heat. She'd grudgingly agreed, in part because she suspected it was the only way he'd take any time off. Would the time off be a half day? A full day? The entire weekend? He'd never given her a firm commitment on that front.

Once she was ready for bed, she expanded her screen and crawled under the covers. She sent a quick message to Bernard to let him know that she planned to stay in New York an extra day or two to cover the Ares Consortium meeting. After that, she sent a note to Paul Caruso at KTI about patching a message through to Shepherd. She made up a vague excuse about a question for a story a colleague was doing—which was true— and added that she'd be at the conference in New York. Maybe they could get together for lunch or dinner if he wasn't entirely swamped?

Then, she settled in to read Shepherd's memoir. She'd thought she might need to message Wyatt with a reminder to send the manuscript. But when she signed into the account, she found the file was waiting in her encrypted box, along with the promised transcript from the speech by Corbin Drexel.

"Okay, Toby," she said. "Let's see just how big of a fraud you are."

FROM AWAITING THE SENTINELS

BY TOBIAS SHEPHERD

THE FINAL WIDESPREAD misperception about our beliefs is that we view the group that we call Sentinels as gods. They are not. They are extraordinarily long-lived, but they *can* die. They have human emotions, or something very close. And they are not immune from madness.

This I know, because I lived with a Sentinel for six years as a child. I watched as he went mad, and I watched them carry his body out when he died. The New Haven authorities deemed it suicide, and they weren't wrong. But he was already dying. Not from any injury or disease, but from the heavy weight of knowledge, of expectations under which he could no longer bear to live. The pills he ingested were simply a quicker, more merciful end.

-2-

The next few chapters are, of necessity, recreations from memory. I suppose that's true of any memoir—it's right there in the word, after all—but I want to stress that I have only a few notes and journal entries from this period. Later in life, I was an obsessive journaler, but this section is about my childhood, and as with all adults, the haze of time has obscured many of my earliest memories. Some of you will, as a result, no doubt view this entire section as suspect. I cannot assure you that the conversations that follow are the exact words that were spoken. (Indeed, there are some things that I have changed on purpose. As I have said before, the terms *Sentinels* and *Administrators* are my own, not the names by which these beings refer to their kind.) But despite lapses of memory and the few things I have altered for the protection of my followers over the years, I swear that the information at the core of these early chapters of my life is true. I would wager that most of the peripheral information is true as well, as the final days of the Sentinel that I chronicle here were traumatic ones for me and were therefore etched quite deeply into my young mind.

One event that I do remember with exceptional clarity is my first glimpse of Allen House. It was the year 2042, and I was a tender child of not-quite-six, a mere sprout in the garden of life. To my wondering eyes, the house was a castle from tales of yore, complete with a pointy turret that reminded me of a wizard's cap. It was a more somber castle than the colorful sort I'd seen in books and videos, to be sure, with its burgundy brick exterior and black iron trim, but it was every bit as intriguing.

Would that moment have been so deeply etched into the tapestry of my memory had I not felt the quiver of my mother's hand as she opened the gate? She held such high hopes for this new chapter in our lives. It was just the two of us, as it had been for as long as I could remember. My father took a job in North Texas when secession sentiment was beginning to heat up and then he gradually vanished from our lives. Or from *her* life, I suppose, since I have no memory of him at all.

My mother's new job promised stability and brighter horizons for us both. As we climbed the steps that first day, I remember asking her why it was called Allen House if it belonged to Professor Everett. She told me that she did not know. Neither did I, until I researched it a few years ago and discovered it was named for the architect. The professor could probably have told me this, but by the time my awe of my mother's new employer receded to the point that I was willing to ask him such an idle question, I was convinced that I already knew the answer. The name *Allen House* must have been a clever jest, that first word a single-letter variation that hinted at the true nature of its owner. Because by the time I was comfortable enough to ask, I was already convinced that the professor was an *alien*.

Nathaniel Everett himself was every bit as formidable as his house, a tall, imposing figure of few words and indeterminate years. To me, he seemed ancient. When I admitted as much to my mother, she said he was probably in his sixties, which was actually a bit young to be retired, especially from a physically undemanding field like academia.

"Do you think I'm old, too, Toby?"

I told her that I didn't, which was true. But she was nearly forty years younger than the professor. Or rather, forty years younger than the professor *appeared* to be.

My mother's one complaint about the place was that the grounds were very small. The house took up most of the space on the corner lot, leaving almost no room for me to play outdoors. Most residents of the nearby homes were elderly, and the nearest park was several blocks away. Even that wasn't ideal. She called it an *old-person park*, which was a fair assessment. Children rarely frequented it, possibly because the play area was small and boring, but if the weather was good, there would usually be at least a few people at the chess tables.

Lacking a yard, and being a rather solitary child by nature, Allen House became my playground. There were dozens of rooms and, to my great delight, a hidden passageway. While looking for a spare blanket one day, I realized there was a door at the back of the linen closet adjacent to my bedroom. That closet had once been part of a corridor. When I followed it to the end, I found a servants' staircase that led up to the third floor and on to the attic beyond.

Most of the attic had been boarded off as part of some long-ago alteration, leaving only a cubby in front of a circular window near the base of the turret. I discovered the spot a few years after we moved in and quickly set about to make that little nook my own private retreat. Once the cobwebs were cleared away, I carted a solar charger and a few pillows up to furnish my secret fort. I spent many afternoons in that nook, looking down at the traffic on the street below as I read or watched videos, or just gazing out as the setting sun bathed New Haven's skyline in shades of tangerine and lilac.

Looking back, I can admit that Allen House *wasn't* the grandest home on Whitney Avenue, but I would have fought any child who claimed otherwise during the years that we lived there. The fact that we didn't own it, that I was the son of the house-keeper, did nothing to alter my fierce loyalty to the place. And with the professor often away on travel, sometimes for months on end, I suspect that many people in the neighborhood believed my mother and I *were* the owners, and the professor was merely a relative who dropped in for extended visits.

Even when the professor was there, he kept to himself. My mother ensured that the house was meticulously clean and well-organized. She prepared meals according to his specifications, which he took alone in the formal dining room. He wasn't unfriendly, and he would occasionally stop for a few words with me, asking the usual questions that adults ask of children they do not know well. For the most part, however, Professor Everett existed in his own orbit.

The professor's study, which took up more than half of the third floor, was the only area of the house where I was forbidden to wander. Even my mother rarely entered, as he did not like his papers disturbed. Aside from the yearly spring cleaning, which she actually performed in early summer when I was out of school to assist, she left the floors of the study to the robo-vac and simply collected the occasional bag of rubbish that the professor left in the hallway.

This might have made the study tempting as a forbidden fruit, but I was not a disobedient or even mischievous child. I would, most likely, never even have considered violating the professor's privacy in any way, were it not for the chance occurrence that my hideaway, my small secret nook, sat directly over the professor's study.

Sometimes, when I couldn't sleep, I'd tiptoe up the servants' staircase with a blanket in hand, and lie on my back, staring out through the window at the canopy of stars above as the house lay silent below. It was the closest I ever came to camping out as a child. Once, I even fell asleep up there. Had it been a cloudy morning, I might have been discovered, but the sun woke me mere minutes before my mother rose for the day and I scurried back down to my room.

It was on one of these nighttime odysseys, shortly after my tenth birthday, that I heard the professor's voice in the study as I climbed the stairs and settled into my nook. I could hear him clearly, but not the other person, so he must have been using a headset. It was nearly midnight, long after the time that he normally retreated to his bedroom. He had, in fact, gone up to bed even earlier than usual that night, having just returned from an extended trip to Europe. My mother had remarked as she cleared the table that he seemed a bit glum or perhaps just tired from travel.

The fact that he was in the study at such a late hour was odd enough. What was even more surprising was his tone. He sounded angry. In the four years we'd lived there, I'd never once heard him raise his voice. He wasn't exactly shouting even now, but there was a barely restrained fury beneath his words.

"Because it's going to take a while before I can fully trust you again!"

There was a long silence. I froze in place, barely breathing, both because I wanted to hear and because I was worried that any movement might give away my location above him.

"I'm not questioning the value of our work! What I question is the secrecy surrounding it. What I *question* is the need to keep the other Sentinels in the dark. Surely you can see how this new knowledge that you've granted me might *rankle* a bit, given that I was one of those you kept in ignorance for over a century?"

For over a century?

I tried to convince myself that I'd misheard him, but I was almost directly above his desk and his words were crystal clear. He must be exaggerating, then. Like when people say they've been waiting a million years for something. It seemed oddly specific, though...

My conscience piped in at that point. *You shouldn't be eavesdropping, Toby. This is private. Just go back downstairs.*

I might have listened to that little voice. Might have crept back downstairs, crawled into my bed, and never ventured up to my nook at night again ... at least, not when the professor was home. I even stood and began moving toward the stairs.

But then I heard something unimaginable, something that shocked me so deeply that it stopped me in my tracks.

The professor was *crying.*

It was now summer, and despite the heat, I took to sleeping in my attic hideaway when Professor Everett was in New Haven. Sometimes, when I thought the risk too great to sneak up there in person, I left my tablet behind to record. I was afraid that I would miss some clue to what had upset the man so deeply—and had he really said *for over a century*?

It was mostly curiosity that kept me climbing those stairs each night and creeping back down to my bed before daylight. But in fairness to my ten-year-old self, my actions were also motivated by concern for the professor. What had the person on the other end of that call done that upset him so? It was, perhaps, silly to imagine that I might find some way to help him if I knew, but children have imagined things far more fanciful.

Trying to put myself into his mindset, I thought about the things that might make me sad enough to cry like that, in loud wrenching sobs rather than sniffles. There was only one that I could think of—the death of my mother. I had no one else. Without her, I would be completely alone in the world.

Had the person on the other end of that call been someone the professor loved, perhaps someone who had betrayed him? Whoever this person was, there were no photographs of them in the house, unless they were on his computer. I had caught glimpses of both his bedroom and his study when I helped with spring cleaning. The only thing on his shelves were books, many of which looked very old. On his desk, there was just his computer and several neat stacks of papers. The room, which was fairly large, was otherwise bare, aside from a well-padded chair, a cabinet that I would later realize held bottles of whiskey, vodka, and cognac, and a table with a marble chessboard top. There were no framed pictures anywhere. He had never mentioned children or family. And in all the time we'd lived at Allen House, no one had ever visited him. He did have at least a couple of friends, because I had seen him playing chess with them in the park on a few occasions. Or—and this struck me as both very likely and very sad—did he carry the chess pieces with him to the park on the chance that someone would arrive to share a game?

Was the professor lonely? I thought perhaps he was.

Over the next few months, I climbed the stairs to my nook and listened to his end of at least a dozen conversations, most of them during the day. Usually, he spoke English, but there were other languages, too. Much of the time, he seemed to be listening, as if the person on the other end were giving a report, and he would speak only a few words at the end. He used the word *assignment* often, which seemed odd to me since he no longer taught. I decided these calls must be with former students, or maybe former colleagues.

The ones that struck me as most unusual were the conversations—arguments, truth be told—about science and whether some achievement merited inclusion on their *list*. I didn't consider the list making to be odd, as I was myself a notorious list keeper—favorite books, movies, games, and as I approached adolescence, music. Maybe he was on an award committee of some sort?

If so, Professor Everett had higher standards than the other person or persons on this committee. He almost always argued against this new advancement making their list. Occasionally, I picked up specific terms or companies—I remember SpaceX, ArboTech, GSKR were among them. I looked them up online, but most of the concepts were far, far above the understanding of the average adult, let alone a ten-year-old.

Nothing that I heard answered any of my questions. While he never again lost his temper, never lapsed into tears, these conversations agitated him. He paced the length of the study before and after. Sometimes, he would hum as he paced. It was always the same tune, and I was reminded of movies where you see parents pacing to comfort a fussy child. But he seemed to be both parent and child, both the comforter and the one in need of comfort.

Once, I heard a thud, as if he'd hurled something against a wall. This was followed by laughter, but it was far from a happy sound.

In fact, it frightened me. I feared that the professor was going mad.

-3-

There was no way that I could tell my mother I'd been eavesdropping. Nor could I risk asking any more questions. I'd already asked her if the professor had family, if that was who he visited on trips abroad. She'd told me that she did not know, and it was not her place to ask. The professor had made it clear from the beginning that he was a very private person. If he wished to share that sort of information, he would most likely have done so by now.

Still, she must have shared my concerns. We could both see that the professor was losing weight, and his health was declining. Instead of the long walks that he'd once taken each day, he would circle the block a few times and return to the house. One evening, as my mother was serving the professor in the dining room and I was at the table in the kitchen eating my own dinner, I was surprised to hear her break her rule and ask the professor if he was feeling ill. There was a short silence and then she spoke again, sounding nervous.

"Or maybe you would prefer that I cook something else? I just noticed that you haven't been eating and I was—"

"No, Marisa." His voice was gentle but firm. "The meal is perfectly lovely. And my health is good. Perhaps too good. I am just under some … stress at the moment."

My mother and I exchanged a look when she returned to the kitchen, and I knew we were both thinking the same thing. How could your health be *too* good?

She had done all that she could, however, and left to my own devices, I came up with what I believed to be a clever plan. I asked my mother for a chess set. She was a bit baffled, noting that she'd never learned to play and doubted she'd be much good, so I'd be better off continuing to play against the computer. But I insisted that I wanted a real set, perhaps a portable one that I could take to school when it started up again in the fall, so that I could play with friends. That last word had caught her attention, because I was a rather solitary child, and she frequently urged me to be more social.

The chess set arrived the next afternoon, and over the next several days, I would set up the board in the dining room or occasionally in the downstairs library, anywhere I thought it likely that the professor would notice. It took four days for him to take the bait and ask if I'd like an actual opponent for a change. Looking back, I suspect that I was painfully obvious, and he knew exactly what I was doing. I don't believe he knew *why*, though. He probably thought that I was lonely, and I suppose he was right.

After that, we played several times a week. He was far, far better than I was. While he did not patronize me by letting me win, he always pointed out the moves that I might have taken to avoid losing my rook or my queen or whatever series of mistakes had led to my defeat, and my game improved quickly. But he never spoke of anything other than chess. I made one feeble attempt to push the conversation into a more personal realm, asking if he had learned to play the game from his parents.

He looked up from the game, arching one of his dark bushy brows. "No."

And then he returned to contemplating his next move.

I believe the professor enjoyed our games, but he was not impressed with my portable chess set, with its lightweight plastic pieces that toppled easily, especially under his larger hands. We played in the park on a few occasions in early autumn, but the weather eventually grew too cold. On that first day when we were forced to play indoors, he scowled at the small pieces and then told me to follow him upstairs.

From then on, we played in his study on the marble chessboard. While the professor took his turn, I would scan the titles on the bookshelves, many of them in languages I could not read. Most of the spines were brown or black leather, a scattered few were navy or cordovan, and there was even the occasional cover that might have once been white. There was only one spot of vivid color on those shelves. The book was purple with yellow writing, and the symbols on the spine were arranged in the usual order, with what looked like a title and an author's name. But it was definitely *not* the English alphabet. I tried to memorize the symbols in the title so that I could look them up later, but the professor always countered my chess moves so quickly that I had time for only the briefest of glances.

During one of these games, as snow piled up on the street outside and I labored over my next move, the professor received a phone call. I heard a faint huff as he stared down at the screen and expected him to shoo me out—at which point, I would have scurried up the hidden staircase as quickly as possible because my tablet was not currently in place to record the conversation.

To my surprise, however, he took the phone into the hall. I eventually moved my knight to C3, and then just sat there for the next few minutes, waiting for him to return. I knew that I should probably leave. We could always finish the game later. That was certainly what my mother would have wanted me to do. Instead, I walked over to the bookshelf and tugged at the purple book, not removing it but just inching it out so that I could look more closely at the cover.

It was a children's book. That probably shouldn't have surprised me, given the vivid purple binding, but it did. The fanciful drawing on the cover surprised me even more. I might have been able to connect the Professor Everett I knew to a children's textbook in some foreign language, but this looked like a storybook.

After a quick glance toward the door, I pulled the book from the shelf and began thumbing through the pages, keeping my ears open for footsteps in the hallway so that I could quickly replace it. The drawings were of make-believe characters. I was reminded a bit of this Winnie-the-Pooh book my mother read to me when I was very small, because they looked like stuffed animals of some sort. Except Pooh and his friends were based on actual animals, and these weren't like any creatures I'd ever seen. They walked through strange woods, with a strange sky that held two suns—or maybe they were moons?

You can probably surmise the next part. I became so lost in the odd pictures and scenery that I never heard the professor enter the room. When I looked up, he was seated once again at the chessboard, watching me. He looked more sad than angry. His eyes, which were a pale bluish gray, were now red-rimmed.

But what if he was simply dreading having to tell my mother that she was fired?

"I'm sorry! I just … The cover was … it was purple. And I couldn't resist."

To my surprise, he smiled. "I see. That is a rather odd compulsion that you have, Tobias. Is it only *purple* books that call you to snoop through the bookshelves of others?"

"No … no, sir. But all of the others look like adult books. And this one looks like a book for children. Probably even too young for me, and I can't read this language anyway. I was just looking at the pictures. I'll put it back. Sorry."

"You're right. It *is* for younger children." He held out his hand for the book and when I brought it to him, began thumbing through the pages. "But one day, when you are very, very old like I am, you may find that the stories of your childhood beckon you. And when you return to them, you'll realize that they were…" He stopped for a moment, as if considering his words. "They were the lens through which you viewed all the other tales you read or heard or watched throughout your life. Children's stories are not all that different from most adult tales—they are, in the vast majority of cases, centered around themes of love, sacrifice, loss. A monster to be slain, either real or metaphorical. Such stories transcend time and culture."

This was more words all at once than he usually spoke in the course of a week. That, combined with the fact that he did not seem angry at my intrusion, gave me the courage to ask him more about the book.

"So you can read this language? I've never seen those symbols before."

"I can indeed read it," he said. "Which makes me one of the few people on Earth. It is an ancient script. A variant of the early … Libyco-Berber alphabet."

"Then where did the book come from? I mean, if no one can read this language, why would anyone use it to write a children's book?"

He chuckled softly. "Why, indeed?" After that, he was quiet for a long moment, humming softly as he continued to flip through the pages. "It was a project of mine, years ago, when my daughter was young."

"I didn't know you had a daughter."

"She died."

"Oh." I stared down at the chessboard, avoiding his eyes. "I'm sorry."

"So am I. But it was long ago. I collected these folk stories so that I could share them with her. And, I suppose, to keep them alive in my own memory. There are so few people who know them."

"Why didn't you translate them into English?"

"Eventually, I did just that. She found learning the language tedious, which is perhaps unsurprising. And there was little incentive to learn a language when your only reward was a single book. But I suppose I wanted her to read the stories as I first read them. To see them in her mind as I did when I was her age." He stopped, one side of his mouth twitching slightly. "I mean … as I *imagine* I would have seen them at her age. I didn't find the stories until I was much, much older, of course."

This was a lie. How I knew this for certain, I could not say. But I had no doubt. He had read these stories as a child and wanted to share them with his daughter, the same way that my mother had shared *The Gruffalo*, and the Harry Potter books, and *The Lie Tree* with me.

"In the end, I simply read the stories to her."

"Did she enjoy them?"

He smiled sadly. "I don't believe she did. Or at least, not as much as I'd hoped she would. I suppose there are some memories that we can never truly share. So very much is lost in the translation. Not just the words, but the experience, especially when worlds are far apart."

"Do you think … do you think you could teach *me*?"

He looked a bit stunned by my question. Thinking back, I'm fairly certain there was also a touch of fear in his eyes. Or maybe trepidation is a better word.

It occurred to me then how very presumptuous my request had been. He'd been talking about something he shared with his daughter and while he had no doubt spent countless hours teaching her, that's what parents do. I could only imagine my mother's shock if she learned I'd made such a huge request of her employer. She'd already told him on at least two occasions to feel free to shoo me out of his study if our chess games were monopolizing too much of his time.

"Never mind. I'm sorry. I should go. We can finish the game later."

I waited a few seconds and when he didn't respond, I got up and hurried toward the door.

"Well, which is it, young man? Do you want to learn the language or not?"

"Yes." I *did* want to learn. At that age, I wanted to learn everything.

"Even if deciphering this book is your only reward? Because I can assure you that you won't find any others out there in ancient Libyc."

I grinned. "But that's what makes it cool. Like a secret code that no one else can decipher, right?"

And so he began to teach me, first the alphabet—which was closer to an abjad, as there were no symbols for most of the vowel sounds—and then we moved onto some basic words. Almost from the beginning, though, I knew he wasn't being truthful about the language. I searched online for everything I could find about the Libyco-Berber script. There were very few similarities to the symbols I was learning. They didn't really match *any* alphabet I found online. And once I reached the point where I began trying to decipher the stories in the book, it became clear that there were other oddities. On several occasions when I was stuck on a word, he would give me the name of a creature or an object that made absolutely no sense to me. If I pressed him, he'd get a strange, slightly panicked look. So I started simply jotting these words down in my notebook, along with my best approximation of his answers to my questions.

Still, I might have been able to convince myself, even at that impressionable age, that everything I was learning was the product of Professor Everett's fertile imagination. I considered myself intelligent and reasonable, and surely that was the far more likely explanation for everything that he'd told me. He even admitted that he'd written the book and had sketched out the images to be completed by the illustrator he hired. All of these things pointed toward both the book, which Everett had entitled *Tales from the Aveezi Forest*, and the language in which it was written being pure fiction.

But there were the phone calls that I overheard once or twice a month. The most heated arguments always involved the word *reassignment*. At first, I assumed that this meant reassigning some scientific discovery in terms of its placement on the lists they were keeping, but then, a few weeks before my eleventh birthday, I heard something that I couldn't explain away.

It was another late night argument, one that the professor eventually lost. "Fine. But not Dagen. VersaBio is too close to her current location."

There was a pause before he replied, this time with a hint of anger. "*Because we'd have to alter her too much.* The two of you may have been out of the field long enough to forget how uncomfortable that is, but I still remember my last one clearly. What about Anak?"

The others apparently took his suggestion, because the conversation then shifted to whether any of the other Sentinels had connections at VersaBio, whether they could get this Anak person into place at the new lab by early spring, and whether any of the identity documents currently in their possession would be adequate for the open position as a synthetic biologist.

After this, I couldn't escape the reality that the professor was a spy, a secret agent of some sort. The logical assumption—that he was simply the agent of another country, trying to steal our nation's scientific knowledge—was countered by so many things that I'd overheard. On the other hand, of what use would our secrets be to a people who lived hundreds of years and who had the ability to travel from other worlds?

I toyed with the idea of reporting him and these other Sentinels. But perhaps they were just watching us, like on *Star Trek*, waiting for Earth to achieve some great milestone before they included us in their grand federation. And even if their purpose was malevolent, I could not believe that the professor himself was evil. He was good to me, good to my mother. The mere thought of reporting him was such an act of disloyalty that it brought me to the brink of tears.

The one thing I knew was that I could no longer keep my questions to myself. There was a very real chance that the professor would be angry with me, but each time I heard him down there humming and talking to himself, I wondered if perhaps what he really needed was another soul with whom to share his heavy burden.

TWELVE

WYATT WAS right on at least one front. Shepherd needed an editor.

Claire skipped most of the introduction, which was essentially an ad for the rest of the book—here's why you should bother reading about the life and times of Tobias Alvin Shepherd—and had skimmed the first chapter, which was a rehash of stuff she already knew about the Flock's ideology. The last few paragraphs of that chapter had covered common misperceptions about the group, concluding with the part Wyatt had mentioned about the alien that Shepherd was now claiming to have known as a child.

The next few chapters were told in flashback, and it was a bit like reading a modern-day Charles Dickens story. *Chapter Two: in which our plucky young hero befriends an elderly curmudgeon with a dark secret.*

She *had* been intrigued, though, by the section where he discussed the book he found in the old man's library and how he'd started learning the language. What if Tobias Shepherd was the Rosetta stone they needed? But she knew it was just wishful thinking. All they had was Devin's word that all sections of the book had been submitted to the publisher before Shepherd was ousted as head of the Flock.

And something had occurred to Claire on the 'loop up from New York—even if Devin was right on that account, it was possible that Shepherd had been shown the symbols *before* he left for Mars. Claire had seen them the day she joined Brodnik's team, thanks to the brief video from the camera they'd slipped inside the chamber once they finally managed to get a drill through the walls. She didn't think anyone on Brodnik's team would have leaked the information to Shepherd or any member of the Flock, for that matter—but who knew what contacts his publisher might have?

People from KTI had seen the video, too, including Kolya. And Kolya had told her that Shepherd was onboard the *Ares Prime* because he'd taken him up on a *standing invitation* to travel to Mars. That suggested that the two of them had been in contact for some time prior to Shepherd's apparent realization that remaining on Earth was no longer conducive to his continued good health.

What she couldn't recall was whether the same symbols featured on the cover of the book in Shepherd's memoir had been visible in the video of the chamber taken by Brodnik's crew on their previous trip. Since she didn't have a copy of it, there was no way to check. But Alice Dobroski had said earlier that Holly Leffler saw the video before Brodnik's return to Mars, so Leffler might still have a copy. If Alice could help her get access to that video, she could check to see if these specific symbols were visible.

Of course, even if the symbols in the photo *weren't* visible in that first video, it didn't prove the book in the photo was real. Kolya could easily have had someone drop another camera inside the chamber once Brodnik and her team were on the worker transport headed back to Earth. The most likely answer was still that Shepherd had added this information in an effort to cash in on the expected barrage of publicity surrounding the discovery. Once conspiracy theorists pounced on the connection, he'd end up selling a hundred times as many copies, if not far more.

Claire's eyes began glazing over a little after midnight. She decided to push through to the end of the chapter before sleeping, but then something near the bottom of the page jolted her wide awake. It wasn't the *only* company that Shepherd had namechecked in his memoir, and not the most well-known. In fact, she would almost certainly never have heard of VersaBio if not for the fact that the company had been bought out by Jonas

Labs, back when the name was still Echols Pharmaceuticals, and her grandfather ran the place. Even then, she still might not have heard the name, since the company had played the mergers and acquisitions game quite aggressively under Edward Echols's leadership, gobbling up at least a dozen small firms.

VersaBio was memorable only because it was a case where Echols Pharmaceuticals had swallowed a poison pill in the process. In the late 2040s, the company had released Nuroniq, one of a broad class of cancer-treatments that utilized CRISPR gene-editing technology to precisely target and remove cancer cells. Nuroniq wasn't even the main reason VersaBio was bought out, but about three months after the acquisition, Echols Pharmaceuticals was hit with a class action suit. A rather large subset of patients had begun experiencing severe neurological symptoms—memory loss, tremors, and in extreme cases, paralysis—a few years after beginning treatment, symptoms they claimed were directly linked to their use of Nuroniq. Echols had planned to fight the suit, but ended up settling out of court when it was revealed that VersaBio had ignored certain adverse events during the trial phase in an effort to push the drug to market more quickly.

It was old history, and Claire probably would never have heard the story at all if not for her grandmother. Grandma Echols was usually pretty chill, but every now and then, she'd start berating Claire's dad for spending too much money.

"We could lose the house, Marty! Remember how close we came when your father bought VersaBio? Don't you let Kai talk you into spending money we don't have."

Martin Echols had taken it in stride, placating his mother or ignoring her, depending on his mood. She'd mostly been worried about the cost of building the new campus, but as she grew older, Grandma Echols had trotted out the VersaBio fiasco more and more frequently, often with little provocation, including one memorable occasion when the weighty financial decision in front of the family was whether to order pizza.

Claire read to the end of the chapter and then did a quick search of the entire document for *VersaBio*. Just the two mentions she'd seen in Chapter Three, so it wasn't a lot to go on. But it did provide a tiny kernel of something that she could check. She was pretty sure that HR would have employment records for all of the companies that Jonas Labs had absorbed over the years. While she didn't know the name attached to whatever identity papers this Anak character had supposedly adopted, she might be able to at least find out whether VersaBio had hired a synthetic biologist in the spring of 2047.

Joe or Beck could get the information from HR without any problem, but she'd need to come up with a plausible reason for the request if she involved them. The obvious alibi—research for a story—wouldn't fly, because they both knew she didn't write stories about Jonas Labs. She could say she was getting information for a colleague, but they might want to know who, and then…

But she did know one person in HR, come to think of it. Or at least, she used to. Geneva Wilson, daughter of the sixth floor security guard, had started work there when Claire was in high school, and Wilson had asked Claire to give her a tour of the biodome when she came by to interview for a position as an assistant benefits specialist.

A quick check of the Jonas Labs directory revealed no one by the name of Geneva Wilson. Geneva W. Chatterjee, however, was now one of the assistant directors of the department. Claire typed out a quick email, most of which was basically true. A friend was writing a story and trying to verify the value of a source. One thing they'd told him was that VersaBio hired a synthetic biologist in the spring of 2047. Was there any chance she could confirm that? Hope all is well, many thanks, etc.

Now she just had to wait for Geneva to reply.

There was one thing she could check immediately, though. A quick online search turned up a Dr. Nathaniel Everett at Yale from 2029 until his retirement in 2041. Everett lived in a house on

Whitney Avenue, which had been designed by an architect named William Allen. He'd taught at several universities in Europe prior to joining the Yale faculty. An obituary in the *Yale Daily News* noted that his death was a suicide and made no mention of family. The same was true for the death notices in the *New Haven Register* and the *Hartford Courant*. She might be able to dig up a birth record or local school registration data for Tobias Shepherd, as well. Maybe even the employment records for his mother, but all of that would take time and she'd probably need to pull in the research team at the *Post*.

It didn't seem worth the effort when Shepherd could have made a search similar to the one that she'd just completed and decided that Everett fit the bill nicely for his fictional alien. His mother might even have actually worked for the man, which would have provided him with a ready-made, verifiable setting and character for the book. Because short of digging the professor up and discovering something not quite human in his DNA, how could any critic conclusively disprove the claim that Everett had been an alien?

Claire started to put the book aside and turn out the light. It was late. She should sleep.

But ... maybe just one more chapter. She wanted to find out what had happened to this children's book. *Tales from the Aveezi Forest* was almost certainly something Shepherd had created himself, but on the very slim chance that it wasn't, it could be the key they needed to translate the Martian script.

FROM AWAITING THE SENTINELS

BY TOBIAS SHEPHERD

-4-

I SLEPT in my own bed that night, tossing and turning as I tried to decide how to approach Professor Everett about what I'd overheard. The next day was Saturday and we always played at least one game of chess. There was no doubt in my mind that he would deny everything if I broached the subject. He would surely say that I'd misunderstood his side of the conversation. That meant I would need to stand firm, to hold my ground, if I were to have any hope of learning more.

For a while, I toyed with the idea of sneaking into his study, going through his papers, maybe even cracking into the files on his computer. If I were a few years older, I might have been able to convince myself that my hacking skills were sufficient, but I was barely in double digits. And while the professor might have been a bit rattled at the moment, he was not stupid. He was not the type to leave his password in a drawer, and it wouldn't be something obvious like *5entinels4ever*.

No, my only hope was for him to decide to share the information with me voluntarily, and to accomplish that, I would have to exploit the hint of loneliness that I'd detected in his eyes. Before I fell asleep, I made and discarded half a dozen plans, finally settling on the least horrible of the bunch.

I can't even remember the details of that plan now, or the words I intended to say in opening that conversation, because what happened next erased all of that from my mind. When I climbed the hidden stairs up to my attic nook the next morning to retrieve the tablet that I'd left up there, I found that it was no longer recording, and there was a folded sheet of note paper on top of it. I opened the note with shaking hands and saw that it was indeed from Professor Everett. Short and to the point. Just my name and four terse words—*Come to my office.*

I did as he asked, my face burning with shame and my pounding heart so loud in my ears that I barely even heard him tell me to come in after I knocked. My eyes remained steadfastly glued to my feet and the floor until I was seated in the chair that I always occupied in this room ... the one on the white side of the chessboard. When I finally mustered the nerve to look up, I realized that he was across the study, behind his desk, looking at me with an expression that seemed to be equal parts annoyance, disappointment, and amusement. The desk was far messier than usual, with an assortment of papers and a bottle of vodka that was nearly three-quarters gone.

"Good morning, Tobias. You found my note, I see. I heard noises in the walls last night, and when I climbed the stairs this morning, I expected to find evidence of a rat. Instead, I found the tools of a budding spy. Would you care to explain why you've been listening in on my conversations?"

I didn't answer for several seconds, and the professor didn't push. Perhaps he could see how upset I was.

"Because I was *worried* about you," I finally said. It was the truth, although perhaps not the whole truth. And once I began, the words spewed out in a torrent, stumbling over each other. "I didn't mean to overhear you the first time, really I didn't. I was just exploring a few years ago, and I found that staircase and the nook in front of the attic window and—and it made a good fort, you know? Because I could see everything down on the street, but no one could see *me*. And so I kept going up there to read or sometimes at night to look at the stars. But then one day last year, I heard you down here arguing with someone. You were angry that they'd kept you in the dark for…" I swallowed hard but forced myself to keep going. "For over a century. And then it sounded like you were … crying. Maybe you weren't, but that's how it sounded to me."

I told him everything, ending with the conversation I'd heard the previous night. "And I was actually planning to talk to you about it. Probably today. I was just trying to figure out how. But now…" I shook my head, trying very hard not to cry. "I'm sorry I spied on you, Professor. But I'm also *not* sorry. Because it sounds like those other Sentinels—well, maybe not all of them, but the other two who make decisions? It sounds like they've ganged up against you. And that maybe they're not very nice people. So yeah, I was planning to come down today and ask if it would help to have someone to talk about it. Because I was worried about you. But … yeah. Also because I was curious."

"Ah, Tobias." He sighed deeply. "I suppose I had forgotten how intensely curious children can be at your age. Perhaps because it's so very, very long since I was your age. Your curiosity is both a blessing and a curse, I'm afraid. Because now, I have to figure out what to do about you."

That didn't sound good to me. I sat very still, barely daring to breathe.

But he surprised me by laughing. "Don't look so alarmed. I'm not planning to kill you and bury you in the garden. So … why don't you tell me what you *think* you know?"

"I think you're an alien." It sounded ridiculous when I said it, but it also sounded right. "And so are those others. I think that you have a job to do here, and maybe you used to like it, but now you don't. Maybe they're asking you to do things you don't want to do. That book … I looked up the Libyco-Berber alphabet after that first day, and it's nothing like this one. So I think it's really written in *your* language, the one from wherever you were born, the one you spoke as a child and first learned to read. That's why you wanted to share it with your daughter. What happened to her?"

He looked a bit startled at the question. "I told you—"

"I mean, how did she die? Unless you don't like to talk about it."

"No. It's okay. She was my *step*daughter, actually, although I loved her as my own. Lila was born in 1981. Her mother and I met when she was just beginning to walk, and we parted ways when Lila was in her teens. I would have liked to stay in touch with both of them. But I was given a new assignment that made that … difficult. " He gave a rueful laugh. "The Administrators cautioned us to avoid emotional ties—a caution that I understand far better now that I have joined their ranks. After that, I watched Lila's life from a distance. She had a daughter, and eventually, a grandson. Her life was happy from what I could tell. And then she died about ten years ago."

"How old *are* you? Will you live forever?"

"I'll answer the last question first. No. We are not immortal. There are always fatal accidents. An accident that befell one of my number was, in fact, how I wound up being promoted from one of a few dozen Sentinels to one of three Administrators. As for my age, that's an exceptionally difficult question to answer. I was kept in stasis for a while during travel—do you know what stasis is?"

I frowned. "Maybe. Is it like a … cryrosleep?"

"*Cryosleep*. And yes. Anyway, I'm not sure how that period counts toward age. Then, there's the fact that years on this planet are different than years on my own. Let's just say that I've been here, on this planet, since the late 1950s. And I lived far, far longer than that on my home world before I was selected to serve as a Sentinel."

"Did you want to be a Sentinel?"

He considered for a moment. "I did. For one thing, some form of service to the Empire is required, and I have always enjoyed travel. Enjoyed learning about new cultures. We were taught that Sentinels have the privilege of observing civilizations on the brink of great transformation, on the precipice of achievements that would allow them to join our alliance."

"That sounds good."

"It does. That's why I enlisted. But it was a lie."

My heart sank. "Why would they lie to you?"

"Because any civilization that reaches that level of advancement is perceived as a potential threat. A threat to the established order, a danger that must be eliminated before they become colonizers. Which is precisely what our *own* civilization did, long long ago, though we conveniently overlook our history in that regard."

He drank deeply from the bottle before continuing. "I met someone a few decades after I arrived on Earth who had served in the American military. The man claimed that he had been lied to by an Army recruiter, but that he wasn't alone. He joked that the longest book in the English language was entitled *Lies My Recruiter Told Me*. I have recently discovered that my own people —the very Administrators that I trusted—engage in similar behavior. And now that I am one of them, I am expected to carry on this great and glorious tradition."

Even at my young age, I detected the sarcasm in those words. "Are you allowed to quit? If the job makes you unhappy, maybe you should just tell them you don't want to do it anymore. That's what my mom did at her old job when she took this one."

"One can always find some way to leave employment they find unsuitable, Tobias. The only question is whether the cost of staying is higher than the cost of leaving." He frowned, for the first time looking like he might be truly angry at me. "But ... my job satisfaction really is *not* the most important thing here. Have you missed the point entirely? Don't you understand the implications of what I've just told you?"

I suppose I *had* missed the point before that, but it hit me fully then and I began to cry. "You're saying the planet will be destroyed. And I know you don't want that to happen, so you *should* quit. Tell someone. Like, someone in the government. Maybe *all of* the governments. So that we can fight back."

"Telling them wouldn't help. Even if they were able to set aside their differences and work together, they couldn't begin to match the forces that my people can bring to bear against them." He sighed and rubbed his temples. "This isn't something a boy your age should have to worry about. I'm certain—or at least *almost* certain—that *none* of this is going to happen in your life-time. I shouldn't have even told you, but..."

"We have to do *something*! You can't just give up. There has to be some way to change this."

He closed his eyes and was silent for so long that I was begin-ning to think he'd fallen asleep. Or passed out, I suppose, given the now-empty bottle. When he finally spoke, his voice was very tired. "Your people cannot win in a fight against mine. But there *is* a way to avoid the fight in the first place. It won't be easy, but you are a bright boy. If you work hard, and get others to do the same, maybe you can keep your world from ever reaching those mile-stones. Teach people to be happy with what they have *now*. To protect *this* planet, instead of looking to the stars. Because you still have time. I don't know how much exactly, but it is decades, at the very least."

"But what if people won't listen? And won't these Sentinels be angry if I tell everyone what they're doing?"

"They might. But people don't need to know everything. Maybe what they need is a symbol, a beacon to rally around. Maybe they just need hope. Life is so very bleak without ... hope." He hesitated on that last word for a long time, and then came over to sit across from me at the chessboard. "And the Sentinels are not without mercy, Tobias. If you can get people to make an effort, an *actual effort*, to reverse this tide, they will take notice. Even if you fail, even if you cannot convince enough people to save this world, they wouldn't be so cruel as to abandon those of you who tried your very best to save it. They will find a place for you."

"They'd come and rescue us? Really and truly?"

"Really and truly." He smiled then, and I remember how kind his eyes were. But I also remember that he did not hold my gaze for long, glancing instead down at the chessboard which held the game we had abandoned the day before when his phone rang. "Shall we continue this match? Or start over?"

"Whichever you want."

"Personally, I think a fresh start is in order."

And so we reset the board for our very last game together.

-5-

The next morning, the professor did not come down for breakfast at his usual time. He was normally an early riser, but seven-thirty came and went with no sign. He had slept in on a few occasions in the past, so my mother did not become concerned immediately. She simply put his plate on a warming tray. I found her cleaning the pans when I came down for my own breakfast. Later, a little before nine, as I sat at the kitchen table mopping up the last of my eggs with a slice of toast, she told me that she was going to go tap on his door.

"Maybe he went out," she said. "He might have had breakfast plans and forgot to mention them to me. Or he could have told me, and I just forgot. Wait here."

She didn't come back for a long time. I heard her go up the stairs and tap on the door, timidly at first and then with greater urgency. Then she went up to the third floor, her steps much more rapid now. When she came down again, she was crying. And then I was crying, too, and she was holding me.

Later, I would learn that she'd found his body in the study. I expected an ambulance to arrive, but my mother said that he'd left specific instructions for her to call his doctor directly in the event of a serious accident or death. The doctor did not arrive for more than two hours, during which my mother paced nervously, terrified that she would be in legal trouble for not calling emergency services.

When the doctor did arrive, we were both relieved to see that he brought an entire team of EMTs with him and also a woman who identified herself as Professor Everett's personal attorney. They asked no questions of my mother aside from where the body was and then the doctor told us to wait downstairs. About half an hour later, they came back down, this time with the professor's body on a stretcher.

The attorney said that someone would be in contact with my mother about final arrangements, her severance pay, and so forth.

The doctor said that it was a brain tumor, that the professor had known he was dying, and that it was a blessing he'd gone with so little pain.

Of course, I didn't believe the doctor. It seemed impossible that it was a coincidence. He'd died just one day after learning that I knew his secret. But I was far too frightened and wracked with guilt to say anything.

There was no funeral. No memorial service. No chance to say goodbye. Nothing but a short obituary in the papers. Later, someone who claimed to be from the university arrived to carry away the professor's books and computer. We were told that these were his wishes, and perhaps they were.

It was only a few months until the end of the school year, and we were allowed to stay in the house until then. My mother busied herself with the final tasks requested of her by the professor's attorney—disposing of his clothes and other personal items and readying the house for sale. To her surprise, Professor Everett had left her a sum that was more than twice her yearly salary, which she eventually used to start the meal delivery service she ran for the next few decades.

On the day before we were scheduled to leave Allen House, I finally screwed up the courage to go up to my hideout and collect the blanket and the other items that I'd left up there including a banana that was now black and shriveled. At first, I thought that the folded piece of notepaper on the window seat was the terse message I'd found the last time I was up here, telling me to come to his office. But I had carried that down with me, twisting it in my hands as we spoke, and later, tearing it into tiny bits and flushing it away to ensure that my mother never found out, so it couldn't be. There was also a package sitting next to the note.

I opened the note first, hands shaking, and read Professor Everett's final message:

Tobias – I hope you will not think badly of me for what I have done and, most importantly, that you will not blame yourself. I had been contemplating this for some time now and it is better this way. As I told you earlier today, one can always find some way to leave, and this was my one sure way out now that the cost of staying in this job has become more than I am willing to bear. My only regret was not finishing our translation project, and I didn't want to leave you wondering about how the stories turned out. This must, however, remain our little secret. Please remember what I told you and do not despair. I have great faith in your powers of persuasion.

   Affectionately,
   Nathaniel Everett

The package contained the professor's copy of *Tales from the Aveezi Forest*, along with a stack of printed pages in English.

I left the attic with a lighter heart. I'd assumed the book had been whisked away by the university with all of the others in his library, and now I had something to remember him by. But it also gave me something concrete that I could take to my mother. As much as I dreaded telling her what I'd done, the guilt was eating away at me. And the professor had left me with a charge that was far beyond the ability of an eleven-year-old boy.

And so, on that last day at Allen House, I bared my soul to my mother. Not just what I'd done, but also everything that the professor had told me about the Sentinels and the impending doom that loomed over our world. She was quiet until I finished, and I held my breath, expecting anger, shock, or disbelief.

Instead, she took my face in her hands. "You should have told me this much, much earlier. I hate that you've been carrying this around inside you. Honey, brain tumors do strange things to a person's mind. They can cause hallucinations and personality shifts. I'll admit that I didn't notice anything aside from his weight loss. He even seemed to perk up a bit after the two of you began playing chess. But what I'm trying to say is … this story? Everything you've told me? It was a product of his illness."

"But what about this? The book? The note?"

"The book could be part of his delusion. You said that he admitted he wrote it, right? Or maybe it really is a storybook from this ancient script, as he told you to begin with. I think you're right that he may have taken his own life—I don't see any other way to explain this note. Maybe the doctor and his attorney decided to hide that. It could be a religious thing. He didn't seem religious, but I know that some faiths do have odd teachings about suicide. He was absolutely right about one thing, though. You can't blame yourself, Toby. None of this was your fault and it's clear that spending time with you made his last days happier. And I'm so very proud of you for that."

I realized two things then as we sat there amid the packing boxes in my little room at the end of the hall—the only bedroom I could remember in the only home I could remember. First, I wanted to believe her. I so desperately *wanted* to believe that everything he'd told me was a figment of a dying man's imagination. But deep down, I knew. The alien script that we had studied together, the phone calls, even the odd behavior by the doctor were all evidence that the professor's tale was more than just a fabrication. The second thing I realized was that I wasn't going to be able to convince my mother of what I knew to be true. If I was going to take on this task, I would be doing it on my own. She might help me—and indeed, she *did* help me in many ways over the years—but it would be because she loved me, not because she truly believed that Professor Everett had been an alien and that the Earth is in imminent danger if we can't find a way to roll back the tide of so-called progress.

As the years passed, I will admit that I began to wonder if my mother was right. Surely hers was the more rational explanation. I did become active in environmental groups, working with them in the summers as a teen, but if you'd asked me back then, I'd have said it was just one interest among many. If pressed, I'd probably have added that I did the work in the memory of someone I knew as a child, but I would never have told anyone the full story. It was just too strange.

In fact, I'm fairly sure that I would have managed to forget the promise I made to Professor Everett if not for the woman who showed up on our doorstep shortly before I graduated high school. She was an attorney. Not the one who had bustled into the house with the doctor and EMTs that awful morning. She said that the professor had hired her shortly before his death. The trust he established provided for my education—he hoped I would attend Yale and had even left a letter of recommendation that I suspect is the main reason I was admitted. In addition, he left behind a fund to help establish a group to be known as the Earth Watch Alliance. The final part of the bequest was the deed to Allen House, which as some of you may know, became the original headquarters of the EWA.

With the professor's final act of generosity, I now had the resources to at least *begin* the work I'd promised him I would attempt. It became, at that point, a question of faith. Because I did have doubts. I still have doubts. Not about his identity. He was a Sentinel, he was an alien, and he gave up something close to immortality because he could no longer bear to continue playing his assigned role in the coming demise of this planet. But each time that I revisit the memory of my last conversation with Professor Everett, I wonder about the shadow I saw in his eyes. Did he truly believe that the Sentinels would show mercy to those who fought to save this world? Or were those words only a gentle lie that he felt compelled to utter, in order to provide me with a spark of hope that would allow me to move forward despite the heavy weight of what I had learned?

Faced with this dilemma, I chose hope over despair. I chose to believe. And I continue to make that choice every day. Whatever may come, I will never regret spending my life trying to make a difference.

Before we move on, however, I should offer up a disclaimer about the rest of this book. From this point forward, it is only tangentially about *my* life. It now becomes primarily the story of the EWA—how it began, how it grew, and why I still believe that its ideals are the last chance for Earth to avoid a fate that inches closer to inevitability with each and every day.

But I would be remiss if I did not close this section by correcting one final misperception that I did not mention with the others in the first chapter of the book. I am often called the "Father" of the EWA but, if I may be allowed to borrow the play on words that the media so enjoys, I am merely Shepherd to the Flock. Its true progenitor was the Sentinel I knew as Professor Nathaniel Everett. If we survive into the next century, it will be because he chose compassion for our kind over duty to his own.

THIRTEEN

CLAIRE AWOKE a little after seven thirty the next morning, still groggy, but unable to fall back asleep thanks to the thin curtains that let in every bit of the morning sun.

The memoir was still on her mind, so she grabbed her phone and did a quick search through the document for any other mentions of the children's book and the notes that Shepherd had taken when he left Allen House. There was no mention of the documents, so she searched the tax records for the property, which had indeed been the very first EWA headquarters. The building was, in fact, still owned by Tobias Alvin Shepherd. Apparently, he had treated the requirement that all Flock members forfeit private property as one of those *rules for thee but not for me* situations. It had recently been listed for sale, though. Given the emotion with which Shepherd had written about the place, that seemed like a clear indication that he'd given up any hope of ever returning to Earth.

She checked her messages and found two more automated drone reports from Apex Security, along with a terse *OK* from Bernard about the conference, which was a good thing since she'd already submitted a press access form on the Ares Consortium website.

There was also a response from Paul Caruso:

Claire! So great to hear from you. We've had some issues with dome-to-dome communications during lockdown so you may have a hard time reaching Shepherd. Send your request to me and I can forward it. Glad you'll be at ACon. Kolya has MAJOR announcement in his keynote speech on Tuesday so things may be a little hectic. We should definitely get lunch. Or at very least coffee if our schedules don't mesh up. Can't wait to see you!

She sat down on the edge of the bed and, after a few minutes, came up with a message that she hoped would convey her actual question to Shepherd without Paul or any of the KTI censors or anyone else who might be monitoring it on that end having the slightest clue what she was talking about.

Once she'd forwarded the message to Paul, she brushed her teeth, pulled on one of the bathing suits and an oversized T-shirt from the closet, and headed downstairs. If Joe was awake, she'd see what was in the kitchen that they could cook for breakfast. If he was still sleeping, as she suspected, she'd head out to the pool for a swim.

To her surprise, the couch was empty aside from the rumpled blanket. Maybe he'd gotten uncomfortable and gone up to bed? Then, she noticed that the note she'd left for him the night before had been flipped over and he'd scrawled a message of his own, most of which would have been unintelligible if she were not fluent in Joe-speak.

Change of plans. Breakfast on Olympus. Bring your suitcase. Beck is picking up ambrosia. Want to show you something big.

YES, I will take the rest of the day off after that. Tomorrow, too.

~ J

PS: Blood bomb alert. Try to leave before nine. Victoria in garage. Code: D's DOB flipped.

Enjoy the ride. ;)

Mount Olympus was the employees' not-so-secret nickname for the top floor at Jonas Labs, which housed Kai's offices on one side and Joe's on the other. Ambrosia *usually* meant coffee, but they had good coffee at the lab. If he'd asked Beck to pick something up it probably meant French toast bagels from the deli a few miles away. Absolutely everything Joe was working on was *something big* in his estimation, although to be fair it was generally true. The part about him taking the next day off was almost certainly a big fat lie. As for the blood bomb alert, that meant there were protestors at the main entrance of Jonas Labs. They loved to torment employees but were even happier if they managed to harass an owner or member of the management team, as she'd learned from her previous unfortunate encounter.

She deciphered the rest of Joe's message based solely on context. Victoria must be a family vehicle preprogrammed for admission to the underground employee parking area, which she should take instead of calling a car if she wanted to avoid the protestors. But getting out before nine wasn't happening. She still had to shower and change. And pack, apparently, although that wouldn't take long.

When she reached the garage about twenty minutes later, she found that Victoria was a sleek black SoloV25. Claire typed in the numbers 815180, having deciphered *D's DOB flipped* as the inverse of their father's date of birth, tossed her bag into the storage area, and slipped into the seat.

A cheery female voice greeted her. "Good morning. I am Victoria. Where would you like to go this morning, ClaireBear?"

She rolled her eyes at the nickname. "Good morning, Victoria. Lab, please."

"Certainly." As soon as they were in the drive, the garage door closed behind them, and the voice continued. "Estimated time until arrival is thirty-two minutes. I will now play music from the list entitled *Claire's Favorites*."

"Okay..." she said a bit hesitantly, trying to remember what would have been on the last playlist she assembled when she lived in this house and hoping it was *after* her brief cybergrunge phase. She really hadn't had enough sleep for that.

The first few notes sounded vaguely familiar. It was a live recording, because she could hear screams from the audience, but she wasn't able to place the song until the music came to a discordant halt. Five male voices chanted "Out of sight, out of mind is a lie, lie, lie." The screams from the audience grew even louder as the synthpop music began once more.

"Oh my god. Skip, skip."

Hell's Gravity. The boy band that Joe had taken her and several friends to see, and which she had grown out of right around her fourteenth birthday.

"I'm sorry, ClaireBear," the car said. "This playlist is locked."

"Then turn the volume to zero."

"I'm sorry. I can increase the volume, but I cannot turn it down."

Laughing, she pulled out her phone and called her brother. He didn't answer, so she left a message.

> "Enjoy the ride"??? I should have killed you in your sleep.

Her smile faded when she looked up from the phone and got a closer look at the other houses in the neighborhood. In the light of day, they looked completely abandoned. A pair of wicker rockers had sat on the porch of the house next door for as far back as she could remember. The gazebo from one of the other houses was also missing. No cars, no people. A couple of the lawns were even overgrown, and this wasn't the sort of neighborhood where that was tolerated.

As the car approached the gate, she got a clue as to why everyone might have left. Joe's blood bomb warning hadn't been about getting into the lab, but about getting out of the neighborhood. Three vehicles were now parked at the curb across the street. One of them had a portable marquee on top with a phone number and the words *FIVE MILLION* flashing above it. A woman in a blue visor was leaning against one of the other cars. Her head shot up as soon as she spotted Claire's vehicle, and she hurried toward the gate. Three others followed, triggering the pedestrian sensor as the V25 began a right turn onto the road. The car alarm sounded, followed by the voice of the security guard who was now out of the kiosk and rushing toward them.

She could barely hear anything over the pedestrian alarm and Hell's Gravity, but she could see just fine. The guard had a dark cylinder clutched in his right hand. Almost certainly a stun gun.

One of the men gave the guard a wary glance, then quickly tapped on the car's window and wedged a business card into the gap between the glass and the frame. "My client is in group twelve! Twelve! Five million if you can get her into the first group."

"Get away from the vehicle!" the guard bellowed. "I mean it. Clear the road, right now, unless you want me to use this thing."

The woman wearing the visor, who Claire could now see was quite elderly, elbowed the attorney out of the way. She moved her face closer, peering to see through the darkened glass. When she caught Claire's eye, she gave her a nasty grin and spat on the window.

Everyone else retreated to the other side of the road, but the woman stood her ground. She placed both hands on the frame and shoved the car. Either she was stronger than she looked, or the car was extremely light, because Claire could actually feel it shake. Then the woman stepped back and spat again, almost as if she were daring the guard to stun her.

As it turned out, the guard was happy to take that dare.

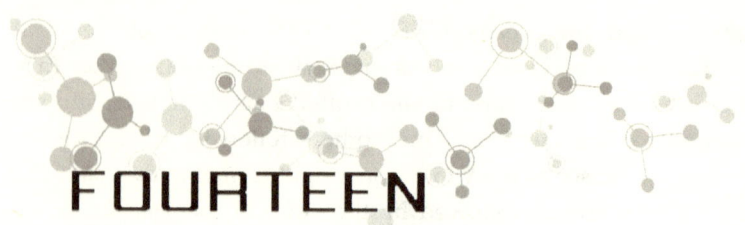

FOURTEEN

THE WOMAN DID NOT FALL to the pavement, as Claire had feared, but merely yelped, grabbed her arm, and backed away.

Claire lowered the window and the attorney's card fluttered to the ground. "What the hell are you doing?" she shouted at the guard. "There was no call for that."

"I have my orders, Ms. Jonas."

"Ms. *Echols*."

The guard glanced at the car's dash, where music continued to blare from the speakers. "Echols. Fine. That was the weapon's lowest setting, Ms. *Echols*. I'm authorized to go up to level five. This car is property of Jonas Labs. We can't stop these idiots from protesting, but we absolutely *can* stop them from damaging company property."

"You didn't have to stun her. It's just spit. It will wash off." Claire looked over at the woman, who was now on the other side of the street. "Are you okay?"

She was okay enough to respond to the question with a one-finger salute. Claire took that as a yes.

The pedestrian alarm was now silent, and the car began moving forward. She gave the guard one last annoyed look and raised the window, then slumped down into the seat and closed her eyes.

Had encounters like this become a daily routine for Joe? He'd sounded more amused than annoyed the last time they spoke about it, but that had been over a week ago.

She reached behind the seat to get her earphones out of the

daypack. The Solo was too narrow to pull the bag around the side and into the front seat. So, she fished around blindly, feeling for the side pocket where she usually kept them. It was only when her fingers brushed across the smooth surface that she remembered this wasn't her old pack, the one that she'd used for several years. This was the pack that Paul or someone at KTI had bought to replace the one that had been destroyed during the bombing at Icarus Camp. A nicer bag, actually, but no side pocket. She finally found the zipper on the front, her fingers identifying a tin of mints, an empty gum wrapper, a tube of lip balm, and a nubby bit of fabric at the bottom that was probably a scrunchie. No earphones, though.

Pulling over to the curb was more trouble than it was worth, especially when she was still feeling a bit unnerved by the crowd outside the neighborhood gate. One of those crazies might even be following her. Resorting to earphones would have been a bit like admitting defeat anyway, so she resigned herself to enduring Joe's little prank. To her surprise, she found herself humming along after a few songs. Aside from that opening number, the group really wasn't *that* bad.

Her phone buzzed with an incoming message shortly after the car merged onto I-95. It was Geneva Wilson. Or rather, Geneva Chatterjee.

Claire!

How wonderful to hear from you!

A quick check of the archives turned up one synthetic biologist, Noah O'Brian (Ph.D., Trinity College Dublin, 2033) hired by VersaBio on June 3, 2047. After the acquisition, he continued working for Jonas Labs (although, back then, it was Echols Pharmaceuticals), remaining with the company until 2058, when he resigned to take a teaching position. I can also check for photographs or a last known address if you think that would be of use to your colleague?

My dad absolutely adores the Martian opal tie clip you brought back for him, by the way. Given recent events, he's decided it's his lucky charm. It was so sweet of you to think of him!

Genni

Claire wasn't sure what *recent events* referred to, but she was glad that Wilson liked the tie clip. This information Genni had provided was already far more than she'd expected, but she messaged back that a last known address would indeed be helpful. She wasn't sure if she'd actually try tracking the guy down, but it would be nice to have if she did. He'd have to be pretty old, if he was still alive. On the other hand, if Shepherd's claims were actually true, he might not be old at all. He could be even younger than she was if he'd been reassigned and taken on an entirely new appearance.

Either way, what would she say if she found him? *Excuse me. Are you Noah O'Brian, the Sentinel formerly known as Anak?*

Genni responded almost immediately with an address in Chicago. A quick search of deaths in Cook County, Illinois brought up a record for Noah O'Brian at that same address and in the very same year that he left his position at Echols Pharma. At age forty-three.

So, O'Brian had indeed been reassigned.

The fact that this was the first thought that popped into her head made her laugh out loud. Sure, the timing seemed a little odd. But it proved *nothing*. People do occasionally die young. The guy could have stepped out in front of a bus for all she knew.

When the car took the exit onto Audubon a few minutes later, she discovered that the protest outside the neighborhood was nothing compared to the gathering near Jonas Labs. It actually looked more like an organized rally than a typical picket line. Security had at least managed to get them off the main grounds, but that didn't seem to have discouraged anyone. A few dozen were congregating on the grassy strip of land that separated the lab campus from the upscale shopping center next door, which was the only property between the lab and the hyperloop terminal. Most of the crowd, however, was clustered at the closest end of the shopping center's parking lot.

She was surprised to see that the vast majority of them didn't appear to be part of the Flock, whose members were always easy to pick out of a crowd. Even under Corbin Drexel, the group had kept its uniform— jeans or a skirt, topped by a T-shirt or a hoodie with the EWA logo, which was a big eye with the Earth superimposed over the iris. You could always spot their transportation, too, and there it was on the far side of the lot—a retrofitted school bus painted green with the EWA eye on the side. In keeping with their low-tech ideology, the Flock also made and carried their protest signs by hand, along with the blood bombs and caged rats and whatever other implements of annoyance they planned to use against their target.

Today, however, two large portable marquees hovered in the sky.

God will not be mocked! (Galatians 6:7).

Jonas (Judas) Labs is the Antichrist! Rejuvesce is US Patent #666!

Claire laughed, but then remembered the drone's high-pitched *thou shalt surely die* and barely repressed a shudder. For the first time, she wondered if the Flock was actually the group—or the *only* group—sending out bugbots?

A bus far longer and more expensive than the Flock's sat directly beneath the signs. It caught Claire's attention mostly because of the image plastered on the side—a youngish couple with blindingly white smiles standing in front of a massive Gates of Destiny Cathedral. It was probably a group from the Boston area, although it was hard to say for sure. There were one or two in most major cities and their buildings all looked pretty much identical. Their preachers, too, for the most part.

The V25 zipped past the sea of protestors without incident and crossed the public parking area out front. Then it navigated around to the opposite side of the campus, which backed to what had once been a lake, but was now either an overgrown field or a marshy swamp depending on the time of year.

When Martin Echols designed the Jonas Labs campus, he'd focused on allowing for growth. In the beginning, the main building that faced the highway had held everything— administrative offices, labs, and manufacturing. A second building provided convenient, affordable housing for employees, although the smart ones (or those with more expendable income) usually took an apartment farther away so that they couldn't be called back to work on a whim. The two remaining buildings had been leased out to other businesses for the first few years, but Jonas Labs had expanded into one of those buildings shortly after the launch of Arvectin and would be taking over the final building when the tenant's lease expired the following year. And the vast majority of manufacturing now took place off campus, in one of the facilities the company owned directly in various parts of the world or through one of its many subcontractors.

Each of the four buildings on the campus was slightly curved, and clustered together to form a loose torus. The entrance to the employee garage was tucked away between two of these buildings. A garage door lifted automatically as Claire approached, and the little car zipped through the tunnel and into the underground lot. It cruised past a sunlit staircase on the right, which led up to the biodome, and then stopped in an assigned space directly in front of the private elevator that would take her straight to Joe's lab.

Claire gave the elevator a quick glance, then veered off to the right, surrendering to the lure of sunlight and the faint sound of birdsong and children's laughter from above. She wouldn't keep Joe and Beck waiting for too long. But her last few visits had been short and hectic, and she'd never made it down here. After the past few days, the confrontation outside the neighborhood earlier, and the chaos of Hell's Gravity blasting out of the speakers on the way over, she needed a bit of serenity. A walk through the biodome and a few minutes at the lake would help clear her mind.

The stairs led up to a wide meadow. A playground shared by the childcare center and the apartment complex sat on one side, along with basketball hoops, tennis courts, and a multipurpose game field. The dome above was oblong, pitched lower here than at the opposite end, where it arced upward to accommodate the trees in the tropical forest.

Several dozen people were roaming about in the meadow. Most of them were children, but there were also a few workers out for an exercise break. As Claire continued along the path, a young woman jogging toward her smiled and started to wave, then dropped her hand awkwardly—no doubt realizing that the person she'd *thought* she recognized was not, in fact, Kai Jonas. Claire waved back anyway.

This biodome wasn't nearly as large or as diversified as ones that she'd visited on school field trips. It was barely even a speck compared to the massive domes she'd seen on Mars. The one around Daedalus City covered more than seven hundred square kilometers, and it was even smaller than the domes at Nepenthes Station. But it had seemed enormous when she was young. Claire had spent more time here as a child than she had in her own back-yard at Everly Estates. She'd watched as the biodome morphed from vague sketches on her father's tablet into design videos he shared with a team of biologists and landscaping professionals. He'd brought her along with him most afternoons when she got out of school so that they could watch the gradual transformation of the biodome from a bare space between the buildings into a tropical oasis. He'd even let her help pick out some of the birds and the fish for the lake as long as she stuck to the list that the biologists had suggested.

Grandma Echols had called the dome *Kai's Folly*, complaining that it more than doubled the construction costs for the new facility and, even after it was finished, would require a full-time maintenance crew. Claire had never taken a look at the final figures, and her grandmother's financial criticism might well have been valid. But she loved the biodome too much to ever think of it as a folly and Kai had very little to do with it.

Although, thinking back, her mom *had* been excited about the dome when it was under construction. She remembered how her father's face would light up on the days that Kai dropped in to check on the progress. And Kai was still proud of the place. She always showed it off to high profile visitors, pointing out the children's play area, the sporting fields, and the hiking trails as evidence of the company's firm commitment to a healthy work-life balance. Then she would lead them on a short walk through the tropical gardens, allowing everyone a few minutes to appreciate the rainbow eucalyptus and the twin waterfalls that cascaded down from the fifth floor terraces into the gentle streams that fed the lake, before whisking them back into a conference room to discuss the things most near and dear to her heart, like mergers and profit margins.

Had Kai ever come down to just enjoy the place once it was completed? Claire couldn't remember a single time, not even before her father died. It was almost as if her mother lost interest in the project once the dream became reality.

Claire had never gotten the sense that this bothered her dad. He was just over fifty when she was born, and approaching sixty by the time they moved the company to the new campus. After it was completed, he went into semiretirement, taking on only a few new projects during the next seven years, including a design for an experimental school that was left unfinished when he died. But the Jonas Labs campus had been his passion project, his masterwork, and he never seemed to be quite as on fire about any of the others.

Was her mother's attraction to that sort of fire the thing that had sparked her interest in Kolya? Martin had wanted to turn a few acres in New England into a tropical forest ... a dream that was fairly easy to achieve with a bit of time and a whole lot of money. Kolya dreamed of transforming an entire planet, so there wasn't much risk of him achieving that goal quickly and losing his drive. Or had it been another sort of drive entirely that interested Kai, given that she was twenty years younger than her husband?

And why does it even matter? God, Claire. Let it go.

She mentally shoved the ghost of her angry teenage self aside and took a seat on the stone ledge near one of the feeder streams. Without even thinking, she scooped up a small handful of pebbles from the water's edge and slipped into her old meditation routine, dropping the pebbles one by one into the water and watching the ripples radiate outward. When the pebbles were gone, she focused on the blips of vibrant color as the fish weaved in and out of the eelgrass at the bottom of the lake. Then she closed her eyes, breathing in the faint camphor scent of the trees, savoring the coolness of the water beneath her fingers, and slowly releasing a bit of the tension that had accumulated over the past week.

"Careful... I heard Joe finally convinced the groundskeepers to add those piranhas you requested."

FIFTEEN

CLAIRE JUMPED AT THE SOUND, even though she recognized the voice almost immediately. She turned to find John Beckett leaning against the prismatic trunk of a eucalyptus tree, holding a small paper bag.

"Joe is such a liar," she said with a laugh. "I did *not* ask for piranhas. I asked for *betta fish*, because I was eight years old, and betta fish are gorgeous. But the biologist said I'd have to pick something else, because bettas are also pugnacious as hell and do not play well with others. Did he send you down to fetch me?"

"Not exactly. I got upstairs with the bagels a few minutes ago and realized I'd left the cream cheese in the car. When I came back down, I noticed the V25 next to mine in the garage. That was a bit of a mystery, since you weren't upstairs and there's just the one elevator going up from the garage to the lab so I couldn't have passed you. The biodome was the only other logical possibility and, well … I thought I might find you here at the lake."

It was a good guess on his part. The lake was where they had scattered her dad's ashes and she'd spent many hours down here in the weeks after he died. She hadn't been aware that this was common knowledge, but then Beck might have been paying a bit more attention to what she did during those weeks than even Joe or her mom. Joe had been distracted by his own grief, and Kai had busied herself with work. Beck had drawn the short straw and wound up listening to her vent on several occasions. He was a good listener.

"I just needed a few moments to breathe," she said. "It's been a rough week."

"If you need a bit longer, I can go back up. Joe is working, so it may be an hour—or a week—before he wonders what's keeping you."

"That's okay. I was about ready to leave anyway."

He extended a hand to help her up. She brushed the leaves from her pants, took one last look at the water trickling over the stones, and followed him out to the path.

"So ... you said that it's been a rough week. Is that because of the drones at your place or your meeting with the professor at Columbia?"

"Both." Claire wasn't sure why saying the word gave her a feeling of déjà vu, until she remembered that it had also been her response when Wyatt asked pretty much the same thing at the restaurant the previous night. She unfolded her phone and pulled up the video of the drone to show Beck. "First, this chatty little cicadabot was outside my house yesterday."

As Beck watched the video, Claire realized Wyatt had been right about the sound. The message was nearly incomprehensible due to the background racket from the garbage truck.

"In case you can't make it out, that's—"

"A bible verse. Or verses, maybe. Sounds like Genesis, chapter two."

Claire raised an eyebrow. "I would not have taken you for a Bible scholar."

"Let's just say I had an ... *eclectic* upbringing. It's from the second version of the creation story, where God cautions Adam and Eve against eating from the tree of knowledge."

"You mean the tree that was placed right in the middle of the garden, so that it could taunt them?"

"That's the one." He frowned. "Joe told me about the drones, but he didn't say anything about them spouting death threats."

"This was the first one with that fun little feature. It struck me as odd for another reason, too, since the Flock has never really been traditionally religious."

"True." He thought for a moment. "Although, if they had to

pick a bible verse as their cult motto, this would be a good candidate. What is science, after all, if not the tree of knowledge? What did you do with the drone?"

"Luckily, I had a gadget to disable the thing and a shovel to scoop it into the trash. But then I got to New York and discovered that the Flock has already moved past mere threats." She filled him in on Leffler's death and her afternoon of interrogation. "Alice—she's Leffler's colleague in the archeolinguistics department who was with me at the hospital? She can't think of any other reason that the Flock would have had to attack Leffler. It has to be connected to the Martian script."

"So … you believe they killed her because she was making progress?"

"The thing is, she actually *wasn't* making progress. In fact, she'd all but told me it was going to be impossible without some sort of Rosetta stone. The entire reason I stopped off in New York was to try and convince her to reconsider."

He shook his head in annoyance. "With all due respect to the deceased, I really hope we can find a better expert. Because I think she's wrong. I've already made a bit of headway—a very, *very* small bit, mind you—using a prototype I purchased from someone at Berkeley. They have a team that's working on a—"

"On a unified theory of language?"

He gave her a sideways look. "Yessss. How did you know *that*?"

"Leffler's colleague mentioned that research as an avenue she wanted to explore. She was, however, planning to go about it in a legal fashion, whereas I'm guessing you've made this purchase off-the-books, given that you already have it in hand."

"Guilty as charged. Official channels would have taken way too much time. Let's just say that someone's tuition has been paid for at least the next few semesters. And if this program ever becomes commercially available, I will happily buy a license. *Ten* licenses, even. At any rate, I've been using the program to run a battery of tests that compare our manuscript to all known languages. The results I've gotten have probability scores that don't even hit single digits, even after adding in what we know or can reasonably deduce about the society, but I'm just tinkering with it. I'm not an expert in this field by any means. So ... if Leffler wasn't making progress, why do you think she was killed?"

"I don't know. At first, I thought they might have been trying to send me a message, but as Ro is fond of telling me these days, I might have a wee touch of paranoia. And why not just target me directly? Admittedly, I now have a one meter no-drone zone that follows me around everywhere and Leffler clearly did not. But drones aren't the only weapons that the Flock has. They're not even the only weapons they've used recently. Which really leaves just the translation project. Maybe they didn't know that she'd decided to abandon it and they were worried she might actually crack the code. Or ... maybe they're not willing to take any chances because they know that there's more than just the etchings in the chambers to decipher."

"I'm not sure how they'd know that. I haven't told anyone. Not even the student at Berkeley. I made up something about a Mayan tablet I purchased, so they probably just think I'm a weirdo with expensive hobbies and way too much time on his hands. And I'm sure Joe hasn't said anything. He's barely looked at the manuscript."

"It's probably my fault," Claire said apologetically. "I didn't *tell* anyone. Not even Wyatt, although I'm going to need to do that soon. But it's possible that I inadvertently gave them a clue if they have a source inside the *Atlantic Post*. Or if they've managed to hack into the *Post's* communication system. I made my plans to travel up here on one of my in-office days, using my personal phone, which is about as secure a device as you can get since Wyatt's friend Kes got hold of it after I returned from Mars. I would have thought that the office would be equally secure, maybe even more than my house, given that they have people working on exclusives and at least give lip service to the belief in protecting our sources. But the drone barrage started right after I made those calls. I assumed it was connected to Wyatt's article on the Flock. And the article may still be what pushed the FBI to start actually questioning people about the bombings. But I was thinking about it earlier and ... you know who Stasia Ljubic is, right?"

"Kolya's former second-in-command. The one who is now working with Drexel."

"That's her. Stasia knew that I was collecting samples for Joe. Which got me to thinking that they could very easily have samples of their own. What if they discovered the same thing we did?"

Beck thought for a moment, then shook his head. "If that was the case, why would they want to kill one of the people most likely to be able to crack the code? You'd think they'd have kidnapped her and put her to work if they believe the message is important enough to kill someone over."

"Unless they already *know* what it says."

"You think they have their own expert."

"Maybe. Or maybe they have their own Rosetta stone."

SIXTEEN

CLAIRE WAS MORE than a little surprised to hear the words come out of her mouth. At what point had she actually decided that Shepherd's memoir might be something other than fiction? Yes, there were bits of evidence that confirmed his story, but he could very easily have built the entire thing around those tiny nuggets of fact.

She quickly held up a hand to forestall the question she could see Beck was on the verge of asking.

"Don't. I can't tell you what I meant by that. It's based on a confidential source. But you'll only be in suspense for a few more days."

"So, Wyatt's about to publish another story about the Flock?"

"What did I just say?"

"Okay, okay. But you can't just drop that on me and expect me to move on to something else."

"Yes. I absolutely can. And now I'm going to change the subject, all subtle-like, so that you won't be tempted to press me for more information." She gave him a prim smile. "Speaking of alien code, I awoke this morning to one of Joe's cryptic notes saying there's been a change of plans. Any idea what's up?"

"That wasn't subtle in the least, but…" He sighed. "I guess we're changing the subject. Vangie, that's Kai's latest assistant, messaged this morning to inform us that they've had to temporarily shut down the Lomas Verdes plant in order to beef up security. There were several protests over the past two weeks, but it seems the one yesterday got out of hand. Which means your mother will be home this evening. And Joe didn't think you'd be comfortable staying at the house with her there."

"Joe is right."

"To be fair, I doubt *anyone* is going to be comfortable around Kai for the next day or two. It wasn't exactly sunshine and kittens around here when she left, and I'm sure you remember how she gets when something upsets her schedule."

"I do, indeed. I'm glad Joe reminded me to pack my things. I guess we can just talk here at the lab. It shouldn't take too long to go over what you've put together, right? I'll get a hotel afterward and maybe we can all grab dinner."

"Actually, we were thinking maybe we could relocate. I don't know if Joe mentioned it, but I'm taking a long-deferred vacation starting … well, starting this afternoon, I guess."

"Oh, he mentioned it. Several times. As if it were some strange, alien concept that he couldn't quite wrap his head around. How long has it been since you took time off?"

"The last vacation was five years ago. Four consecutive days. And I took an entire week about six years before that. When I told him I was taking three weeks this year, he nearly choked. Your mother was baffled, too."

"I'm proud of you, Beck. It must be hard to remain a human being when you are surrounded by automatons."

He laughed. "It can be challenging. Kai asked if this was my way of telling her that I wanted more money. It's not, but I don't think she believes me. Anyway, I have plans to meet up with a few college friends for a short reunion at the beginning of next week. We've been putting it off for much too long."

A cloud passed over his face at that point, almost as if he were dreading this reunion. That piqued Claire's curiosity, but before she could come up with a tactful way to ask why, Beck continued.

"Other than that, however, I'm planning to spend my time off at a little bed-and-breakfast that I own up in Maine."

"You *own* a B and B?"

"Yes. It's an investment I've had for a while now. I don't go there often, because there are usually guests and the couple who run it for me live there full time. When I manage to get away, I'm looking for solitude, so I go to a little cabin I own a few miles from there."

"You have a lot of vacation homes for someone who never gets a vacation."

"True. But it's only a little over an hour away, and I still—occasionally—get a weekend off. The B and B is an investment, but the cabin is my quiet place. It's tiny and rustic, in the middle of the woods near Mount Agamenticus, and you can actually see the stars at night. Feels like you're the only person on the planet. Anyway, the couple that manages Bellamy House for me have been wanting to take some time off to visit their daughter in London, so I blocked the entire month of September from the rental schedule. They left a few days ago, which means we'd have the place to ourselves. There's a little river out back, a decent-sized swimming pool, and it's easy biking distance to the beach. Mostly though, it's a place where we won't have to deal with protestors. And it's only about an hour from here by car. Maybe twenty minutes from the Portsmouth-Kittery terminal so we can easily get you back on the hyperloop to DC when you're ready to leave. I was planning to head up this evening anyway, so if you're game..."

"It sounds great. To be honest, I really wasn't looking forward to going back to the house, even *before* knowing Kai would be there. Joe really downplayed how crazy it's gotten here. Just getting out of the neighborhood this morning was insane. The guard actually *stunned* an elderly woman who touched the car. I mean, yes, she was being obnoxious. Maybe even a little threatening. But she was probably in her seventies and..." She shook her head. "Do you know what happened? To the neighborhood, I mean. It looks like a freakin' ghost town. Joe said they'd ramped up security a tiny bit—I'm pretty sure those were his *exact* words, in fact. But it looks like all five neighbors packed up and cleared out."

"They did. After a few weeks of dealing with complaints from them about the noise and hassles getting out to the highway, your mother decided to just have the company buy everyone out. They can always sell the houses again once things calm down, although they won't get nearly what they paid for them since Kai told them to go way above market price just to be done with it. This way, Jonas Labs security can handle everything. The families in the neighborhood have been gradually clearing out over the past few months. I think the last bunch moved about a week ago. Was the woman okay? The one the guard stunned, I mean."

"Yeah. She seemed fine. The guard said the weapon was on the lowest setting, but still…" She shuddered. "On the plus side, though, if you've got some extra Rejuvesce sitting around, I think I know a way we can split a cool five mill."

He made a dismissive sound. "Five million is low-ball compared to some of the offers we've heard."

A little girl on a bike was heading toward them. She looked a bit wobbly, so they stepped off the path to let her pass. Beck turned back to watch for a moment, apparently worried that the kid might take a tumble. But the girl righted herself and they continued toward the garage.

"I'm just amazed that you got Joe to agree to travel to *Maine*. Or anywhere for that matter. I can barely get him to meet me in New York these days."

"The trick with Joe is to make him an offer he can't refuse."

Beck mumbled the words, almost as if he had a mouth full of marbles. She had the sense that he was making a joke and smiled. Her face must have shown her confusion, though, because he laughed.

"Sorry. I watch too many old movies. I just meant that I bribed your brother by telling him that while I had officially put in for the full three weeks' vacation, I would come back a day *early* for every day he takes off."

"That's … downright devious. I'm impressed."

Beck gave her a gracious little nod. "I try. But, to be honest, I think even Joe realizes he needs to get out of here for a bit. And maybe get his mind on something other than Rejuvesce. Kai was in a pissy mood even before this. The annual stockholders meeting is less than a month away and she'd like to be able to announce … well, I'll let *Joe* give you more on that. Let's just say that she would like something big enough to offset the general annoyance at the decision to release the patent ahead of the expected schedule."

"So Joe doesn't want to be here when she gets back, either."

"Exactly. But the past few months have also been pretty rough on him. I've had a distraction. It took time for me to extract the manuscript from the non-coding DNA and get it into a version that allowed me to run the program I purchased. And I can still go out to the store or whatever and *usually* manage to avoid being recognized. Guess that's an upside to being kind of generic looking. But Joe … the crazies can spot him a mile away. I don't think he made it out to the beach all summer, and that's the one thing that he usually makes time for. He can't even go up on the roof anymore without someone shouting at him through a portable PA system."

Claire wouldn't have described Beck as generic looking. In fact, she'd crushed on him pretty hard when she was in her upper teens, at least in part because he was in his mid to late twenties at that point and therefore, forbidden fruit. Even more off limits if you added in the fact that he was Joe's research partner. But it was fair to say that he could blend in with a crowd much easier than a dark, hulking, six-foot-seven wall of muscle like Joe. When Joe walked into a room, everyone noticed him.

And if the protests were keeping Joe from going up on the roof, that wasn't good. The roof was Joe's haven, the place he went when he needed to pace around and think. Even though there was a fully equipped gym in the building and at least a mile of trails winding through the biodome, there were *people* in those places, and people were the very last thing Joe wanted when he was trying to clear his head and focus. No wonder Beck needed a vacation. If Joe wasn't getting his rooftop time, he had to be grouchy as hell.

"Can't security do something about the situation?" she asked.

Beck shrugged. "Security is part of the reason he's not out on the roof. One of the more recent and credible death threats explicitly mentioned watching him pace around up there through the scope of his rifle. Even included what he was wearing. Wilson put a lock on the roof exit after that and won't give him the password."

"I'm surprised he didn't go over Wilson's head."

"Oh. You don't know about the promotion then. Carmichael quit about a month ago. Well, technically, he retired, but we all knew he was tired of dealing with the ramped up threat situation. Anyway, Wilson put in for the job and got it."

"Good for him! And he's right. What good is a few extra decades of life if someone guns you down? Rejuvesce can't stop a bullet."

"That's pretty much what Wilson told him when he complained. Security *has* been really good about keeping the lunatics off the property, but as you no doubt noticed on the way in, when someone runs them off, they just set up camp next door. Kai personally asked the owner of the shopping center to do something about it, but it turns out that he's in sympathy with the protestors, since he turned seventy a few months back. The police come by and chase them away if they use the PA too much and trigger a noise violation. But they just show back up again a few days later. And different groups come in at different times. Different people *within* the same group, too, so the police seem to mostly be letting them off with a warning. Wilson and I both suggested to Kai that we should have the legal team work on getting a more expansive restraining order, but Joe agrees with your mom's position—if we ignore them, they'll eventually go away."

That drew a dry chuckle from Claire. "I would have told you that my housemate and my mother had absolutely nothing in common, but they apparently have very similar philosophies on how to handle the Flock."

"Yeah, well, they're both wrong. Zealots don't back down. Once people become convinced that they know the truth—the one and only, absolute, unshakeable truth—they're generally in it for the long haul. I just ... I'd never have imagined Jenelle Tuller. Why didn't you think to mention last time that she's the one who ousted Shepherd? It was a bit of a shock—for me and Joe both—to see her face pop up in Wyatt's article a few weeks later."

"His story was still pending when I was here, and..." Claire frowned. "Why? Do you guys know her?"

To her surprise, Beck blushed. "Um, kind of? She used to be sort of a ... I guess you'd call her a science groupie? I mean, that's how she wound up with Kolya eventually."

"A *science groupie*? Is that actually a thing?"

"For scientists at Kolya's level? Absolutely."

"Well, yeah." Claire laughed. "Kolya's insanely rich. Wouldn't that make her more of a money groupie, though? I thought you were talking about followers who ... I don't know ... hung out in lab hallways and chased down the authors from the latest issues of *The Lancet* or *Nanotech Monthly*."

"I'm not saying there are hordes of them. And Jenelle had plenty of money of her own, so that wasn't the reason she was attracted to Kolya. She's also very smart. A bit quirky, but I would never have imagined her going completely off the deep end like this. I guess anyone can have a breakdown, though."

"You think she's insane?"

"I don't ... I mean, I haven't talked to her in a couple of years. I certainly don't know her well enough to say for sure, but it kind of sounds like it, right? The only reason I mentioned it was because... Jenelle was..." He stopped, clearly measuring his words. "Around the time I started at Jonas Labs, she seemed to have her sights set on Joe."

"You're kidding. He was barely legal."

"He was twenty. Maybe even twenty one."

"Yeah, but ... how old is she?"

"I don't know. I'd have said mid-twenties at that time, so add a decade."

Based on Claire's one face-to-face encounter with Drexel and the photographs she'd seen at Kolya's house when she was at Ehden, she would have guessed early thirties. Which actually wouldn't make her that much older than Joe. It would make her considerably *younger* than Kolya, however, calling into question his previous claim that he wasn't generally attracted to younger women.

"Anyway, your mom was still trying to get Joe to do corporate events back then, to show off her wunderkind. Jenelle was really good at getting herself invited to those parties. Like I said, she's got money, and she likes to invest in the next big thing. And she thought Joe was the next big thing." He chuckled. "In more ways than one. There was this picture of the two of them that wound up online, with her clutching his arm and staring up at him all doe-eyed."

Claire gasped. *"That's* where I'd seen her before! She seemed vaguely familiar even when she bumped into me at Columbia and tagged my messenger bag with the listening device."

"She did that personally? I assumed one of the Flock would be tasked with that sort of thing."

"Yeah. You'd think, right? Maybe she was just in the area." They headed down the stairs into the garage. "So what happened between her and Joe? No, let me guess. He was completely oblivious."

"Well, no. He *noticed* her. It was kind of hard not to. She's gorgeous. He said they had dinner once, so I think he was even tempted. But she was just not as tempting as going back to the lab, you know? Eventually, she gave up on Joe and later that year, she ends up married to Kolya. I think your mom was more upset about it than Joe."

"I'll *bet* she was." Claire quickly added in response to Beck's raised eyebrow, "I mean, you know Joe's standard response to any questions about dating and relationships. *Too busy now. I'll have plenty of time to worry about all of that later.* I'm just afraid he'll still be saying that when he's a hundred and it will be too late."

"Yeah. Could be." Beck's response seemed innocuous enough, just a casual agreement with her point. And if he hadn't turned at that exact moment, stepping aside to let her enter the elevator, she might have missed the laughter in his eyes.

What exactly was he laughing at? Joe wasn't just Beck's research partner. And it was very much out of character for him to be amused at the possibility that his best friend might be so focused on work that he missed out on life.

Maybe Joe was already seeing someone and hadn't told her? She couldn't imagine how or when. Not unless he'd managed to grow the perfect companion in his lab. Beck was pretty much the only person he interacted with these days, and they were both straight, to the best of her knowledge.

Or maybe Beck was reacting to her own snarky comment about her mother. Was it possible that he knew about Kai and Kolya?

FROM THE ATLANTIC POST OPINION

(SEPTEMBER 1, 2084)

Your recent article about the equity issues surrounding the distribution plan for Rejuvesce ("Waiting Line at the Fountain of Youth," August 27, 2084) ignores one glaring injustice: the arbitrary cut-off age. Obviously, the government faces constraints due to the limited supply, which means that difficult decisions must be made. But the current lottery system is a blunt ax in an enterprise that would be far better served by a scalpel.

According to the rules of the lottery, all individuals between fifty and sixty-nine receive priority due to the fact that the drug has shown increased efficacy among patients under the age of seventy. We have been informed that as supplies increase, the cut-off age will be expanded to include older citizens, as well.

There are several strong arguments for why this is unfair. First, the manufacturer and the US Department of Health both acknowledge that the drug does still work for those beyond seventy; it simply has a "higher" rate of failure. Most medical treatments have variable success rates across populations. What if we denied cancer patients treatment based solely on success percentages? Such a system would be decried as unjust, and right-fully so.

Secondly, those above the age of seventy are in greater need of the drug. The odds of an octogenarian surviving until there is adequate supply for all are far lower than the odds of those in their fifties surviving that long. Surely some consideration should be given to the balance between efficacy and need?

Furthermore, the current system fails to consider the health of the patient. Where is the data showing that the drug is less effective for a seventy-year-old who exercises regularly and has no harmful habits or comorbidities than it is for a sixty-nine-year-old who is sedentary and engages in habits harmful to his or her health? And does the success rate of the drug suddenly plummet at midnight on a person's seventieth birthday?

These issues are important considerations for a society that claims to value justice but also venerates youth. The current distribution method reinforces harmful stereotypes that sideline the elderly, perpetuating the idea that older individuals are expendable, and have little to offer. A full review should be undertaken immediately by the WHO and the US Department of Health, to ensure that the distribution is handled with justice, compassion, and a recognition of the inherent worth of *all* individuals, regardless of age.

SEVENTEEN

WHEN THE ELEVATOR reached the sixth floor, an unfamiliar face was at the guard station. She was glad that Wilson had gotten the promotion but had to admit that she'd miss seeing him there.

That thought hadn't even had time to leave her head when Wilson rounded the corner, not in his standard uniform, but in a suit, complete with the tie pin she'd brought back from Mars.

"Miss Claire! Joe told me you were coming by, but I was worried that I might miss you."

Beck gave her a little wave and headed down the hall so that she and Wilson could catch up. But Wilson pushed the down button, clearly in a bit of a hurry.

"Yeah," he said when Claire asked where he was heading, "I got a meeting with Jack Perry, the man who owns the shopping center next door. Hoping I can finally convince him to stop letting those crazy sonsabitches camp out in his parking lot."

"I thought they already tried to reason with him."

He gave her a crooked smile and lowered his voice. "You been on the receiving end of your mama's attempts to reason with someone, right?"

She laughed. "Yes, unfortunately."

"Well, let's just say that the guy who had this position before me had pretty much the same negotiation style. I'm going to focus a little more on our mutual interests. I might come back across the lot with my tail between my legs, but he agreed to meet, so I figured it's worth a shot."

"Let me ride down with you since you're running late. I need to ask you something."

"Sure."

She followed him into the elevator and told him about the confrontation outside Everly Estates, including the guard stunning the old woman.

"I'm not trying to get the guy in trouble. I know he was just doing his job. But … she was old, and she could have been seriously hurt. I just thought you might want to know."

"I think I know which guy you're talking about. He's a little on the gung ho side. I'll have a chat with him. But in his defense, things have gotten a bit crazy around here. I'm pretty sure I know the woman you're talking about, too. She's been out there every day for the past few weeks. Kind of sad, really. She's a few years younger than her husband. She made the age cutoff for the lottery, but just barely."

Claire winced. "So he didn't make it?"

"You guessed it. That's one of the things the bureaucrats didn't think through all the way, but I guess you've gotta draw the line somewhere."

She debated asking Wilson if he'd had anything similar to her bugbot infestation, but they were already at the bottom floor. So she wished him luck with the shopping center owner, then headed back up to Olympus. And for the second time in recent memory, she entered Joe's lab to find herself already there.

The holographic body currently hovering in the middle of the room was, for all intents and purposes, hers … or at least what hers would look like in about ten years. She'd been one of Joe's first subjects back when she was in middle school. It hadn't involved much of a time commitment on her part. Aside from undergoing a full body scan, answering a series of lifestyle questions, and offering up a variety of bodily fluids for analysis, everything else had been handled by the computers. Her *in silico* double had been uncannily accurate in predicting a few minor health issues, including the appendectomy in her early twenties. At the time, however, she'd just been happy to get concert tickets out of the deal.

"Well, that explains why Hell's Gravity was on your mind," she told Joe, nodding toward the hologram.

He looked up from his screen, his face a picture of innocence. "I have no idea what you're talking about."

"Yeah, *right*. Why have you been running Virtual-Me so much lately? Isn't she a bit outside the age range of your research?"

"Maybe. How old do you think you are here?"

Claire examined her virtual self a bit more closely this time. There were faint lines around her eyes. A slight softening at the waist and the jawline. Judging from the scars on her left leg, the *in silico* model had been updated with her latest medical information. As the model turned, she saw another faintly discolored line a few inches from the spine on her left. That was from the second injury she incurred in the chamber, the one that had very nearly killed her.

"Can you display stats?" she asked.

"I was shooting for more of an off-the-cuff assessment, but hey, if you want to make a full study, have at it. Holo2, display all information about current subject except age." Several columns of data popped up to the right of the hologram. "Where'd Beck go?"

"I believe he's toasting a bagel."

"An excellent idea. I'll leave you to it, professor."

"Put one in for me, okay? And don't burn it."

"One bagel, barely warm, coming right up."

Claire had no clue what half of the data on the screen even meant, but after skimming through for several minutes, she finally found a few stats for which she more or less knew her current readings. Blood pressure seemed about right at 115/75. Her weight was a tiny bit higher, but BMI still well within the green zone. Cholesterol and blood sugar were also in the green zone, and while her triglyceride count seemed a *bit* higher than usual, she couldn't have sworn to it.

If she'd seen this information without having any clue about the nature of her brother's work, she'd have said the model's age was mid- to late-thirties. Early forties, at the outer limit. But she now had a decent idea what he'd meant by a stretch goal. Extending the lifespan by a few decades would be much better if you began to slow the aging process when the body was still relatively young and healthy.

She crossed the hall into the break room, where Joe was waiting for his bagel to pop out of the toaster. Hers was already out and smeared with way too much cream cheese. She took the plate, discreetly scraped about half of the spread back into the container and joined Beck at the table.

"So ... what's the verdict?" he asked.

"I'm going to round up a bit and say ... fifty?"

"Guess again." Joe leaned back against the counter, his grin growing wider as she increased her guess by increments of five and then ten years.

She stopped at eighty, shaking her head. "You've got to be kidding me."

"Nope."

She looked at Beck for confirmation.

"He's right. Assuming you begin Rejuvesce by age thirty-five, that's what you'll look like on your ninety-ninth birthday."

Well, that explained what Beck had been smirking about in the elevator when she suggested that Joe might put off dating until he was a hundred. If her brother was even close to the same shape as Virtual-Claire at that age, he'd have plenty of time left.

Joe slid into the seat next to her. "We cut it off at max plus-ten. Barring accidental death or injury, the system had you living to eighty-nine."

Beck sighed. "Seriously, Joe? Maybe you could have given her a spoiler alert first?"

"Why?" He asked around a bite of bagel. "That was her projected maximum age *without* treatment. At the current rate of production increase, she can almost certainly start a few years before that."

"If that's me at nearly one hundred, and those are my

projected readings at that age, then that's well beyond the twenty-five year increase in life expectancy that you initially predicted."

"Twenty-five years is still pretty accurate if treatment begins by age fifty," Beck said. "But yeah. Begin fifteen years earlier and it's a very different story."

"So … how far out have you run the projections?"

Joe glanced over at Beck. "Since you were ragging me about spoilers, I'll let you field this one."

"Okay." Beck considered for a moment. "We're thinking it could triple life expectancy or a little more. So a ballpark figure would be around two hundred and eighty years."

"Holy…" Claire shook her head. "That's just…"

Having now reached a complete lack of words, she went over to the counter to brew a cup of coffee, hoping to give her brain a bit of time to process what they'd just told her. Twenty to twenty-five extra years of life wasn't that much of a mental leap. People were, on average, already living about twelve years longer than they had at the beginning of the twenty-first century. Life expectancy had increased even more rapidly during the century before that, but that increase was largely due to improvements in infant mortality. Rejuvesce was notable because it promised a fairly rapid increase in *adult* life expectancy, but before now, it still seemed like a relatively incremental change.

Tripling the average life span, though?

"And it gets wilder—" Joe began.

Claire held up a hand. "Give me a sec, okay?" She pushed the button on the coffee machine, then turned around to face him. "You're telling me something is *wilder* than tripling life expectancy?"

"Triple is our prediction if treatment begins by age thirty-five," he said. "If we begin earlier … I don't think we can rule out the effects being indefinite. We've got rats in the system that I started on the protocol at seven months, which is roughly equivalent to twenty years in humans. That was *twelve* years ago. They should have been dead two or three years back, but their cells are still showing almost *no* signs of senescence. The same is true for the tests on higher mammals, too."

"That's the kind of statement that gets the Flock and other groups all riled up," Claire said with a sigh. "Say it with me, Joe. *In silico rats. In. Silico.*"

There hadn't been a live test subject in Jonas Labs in decades. What Joe had in the system were several thousand simulated rats, along with various other mammals, and *twelve years ago* meant twelve years inside the simulation. That was probably only a few weeks in real time.

"Fine, fine. *In silico.* But you knew what I meant."

"What about the human *in silico* models?" she asked. "Are they showing similar results?"

"That's kind of the problem," Beck said. "Virtual Claire is the youngest subject we have full permissions to use, but the early tests on you seem very promising. The version we're running now has been updated with your most recent records, including lab results from your last physical and the data we got from the medical staff on the *Ares Prime*. At twenty-eight, you've already experienced some cell deterioration but–"

"*Smooth,*" Joe said. "Never let anyone tell you John Beckett doesn't know how to charm the ladies."

Beck gave her a slightly embarrassed smile and then continued, "Not *visible* deterioration, of course. But cellular death begins around age twenty-five, so ideally, treatment should start a bit before that."

"That's okay. I knew what you meant. So the next step is reverting to the data from when I was thirteen?"

"Yes," Joe said. "Those models are Beck's area of expertise, though, so I guess we'll have to wait until he gets back from his vacation before we start."

There was a note of reproach in her brother's voice, which Claire didn't think was at all fair. She didn't say anything, but she did shoot him a look, which he either missed or ignored.

"I already told you how to make it quicker," Beck said, grinning.

"Yes," Joe said. "I meant when *we* get back from vacation. Anyway, if it all goes as I think it will, within the next month or so, we should be able to start recruiting a few thousand young volunteers for a screening process similar to the one you went through. College age, or even younger if we can get approval to include adolescents. And then the whole dance with the government starts again."

"But it shouldn't take as long for it to get final approval, right? I mean, it's not even an entirely new application of the drug, just a new population being treated. And once you have the *in silico* volunteers, won't it simply be a matter of running the data?"

"Yes," Joe said. "A drop in the bucket compared to what it would have been a few decades back. But we could still be looking at as much as five years from start to finish."

"Which I keep telling him is a *good* thing," Beck said. "Five years gives us more time to deal with supply issues. More time for other companies to begin work on biosimilar versions. Frankly, ten years would be even better. Unfortunately, rumors are going to spread once we start recruiting younger volunteers for the scanning process. Even if we're vague about the nature of the study, if they find out Jonas Labs is behind it, I think it's inevitable that people will put the pieces together and realize that we're talking about an extension of more than just a couple of decades. Do we really want that to get out before *all* countries have at least some level of access to the drug? Because I'm thinking that could be somewhat … destabilizing."

Claire sank back down into her chair at the table. Beck was right, although she thought *somewhat destabilizing* was putting it very mildly. Her mother had risen to demigod status simply by following in the footsteps of many, many other researchers and beating the last, most stubborn form of cancer.

Joe was talking about potentially beating *death*.

EIGHTEEN

THEY TOOK two cars up to Maine, since Joe still wasn't willing to commit to exactly how long he'd be away from the lab. Claire rode with her brother so that she could fill him in on everything that she'd told Beck in the biodome. When she reached the end, Joe fell silent. She knew him well enough not to push, so she just let him stare out the window as he thought through what he wanted to say.

This was one of the main reasons Joe didn't like crowds or public speaking. He had two default modes—saying next to nothing or going into so much detail that it often left the listener feeling assaulted and confused. Kai still pushed him to do public events. She had even gotten a full ten words out of him on video at the Rejuvesce launch. But he'd probably had to spend an hour or more thinking those ten words through before he showed up at the party, and Beck was almost certainly the only person he talked to for the next few days after that.

Joe was at ease with Claire. Willing to joke and tease. He was possibly even more relaxed with Beck. But that was only because they both knew when to shut up and let him percolate. Kai was more stubborn, but even she knew better than to push Joe too far if she didn't want him to retreat to the lab and refuse to talk to anyone.

They were off the interstate now, so Claire followed Joe's lead and watched as the stretches of balsams that lined the narrow road flew by. Occasionally, the view was punctuated by a house, a charging station, or some other sign of civilization, but for the most part, it was just one long viridian blur.

"Okay," he began, after a couple of minutes. "Don't you think maybe you and Beck are making too much of all this? I mean sure, when we first found that there was a manuscript hidden in the DNA of that sample, I was impressed—and yes, maybe even a little alarmed— by the fact that someone had gone to that much trouble in order to disseminate the document. But as I believe I said even then, what if that's just how this ancient Martian civilization distributed information? The organisms are self-replicating, after all, so that would be a pretty convenient way to spread something far and wide with minimal effort. They could have done that for even the most mundane documents. This could have been their equivalent of a sales catalog for all we know."

"If that were the case, though, why would we have found only the *one* book? It's the same manuscript, coded over and over throughout the sample."

"Easy. Almost every trace of life was erased from the planet. What if they used different hosts to code different documents? It could even have been a classification system of sorts, by domain, kingdom, phylum, and so on. *Chlorobium* houses the gardening books, Norse mythology is in *Lokiarchaeota*. And so on. I know those are Earth-centric examples, but you get the point. There could have been tens of thousands or even millions of other documents distributed through the non-coding DNA of other lifeforms. Maybe this is the only one that survived simply because *Deinococcus aganippe* was the hardiest host out of the bunch. For all we know, Kolya could have wiped out a few hundred more— thousands, even—during the early stages of terraforming. I'm just saying that the fact that this document survived whatever destroyed the planet is *not* evidence that it's important."

"I will agree that it's not *conclusive* evidence. But someone went to a great deal of trouble to preserve that specific document."

"Again, it could just be the only one that survived."

"To actually leave us *directions*," Claire continued, ignoring his interruption, "by using a symbol that we'd recognize even if we couldn't read their language. And now, someone else seems to be going to a great deal of trouble—maybe even murder—to keep us from deciphering it."

"You don't know that for certain."

"I don't. But it really doesn't feel like a coincidence that two people I've been in close contact with were attacked by neurotoxic drones over the past few months. One of them is now dead, Joe. Her only connection to the Flock, as far as I can tell, is the fact that she was attempting to translate something written in what appears to be the very same script that we found hidden in those samples. The other person would have died, too, if I hadn't spotted the bugbot that attacked him, and he's now hiding out on another planet because he's pretty sure that staying on this one would get him killed."

"But how is he connected? I mean, aside from the fact that he was on Mars when the chamber was excavated, Shepherd doesn't have anything to do with the code."

"I would have agreed with you on that point a few days ago." The truth was, she'd have agreed with him on that point when she left New York. She had still been leaning heavily in that direction when she left the house a few hours earlier. Geneva's information about the VersaBio hire wasn't proof of anything, but after a bit of time to think about it, Claire realized that Noah O'Brian's unusually early death shortly after leaving the company had tilted the balance just enough that she could no longer dismiss it. "I can't go into details yet on what changed my mind. It's confidential. But … yes. I think the attack on Shepherd was connected. Maybe the bombing on Mars, as well."

Another long stretch of silence, and then Joe shrugged. "I obviously can't argue the point since you have information you can't share. But here's my issue with the entire project—is it worth the effort when the odds of it ever being translated are so slim? You hate puzzles that can't be solved as much as I do. From what you said, this professor at Columbia didn't think this one was solvable. And she was the top expert, right?"

"*One* of the top experts. But not the only one. Maybe not even the one best suited to unravel this. The member of her department I met yesterday wasn't nearly as pessimistic as Leffler about the prospects. She actually seems excited to take on the task. The main obstacle she was worried about was that she had such a tiny sample to work with for frequency analysis and so forth. And we have the larger sample that she needs, plus the software she needs to analyze it."

"Aren't you worried about getting another person involved? If you actually think the Flock killed Leffler, that seems risky."

"Alice Dobroski is very savvy about personal security. But sure. If we decide to pull her in, I'll make sure that she's fully aware of the risks. While we're on the subject of the Flock, though … you dated Corbin Drexel?"

Joe groaned. "Beck exaggerates. I didn't *date* her. We had dinner once. And then we got thrown together at some corporate event, which was more Mom's idea than mine. Jenelle was thinking of investing in Jonas Labs but then she sank the money into KTI, instead. I think Mom kind of blamed me for that, but Jenelle and I just didn't click. She's very intelligent, though. Better versed in synthetic biology than some people with PhDs in the field."

"Which makes it doubly weird that she's leading a group like the Flock."

"Maybe, but…" Another long pause, and then, "You know how some people who are the staunchest atheists suddenly throw themselves wholeheartedly into religion? And vice versa? Or how they swing from one side to the other on the political spectrum. Some people just aren't happy being in the middle. Extremophiles of another sort, I guess. I could see her being one of those. Can't say I would have pegged her as a terrorist, though. It was weird to see her face on the news." His jaw tightened. "And to find out that she actually planned the attack that nearly got you killed. Did you know who she was when you came up to deliver the samples?"

"I did, but I couldn't say anything yet. And it didn't seem especially relevant. I had no clue that you'd even met her."

"Do you think it's … I don't know … multiplicative? That the Flock is going after you because you're involved with the Mars thing and also with Jonas Labs?"

"The thought had occurred to me, especially when you add in my relationship with the reporter investigating them. But I still think it's ultimately connected to the effort to translate the Icarus documents."

Another extended pause, and then Joe shook his head. "Even if it *is* all connected, I still don't get the rush, Claire. Sure, the document is a fantastic discovery. I can understand why *you* want to push ahead, given that you were literally there when it was dredged up. Obviously, I have no objection to that. I just wish you wouldn't encourage Beck. We've got enough going on right now without him getting sidetracked."

"What? I haven't *encouraged* Beck to do anything. He's just interested."

"You brought him a puzzle. And he's always had a bit of a soft spot where you're concerned."

Claire took a deep breath, praying for patience. Joe didn't get into these moods often, but when he did, she kind of wanted to smack him. "In case you've forgotten, I brought the samples back for *you*. Per your request, in fact. I didn't bring them back for Beck, although I will admit to knowing that you two are inclined to share your toys."

"Okay, okay. You're right. And I *am* looking forward to checking out the other stuff you brought back at some point. I just didn't expect one of the samples to have a mystery in the middle that would derail our research agenda."

"It's not derailed."

"It is for the next few weeks. Did he tell you about our bargain?"

"That he'd come back a day early for each day you take off? Yes. I was very impressed with his resourcefulness."

He grunted and lapsed into another stretch of silence.

"Okay," he said after a few minutes. "Maybe I'm off base. Maybe it isn't even about the manuscript project. Beck could just be using it as an excuse. But either way it *feels* like he's trying to slow-walk this next stage of research."

"Or maybe he needed a break after literally *years* of work. And maybe you do, too. Maybe, just *maybe*, he's your friend and he's worried about you?"

More silence. And then, finally, "Deciphering the script is a time suck, Claire. A distraction. I need to be done with it."

She went back to staring out the window. From what Beck had told her, Joe had barely looked at the sample over the past few months. What he was really saying was that he needed *Beck* to be done with it. And there was no way she was getting into the middle of that.

NINETEEN

THEY TURNED onto a gravel path between two long stretches of white split rail fence that ran along the edge of the two-lane road. The path wound through what might once have been farmland, ending in a circular drive in front of a large gray stone house built into a slight hill. Long tendrils of ivy hung down over the iron rails of a second-level patio on the right. On the left was a covered entryway, with two stout gray columns framing double doors of burnished wood, each inset with stained glass panels.

The garage was open, and a car that Claire assumed must be Beck's was already on the charging pad. They parked next to it, grabbed their bags from the storage compartment, and followed the arrow on a welcome sign that they'd spotted on their way in. It pointed to a stone alcove off to the left of the garage, where firewood was already piled high against the wall in preparation for the winter, which despite the current heat wave, would probably come pretty early this far north. Another sign—*Welcome to Bellamy House*—was propped on the ledge of an arched window next to a black wrought iron bench.

The ocean was too far away to see, especially with the trees in back of the house, but it was less than a kilometer away as the crow flies, close enough to catch a whiff of salt in the breeze. Claire could see Joe's sulky mood slipping away as he pulled in a deep breath and she again flashed back to that last family vacation before their father fell ill, eating scuppernongs and watching Joe try to wrestle the kayak out to the calmer water beyond the waves. He loved the ocean. There were several beaches within a few minutes' drive of both the house and Jonas Labs, and on a clear day, you could actually see the water from Joe's rooftop track. She'd always suspected that was one reason he liked it up there.

"Did you get out to the beach at all this summer?" she asked, even though she'd already gotten the answer from Beck.

"Nah. Too busy with work. The beaches were way too crowded, anyway, this time of year." He stopped to look up at the windows on the second level and grinned. "So...how do you think Dad would classify this place?"

It was an obvious attempt to change the subject, but she let it go and joined in the game. "Well, he definitely wouldn't call it a McMansion. I'm going to say … French Normandy?"

Joe nodded. "Yeah. I can see that. Although it has English touches, too. The windows, for example."

Claire tapped the stone archway. "He would grumble about the supports being composite rather than actual stone, but otherwise, I believe he'd give it two thumbs up."

Beck's voice came from behind them. "If you've finished your architectural critique, why don't I show you to your rooms? Then I can give you the grand tour and we'll decide whether to work or swim first."

"Swim first," Joe said immediately. "While there's still plenty of sun. And then food. We can play interplanetary literary detective after dinner."

Claire was fine with that. Joe's mood was always better when his stomach was full.

They spent the next few hours goofing about in the pool. It was actually larger than the one at Kai's house, long enough to do laps. Beck managed to ensure that Joe would take at least the next few days off by telling him that he'd rented a boat for the week so that they could explore some of the small islands along the coast. Her brother was psyched about it, so Claire kept her lack of enthusiasm to herself. Beck couldn't have known. Even Joe had apparently forgotten the vacation trip where she had spent half a day barfing over the side of a boat. As much as she liked the possibility of spotting whales, it would mean dosing up with anti-nausea meds that might or might not work but would definitely leave her too groggy to really enjoy the day.

She did a few more lazy backstroke laps, eyes closed, enjoying the sun on her face. But Joe was asking her something from the other end of the pool now, so she righted herself and turned around to get him to repeat the question.

"I said do you want to get take out or see what's here to cook?"

Claire froze, unable to answer him. A bright green dragonfly hovered about two feet above the water, positioned almost directly between Joe and Beck. The drone zapper was in the pocket of her shorts. There was no way she'd be able to reach it before the thing attacked one or both of them.

But it was just a dragonfly. At least, she *thought* so. It dipped closer to the water, hesitated, and then darted back to the side of the pool.

"Hey," Beck said. "Are you okay?"

She nodded, watching as the insect hovered near the fence for a moment, then continued on toward the river.

"Yeah. Just a little disoriented. Must have stood up too fast. And I'm fine with either, as long as there's something we can cook fairly quickly."

The couple who ran the place had stocked the fridge with several days' worth of meals before they left, including the ingredients for lobster rolls. Claire had just finished chopping up some peppers for a salad to go with them when her phone vibrated with an incoming text from an unknown number. The message that she'd asked Paul to forward to Shepherd was pasted at the top.

Dear Dr. Shepherd: So sorry to bother you, but a colleague at the Atlantic Post is working on an article about how comparing versions of folktales can be a key to understanding the similarities and differences between cultures across time. It reminded me so much of the conversation we had onboard the Ares Prime. You mentioned a copy of folktales that you helped a former professor translate into various languages, including one that was quite old. Do you by any chance still have a copy or know where she could obtain one? Hope things are going well for you. ~ Claire Echols

Shepherd's reply was below. It was short, and so cryptic that Joe could have written it.

I do remember that conversation, although I thought we discussed it at Ehden. Folktales are indeed the fabric of culture, the very ties that bind us together.

On the one hand, she was relieved that he hadn't exposed her subterfuge. Even if Shepherd understood what it was that she was asking, there was no reason for him to trust her. She had thought it quite likely that he would send something back saying he had no memory of any such conversation and then she'd have had to find a way to explain the whole thing to Paul.

On the other hand, Shepherd hadn't answered her question. And given the time it took for her message to get to him on Mars and for his response to get back to her, it was annoying that he seemed to want to do a complex dance around the subject rather than getting straight to the point. Or, as straight to the point as you could get while trying to fool censors.

But, *fine*. She messaged back:

That's so true, Dr. Shepherd. If I remember correctly, you said the script was Libyco-Berber? My colleague would need to find the English translation, too, of course, so that she can compare them. Any help you can give would be greatly appreciated!

Then she folded the phone back into her pocket. It would be at least half an hour before she heard anything further.

She had a false alarm about halfway through dinner, but it was just the daily digest version of the drone report from Apex Security. They lingered outside on the front patio after dinner to catch the views of Mount Agamenticus, where Beck's more rustic cabin was located, and the nature preserve to the west. Then, as they were clearing the dishes, nearly an hour after she sent the message to Shepherd, her phone vibrated again.

Joe and Beck were well into one of their ubiquitous arguments, this time over whether what they'd just eaten was a lobster roll or a lobster *salad* roll, given that it was made with mayo rather than melted butter, so she stepped into the hallway in order to better focus on Shepherd's response.

> Unfortunately, I don't have the book with me. I managed to get away by only a hair's breadth, as you are probably now aware. There was barely enough time to pack a bag, let alone to go home and scour every hidden nook in my attic for my memoirabilia. I wish that I could retrieve it, as it is one of my most cherished belongings that ties me to the past. But even though I hate the thought of it being tossed out when the house is sold, a wise person would say you should simply cut the tie.

She read through the response several times, trying to decipher its meaning. Two words jumped out at her. Shepherd had called the little room in the attic at Allen House his *hidden nook*. And while *memorabilia* wasn't so common a word that a misspelling was out of the question, a misspelling that incorporated the word *memoir* seemed a bit too on the nose to be coincidental. The last part was baffling, though. Her best guess was that he was suggesting that she retrieve the book from Allen House, but he also didn't have much confidence that she would be able to do so.

Either way, it confirmed that he *had* written the memoir. So she sent him a vague *thanks-anyway*, and messaged Wyatt with the news. He responded immediately, which was fairly typical, but it still felt like a minor miracle of technology after dealing with the Mars-Earth lag.

> Thanks! Any chance you can give me a tiny bit of proof for Erica? You know how she is. Trust, but verify.

Claire snorted. Erica had probably leaned a lot more heavily toward the trust side of that equation before she started working with Wyatt.

> What he sent me is kind of vague, so you may need to explain it to her. But I really don't want any communication about this going through the Post right now. Does she have a private connection that you trust?

> Better yet, I can hand deliver. I'm in DC until Tuesday. Working on the Ohio militia case. Erica and I are supposed to meet for lunch tomorrow.

She sent him the exchange with Shepherd, thought for a moment, then added:

> I may know where to find the book in the photo, too. I'm going to check something out tomorrow and I'll let you know.

There was a longer pause this time.

> Just to be clear, you think there's an actual book? That it's not just a cover that Shepherd or the publisher faked?

> Not 100% sure yet. Gotta go. I'll keep you posted.

Claire did a quick search for the agent that was marketing Allen House and sent him a message using a generic email and rerouting number she'd set up in case she ever needed to fly under the radar for a story. She told him that she would only be in New Haven for a few hours the next day, but really wanted to view the property. Hopefully, he would be eager enough for a sale that he'd get back to her before morning. New Haven wouldn't be much more than an hour away by hyperloop. If she got an early start, she could be back by mid-afternoon. And as an added bonus, she now had a good excuse to avoid the boat trip and eight hours or so of potential misery.

TWENTY

JOE SHOOK his head in mock dismay when Claire came back into the kitchen. "Perfect timing, as usual. You saunter in to join us right *after* we finish cleaning up."

"I was gone *five* minutes, tops. And we were almost finished cleaning up when I left. So who won the argument?"

He shrugged. "We looked it up and we're both right."

"Nope," Beck said. "You're still wrong, because we are not in Connecticut at the moment. We're in *Maine*, which means those were *lobster rolls*."

"I swear, you guys would argue over whether water gets wetter on the weekend."

"Oh, come on," Beck said. "That's ridiculous. We wouldn't argue over that."

Joe nodded. "He's right. No argument to be had. Water is a liquid. It can't *get* wet, no matter what day of the week it might be."

"Nope, you are not pulling me into any pointless debates." Claire grabbed a sativa seltzer from the fridge. "Come on. I've waited long enough. I want to see our Martian book."

They went into the living room, where a large picture window took up most of one wall, showing the pool and the trees beyond. Further off in the distance, you could see a ribbon of ocean, now painted scarlet and orange with the last rays of the setting sun.

Beck tapped a button on the side of the window. The glass shimmered slightly and then the view was gone, replaced by a wall screen. A few taps later and two pages of script appeared, side by side.

When Claire had last seen them in the lab, the symbols now on the screen had been magnified a few hundred million times in order to be visible, and their edges had been misshapen because they were really clusters formed from tiny purple particles inserted into the non-coding DNA. They had even moved slightly, leaving Claire feeling a little queasy if she stared at them for too long.

These symbols were far more regular. In fact, they looked like the sort of characters you might find in a dingbat font.

"I'm impressed," she said. "They're a lot more legible now."

"That's because these are actual static symbols and not a bunch of nanoscopic particles zigging around," Beck said, pulling up a separate file. "I'm fairly certain that these are the thirty-one primary characters—letters, I guess—that make up the script. Although, there may be only thirty. Two of the symbols…" He squinted slightly, then pointed out two characters that looked like an upside down U and an upside down U with a dot in the center. "These two might be the same, if the dot is an artifact. But I can enter that into the decryption program as a variable to consider. There are another twelve characters that I think may be numbers. They only appear as a sort of … I guess you might say a section break? … within the manuscript. They're usually in this same pattern—two symbols, a dot, two symbols, a dot, then three symbols at the end. I'm thinking maybe the clusters are a date, in which case this might be a diary. So that's forty-three characters in all. Given the relatively small number, I think that we can safely assume this is an alphabetic script."

Claire nodded. "Leffler seemed pretty confident that it was alphabetic, although that was about as far as she was willing to go. Were you able to confirm your earlier assumption that the manuscript in the *Deinococcus* sample from the second chamber is the same as the one in the two samples that were collected from the surface? I mean, I know the other samples were in much worse shape, but…"

"They're the same. Over a ninety-eight percent similarity score between the one from the chamber and the sample from Arsia Sulci. The Hyblaeus Dorsa sample had a ninety-two percent correlation. I'm guessing it was collected from an area that was more exposed to the elements than the other two over the past ... however many millions of years."

"At least eighty-four million," Claire said. "Give or take. That was the reading Ben Pelzer got from the olivine sample on the outside of the upper chamber. But who knows how long the chamber was buried before a bit of molten rock happened to shoot up and attach itself to the metal?"

"Probably around two *billion* years," Joe said. "Since that's when most scientists think Mars became uninhabitable. But ... okay. We have an alphabet. I guess that's a start."

Claire shot him a look, wishing he would lose the dismissive tone. "So, what happened when you ran everything through your purloined software?" she asked Beck. "Did your criming yield any notable results?"

He laughed. "It did. But I need to caution you that this is very much a first cut, and a very shallow one, at that. I ran a frequency analysis on the entire document, searching for repeated words and patterns that are seen in various languages. I also added in a few fairly safe assumptions we can make about the individual or individuals, I suppose, who wrote it."

"Seems to me that last part would have to be almost entirely speculative," Joe said. "I mean, can you really make any *safe* assumptions on that front?"

"Of course we can." Beck's voice had now taken on a trace of the tone that a teacher might use with a difficult student. "We *know* that their planet had water, for starters. They appear to have had burial customs not entirely unlike our own."

"Except they've only found one crypt," Joe said. "Not sure that counts as a *custom*."

"We *know* that their planet had one sun," Beck continued, ignoring the interruption, "since we're in the same solar system. We know that the civilization was technologically advanced enough to understand and modify DNA. Beyond that, we can also assume that the words we saw etched above the water molecule symbol in the chamber were something along the lines of *just add*, since adding water dissolved the polymer and allowed us to extract it. It's not much, I'll admit, but it's also not *nothing*."

"Okay, okay," Joe said. "You're right. Go ahead."

"Thank you. I assigned a probability to these assumptions, indicating which ones I had the most confidence in. Anyway, once I had everything in the model, I asked it to translate a tiny, tiny section as a test. This is what it came up with."

Beck pulled up another document, which was divided into four paragraphs. Each of them was followed by a confidence interval in parentheses.

The men argue loudly in the field, their words sharp as the clash of swords. (Confidence interval: 00.06%)

The children play tag in the yard, their shouts loud with the chaos of battle. (Confidence interval: 00.06%)

The group advances on toward the town, their cries a warning of the coming siege. (Confidence interval: 00.06%)

Hoping to harness a breeze for the journey, they tilt the sails toward the east. (Confidence interval: 00.04%)

"They're all less than one-tenth of one percent," Joe said. "And all very, very different. Are you sure this really counts as progress?"

"Oh, shush, Joe. We're at the baby steps stage." Claire moved closer to the screen. "And it does at least look like the program figured out one word. The order is a bit different on the last one, but each of the four translations has three iterations of the word *the*."

Beck grinned. "Yes. It also seems pretty close on *they/their*. Those are two of the three words it seems fairly confident about. In fact, taking the manuscript as a whole, it gives about a sixty percent probability that this two symbol cluster translates as *the*, which means we can assume it's a language that has definite articles. The last sample assumes that it's a script read right-to-left and, as you can see, the model still translates that word as *the*."

"*With* a probability of just over one half of one percent." Joe shook his head, clearly not impressed.

"Yes," Beck said. "As I've already acknowledged. But this is on the basis of maybe fifteen hours of work, including getting the script digitized. And I'm not exactly an expert in the field."

"Which is kind of my point," Joe said. "Did Claire tell you that she may *have* another expert interested in picking up the project?"

Beck nodded. "She did. She also made a rather cryptic mention of a potential Rosetta stone."

"Which I have a new lead on," Claire said. "But that's still all I'm going to say about it. As for Alice Dobroski, though, I do think we should pull her in. In fact, I may message her tonight to see if she wants to help me follow up on that new lead. I only spent a few hours with her, but I liked her. And she's eager enough to work on this that I'm pretty sure she'd sign anything we asked her to about holding off until we're ready to take the manuscript public. To be honest, though, I'm not sure she can make headway much faster than you have, Beck. She doesn't even have access to this software."

"Well, she *could* have access," Beck said. "If you don't think she'll be too upset about its … unlicensed nature. From what you said earlier, I'm guessing that could be an issue for her?"

"What?" Claire frowned. "Oh, no. Alice was talking about the project being a possible collaboration between Columbia and Berkeley. I just meant that she'd need to keep it all aboveboard if she went through the university. But if we were to hire her as an independent consultant, I don't think that would be a problem for her at all. In fact, I'd pretty much guarantee that several of the apps on her armscreen are only available on the black market."

"If you trust her, then why don't we just turn it over to her completely?" Joe asked. "That way, she could even *go* through the official channels. She'll probably need to do that anyway if she ever wants to publish anything on the subject, right? And you'd still be able to write it up for the *Post*. I just don't get why the two of you seem to think we have to treat this manuscript like it's some sort of deep, dark secret. The public already knows there was a technologically advanced civilization on Mars. They already know that a message was carved into the walls of those chambers. A second document really isn't going to come as that much of a surprise. And as I've explained to both of you, there's *no* reason to assume that this document is important simply because it's the only one that we found."

TWENTY-ONE

CLAIRE AND BECK EXCHANGED A LOOK, and she could tell that he was thinking the same thing. In matters like this, Joe operated almost entirely on a rational level. And if you looked at it on a *purely* rational level, he was right. Their argument for believing the manuscript contained a message of any importance was built on a rather shaky foundation. That went double for their assumption that the message was time sensitive.

She liked to think of herself as a rational actor, too, for the most part. But her gut was screaming that Joe was wrong, that this document was actually important. That had been true to some extent even before she read Shepherd's memoir and began to suspect that these Sentinels could be more than a fiction that the man had concocted to build himself up as a religious guru and bilk thousands of credulous people out of their life savings. And while she wouldn't have pegged Beck as someone who went with his gut feelings in most cases, he clearly agreed with her.

Joe must have realized that, too, because he didn't give either of them a chance to respond. "I'm not saying that the document isn't important," he said. "It *might* be. But come on, Beck! Are you seriously trying to tell me that anything it contains could possibly be more important than what *we're* working on? You said yourself that you're not an expert in this field. Do you really think that trying to reconstruct a long-dead language so that you can learn about a long-dead civilization is a better use of your time and talents than what we're on the very threshold of accomplishing?"

"No," Beck said. "And if we were simply trying to decipher

the language to advance our knowledge about ancient Mars, you'd be completely right. But that's *not* why we're doing this."

Joe heaved a massive, theatrical sigh and sank back into the cushions of the sofa. Claire expected one of his protracted silences to follow, but to her surprise he popped back up almost instantly.

"Can I be honest?"

"When are you ever less than honest?" Beck said. "I'm pretty sure I know what you're going to say anyway."

"Fine. I think your *main* purpose is to slow our research down. I'm not saying that's the only reason you're interested in this, but you've already said you think we're going too fast."

"Come on, Joe," Claire said. "You're not being fair."

"No. It's okay. Let him get it out," Beck said.

"You keep telling me that you want to take it slow. But … you're not the one who has to deal with Kai."

"I know. Do you want me to talk to her? Because I will. Someone needs to tell her to stop and reflect on the lesson of *Jurassic Park*."

Joe raised an eyebrow. "Don't resurrect dinosaurs? That ship sailed decades ago."

"That wasn't the lesson," Beck said. "Okay, that was the *applied* lesson, but not the philosophical truth underpinning it. The Jeff Goldblum guy says something like *you scientists were so busy figuring out whether you could do it that you forgot to consider whether you should.*"

"Are you seriously saying we *shouldn't*?" Joe asked. "Seriously?"

"No. But I *am* saying we shouldn't go so fast. You'd think Kai would understand that. It isn't unheard of for governments to take over a company or even an entire industry for purposes of national security. Even from a strictly financial perspective—"

Joe threw out his arms in frustration. "I don't *care* about the financial perspective! You both know that if I had my way, we'd jettison that damn patent right now. Jonas Salk had the right idea —discoveries like this belong to the world. You keep saying that pushing too fast could be destabilizing. I'm not denying that. But what about the moral considerations of intentionally slow-walking this research? Have *either* of you thought about that?"

Claire shook her head. Joe was clearly trying to get her to jump into the fray on his side. "Hey, I'm Switzerland here."

"But you're *not* Switzerland," Joe said. "You're a stockholder. You do have a stake in this."

"I'm a *stockholder* who gave you my proxy years ago."

"It's me that you're pissed at," Beck said, "so stop giving Claire grief. And of course, I've *thought* about it. How could I not think about it?"

"Good," Joe said. "But have you run the numbers? Because I did. At the current global death rate, delaying our research by a year would deny several extra *centuries* of life to three hundred and eighty-five million people. That's more than a million people for each day we drag this out. Stretch it out to five or six years, and you're getting close to half a *billion* people. Even if this desta-bilization you're talking about causes another world war, it wouldn't result in that many unnecessary deaths. Do you really want that on your conscience? *Because I don't.* If the research agenda had been in my hands when Jonas Labs began working on Arvectin, I'd have had it on the market two years earlier. Dad would probably still be alive, and maybe five thousand other people with cancer would have had a shot at two or three extra *decades* of life. In this case, though? Delaying will rob *millions* of people of a few extra *centuries*. Maybe even more. And yes. People will blame me for those who didn't get the cure in time." His eyes shot toward Claire for the briefest instant, then back to Beck. "For the rest of my life, I'll have to deal with that. And the only way I can be completely okay with it is if I *know* that I did everything I could to get this out to as many people as I can, as quickly as I can."

Joe's words hit Claire hard, especially that tiny shift of his gaze toward her on the word *blame*. If their dad had been able to hold on six months longer, he'd have been alive for the human trials phase of Arvectin. She knew that Joe shared Kai's sense of failure over that, but he'd barely finished grad school at the time. He'd started work at the lab a little over two months before their dad died.

"You can't actually think that I blame you for the delay with Arvectin?"

Joe shook his head. "No. I know you don't. But you do blame *her*."

It was the truth. They both knew it, so there was no point in denying it. But it wasn't the *whole* truth. Joe was missing a huge part of the picture.

"Yes. But I blame her a whole lot more for not being there with him at the end. You *were* there those last few days. You know how he was. He asked for her, and she couldn't be bothered to..." Claire shook her head, pushing back the temptation to spill everything she knew. But it would just make things worse. And was it even relevant? She'd blamed her mother plenty even before she knew about the affair with Kolya.

"I'm not saying it was the right choice for Dad or for us," Joe said. "It's not the choice that I made back then. Like you said, I was *there* those last few days. But back then, I wasn't the one making the life or death decisions. Maybe Mom was thinking of the people that she *could* save. The ones who *might* make it, but only if she pushed harder. Faster. Maybe she was trying to spare dozens of other families from going through what we were."

"Did she tell you that?"

Joe laughed humorlessly. "You actually think we have heart-to-heart chats? That she talks to me about her feelings? She's mentioned Dad's death to me *twice*, and both times were connected to business."

He sighed again, and the energy seemed to drain out of him. "I'm sorry, okay? Both of you were right in saying that I need a break. I'm not being fair to either of you, and yes—I've been a complete ass about the vacation thing. We both know I've got stuff I can be working on even if you're not there, Beck. I *am* going to take a couple of days off. I could definitely use a few nights of solid sleep and a bit of time outdoors where I don't have to listen to those Luddites yelling at me constantly. But … a million people a day. A million people."

Claire wanted to point out that it was a drop in the bucket compared to the number of lives that his research would extend, but she kept quiet. Would that logic have made her feel better if someone she loved was among those who died in the interim? Almost certainly not. And Joe wouldn't be swayed by it anyway. When it came to this sort of thing, he was very much a glass half empty kind of guy. He would only see the lives he could have saved but didn't.

"I know you've got the school reunion thing next week," Joe said to Beck. "And if you need the full three weeks … take it, man. Just take it. No hard feelings. I guess that includes this side project, too. Do what you need to do. But I have to do the same. For me, that means that come Tuesday morning, I'll be back in the lab. Anyway … I think I'm going to turn in now so we can get out on the boat extra early." As he crossed behind the couch, he leaned down and pressed a kiss to the top of Claire's head. "You, however, should probably skip it. Unless you think your vestibular training for the Mars trip cured your seasickness?"

"It helped. But I still had to use an ear gadget … which is back at the house."

"We can do something else," Beck said. "I didn't know that you—"

"No, no. You guys should *definitely* go. I got a message earlier and I need to take a short day trip anyway. I'll probably be back before you are."

And with any luck, she thought, *I'll be coming back with our Rosetta stone.*

FROM THE JOURNAL
OF EBERIN DAS

21.03.507

THE OFFICIAL ANNOUNCEMENT was made today with considerable fanfare. This civilization has now achieved one of the great milestones, and I know from my own work over the past few years that they are close, so *very* close, to the second.

Their aims are not evil. They are innocents, even now. But they will soon, inevitably, become a threat. This I have been taught. And even as I question my next steps, this I do, in fact, believe.

A small voice inside my mind reminds me daily that [Literal translation: "the *abeeda* has a sweeter peel" From notes: the cloud has a silver lining?]: no one else has to die by my hand. I have already done the unthinkable ... not once, not twice, but three times. Duty will never require that I look at the two files—two lives—I am given and weigh their worth.   This should reassure me. It should make it easier to simply carry on with the last stage of our assignment.

If I do that, if I remain silent and simply carry on as usual, I will eventually arrive home. And once on Ufretas, I could leave all of this behind. I could choose work that heals, and, in time, I might be able to live with the awful choices I made here.

But I would know that an entire world had been killed by my silence. An entire world that might have been saved if I spoke out.

If I gave them the tools, the information that they need to save themselves.

How many [ages? iterations?] of healing work would it take for me to forget that? How long would I have to atone if I didn't even bother to try?

(Confidence interval: 94.2%)

TWENTY-TWO

IT WAS ONLY a few minutes after nine, so the chances of Claire being able to fall asleep were pretty much nil. Joe was a napper—an hour here, four or five hours there. He rarely bothered with a full eight, and almost never at the times when most people slept. Beck seemed to keep to a similar schedule, although whether that was by preference or necessity, Claire wasn't sure.

She thought about doing a few laps in the pool, but the massage jets in the hot tub were calling her name a whole lot louder. So she grabbed another drink and her phone, then sank down into the warm water before checking to see whether the real estate agent had gotten back with her.

Still nothing, but she did have a message from Ro that had posted a few minutes earlier.

> Send me all of your patience vibes ASAP.
> Otherwise, I may end up in a Canadian prison.

Claire texted back that if she *had* to wind up in prison, Canada was far from the worst country for it. She started to follow up with a question about what was going on but thought again and hit the call button instead.

"Sounded like you might need to vent," she said when Ro answered.

"That's for certain. But this is probably not the best time."

"That's Claire!" Jemma said in the background. "Can I talk? Oh … and can you put it on video so I can see Siggy? I miss her *so* much."

"Sorry, sweetie. I'm not at home. Siggy had to go stay at the kitty hotel for a few nights. You should have seen me trying to wrestle her into the carrier."

"Ooh. I bet she was *mad*."

"Yep. And I have the scratches to prove it. Steam was pouring out of her furry little ears just like in the cartoons. Are you having fun with your grandma?"

Jemma gave a loud, dramatic sigh. "No. She's really really mad at me because I'm not supposed to *call* her that anymore but I really did forget. It wasn't on purpose like she said. And Mommy was going to take me to the beach today, but it rained *all day long*, so we had to go to the museum and now they closed and we have to go back to *her house*."

The part of Jemma's spiel about her grandmother and the emphasis on those last two words was almost certainly connected to Ro's need to vent, so Claire sidestepped the issue and redirected her to more neutral ground. "What kind of museum did you go to?"

"One that's shaped like a giant ball. It has dinosaurs and sciency stuff. There's a splash table and these little boats that go down a waterslide but it's not big enough for kid butts so I couldn't ride on it. And there's a room that has different kinds of mud so you can build stuff. It was pretty fun but not as good as the beach. You would have liked it, though."

"I'm sure I would have."

"Hopefully we'll get at least a little patch of sunshine tomorrow morning," Ro said. "Because I did promise her a beach trip while we're here. I'm thinking we may have to settle for a drive over to Ocean City once we're back home, though, because unless things get a whole lot better really quickly, we're heading back early."

"How early?"

"Unless there's a full and heartfelt apology forthcoming? As-soon-as-I-can-get-a-plane-out early. Might not be easy given the holiday weekend, though. We're going back to her house, but if

Aunty Nina hasn't chilled out by the time she gets back from her date tonight, I may be packing Jem up and heading to a hotel in the interim."

"*Aunty* Nina?"

"Long story. And little pitchers..."

Jemma, who had heard that expression more than once, said, "I'm not a pitcher and I don't have big ears."

"Yes, you do. Great big giant elephant ears. With mud behind them, in fact. She got a bit carried away with the clay exhibit," Ro told Claire. "How about I call you back once I have her in the tub?"

"Sure. I'll be here. I need to chat with you, too, especially if you're coming home early. There have been some ... developments in the drone situation."

"Are we talking good developments or bad developments?"

"Let's just say the folks at the FBI seem to be taking my complaints more seriously now. But, like you said, little pitchers. Call back as soon as you can. Tell the cheeky monkey to enjoy her bubble bath and give her a big goodnight hug for me."

Most of the time, those words would prompt a loud protest from Jemma that she wasn't a cheeky monkey and then Claire would say *oh yes you are*. It was one of their regular call-and-response routines generally accompanied by tickles and giggles. Today, though, Jemma mixed things up a bit by making monkey noises and demanding a banana just before Ro cut the call.

Claire folded her phone and was placing it in the caddy on the side of the tub, when she spotted Beck standing in the doorway, still in his swimsuit and holding a beer. He had an odd, pensive look on his face.

"Sorry," he said. "I didn't mean to eavesdrop."

"Oh, that's okay. It was just Ro. She's going to call me back in a few. Jemma was listening and ... there's some sort of issue with Ro's mom, so they're coming back early." Claire grabbed her drink and phone and slipped over to one of the other seats in the tub so that Beck could get in more easily. "Which means I need to tell her about Leffler and let her know that the drones now come with death threats. Were we too loud? I didn't think about the fact that the sound might carry to the upper floor. Jemma can get a little wild when the sillies hit, and I think she's had a rough day."

He shook his head and climbed in. "No. I didn't even know you were out here until I got downstairs. I'm just a bit too wound up to sleep and thought a soak might help. I envy your brother's ability to nod off in an instant."

Claire laughed. "He's always had that knack. On vacations, we would be on a plane for five minutes and he'd be completely out."

"Maybe it's due to the unwavering focus of his moral compass. I don't think Joe ever lies awake at night considering the various shades of gray."

"That's probably true. Although, I'm now thinking he lay awake more nights than I imagined feeling guilty about Dad's death."

Beck was quiet for a moment, and when he finally spoke, she had the sense he was still weighing how much he could say without violating confidences. "Joe doesn't feel *guilty* about that. Not really. We've talked about it a few times. He knows there wasn't anything more that *he* could have done. Hell, he was barely out of school when it happened. I'd been at the lab—what? A month? Two at the most. But like he said, he knows that there was more that *Kai* could have done—maybe not by the time your dad was diagnosed, but he feels like she ... didn't have her priorities straight *before* the diagnosis."

Amen to that, Claire thought.

"The current situation with Rejuvesce is stirring some of that up again," he continued. "Joe thinks she should have taken some resources away from the drugs that were making money for the company in order to focus on Arvectin, given its potential to save lives. He knows Kai feels like she didn't do enough, and he doesn't want that for himself."

"Can you blame him?"

"No." He took a long sip of his beer before continuing. "I just don't think he grasps how monumental a change this is going to be. Resource allocation, for one thing. Retirement policies, for another. I mean, think about the people who are planning to retire assuming those funds have to extend for a few decades. Most of them are going to think they should still be able to retire as planned, so they'll be living on the basic income subsidy after that, which is going to put the system under an incredible amount of strain. That's short term, though. And then there's the issue of family structure. I was thinking as I heard the little girl—Jemma— laughing a minute ago that it's a sound that is going to become increasingly rare in the coming years, as governments start limiting children. Probably not immediately, but over time they won't have any choice. Space on the planet is, after all, finite. Even with outlets like the Mars colonies, Earth will quickly get to the point where it's bursting at the seams. All of this is just going a lot faster than I imagined it would. I thought there would be at least a decade between the launch of Rejuvesce and any push to extend the research." He made a sound somewhere between a sigh and a chuckle. "Yeah. I know. I've worked with your brother for long enough that I should have known better. Between Joe's drive and your mother's ambition…"

"Which are flip sides of the same coin. Maybe Joe would have a life outside the lab if she hadn't kept pushing him to work every waking hour. You'd think that maternal instincts would kick in at some point, that she'd realize it's not healthy for him."

Beck's mouth twitched, as if he were holding back a laugh.

"What?" Claire asked. "You don't agree?"

"No. It's just…" He shook his head. "You know I'm not a member of the Kai Jonas fan club. But as tempting as it is to blame her, like I said, I've worked with Joe for a long time now. Nearly every day for over a decade. If his drive is your mother's fault, it's only in the genetic sense. Joe loves his work. You know that. And I really do think he'd push himself just as hard even if she wasn't in the picture."

Claire gave a tiny nod of admission. It was true. She'd thought the part about Joe's enthusiasm for his work often enough herself. On the other hand…

"You weren't around when we were kids, Beck. As the twig is bent, so grows the tree."

"Fair enough. But I think you're missing what it is that's tormenting him right now. It's not the work. It's the fact that he feels like everyone is holding him back in some way. I'm trying to get him to slow down so that the world doesn't … implode, I guess? … as a result of such rapid change. And Kai—"

"I thought he said Mom was pushing him to go *faster*?"

"Well, yeah. She wants him to speed up the research so that she can have her big announcement to make the stockholders happy. But she's holding him back in a different way, by keeping him from getting the drug to as many people as possible. She really did *not* want to relax Jonas Labs's hold on the patent. He fought hard for that two-year release window. Told her he'd quit, although she has to have known it was an empty threat."

"Because he wouldn't have been able to take his research with him?"

"Exactly. So it was about as credible as him threatening to rip out his own heart. He couldn't do it even if he tried. So, yeah. He's got different forces slowing him down in different ways. And he has that infernal ticker in his head. Each day, that's a million more people that he thinks are doomed to die early because of his failure to save them. I told him he has a messiah complex. And he told *me* that I have a Cassandra complex."

"Seems like he may be missing a key point there. Weren't Cassandra's warnings always right? Her curse was that nobody believed her."

"Yep. That's me. Cursed with always being right."

He grinned, and Claire remembered exactly why she'd had such a huge crush on him. Which stirred a twinge of guilt concerning Wyatt—but no. She was not going to think about Wyatt right now. The man was too much work.

The hot tub timer ran out. Claire reached over to the control panel to start it again, letting the water jets lift her feet to the surface. "I'm just glad that you managed to get him away from the lab, even if it is only for a day or two."

"So am I. Although it's probably a good thing that I'm not going back for a few weeks. Kai should be getting back to the lab about now and I wouldn't want to be anywhere near her when she realizes that Elvis has left the building."

Claire smiled at the archaic turn of phrase. Joe called them Beckisms. The guy had an entire library of them, which he said were the side effect of being raised by elderly grandparents. "Wait 'til she hears that Elvis has left the entire *state*."

"It's the only way he had any hope of getting outside at all. And even here… The main reason I reserved the boat was so that he'd be able to spend the entire day outside with no risk of anyone recognizing him. But I'd have thought of something else if I'd known you had motion sickness."

"No, I'm glad you're going. He'll love it. And I was telling the truth. I really do need to run down to New Haven for a few hours."

Beck raised his eyebrows when she mentioned New Haven and Claire wondered if he knew that was where the Flock got its start. Probably. He'd paid far more attention to the group over the years than Joe, who had tended to dismiss them as a minor nuisance, at least before their schism and tilt toward violence.

"I should be back by mid-afternoon, though. Maybe even before you get back."

"That's good," Beck said. "Because I think Joe needs to be around *you* more than he needs to be around me right now. And not just because he sees me all the time at the lab, or because he's annoyed at what he sees as my foot-dragging on Rejuvesce." He hesitated, seeming to search for the right words. "I've been trying to lure him down to the biodome for the past few months. To get him to watch the kids on the playground. To watch the interaction between parents and children, so that maybe he'll understand how hard some people are going to resist the changes this will bring."

"You really think that many people are going to refuse to take the drug? I mean, right now it just seems to be a few scattered religious types. And as Wyatt was saying the other night they'll probably cave as soon as their lottery number comes up."

"Oh, no—Wyatt is right about that. People won't resist the Rejuvesce part. The demand is almost certainly going to increase when they learn that what's really at stake isn't just a few more decades of old age, but something close to immortality with bodies still in their prime. But the changes to the social structure and the end of the nuclear family? They'll fight that tooth and nail, even though I think it's going to be inevitable. Joe practically sticks his fingers in his ears when I mention anything of that sort, which means the only hope is to present him with an object lesson. So if your friend decides she needs to get out of Vancouver, maybe you should have her bring Jemma here. We've got a beach nearby, a pool, and plenty of room."

"I can suggest it," Claire said, thinking that Beck must have heard quite a bit of her conversation with Ro. "But I doubt she'd accept. And if she did, she'd probably insist on paying you."

"Tell her she'd be doing me a personal favor. Maybe it would help Joe wrap his head around the tradeoffs. Sure, a million people will die every day he delays. But a million more—give or take—will be born. After Rejuvesce is fully implemented, the birth rate will need to start dropping pretty fast. Anyway, suggest it to her. If she says no, I'm still hopeful that Plan B will have some effect."

"What's Plan B?"

"You."

Claire laughed. "Not sure if you've noticed, Beck, but I'm only a few years shy of thirty."

"I know, I know. You're ancient. But … I had an ulterior motive for getting you to visit so that we could discuss all of this face-to-face. Being around you reminds Joe of when he was a kid.

Or more to the point, it reminds him of when *you* were a kid. And that's another thing that will change. Having siblings is about to become exceptionally rare."

"Yeah. I guess that's true. What about you?" she asked, realizing that she knew very little about his family. "Do you have any siblings?"

"Nope. I was an only child."

"What about the grandparents who raised you? Are they still around? Or your parents?"

There was a slight hesitation, but he shook his head.

"So, no relatives at all?"

He shrugged. "Everyone has relatives. Mine are just of the very distant variety. We don't keep in touch. Which is probably a good thing, given my work schedule."

"Well, I'm glad you keep up with friends from college then. Where is the reunion?"

"New York. One of them has a place in the Bronx. Some are arriving over the weekend, but we're all supposed to be there for an event on Monday night."

"We'll be in the city at the same time then. I'm covering the Ares Consortium conference on Tuesday. Maybe you could get away for a few hours on Wednesday to meet with Alice Dobroski? It might make more sense for you to explain the work you've been doing instead of relying on me as the go-between. I mean, I haven't used the transcription software at all, so I wouldn't be able to answer any questions."

"Yeah. It's kind of tricky, and given how it was obtained, I don't have a lot of documentation. Wednesday should be fine."

Claire's phone rang as he was speaking. Beck started to get up, but she put a hand on his shoulder.

"It's okay. I'm going in. This might take a while. I'm hoping I can talk her down from the ledge so that she'll stay in Vancouver at least until I'm back in DC."

"Hey, like I said, the offer stands. If we can't bring Joe to the mountain, maybe we can bring the mountain to him."

TWENTY-THREE

THE CAFÉ SAT ALMOST DIRECTLY opposite Allen House, so Claire took a chair facing Whitney Avenue and compared the building to the description in Shepherd's memoir. It was a solid match, which wasn't surprising in the least now that she knew he'd owned the place for the past few decades. Her father would have had no trouble at all categorizing this one—it was classic Victorian, and probably *had* looked a bit like a castle to a five-year-old kid looking up at it from the sidewalk. After a minute, she made out a tiny circular window at the base of the smaller turret, where Toby Shepherd claimed to have hidden out and spied on his friendly alien. If all went as planned, she would be on the other side of that window in a little over an hour.

"I'm meeting someone in about ten minutes," she told the waiter as he approached the table with a pitcher of water. "Is it okay if I just wait here on the patio until she arrives?"

"Sure. I don't think we're going to have many people clamoring to eat outside in this heat." He stared at her for a moment, head tilted slightly to the right. "Hey, I *know* you. You're ... the Mars reporter, right? The buried chamber?"

Claire sighed and gave him a tight smile, wishing that she'd left her shades on. She'd been recognized occasionally before the Mars trip, either because she looked so much like her mother or because someone actually watched her *Simple Science* videos. Both kinds of encounters made her a little nervous, but she'd never actively dreaded talking to those people. These days, however, there was about a fifty-fifty chance that she'd have to deal with a conspiracy theory of some sort before she managed to extract herself from the conversation.

She was tempted to lie, but he'd probably figure it out when she paid her tab after lunch. "Yes, that's me."

"I *knew* it! So … tell me the truth. Was it real? Because a lot of people are saying it's fake. My dad says *everything* on Mars is virtual reality. That Kolya guy and all the others are just pocketing the investment money."

It wasn't the first time Claire had been asked this over the past few months. The person inquiring almost always said they had a family member or a friend who was suspicious, even though she could usually tell that they were the ones with doubts. Never mind that thousands of people were currently on Mars now as workers and thousands more had traveled there as tourists. If you pointed that out, they'd just counter that those people were paid. Or tricked … they thought they were on Mars, but it was actually a VR. Or something Kolya had built out in the desert. It was all a giant pyramid scheme, they claimed, and they knew that was the truth because they had a cousin whose girlfriend knew a guy whose mother made two thousand bucks to tell everyone she went to Mars on vacation. One woman even went so far as to ask Claire how much they were paying her to keep telling their lies.

Nothing she could say was going to change anyone's mind, so she pulled out one of her stock responses. "If that was VR, somebody needs to work on the safety features. I spent two weeks in a hospital bed and came back with a pin in my ankle and several fun little souvenirs." She tugged up the hem of her pants to show him the scar that snaked up her shin, which was no longer red but still a vivid pink. "See?"

"Oh, wow," the waiter said, his face going nearly the same shade as her scar. "Yeah … um … sorry about that. Hey, you can wait inside if you want. Lunch rush won't hit for another half hour."

She shook her head, feeling a little bad that she'd made him uncomfortable. "It's okay. I'll stay out here. I may need to make some calls."

"Sure. No problem." He poured her a glass of water and headed back inside, flipping on the swamp cooler as he passed by and sending a slightly chillier stream of air in her direction. The patio still wasn't cool enough that she'd be eating out here, but it was an improvement.

The stars had aligned surprisingly well so far, given the spur of the moment nature of this trip. Alice messaged back the night before that she was free for most of the day and would be happy to meet in New Haven to talk about translating the chamber text and what Claire had billed simply as a *related side project.*

She'd decided to wait until Alice arrived to find out whether she was willing to assist with a bit of sleuthing over at Allen House. It wasn't the sort of thing you generally asked someone on short acquaintance, even if you were about to hire them. She'd been reluctant to ask her at all, but her choices were limited. Beck would have been willing, but there was no way she was going to ask him to cancel the boat trip, and she thought he and Joe might have a bit of bridge mending to do. The two of them were like brothers in that they argued good-naturedly about pretty much everything, but last night was the first time that she'd heard them exchange anything close to harsh words.

Wyatt had been another possibility, but he'd said he had the meeting with Erica. And she hadn't really wanted to ask him anyway. Just thinking about it had started their conversation at the restaurant replaying in her mind, along with all of his possible responses. He'd tell her this was a bad idea. Too dangerous. That he'd take care of it himself. That she should be a good girl, go home, and stay out of trouble.

Which was crazy. Wyatt would never use those words. If she was being honest, she couldn't even imagine him *thinking* those words. But she was now almost certain that it was what he wanted, even if he wouldn't say it. And she was not ready to deal with all of the ramifications of that knowledge with everything else going on.

Even if Alice wasn't game, Claire thought that she'd probably be able to handle things solo. The listing agent that she'd contacted the night before had left a voice message on the burner number she provided saying that he'd *try* to squeeze her into his schedule but couldn't promise anything.

"I've got an appointment at ten and two more in the afternoon. And … to be honest, I'm hesitant to show the place at all. In fact, I just pulled it off the listing service temporarily because it was hit by some vandals a couple of days back. No *major* damage," he'd added quickly, clearly realizing that vandalism might raise red flags for a potential buyer. "That sort of thing isn't at *all* common around there. Very nice neighborhood. But it can happen anywhere when a place is unoccupied for a while. I got someone out there to replace the windows yesterday, but there's still a bit of broken glass and debris on the inside. Are you sure you can't come back next week? It's a lovely place, and I'd hate not to show it in its best light. Alternatively, I know several others on the market that are ready right now and might better suit your needs."

Claire had called him back on the way to the hyperloop that morning, explaining that her schedule was packed, her heart was absolutely set on that *specific* house, and that she was capable of seeing beyond a bit of graffiti and rubble.

"Well," he said, "I suppose we *do* have another option since the place is unoccupied. If I find that I can't make it by noon, I'll send you the lockbox code and you can view the place on your own."

Claire told him that would be perfect, sending up a silent prayer that the man's morning appointment would drag well into the afternoon, and he'd have no choice but to send the code. It was going to be hard enough for her to find a plausible reason to snoop around for hidden passageways with the agent underfoot, let alone sneak something out. That was the main reason she'd had the idea to bring along an accomplice. If Alice could distract the guy for a few minutes, hopefully that would give Claire enough time to find the secret stairway to the attic, locate Shepherd's hidden nook, grab the book, and slip it into her bag.

Assuming, of course, that it was even there. That it even existed. Her gut instinct and the rational side of her brain were still at war on that issue.

Since she had a few minutes to kill, she checked her messages to see if there was an update from Ro. They'd barely started talking the night before when Ro's mom showed up at the house, determined to continue their argument, and Claire now totally understood why they needed to get out of there. She'd been ready to fly to Vancouver herself and punch the woman after what Ro told her in their brief conversation. Asking a five-year-old to lie to the guy she was dating in order to protect her vanity was bad enough. But getting angry at Jemma when she slipped up and forgot that she was supposed to say Aunty Nina rather than Grandma was next level. And then she'd actually had the nerve to say Jemma did it on purpose, which had reduced the kid to tears. Claire and Ro had bonded over comparing maternal horror stories, but this one pushed Nina into first place in the Evil Mom Hall of Fame.

At some point after Claire fell asleep, Ro had messaged that she and Jemma were at a hotel. The only thing she'd gotten since then was another drone digest from Apex Security, which she scrolled past without opening.

It was still kind of early on the West Coast, especially since Ro apparently hadn't checked into the hotel until well after midnight. They would again have the "little pitchers" problem if Jemma was awake, and Claire would be too busy to talk once Alice arrived anyway. So she started composing a message to explain about the cicada drone and Leffler's death and why it would be a bad idea to return home early. She offered to cover the hotel, but she doubted that Ro would accept it any more than she'd have accepted Beck's invitation. Claire didn't even mention that, since she suspected the offer was based more on beer and Beck's melancholy frame of mind after the argument with Joe than on a sober reflection of what having a five-year-old underfoot would do to his prospects for a quiet vacation.

She'd almost finished the message when a car pulled up to the curb. Alice had traded in her orange-framed glasses and business casual for purple tortoiseshell frames and a sundress that hugged every curve.

Claire saved the message and stood up to wave Alice over. "I'm glad you could make it. Sorry for such short notice."

Alice arched an eyebrow. "Are you kidding me? You plied me with the archeolinguistic equivalent of catnip with that cryptic mention of a *related side project*. I'd have come all the way up to Boston if you wanted. On my *knees*. Even without the financial incentive."

"You'd have had to crawl all the way to Maine, actually. We had a change of plans." Claire grabbed her daypack and the glass of water from the table, then nodded toward the café door. "Let's get some food while I give you the details. And after that ... I may need your help with a tiny bit of larceny."

TWENTY-FOUR

THE BUSINESS ARRANGEMENTS were settled by the time their lunch was served. Alice seemed more than happy with the financial offer and had no problems with signing a temporary non-disclosure agreement. Claire had put that together on the trip down to New Haven, along with a basic contract, feeling a deep sense of irony as she pulled paragraphs from the NDA she signed for Kolya Terraforming.

Before Claire slid the contract across the table for Alice to sign, she said, "You already know that I think there may be some danger involved in this project. But I want to be crystal clear, so that you don't go into anything under false assumptions. I believe that the Flock's new leadership killed Dr. Leffler. And if you sign this, they may well come after you, too. If you need additional security at your place, we will provide it."

"I'll be fine."

"I just don't want you to underestimate the—"

"Really. I will be fine. I had a…" She pushed a bit of salad around on her plate for a moment, then looked up. "I had a stalker when I was in college, okay? An ex who didn't want to be an ex, who apparently *still* doesn't want to be an ex. He has a nasty temper, absolutely no understanding of *boundaries*, and a family with money and connections. After a very scary close call, I decided that I would rather become someone else than become dead."

Claire winced. "God, Alice. I'm so sorry."

She shrugged. "You do what you have to do in the face of absolute crazy. In my case, that meant my mother and I relocated, changed our appearance, and changed our names. I applied to a graduate program in London, in a field that was only tangentially related to my undergrad degree. When I discovered he was still looking for me, I logged in under my mom's old accounts and switched all of my former self's social media to memorial status claiming that I had been killed in a car accident. And the crazy bastard *still* logs onto one of those accounts to light a virtual candle at least once a week." She nodded toward the screen on her forearm. "So you now know why I have an entire fleet of privacy apps. And *no one* gets into my apartment. My mom calls it Fort Knox."

"Okay." Claire pushed the screen over for Alice's signature. "Although after hearing all of that, I feel like I should be the one signing the NDA."

Alice smiled. "Not necessary. I do background searches on everyone I meet. You and your housemate both volunteer with the House of Ruth in Maryland."

Claire nodded. The women's shelter was connected to Johns Hopkins, where Ro was doing her residency. Ro had spent several months the previous year working in the shelter's health clinic, and Claire had volunteered to emcee a fundraising event.

"You also received a rather effusive special thank you in one of their newsletters last year, so I'm guessing you've contributed financially. If I thought there was any chance that you weren't safe, I wouldn't be here."

"Fair enough."

The waiter returned to top off their iced tea. He was being very solicitous now, perhaps worried that his tip was in jeopardy after his earlier suggestion that Claire was involved in some sort of interplanetary Ponzi scheme.

Once he was gone, Claire glanced at the screen on Alice's arm. "Can I assume that your audio scrambler is on?"

"Always always."

"Good." She made a mental note to order one for herself. Maybe an arm phone, too. They'd always felt gimmicky, but then she remembered that moment of panic in the pool the previous day when she'd realized she didn't have time to get to the zapper gadget. Not that it would have done any good against an actual dragonfly.

"Anyway," she said, "I wanted to emphasize the safety issues because I think they're even more relevant now. I believe the Flock may have targeted Leffler not just because they were worried about her translating the messages inscribed in those chambers, but because that would lead to her translating the longer document that I inadvertently carried back from Mars."

Alice's eyes lit up. "That's the side project?"

Claire spent the next few minutes bringing her up to speed on the manuscript, the not-entirely-legal software that Beck had purchased, and the preliminary work that he'd completed.

"I think Beck has gone about as far with it as he can at this point, so if you're game, I could bring a copy of it, along with the software I mentioned, when I'm in New York to cover the Ares Consortium conference. Beck might be able to meet up with us, too, so that he can update you on the tiny bit of progress he's made so far. And if all goes well in..." She glanced at the screen to check the time. "In about fifteen minutes, there could be a second additional document."

"First, you have me completely sold on the project. I'm in. But … is this second document where the larceny you mentioned comes into play?"

"It is. And your participation in that is completely optional."

Claire gave her a very barebones description of what they'd be going after, leaving out any details that might break her promise to Wyatt. Alice might well be able to fill in those missing pieces on her own, and that probably did violate the *spirit* of her promise, but she was determined to at least stick to the letter of it.

Alice dabbed a bit of salad dressing from the corner of her mouth. "So, you think this document in the house across the street is in the *same* script as the ones on Mars? How is that even possible?"

"The same or at least fairly similar. I can't give you the full details on where it's from or how I know about it at the moment, but you'll know most of that in a couple of days. For now, I'll just say that what I've dug up has taken me from a complete skeptic on that point to fairly certain in less than forty-eight hours."

"Okay. What do you need *me* to do?"

"Hopefully, nothing. If we're lucky, it will be just the two of us going in. But if the real estate agent *does* show up, I need you to distract him for a bit while I hunt around for a secret door and a servants' staircase. If I've interpreted the message from the owner correctly, the book is in a hidden section of the attic."

"Well, now I'm disappointed," Alice said with a fake pout. "I was all geared up for an armed heist. I'm not even sure you can call it *larceny* if the owner of the property asked you to retrieve it."

"Not *grand* larceny, but it probably qualifies as the petty variety. And the owner only *might* have asked me to retrieve it. It's entirely possible that I misinterpreted what they were saying since we were trying to slip the discussion past Kolya's security team, which seems to monitor everything."

Alice grinned. "So the owner of the house is someone who works for Kolya."

"Nice try, but they actually do *not* work for Kolya."

"Then why are you worried about Kolya's people finding out? I mean, I know his ex-wife is leading the Flock now, but he came out pretty forcefully against her. Do you think he's actually working *with* the group?"

The thought had crossed Claire's mind, in part because coincidences didn't sit particularly well with her and far too many of them seemed to have been happening over the past few months. For one thing, the Earth Watch Alliance had generally cast a wide net in terms of their protests, targeting not just private companies, but also universities, think tanks, and federally funded labs. Now they seemed to have narrowed their focus to two companies—Jonas Labs and KTI—and she was connected to both of them. It could simply be because they were the two companies that were in the news right now, and the Flock was aiming to maximize their media coverage. But something about the whole thing felt off.

And then you had the fact that Kolya had whisked Shepherd off to Mars when his ex-wife was in the middle of staging a coup against the guy. He'd even told Claire during their dinner at Della Luna that his goals and Shepherd's were largely the same—they were both trying to ensure the survival of humanity. The only difference was that Kolya believed that the Flock's insistence on simplifying lives and abandoning scientific progress was, at best, a stopgap measure. He was convinced that long-term human survival had to include spreading out to other planets, and eventually, beyond.

It wasn't *entirely* inconceivable that Kolya had worked with Drexel to get Shepherd out of her way, but Claire couldn't believe that he knew about the terrorist attacks. He'd nearly gotten himself blown up trying to stop Kimura. And there was no way that he'd known that Stasia Ljubic was involved. Claire had seen the very real pain on his face at the thought of her betrayal. Anton Kolya had many, many flaws and she didn't think he was averse to a bit of violence in order to further his goals—although he'd probably contract it out to Macek and the rest of his security team. But he hadn't known about the attacks.

"I really don't think he's working with her," she told Alice. "But the situation is kind of complicated right now. The one thing I *do* know is that any claim I make that I'm in that house on behalf of the owner won't help us much if the agent finds me sneaking out with something and reports us to the police."

TWENTY-FIVE

THE REALTOR MESSAGED Claire to say that he was running late but could be there in half an hour, maybe sooner if traffic wasn't too bad. Claire messaged back asking if there was any way he could send the code so that she didn't have to wait in the heat. She could almost hear the man's annoyed sigh, but he sent her the code.

Claire paid their tab and headed to the door to wait for Alice, who was in the restroom. The waiter gave her a little wave, clearly happy with the extra generous tip—which he would no doubt tell everyone was hush money to keep him quiet about her role in the Mars hoax.

"We need to hurry," she told Alice as she ushered her toward the sidewalk. "I have the code, but we're going to have company a bit sooner than I'd hoped."

"Don't worry. You'll have plenty of time to search. I did two years of improv theater in my previous life. I can keep him distracted."

When they reached the front of the house, Claire entered the code into the pad on the door, remembering Shepherd's comments about his mother doing the same thing, her hand shaking because she was so eager for the job to work out. The pad gave a cheerful little chirp and then the lock clicked, and they stepped into the foyer.

Aside from a bit of broken glass on the floor and a slightly rancid smell, there were no immediate signs of the vandalism the realtor mentioned. As they entered the first room on the right, she noticed that two walls were lined with shelves, so it was probably the downstairs library that Shepherd had mentioned in the memoir.

Claire's stomach sank when she stepped inside and saw the other two walls.

One of the windows was still broken, despite what the agent had said about having them replaced. And the rest of it…

Alice turned around in a slow circle, taking everything in. "Is that … blood?"

"Not real blood. Or at least, I don't think so." Claire pointed at the balloon remnants on the floor near the baseboard. "My brother calls these things blood bombs. A favorite toy of the Flock. And *that*?" She nodded toward the words scrawled in the red goop on the wall behind Alice. "That's the same bible verse the drone was quoting outside my house the other day. Or a part of it, at any rate."

"*For in the day that thou eatest thereof...*" Alice read. "Kind of weird that they ended it there."

"Yeah. If they weren't going to smear the entire message on the wall, you'd think they'd have opted for the actual death threat."

"Maybe they were interrupted. Or they might have gotten spooked. Which I kind of understand, at the moment." She pulled up something on her screen and tapped a few times. "Do you still think the book is here?"

"Probably not, since the Flock seems to have beaten us to the punch, but … they may not have known where to look. I should probably check to be sure. I'm just a little concerned that the people who did this might still be hanging around."

"That's what I was just checking. They've already gone. I'm not detecting anyone but us in the building. I'll set an alert, though, so that I'll get a beep if someone else shows up."

Claire added that app to the mental list of upgrades she was going to ask Kes to install when she got back to DC. Or maybe she'd just turn her phone over to Alice and ask her to load it up with the works.

She pulled the drone detector out of her pocket and extended the range to maximum. That would cover the better part of the block, but they'd need to hurry. DC monitor drones, like those of most cities, were programmed to call in any dead zones they detected that exceeded one meter. It made sense—anyone trying to hide illegal activity would want to keep police drones at bay. If New Haven had similar laws, any monitor drone that happened by on patrol would report the address, and she and Alice would very quickly find themselves explaining things to the local police.

"The entrance we need to find *should* be on the second floor," Claire said as they headed up the staircase near the end of the foyer. "If we don't locate it there, we can come back down and see if there are any bedrooms on the main floor. We're looking for a linen closet. There's a door at the back that opens to a hallway and a hidden staircase that goes up to the attic."

"So ... you've seen the floorplan?" Alice asked as she tapped something on her screen.

"No. The owner said the closet was adjacent to a small bedroom. Possibly a *very* small bedroom, since I think it used to be servants' quarters."

When they reached the second floor, two hallways jutted off in opposite directions. The one to the right had only two doors. The longer one continued straight ahead, with five doors and what looked like another hallway on the left at the far end.

"I'll check this side and then catch up with you," Alice said, nodding to the shorter section.

The vandals apparently hadn't bothered with the upper floors. Each door that Claire opened revealed rooms that were clean, empty, and judging from the smell, freshly painted. The third door down opened to reveal a laundry closet with a washer and dryer and shelves, but there was no door at the back of the room. She stepped inside and ran her hands over the wall to check for any seams or other evidence that might suggest that it had been painted over, but she was pretty sure this wasn't the right place, since the bedrooms on either side of the laundry closet were both quite large.

Alice was waiting when she stepped back into the hallway, eyes down, reading something on her screen. "Nothing on the other side," she said. "I'm going to guess that you already know that this place was the first EWA headquarters, right? The entire Flock lived here for about five years until the city issued a citation for too many unrelated people living in a single family home. The article says that's when members of the Flock started changing their last name to Shepherd as sort of a protest against the city's definition of family. So ... I'm guessing that means the owner of this place is Tobias Shepherd."

Claire sighed. "In the interest of protecting sources, I can neither confirm nor deny."

"No need. I just pulled up the tax records."

They checked the two remaining doors in the main hallway, finding nothing. The small hallway on the left had only one door, which seemed to rule it out based on Shepherd's description. But when Claire opened it, she found a small empty bedroom with two closets, the first of which was indeed a linen closet, with shelves built into the side of one wall.

"*Adjacent to* doesn't mean *inside*, Toby," she said under her breath.

The closet was much deeper than she'd expected. And sure enough, there was a door at the back, clearly outlined against the wall of the closet by a faint yellow glow. Either there was a window on the other side, or someone had left a light on.

"Maybe you should wait here," Claire said to Alice as she flicked on the light switch. "We've got maybe five minutes before the agent is supposed to arrive, and it will be easier for you to head him off if you only have to run down a single flight of stairs to do it."

"That's perfectly fine by me. I'm not a fan of tight spaces."

"This is just a formality, anyway. I can't imagine the book is still here given what we saw downstairs."

Claire turned the knob, planning to pull it open. But the door swung free on its own, smacking hard against her knee. She tried to step out of the way, but lost her balance as something—no, some*one*—crashed through the doorway into her legs, causing her to fall to the floor.

Alice screamed and stepped forward, producing a pistol seemingly out of thin air. It was pointing at the man now lying face down on the floor, with one stiff, cold arm draped over Claire's ankle.

"It's okay," Claire said. "You can put that away. He's dead."

The man was wearing an EWA hoodie. Both the hoodie and his long blond hair were flecked with blood. She knew who he was before she even saw his face.

And on the inside of the now-open door, someone had scrawled the rest of the bible verse—*thou shalt surely die*—in Devin Shepherd's blood.

PART II

FROM THE JOURNAL
OF EBERIN DAS

14.13.508

One drawback to this life that we have chosen is isolation from our own kind. It is acknowledged in our training, and we are encouraged to spend what free time we have in communion when possible. Group retreats are encouraged, but aside from our mandatory [conventions? meetings?] it is hard to synchronize our schedules. Gatherings of more than two or three are uncommon. We send messages, we hold virtual conversations, but it is not the same.

Friendships that were strong at the Academy can wither in this environment, but I have been fortunate to maintain a strong tie with Bodae. We continued to meet two or three times a year during my first two assignments, and we still meet at least once every year. Our conversations during training—sometimes raucous, sometimes quiet and philosophical—often ran long into the night over many [from context: a narcotic substance?] that we regretted if we had duties the next day. No subject was taboo or off-limits between us then. I would have trusted him with my life, but there was never any need. We faced no real danger at the Academy.

So when I found myself in need of an ally here, I naturally turned to Bodae. It was a mistake, and one that I regret deeply. Not merely because it has me on the run from those who were once my brothers and sisters, but because I know that his affection for me was as genuine as mine for him. Telling the Triad what I told him in confidence could not have been easy.

I hope that you never read this, Bodae. Because if you read this, I will have failed.

But I do wish there was some way for you to know that I regret putting you in that position. I hope that you do not blame yourself for my end. I wish I could tell you that I forgave you. And I hope that you eventually find a way to forgive me.

(Confidence interval: 86.0%)

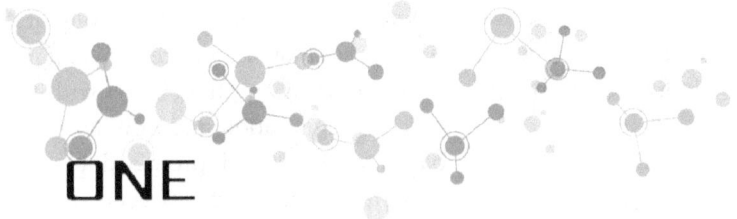

ONE

SGT. ARLEN BRIDGES was a short balding man with a square jaw and the bleary-eyed expression of someone who'd been awakened in the middle of the night. It was a little after two p.m., though, so maybe it was his afternoon nap that had been interrupted by an inconvenient case of murder.

He crossed the lawn toward the ancient patio table where Alice and Claire had been told to wait about fifteen minutes earlier when the forensics crew—one woman and three robotic collection units—arrived on the scene and began scouring the house. A monitor drone tagged along a few paces behind him. It was one of the old-school kind—about the size of a dinner plate, black, and spindly. It reminded Claire of a giant flying tarantula, but that could simply have been because her mind was stuck on bugbots. The thing came to a halt about a meter away when the officer sank down onto one of the ancient patio chairs, which responded with a metallic groan.

"I just spoke to the FBI agent whose name you gave me, Ms. Echols. From what he tells me you've been doing a tour of police stations along the Eastern seaboard this week."

"Not by choice. And I really don't think *one* station constitutes a tour."

"Fair enough, but it's about to be two. I'm going to need both of you to come down to the station and answer a few questions."

Claire took a deep breath, and then decided it might be wise to put Wyatt's advice into practice.

But Alice beat her to it. "Are we being detained, or are we free to go?"

The fact that Alice had been through this particular song and dance before had become clear as soon as the police arrived, and she handed over her gun with one hand and the bullets with the other so that they could check the registration and download the data from the weapon's barrel cam. They'd promised to give everything back when she was released. Devin *had* been shot—a first for the Flock as far as Claire knew—but at least they had proof that it wasn't by Alice's gun.

"Neither of you are *suspected* of anything at this time," the officer told her. "We just need to get your statements."

"So … are you saying we're *not* free to go at this moment?" Claire asked.

"Yeah, I guess that's what I'm saying." He sighed heavily and Claire detected the faintest hint of an eyeroll as he pulled his device out of his shirt pocket and proceeded in a singsong tone. "You are allowed one contact each. I would suggest that it be to your attorneys so that they'll be ready for us to conference them in once we arrive at the station. In the interim, please be aware that this is an active crime scene. You are free to move around here in the yard if you feel the need to stretch your legs, but should you attempt to leave the grounds you will be stopped."

Claire glanced around the postage stamp patio and the narrow strips of grass that encircled it on three sides. Tobias Shepherd's memoir hadn't exaggerated the size of the backyard at Allen House. Sgt. Bridges calling it *the grounds* was almost comical.

"Your movements and all communications are being monitored as of…" He tapped something on his device. "As of this moment. All privacy apps have been disabled. Anything you say or do can be used against you in a court of law should you eventually be charged with this or any related crime, so I would caution you not to say anything to each other or to your attorney or to whoever else you choose to call if you do not intend to share that information with us. When your call is completed, place all communications devices on the table."

"I am here in my capacity as a journalist for the *Atlantic*

Post." Claire held up her phone and continued the litany that she'd memorized her first week on the job, using the same monotone that Bridges had employed. "This device may contain confidential information about sources whose privacy I am ethically bound to protect in accordance with case law pertaining to the First and Fourth Amendments. It is currently powered down and locked. Once I have made a call to arrange for legal representation, I will again power down and lock this device. I will hand it over *only* in the event that I am charged with a crime, and it may be unlocked *only* if a warrant is presented to my employer."

Bridges surprised her by laughing. "Copy that, Ms. Echols. But I'll bet I've had to use my speech more times than you have."

"Unless this is your first day on the job, you'd win that bet."

He turned to Alice. "You with the *Post*, too?"

"Ms. Dobroski is a translator working with me on this story," Claire said quickly, hoping she could extend her journalist's exemption to an assistant.

"Good for you, Ms. Dobroski," he said amiably. "But ... are you officially employed by the *Atlantic Post* or any other media agency?"

"No, sir. I am not," Alice said.

"Okay, then. One call and any devices in *your* possession go on the table." Bridges nodded toward the drone. "I'll leave Timmy here to keep an eye on the two of you while I check the forensics results. Then, I'll give you a ride to the station. I hope to hell the air conditioners are working better than they were this morning." He tucked the phone into his pocket and headed back inside, leaving his airborne pet tarantula behind to babysit.

Alice gave Claire a weak smile. "Were attorney fees covered in that contract I signed this morning?"

"If they weren't, consider it hereby amended. I'm about to contact a colleague who'll get someone to represent both of us, so feel free to use your call however you wish."

"I also turned my phone off as soon as you called 911." She

began rolling the screen on her arm into a cylinder. "I have no plans to turn it back on until we're officially free to go."

"Is this situation going to cause … problems for you?" Claire asked, thinking of everything that Alice had told her over lunch.

"Nope." She smiled sweetly. "There's *nothing* on that device that will interest them. Everything on the phone will show that my life is an open book. And … don't even bother asking me if I want out of the contract. Even though you didn't find what you were looking for in there, I still want to see what I can do with the *other* information that we discussed."

Given the apps that she'd noticed on the device when they were at the hospital, Alice must have done more than simply turn off the phone. She'd probably wiped the system and reset it to the original build. Claire just hoped that Alice's software—and her alternative identity—were as rock solid as she seemed to believe.

Claire's phone began vibrating as soon as she switched it on. Several messages from Apex Security popped up, along with one from Kes. They would both have to wait. There was also a voice message from Wyatt, which she didn't bother to play since she was about to call him. She'd been a little worried that he might be in the meeting with Erica, but he picked up on the first ring.

"Claire. Thank god. I've been trying to reach you for the past—"

"What was the name of that attorney?" she asked. "The one that you said gave you good advice?"

"Um … Jamaal Sellers? He's by far the best that the *Post* keeps on contract. What happened? Are you okay?"

"I'm okay. But I'm going to need you to contact him for me. This is my one phone call. I found a body in the house in New Haven.   It's…" She hesitated, unsure how much she was supposed to say about the crime. But she was certain the officer hadn't explicitly told her to keep the name of the victim secret. And Wyatt needed to know. "It's Devin."

There was a long silence on the other end, followed by a string of curses and a thud that was almost certainly Wyatt's fist connecting with something solid.

"I can't go into details right now. Again, this is my *one phone call*." She stressed the last three words to make sure he understood that they were being monitored.

"Got it. But ... please tell me you didn't break into the place? No. Never mind. Don't answer that."

"Of course I didn't break in! The real estate agent I called wasn't too happy that I used a fake name and number to arrange a showing, but unless Connecticut laws are strange in that regard, I didn't do *anything* illegal. And the *owner* of the house himself told me that it was on the market. Remember? I've even got messages back and forth with him that show—"

"Yeah, you sent me those. Do you know how long ago..." He took a deep breath before continuing. "Do you know when it happened?"

"Not yet. The agent told me earlier that the place had been vandalized a few days ago, but that was just broken windows. I doubt anyone would have found the body then—it was ... hidden. But they'd have seen the message on the walls downstairs. The agent said that the graffiti was new, so I'm thinking it happened last night."

"What have you said to the police?"

"Exactly what you told me to say. Oh, except I did tell them the name of the deceased. And I said to call Andrew West—he's the FBI agent handling the case in Baltimore—to let him know. They said I'm not under suspicion, but I'm also not free to go until I answer their questions. Which is why I called you about the attorney."

"Jamaal is going to say you shouldn't have even told them that much. I'll contact him though and tell him to call the New Haven PD and say he's representing you. Listen, you're going to be fine. They don't have any reason to suspect you're involved. And the real estate agent was there when you found the body, right?"

"No. He came later. The house was empty, so he sent me an entry code. But Alice Dobroski was there."

"Alice … who? Oh, right, right. That's the other professor you mentioned. Why was she there?"

"Mostly I had her meet me here so we could discuss a side project, but I thought I might need her to … translate."

"What did you tell her? And *when* did you tell her?"

She could hear the suspicion in Wyatt's voice, and suspected Alice could hear it, too, even though she was studiously pretending not to be paying attention. It almost made her regret not getting the ear implants.

"I didn't tell Alice anything that you asked me to keep confidential. And she didn't learn about the document I was hunting for until we met for lunch, so only a few hours ago. There's no way she outed Devin."

"Okay," he said. "I'm just a little concerned about the other person I mentioned. The other source. Because if the Flock found out about Devin she could be in danger, too. Not that I'd have any way of knowing."

For a moment, Claire wasn't sure who he was talking about. Her first thought was that he meant his source within the Mars Federation of Labor and her mind began scrambling for a connection. But then she remembered Wyatt saying that Devin had gotten his information from a woman who helped Shepherd prepare the book for publication. No … the *books*. He'd said it was a two-book deal. Was it possible that the second book was the translated *Tales from the Aveezi Forest*? If so, they might also have the original, untranslated version. She made a mental note to get the name of the publisher from Wyatt when they were able to talk freely.

"I need to get Alice an attorney, too," she said, "since she's now working for me."

"Okay. Jamaal might be able to handle both cases. If not, he'll recommend someone. Can you spell her name for me?" After

Claire spelled it out, he paused for a moment, then said, "I take it that the item you were seeking was no longer in the house?"

"I checked while we were waiting for the police. If it was there, the Flock beat me to it." She was about to say goodbye, but then she remembered how he'd answered her call. "Wait. You said you were trying to reach me. What's up? Unless it's something you don't want to tell me in a *monitored* conversation."

There was a long silence and then he groaned. "God. I really hate to pile more on you given the awful day that you're having but … Kes has been trying to reach you. Apex Security called when they couldn't get up with you because you listed them as a backup security contact. Babe … your house …"

"What about my house?"

"It's gone. Someone torched it."

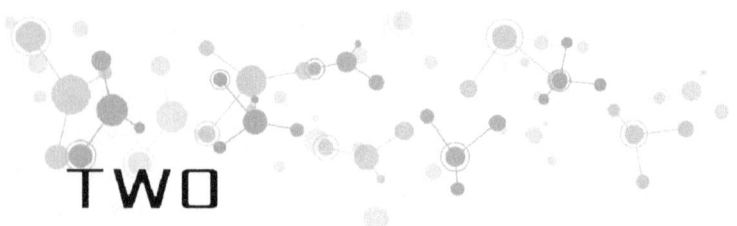

TWO

WYATT WENT on to explain that Claire's fire alarm had gone off around ten-thirty that morning. The fire department barely got there in time to keep it from spreading to her neighbors' houses. It had actually taken out the fence between her place and the house on the left before they got it under control.

"Kes sent me a picture," he said. "It's nothing but ashes."

"Did you hear that?" she asked Alice after she ended the call.

Alice nodded. "I'm so sorry."

"Thanks. Let's go ahead and consider your contract also amended to include the cost of increasing your fire insurance."

"How about life insurance?" she asked with a glance toward Allen House.

"That, too."

As it turned out, Sgt. Bridges was not an unreasonable man. Or perhaps he was moved by the expression of shock that was still on Claire's face when he returned to escort her and Alice to the station. Either way, once he had the two of them in separate rooms, he told Claire that he'd go ahead and take Alice's statement first so that she could make any calls she needed while she waited. They were no doubt monitoring the room she was in anyway, so he probably considered it a win-win situation in terms of collecting information.

Her first call was to Joe, in part because she realized that she didn't actually have Beck's number. There had never been any need for her to ask for it before, since he was invariably at the lab with Joe. She still thought the odds of Ro accepting his invitation were slim, but she wanted to confirm it and ask about getting extra security at the B and B before she even mentioned it to Ro as a possibility.

Her brother didn't answer, and she tried to keep her mind from going to dark places. He and Beck were out on the boat, hopefully enjoying the afternoon. Joe was probably just avoiding calls from Kai. He deserved a few days away from their mother's incessant demands.

She hung up and then debated whether to call back and leave a message. There was nothing they could do at the moment, and she didn't want to spoil the rest of their day. Before she could make up her mind, though, her phone rang. It was Joe's number, but Beck was on the other end.

"Hey, Claire. He's in the water right now, but we're heading in to shore in about half an hour. Are you already back from New Haven?"

"No. I'm going to be a good bit later than expected." She filled him in on both the murder and the fire as best she could, given the fact that the conversation wasn't private.

"Are you heading back to DC, then?"

"Not yet. Wyatt said there was no point, and I don't think I can bear to look at my place right now. He's going to have a friend retrieve our safe and we'll call in a team later to go through the wreckage and see if anything can be salvaged. But ... I still have to tell Ro." Claire's throat tightened at the thought, and she had to fight back tears. "They were planning to fly home as soon as a flight was available. But now ... last night, you said—"

"Yes. I was serious. Tell them to come here."

"Thanks. I'm ... I'm just wondering about security. The two of them will be alone there for at least a day and—"

"Understood. I'll have Joe call and get Wilson to send a security team tonight," Beck said. "I can arrange a private flight to get them from Vancouver, too. Just give us a couple of hours to line things up."

Claire gave a shaky laugh. "I still have to talk her into it. And I can very easily see her deciding that the best place for her and Jemma is far, far away from me."

"Then you need to convince her otherwise. The Flock has groups in every state. They probably saw this Devin guy as a traitor, so killing him may have been as much a way of sending a message to their own people about the price of betrayal as it was about sending a message to you and Wyatt. But that professor … Leffler. She was elderly, and really nothing more than an abstract threat, and they killed her. I would have said before that there's no way they'd kill a child, but I'm less sure now. Drexel and Stasia have clearly lost their minds."

The mention of Stasia was a bit jolting. Claire had been thinking of her as more of a foot soldier, following Drexel's orders, which was bad enough. But Beck was probably right. She'd been in charge of the attacks on Mars. It was perfectly reasonable to assume that she might be in charge of such matters here on Earth, too. Claire didn't know Drexel, so it was far easier to see her as completely heartless. Sure, Stasia had been a bit chilly after they arrived at Daedalus City, but she'd seemed so warm and affable during their conversations at Tranquility Base and onboard the *Ares Prime*.

"You're right," she told him. "There's no guarantee at all. I just hope that I can get that point across to Ro."

"Do you need me to arrange for an attorney, too?"

"No. Wyatt is taking care of it. Technically, since I'm following up on a lead, I need to use the legal team at the *Post*. I'll message back once I've talked to Ro."

She thanked Beck and hung up, feeling a bit guilty to be delegating so much out to others. But there wasn't much else she could do when she was stuck in an interrogation room. And she still had to tackle the hardest task herself—telling Rowan.

Everything that Ro and Jemma owned was in that house. Yes, insurance would replace most of it and Claire could afford to cover everything else, even with upgrades. All of their documents and the most important keepsakes were either digitized or in the safe, so that wasn't an issue. But she knew that Ro had kept a few of Jemma's baby clothes and toys. Those would be gone. Claire also had a handful of things that weren't replaceable, mostly books and a few personal items that had belonged to her dad. She was just so very glad that she'd decided to brave Siggy's claws of fury rather than leaving the cat on her own for a few days. Jemma's WonderKitties curtains could be replaced. Her real kitty couldn't.

The worst thing, though, was the sense of violation, the knowledge that someone had upended their lives in an instant. And Claire had a feeling that this might be the end of their odd little family unit. Ro wouldn't be able to ignore the risks any longer, wouldn't be able to pass it off as Claire being paranoid.

She was half hoping that Ro wouldn't answer, so that she'd have a little more time to figure out exactly how to tell her. But Ro picked up on the second ring and somehow, Claire found the words.

There was nothing but stunned silence on the other end when she finished, so Claire rushed to fill the void. "I'm very, very worried about the two of you being on your own right now. We have a safe location, and we're getting a security team in place. I don't want to say where because this call isn't exactly private, but it's near the ocean so maybe you can still keep your promise to Jemma. A plane can pick you up in a couple of hours, deliver you to the nearest airport, and someone will meet you there. And one tiny shred of good news is that the FBI is going to have to take this seriously from here on out, with two more deaths and now the fire. All of this is just temporary. They're going to catch—"

"*Two* more deaths?"

Claire stopped, realizing that she'd never gotten around to telling Ro about Leffler.

"I was going to tell you last night," she said once she filled in the basic details of the drone attack. "But with the chaos surrounding your mom, I never got the chance. Listen, I know this is all coming down on you and Jemma because of me and I'm sure your instincts are probably telling you to stay far away. And I completely understand if that's your decision long term. In fact, as much as it breaks my heart, that *should* be your decision long term unless things change for the better really soon. But right now, I have the resources to keep you and Jemma safe. Safer than you'd be at a hotel even in Vancouver. The Flock has chapters everywhere. And right now, you..."

She trailed off, not actually wanting to say the words, but Ro filled them in on her own.

"Right now, we have nowhere else to go." Ro laughed, a high, tremulous sound that almost certainly meant she was on the verge of tears. "They're just things, Claire. *Things.* We're all okay and my priority at this moment is keeping Jemma safe. So, yeah. Send your plane to get us. I just hope the East Coast isn't as rainy as the West this week."

THREE

ASIDE FROM THE fact that there was no antique clock on the wall for her to watch slowly ticking off the minutes, Claire's afternoon was a near repeat of the one two days back that she'd spent in the NYPD precinct office.

Alice stuck her head in around two-thirty to say that she'd finished giving her statement and had been declared free to go. Claire promised to call later to set up a place and time for them to meet in New York. She then spent the next few minutes talking to her new attorney, Jamaal Sellers, who had already been fully briefed by Wyatt, and another half hour or so giving her statement to Sgt. Bridges.

While she did tell the truth and nothing *but* the truth, it wasn't exactly the *whole* truth. She relied heavily on *I don't know* when asked about the manuscript, aside from telling Bridges that it was a notebook with the original draft of Shepherd's memoir that she was trying to retrieve for a colleague at the *Post*. She also added and emphasized several times that this was with the express approval of the author and owner of the house. That approval was, of course, based on Claire's interpretation of their heavily encrypted exchange the night before, and it would never stand up to close scrutiny without support from Shepherd. But as Jamaal had noted, it wasn't even relevant since the manuscript hadn't been in the house when she arrived. They weren't likely to charge her with planning to snatch something that the Flock had already stolen.

Jamaal had also noted in their brief conversation before Bridges entered the room that she was under no obligation to speculate. The only time she did so was when he asked why she thought the Flock was so eager to get their hands on the book. She told him that her best guess was that something in the original version might paint the new leader of the Flock in a bad light, since that seemed reasonable and was probably what Wyatt would say when they eventually questioned him, especially if he talked to Jamaal in advance. She omitted everything about a book of folktales and her belief that the Flock had stolen them to keep her from translating a code hidden in ancient Martian DNA. He wouldn't believe her anyway and the story would likely call everything else she'd told him—and possibly her sanity—into question.

The interview with Bridges concluded around four. He told Claire that she was free to go and said they'd be in touch if they needed anything else from her. Before she could make it to the front door, however, he called her back, saying they needed her to wait a bit longer so that she could talk to Agent West who was currently headed north on the Loop from Baltimore. She was given a surprisingly decent cup of coffee and pointed back toward the interrogation room to await his arrival.

That had been nearly an hour ago. Ro and Jemma were probably already en route from Vancouver. At this rate, they'd be in Maine before she was.

Andrew West finally stepped into the interrogation room at about five-fifteen.

"Sorry to keep you waiting, Ms. Echols," West said as he took the seat across from her. He had one of those faces that made it almost impossible to pinpoint his age. Claire went back and forth between thinking he was a baby-faced fifty and believing he was a prematurely bald twenty-five. She also went back and forth on whether he was abrasive because he was overworked or because he was a jerk.

"It's okay," she said. "You had a long commute from Balti-more. The wait was definitely giving me a case of déjà vu, though."

"And why is that?" he asked, frowning slightly. "Have I kept you waiting before today?"

"Oh, no. I didn't mean you personally. I was referring to your colleague with the Manhattan office. The one you asked to speak with me about Professor Leffler on Thursday?"

He stared at her, his frown deepening the lines on his forehead, and she leaned back toward him being a baby-faced fifty.

"Agent Emily Wheeler?" she said. "At least, I'm pretty sure that was the name she gave me."

After a few more seconds of silent frowning, he pushed his chair back and stood up. "Wait here."

"Okay. I was about to bring in my attorney, though. Should I hold off?"

"Why would you hold off? I just need to call the Manhattan office and find out what the hell is going on. Don't tell me you're worried about a few extra minutes of attorney fees?" He chortled at his little joke and Claire had her second answer. The guy was a jerk.

West was actually back before she had Jamaal conferenced in. He stuck his head into the room, holding his phone off to the side. "Are you sure the name was Emily Wheeler?"

"I wouldn't swear to the first name, but I'm absolutely certain about the last. I remember seeing it on her badge."

"Did you get that?" he said into the phone. "Okay. Then what about the other borough offices? … Well, *could you check*? Damn."

He left the room again, and about a minute later, Jamaal called in. She was explaining the situation, or at least what she believed to be the situation, when West returned and sank back down into the chair.

"So … I'm getting the sense that Wheeler *wasn't* with the FBI?"

"You must be psychic," West said, with a bit more sarcasm than Claire felt was strictly warranted. "I didn't call anyone at the New York office after you contacted me on Thursday. The Manhattan branch doesn't have an agent named Wheeler. None of the *other* New York City boroughs have an agent named Wheeler.

Nor do any of them have a record of sending any of their agents over to talk to you. They just took the information that you gave to the NYPD and sent it on to me."

"Is that usual practice?" Claire asked.

"Yes. Despite what you may have read or seen on cop shows, we *do* cooperate with local police. Most of the time."

"So … if she wasn't with the FBI, who was I talking to?"

West shrugged. "Your guess would be better than mine at this point."

"This is why you should never proceed without an attorney," Jamaal said softly.

"Believe me, it won't happen again. But … come on! She showed me her badge. Her tablet even had the FBI logo on the cover."

"Yeah, well, that kind of thing is really easy to forge," West said. "You should have gotten the badge number and entered it into the Bureau's verification site to confirm."

"On that note," Jamaal said, "maybe it would be a good time for us to check yours?"

Claire was about to say she didn't think it was necessary, given that she'd met with West previously at the Baltimore FBI office and had spoken to him several times over the phone. They had already launched into their little authentication dance, though, so she just sat back and waited for them to finish.

"But to be honest," West said, "you're really not the one who should have had to worry about confirming Wheeler's credentials. Whoever let the woman into the precinct should have double checked her ID and I can assure you that we'll be following up on it." He unfolded his tablet, which Claire could see was a newer model than the one Wheeler or whatever her name was had been carrying. Same black cover, though, and the same logo. "Okay. Describe her to me. And then tell me everything she asked you."

"Unusually tall. Close to six feet, maybe even a bit taller. Strawberry blonde hair, long and kind of frizzy, with those choppy short bangs. I think they call them baby bangs. That's pretty much all I can remember."

She spent the next few minutes recapping the interview. "I think I knew something was a little off, even then," she added. "Not that I suspected that she was a fraud or anything like that. I just thought maybe she wasn't much good at the job. Or maybe that she wasn't familiar enough with the case to understand what she needed to focus on. For example, she seemed much less interested in the drone attack on Leffler than she was in how well I knew Tobias Shepherd. She actually said that she would just get the information about Leffler from the NYPD, so she was familiar enough with the Bureau to know that you cooperate with the local police. *Most* of the time."

"What did you tell her about Shepherd?" West asked, ignoring her little jab.

"That I'd had a total of three conversations with the man, only one of which lasted more than a minute. She seemed to be most interested in one of the briefer exchanges, the last time we spoke, after we were both on Mars. I was surprised anyone even knew about it, but then I remembered that there were other people, including a couple of KTI security in the diner, and figured that the Bureau must have finally gotten around to questioning some of them about the events leading up to the bombings at Millex and Icarus."

West's face colored slightly, and she realized that *finally gotten around to* might not have been the most delicate way of phrasing it. But he knew as well as she did that they hadn't exactly been setting speed records with the investigation.

"Was that all?"

"No. She seemed convinced that Shepherd had passed something to me. A data drive. I told her that the only thing he handed me was a scrunchie—that's a hair accessory. One of those fabric covered elastic bands?"

West smiled briefly, possibly the first smile she'd seen cross his face. "I have two daughters. Both with long hair. I know what a scrunchie is."

"Okay. I remembered that it was pink—I'm thinking bright pink with little dots?— because I assumed that was one reason Shepherd spotted it under the sink in the bathroom and thought it might be mine. This was at the diner in Ehden, so it was a reasonable assumption."

"Why? Were you wearing pink?"

"No. I was just the only female there at the time, and the scrunchie was kind of … well, kind of girly-looking. I've probably had it since I was a teenager. Those things last forever."

"And you said you were in … Ehden? Where is that exactly?"

"It's a domed community near Nepenthes Station. Under control of KTI. You know, the dome where Shepherd is setting up his new Flock?"

He asked her to spell it. She did, trying hard to keep the irritation out of her voice. If this man was actually investigating the bombings, if he'd dug at all into the events that led up to the one at Icarus, then he should at least have heard of Ehden.

"Anyway," Claire continued, "Wheeler seemed more interested in the scrunchie than anything else, and asked if I knew where it is now."

"What did you tell her?"

"I laughed. I mean, it's not the kind of thing that you only have one or two of. People even buy them in multipacks most of the time. I don't keep track of them but just grab the first one I find in the drawer or my bag if I need to tie my hair … back."

Several odd phrases in Shepherd's text messages suddenly began running through her mind.

*I escaped by a **hair's** breadth…*

*Folktales are the **ties** that bind…*

*Easier to just **cut the tie**…*

And then yesterday in the car, her arm stretched behind the seat, fingers searching blindly through the unfamiliar pocket of the daypack for her earphones to block the roar of Hell's Gravity. Feeling an empty gum wrapper, lip balm, a tin of breath mints.

And a hair tie.

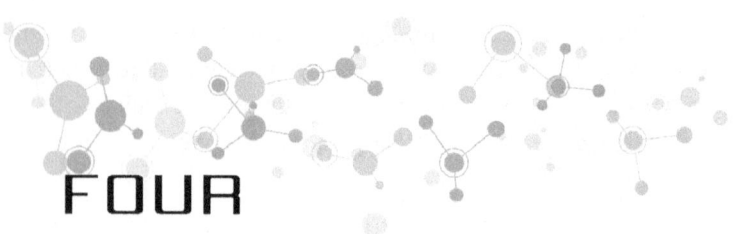

FOUR

"MS. ECHOLS?"

Claire shook her head to clear it, suddenly very conscious not only that both the attorney and Agent West were watching her but also of the weight of the daypack against her right calf.

"Sorry." She laughed nervously. "It's been a very long, very unsettling day. I think I need more coffee so that I don't keep fading out in mid-sentence. What ... what was I saying?"

"Something about Wheeler being very interested in the location of a hair tie," Jamaal said.

"Yes. Thank you. I told her I didn't know where it was. That it might be somewhere in that cave at Icarus Camp, for that matter, since it was in my bag when the bomb went off. But I said my best guess was that it was with the dozens of others I own. At home."

"Meaning your house in Maryland?"

She nodded. "Yes. The house that someone just burned to the ground."

West was quiet for a moment as he entered something into his tablet, and then he asked, "Are you familiar with a company in Virginia called Greenleaf Books?"

"No." Claire had the sinking feeling that she wasn't going to need to ask Wyatt the name of Shepherd's publisher.

"They mostly handle books and pamphlets for environmental groups," West said. "Small company. Really small, in fact. What you might call a mom-and-pop shop. Aside from the printing itself, which they apparently contracted out, everything was done out of the home office of a couple who had lived in the little community of Catawba for close to forty years. I don't know how familiar you are with the area, but that's only a stone's throw away from the Flock's compound at Culpeper."

"What happened?"

"Another house fire, believe it or not. Last night. Only the couple was home at the time. Quite possibly already dead when the fire started. All of their equipment was destroyed, too. So we have three people murdered and two buildings burned, in a span of around forty-eight hours. Maybe four murders, if Dr. Leffler's case is connected, and I've been told that one of her colleagues from Columbia was with you today so I'm going to go out on a limb and say that it is. So ... we have four murders, two cases of arson, and unless I'm mistaken, the same bible verse at the scene of the murder here in New Haven was on the recording of the drone you smashed to bits on Thursday. All, apparently, connected to the manuscript that you were trying to steal from the house where one of those bodies was found."

"Retrieve. Not steal," Jamaal corrected. "Ms. Echols had written approval from the owner."

"I'm not sure that I'm convinced on that point," West said, "but, fine. Let's put all of this in the most benign light possible. Four murders and two acts of arson connected to this document you were trying to *retrieve* on behalf of Tobias Shepherd. So I've got two questions. First, why would Shepherd have you out hunting for this document now, entering on false pretenses so that you can root around in the attic of the house he's currently trying to sell, if he'd supposedly hidden a copy of it inside your hair tie? And second, what could possibly be in this book that would make Corbin Drexel and the Flock go on a killing spree, especially when they know they're already under investigation for the events on Mars?"

Claire had to stifle a laugh. The Flock hadn't appeared to be fazed in the slightest by the fact that they were being investigated. And she wasn't sure she blamed them given the pace at which West and his ... well, she was going to say *West and his team*, but at this point, she was beginning to suspect that he was the only agent assigned to the case, that it was only *one* item on his very crowded agenda, and quite possibly near the bottom in terms of priority. But she reminded herself that pointing this out would probably be counterproductive, and focused on answering his questions so that she could make the next train.

"On the first question," she said, "I don't know. Shepherd is a bit … I'm not going to say paranoid, because they really *are* trying to kill him. Let's just say that he's security conscious. And he doesn't really trust KTI's setup in that regard, so I'm not surprised that he was speaking in riddles to avoid the censors. I did the same thing when I was there. But I don't know why he would have given the manuscript to me when we'd exchanged only a few dozen words, and he didn't say anything at the time that would have made me think he'd inserted something into the hair tie. He just handed it to me. Shepherd *did* know that I…"

She stopped herself on the verge of saying that Shepherd knew she'd be trying to decipher the writing found in the chambers. Suggesting that the manuscript contained anything other than a draft of Shepherd's memoir would just lead to more questions.

Although … maybe there *was* a reason he'd given it to her rather than to anyone else. She didn't see how he could have known about the manuscript in the *Deinococcus* sample. But he could easily have seen and recognized some of the symbols in the images of the chambers from his own translation project. Claire and Wyatt had both noticed similarities and Shepherd was far more familiar with the script than they were.

And what had he done right after he handed her the hair tie? He had thanked her for saving his life. Giving her a clue that could be useful for translating the text from the chambers might have been Shepherd's way of expressing his gratitude. It would have been nice if he'd bothered to *tell* her that he'd hidden the clue inside the hair tie … but maybe he was holding off in order for whatever story she wrote to sync up with the publication of his memoir?

"He did know that I'm a journalist," she said. "If he wanted to get publicity for his book—or maybe just have a spare copy around as insurance if he was worried about something like this happening—then sneaking a copy off planet with me would make a lot of sense. As for why they're so determined to destroy the document I was looking for today, I'm afraid you'll need to save that question for Corbin Drexel. Or Dr. Shepherd, I suppose. If he has backups or if there are copies at the printer that Greenleaf Books contracted out to, then maybe you can read it for yourself and draw your own conclusions. But I can't help you there because I've never read it. Neither has my colleague."

Claire felt a tiny twinge at this, because she had definitely given West and the police the impression that the document she was retrieving from Allen House was Shepherd's memoir, which both she and Wyatt had read, at least in part. But they hadn't read *Tales from the Aveezi Forest* or Shepherd's translation notes, and she was certain that those documents were actually the ones that the Flock was willing to kill to keep hidden.

West wrapped up the interview a few minutes later, saying that he wanted to get over to Allen House and check out the crime scene before dark. As he was heading toward the door, she asked if the fire at her house was now part of the FBI's investigation into the Flock.

"Yes." He didn't add the word *unfortunately*, but it came through loud and clear in his tone. "We're coordinating with the Howard County Fire Marshal. I'm sorry for your loss, Ms. Echols. But I have no doubt that you were *more* than adequately insured."

There was something in his tone that irked her. It almost sounded like he was suggesting that she'd had her house burned down for the insurance money. But no, that wasn't it. He was just thinking that she could *afford* it—not just the insurance but the disaster itself. Which was true but also obnoxious as hell.

Or maybe he was reflecting on the fact that Claire had been exceptionally lucky compared to the other victims. Unlike the couple who was publishing Shepherd's book, her house had been empty at the time of the attack. Four people were dead, and despite the fact that she seemed to be at the heart of whatever was going on, she was still alive.

She pushed her annoyance aside and asked if the investigators knew how the fire started.

He flushed slightly. "Your security service said a swarm of microdrones dipped down into your safety perimeter from above at around ten fifteen this morning. Apparently, they'd been doing that on and off for the past two days."

"More like *twelve* days, if you look back at when I first called you to report the problem."

"No, Ms. Echols. You never mentioned *swarms*. You said that individual drones were setting off your perimeter alarm. Right?"

"Right…"

West nodded firmly. Apparently, he thought the fact that the arsonists started out testing her defenses with *single* drones, rather than swarms of the things, somehow excused both his office and the local police shrugging off her complaints as being mere harassment or falling outside their jurisdiction.

"The guy I talked to said the place went up quickly," he added, in a tone that sounded like it should be some consolation to Claire that her house hadn't lingered in pain. "He thinks there might be some stuff that's salvageable down in the basement, but there's not much left on the upper floors. Once the county team finishes, we'll need to get our arson squad in there to check everything over. That's scheduled for Wednesday morning—things are a bit tight with the holiday weekend. I'll have someone let your security team know when you can get back in to assess the damage. I'm guessing that will be late afternoon Wednesday or early Thursday." As he went through the door, he tossed one final snide remark over his shoulder. "And I'll tell them to be on the lookout for a pink scrunchie in the debris."

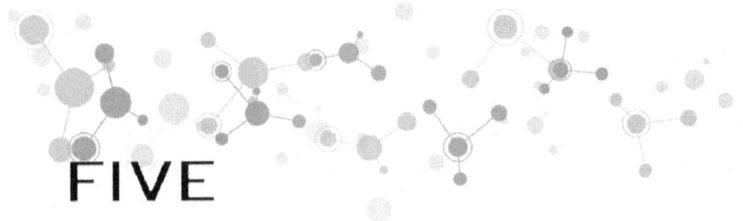

FIVE

CLAIRE GRABBED her daypack from under the table, double checked with the officer at the desk to make sure she was free to go, and then headed toward the hyperloop terminal. It was about six blocks away from the police station, and she had plenty of time to make the 6:10 northbound but she found it hard to keep her pace below a jog. When she spotted a coffee shop on the corner of Water and Brown, she went inside and while the barista was preparing her drink, she slipped into the bathroom, which was one of the few public places where you could still be sure—or at least, *reasonably* sure—of a modicum of privacy.

Once she was inside a stall, she unzipped the daypack's pocket. The light was dim, but she could still make out the tin of mints, a tube of Red Dahlia lip balm, and at the very bottom, a bright pink scrunchie. Not polka dots, as she had thought, but dotted Swiss, which was why the fabric had felt nubby when she was searching through the pocket for her earphones the day before.

She didn't pull it out, just in case her assumption of privacy in the stall was mistaken. Instead, she ran the fabric slowly between her fingers, working her way around the elastic band.

About halfway through, she felt something. It was so small that she initially thought it was one of the raised dots on the fabric, but when she went back and pressed it between her fingers again, she could make out a thin square maybe ten millimeters across. Moving forward again, she found a tiny frayed area along the seam and began pushing the square chip toward the hole. A few seconds later, a minuscule tab of metal and plastic popped into her palm.

She stared down at it, marveling at the surreality of the Flock burning down her house in an effort to destroy something the size of her pinky nail. They had killed at least four people to keep whatever was contained on this drive a secret. Had the attack on Shepherd also been part of that effort? It seemed increasingly likely, and Agent West's second question echoed in her mind. What could be so important that the Flock would go on a killing spree to keep it from being uncovered?

She slipped the drive back into the hair band—not an easy task with shaking hands—and then, after a quick check to make certain she was still alone in the bathroom, she called Wyatt. Messaging would probably have been wiser, but she really wanted to hear his voice.

"I'm out," she said when he answered.

"Thank god. What took so long?"

"Had to wait for Agent West to arrive from Baltimore. I'm guessing he'll be contacting you soon. Did you hear about the fire at Greenleaf?"

"Yeah. About half an hour ago. Did you hear about the fire in Richmond last night?"

The faint slurring of Wyatt's consonants suggested he'd had several drinks, and she knew he was blaming himself for Devin's death. Maybe for the others, as well.

"Let me guess," she said. "A printing company?"

"Ding ding ding. Fortunately, that building was unoccupied." He hesitated for a moment, then said, "Any chance you can get in touch with Shepherd again? He strikes me as the kind of guy who backs up his files."

"He is. And yes, I'm going to try to reach him tonight. But, Wyatt—"

"This isn't just about supporting my claims in the article, okay? It's more that I can't see anyone going to this much trouble just to hide what's in that memoir. I'm thinking it has something to do with the message you found in the chambers. Because there has to be something more to all of this …"

"*There is.*" She paused, letting her silence hammer the point home. "I don't know everything yet, but … how firmly are you holding me to the promise of confidentiality I made the other night?"

"You want to share the memoir with that linguistics expert? Alice …?"

"Dobroski. Eventually, yes. But right now it's Joe. And Beck. I promise you it's not just so they can chuckle at Shepherd's purple prose. I need their help."

She strongly suspected that she'd actually only need Beck's help. Joe had made it clear that he was done with the project. But Wyatt had never met Beck, and since Claire had admitted in a slightly tipsy moment when they were talking about adolescent crushes that Beck had been one of hers, tossing Joe's name into the mix seemed like a good idea.

Wyatt was silent for a few seconds, then he laughed harshly. "Sure. Even if it was just for entertainment purposes, I don't see any reason to hold you to it. It's not like I have a source to shield anymore. I'm guessing Devin's contact was exposed, too, but he never gave me her name, so I doubt I'll be able to find out one way or the other. Just use your discretion, babe. But … when you say there's *more* going on—"

"I'll call you tonight, okay? Any chance you can meet me in New York on Tuesday?"

"You're still going to the conference? Because I've got a backup plan if you need to bow out. And you probably *should*—"

"I'm going," she said, trying to keep the frustration out of her voice. "I told Bernard I was covering it. And I already told Paul that I'd be there."

"I'm sure they'd understand, given everything that happened today."

"They probably would. But Anton Kolya is also going to be there and *given everything that happened today* I'm going to set personal reasons for avoiding the man aside. He was married to the woman who apparently ordered my house burned down and also had a bunch of people killed. And then there's Stasia, right there in the middle of it, and she worked side by side with Kolya for years. So … I've got a few questions for him. I'll keep an ear out for information about Millex, as well, but it's not my only or even my main reason for going. And as I told you the other night, you aren't the reason I'm in danger right now. Encasing me in bubble wrap isn't a viable option."

"You're right. It's just…" He sighed. "This is new for me, okay? I'm usually the one who's out there pissing off the people with zero compunctions about killing."

"I know. And I'll be careful."

"Okay. I've got to admit that the bubble wrap part sounds like fun, though. I could take my time, popping each little bubble…"

That pulled a laugh from her, even though she was trying to be serious. "I have to go, okay? Don't kick yourself too hard over all of this and don't take any chances that you don't have to. I love you."

She ended the call then, not waiting for a response or putting him in a position where he felt pressured to make one. It wasn't the first time she'd said the words to him, or vice versa. But neither of them had ever used it as a stand-alone statement. It had always been lighter, more casual. More ambiguous. They were best friends, after all, and had been for nearly a decade. *Of course,* she loved him.

But she was tired of playing games. They were either friends or they were more. She couldn't keep ping ponging back and forth. It was time for a long talk and a decision.

Assuming they both made it through all of this alive.

Claire slung the daypack over one shoulder and gripped the strap firmly. But then she caught her reflection in the mirror as she stepped toward the door. It would be so very easy for someone to rip it from her grasp. So she ducked back into the stall, reached into the pocket, and wrapped her hand around the hair tie.

Feeling as if a thousand eyes were watching from every corner of the empty stall, she removed the scrunchie, slipped her hand inside her shirt, and tucked it into her bra.

Then she hurried from the bathroom and out the side door, clutching the daypack to her chest even though she knew there was no way anyone could see the hair tie through her shirt. Resisting the urge to peek over her shoulder every few steps, she walked the two remaining blocks to the terminal. Fifteen minutes later, strapped into her seat on the train and still clutching the daypack, she realized she'd bolted from the shop without even grabbing her coffee.

SPEECH BY CORBIN DREXEL

(PARTIAL TRANSCRIPT—CULPEPER,
VIRGINIA—MARCH 5, 2084)

I'm going to keep this brief, but I wanted us to gather as a group
before I head back to Ohio and leave you under the guidance of
Anthony. I've already spoken with many of you individually. I
know that some—maybe even most—of you resent me. I understand. In your place, I would likely feel the same.

Some of you remain loyal to Tobias Shepherd. You feel that I am a
usurper, that I have stolen control of the organization that has
been his life's work.

And you're right. I did not build this group. I don't deny that.
Without Shepherd's dedication and vision, the Earth Watch
Alliance would *never* have been created. Shepherd, and all of you
who have worked under his guidance over the past few decades
have so much to be proud of in terms of raising consciousness and
gathering the resources we need for the fight ahead.

Because … that's the problem. *That's* the problem and also the
reason that Shepherd can no longer lead. We have a *fight* ahead.

Not a debate, not a lecture, not a gentle persuasion. A *fight* that could well end in death, and not just our own. I'm talking about the death of every human. Every creature. Every hint of life on this planet.

Shepherd would have you believe that these beings he calls the Sentinels are your friends. That they will swoop down and rescue those who fought the good fight, the faithful few. I will not ridicule his belief, because I held one even more naïve. I believed that they would save the entire planet, that Earth's progress would be welcomed and applauded. That Earth would be pulled into the Alliance, rather than becoming its target.

Your former leader is a good man. But he believes that this is a struggle for people's hearts and minds. I suppose that at one point, he may have been right. Maybe when he first began it was still possible to convince people through solely nonviolent means to … well, I was going to say turn back the clock, but that's not right. Our task is smaller. We only need to *stop* it. This far and no further.

But the time for peaceful change has passed, my friends. We are now on the very brink of destruction because persuasion has not been enough to halt the combined engine of ambition and greed. I tried. As soon as I understood the gravity of the situation, I tried persuasion. I literally begged the man who may well wield the killing blow to this planet to listen. Simple persuasion will not work.

One of you asked me earlier today how we are supposed to fight beings who are so much more advanced. The answer is that we cannot fight them. All we can do is fight the forces who are pushing us into the path of their destruction.

In my last discussion with Shepherd, he told me that his Flock is not an army, that you would not fight. I don't think he meant that as an insult in any way, and I'm fairly sure he didn't believe the most important parts of what I told him, so you shouldn't hold the words against him. But he told me that your pacifism runs too deep, that you would resist using the tools that are necessary to win.

I hope he was wrong. There is nothing wrong with pacifism when the stakes are low. There's nothing wrong with being a pacifist if it is only your own life that is on the line. But to cling to pacifism when the lives of others are in your hands? That's creeping onto some shaky moral ground. And to cling to it still when we're talking about the survival of the planet? The only moral course of action in that case is to fight tooth and nail, to your very last breath.

Simply put, Tobias Shepherd believed that you are a flock of sheep. And maybe you were, before. Our survival, however, depends on you becoming a flock of *geese*. You've all worked on these farms, so I'm guessing most of you understand what I'm saying. Geese are generally tranquil until you rouse their protective instincts. If you threaten those in their care, they *will* attack, even at great personal risk. Geese are brave. They'll go up against an elephant to protect those who are depending on them.

I'm going to end by paraphrasing the Bible. Or an old song by a group called The Byrds, if you're not of the religious persuasion. I don't remember the words exactly, but it's something like:

> *To everything there is a season. A time to be born, a time to die. A time to sow and a time to reap. A time to break down and a time to build up. A time of war and a time of peace.*

The song version ends by saying that they swear it's not too late for peace. And I hope that they are right in the long run. But to *get* to that peace, that greater peace that ends with the survival of the planet, we must first fight.

In the coming battle, some of you will be asked to do things that may trouble your conscience. When that happens, I ask that you remember that these are not acts of aggression. They are acts of preservation. We are doing this to safeguard our planet, our home, and the billions of people who are now, through a twist of fate, under your protection.

The outsiders? They call you Toby's sheep. But you are not sheep.

You are geese. And I know that you will do whatever it takes to protect those in your care.

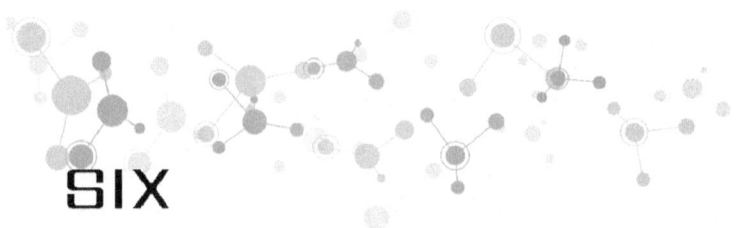

SIX

CLAIRE HAD all but forgotten that Wyatt sent her the transcript of Corbin Drexel's speech along with Shepherd's book. She'd actually planned to read another chapter or two of the memoir on the short ride north to Maine, but when she opened the folder, she spotted the other file and opened it instead.

What struck her most about the speech was how much it reinforced what Shepherd had said in those early chapters she'd read. In one sense, that wasn't surprising. Drexel was, after all, taking over an established organization with several decades of history. It made sense that she'd incorporate as much of their mythology as possible, while at the same time trying to push them in this more extreme direction.

She understood now why Wyatt's editor had been leaning heavily toward the memoir being a fake written by Drexel's faction, given that the speech basically echoed the warning that he claimed to have been given by Nathaniel Everett. If Claire had read the speech before her messages back and forth with Shepherd, she'd have been leaning in the same direction.

Her phone buzzed. It was Kes, returning her earlier call.

"You're talking on the hyperloop?"

"Yes." Claire was tempted to ask how Kes had known she was on the loop, but they owned as many gray market security apps as Alice so who knew what sort of information was being displayed on the other end of the call. "Is that a problem?"

Kes considered for a moment. "Not if you just want to ask me about the fire. All of that information is public record. Or it will be eventually."

"Is there something else that I *should* ask you about?"

"Not while you're on the 'loop."

"Then why don't you tell me what you've found out about the fire."

That had, in fact, been the only thing she'd planned to ask about when she called Kes back at the police station, but she made a mental note to check in again later.

"Okay. This is what I've managed to put together between a chat with one of the firefighters and some … security footage I obtained. The drones upped their activity shortly after you left, at least in terms of the number showing up at any given time. This last swarm was armed with a slew of tiny chemical explosives, basically souped up versions of things called dragon's eggs that firefighters and private landowners sometimes use in controlled burning of dead brush and so forth to prevent wildfires. Anyway, these were military grade. The firefighter called them double-yolked. Although he said they might even have been triple. Dragon eggs are stable until impact, at which point the barrier between the two chemicals shatters, thus combining them and causing the fire, and in this case also releasing a second egg. The first yolk burns a hole through the roof, then the other one drops through and starts a secondary blaze inside. It's designed for surgical strikes, usually in urban or residential areas where you want to take out an enemy target but need to avoid collateral damage."

"But how did the drones get past our perimeter? Shouldn't the system have brought them down as soon as they breached the barrier?"

"Based on the security cam footage, it appears to have worked just fine. The whole swarm dipped down close enough for the barrier to disable them, and then gravity did the rest. All of the drones dropped like rocks, and since the chemical reaction is set off on impact…"

"The dragon eggs ignited when the drones hit the roof," Claire finished.

"*Exactly.* The smarter thing would have been to stay above the barrier and simply release the payload. That way, they could have avoided sacrificing the drones. Looked like there were fifty or sixty to me, and those things aren't exactly cheap. But the dragon eggs are light and any wind or even the turbulence from that many small drones in a fairly tight formation might have sent the eggs off course. Which suggests they were trying to limit damage to just the one house and—assuming they knew your place was empty—avoid having any casualties."

"Have you talked to Wyatt in the past few hours?" Claire asked.

"Uh … no. He did message to say he'd gotten up with you to let you know about the house. But nothing after that."

"Call him. Maybe even go by and check on him. I think he might need to see a friendly face. For now, I'll just tell you that after today, we can safely say that the people who did this aren't especially worried about casualties." She thought back to Drexel's speech. "They see this as a war. Did any of their drones survive the fire?"

"I doubt it. The firefighter didn't mention them when I collected your safe, and … I don't think much of *anything* could have survived that fire. Most of this is just speculation based on security cam footage."

Claire was pretty sure her system didn't have security cameras on the roof or far enough from the house that they'd have a clear shot of anything happening just above it. And Elkridge was a community that tended to prioritize privacy over safety, so there were no neighborhood watch cameras in the cul-de-sac. That meant Kes's assessment was probably based on the doorbell cams of neighbors. The footage *might* have been obtained through proper channels, but she had a strong suspicion that shortcuts were taken. Kes had gotten the footage in a matter of hours. And Kes had also claimed on more than one occasion that most door-bell cams were extremely easy to hack. Either way, she wasn't going to ask, not on the hyperloop and not ever. Plausible deniability was clearly her best course of action in all things involving Kes.

"Personally, I'm thinking that they wanted the drones to be destroyed," she said. "That way, they leave behind no evidence and there's no risk of cameras tracing the swarm when they return to their point of origin. Given everything that's happened in the past few days, I'd guess that limiting collateral damage was a whole lot less important to the Flock than covering their tracks."

SEVEN

RO AND JEMMA didn't quite beat Claire to Maine, but their plane was due to arrive about ten minutes after her train, which meant that Joe and Beck had to head out at the same time to pick them up. Joe wasn't a complete stranger thanks to occasional video calls with Claire, so Beck had suggested that Joe retrieve Ro and Jemma from the airport in Portsmouth while he picked Claire up at the Kittery terminal.

Claire was pretty sure that Beck also had an ulterior motive in maximizing the amount of time Joe spent around Jemma, given their conversation in the hot tub. Not that she was complaining. The drive back would give her time to talk to Beck about Shepherd's memoir and the book of presumably alien folklore. She intended to tell Joe, too, but she was no longer sure how seriously he'd take it and preferred to talk to Beck first without her brother interrupting to remind him that they had more important work back at the lab.

Claire had felt a bit ridiculous—and yes, *paranoid*—for asking someone to come get her in the first place, given that she had driven Joe's car to the station that morning. It was right there in the lot waiting to take her back to Beck's place. But that was precisely what had her worried. The people who left that message and Devin's body at Allen House had known she was coming. Had they also known where she was coming *from*? If so, the car had been parked in the lot since early morning, leaving plenty of time for someone to tamper with it.

Beck was waiting on the platform when she got off the train. Even in the fading sunlight she could see a vivid pink splotch on his left cheek and her breath caught in her throat. It looked almost identical to the mark on Leffler's neck.

But Beck seemed fine. He was moving through the crowd toward her, quite possibly attributing her alarmed expression to general upset over the events of the day, because as soon as he reached her, he pulled her into a long hug. And maybe he wasn't that wrong about her emotional state. She'd been holding it together fairly well, but the sight of a familiar, sympathetic face had her fighting back tears.

"I'm sorry," she said as they began to weave their way through one cluster of people trying to board and another group moving toward the parking lot. "I should have just taken Joe's car back. Or called for a ride. But after everything else that's happened today…"

"Don't be silly. If I'd been thinking straight, I'd have suggested it myself. Joe asked Wilson to send two guards up from the lab to cover Bellamy House, along with a few perimeter bots. He made the call when we were still on the boat, so they were actually at the house by the time we got back. One of the guards gave me a ride here to the station. He's checking Joe's car now. And you have every reason to be extra cautious about personal security at the moment."

"It's not just *personal* security I'm worried about," she said. "I've got … cargo."

"Cargo?"

"I'll explain once we're out of here. What happened to your face?"

He raised his hand to the pink splotch. "Oh, that. Yeah … I burn after five minutes in the sun. Usually, I'm good about applying sunscreen every few hours, but I must have gotten distracted. Missed a spot on my side, too. Your brother said I look like someone slapped me."

"You kind of do," she said, again picturing the pink handprint on Leffler's neck from where she'd slapped the drone. "That's one area where I'm *glad* that I inherited my mother's genes."

"Tell me about it. Joe spritzed something on his face and shoulders *once*, just before we got on the boat, and he was fine for the entire day. I have a UV-protection implant and *still* have to reapply the stuff multiple times if I'm outside for more than an hour."

A blue and gold Jonas Labs cruiser was parked on the other side of Joe's car when they reached the lot. The guard gave them a thumbs up and said there were no issues. Claire slipped into the right side of the car, still feeling a bit ridiculous for making him check in the first place. Beck stayed outside for a moment, to ask the guard what he liked on his pizza and then waited a bit longer while he called the other guard to get his order.

Claire took advantage of the moment of privacy to pull the hair tie from her bra. For one panicky moment, she couldn't locate the nanodrive. Had it slipped out during the trip? Or maybe she'd only imagined it was there in the first place. She knew better, but her heart didn't start beating normally again until her fingers finally closed around the tiny square.

Beck got in on the other side and handed her his phone, which displayed the pizza menu. "We've got seven mouths to feed counting the guards so this seemed like the best option. Are you comfortable ordering for Ro and Jemma? I already know what Joe wants."

"*All* the pizzas," Claire said, dropping her voice a few octaves in a decent imitation of her brother.

"And heaven forbid you forget the garlic bread," Beck added.

He gave the car their destination while she added her choices to the order, including a small pizza with just pepperoni so that they didn't have to pick everything else off for Jemma. Once the order was placed and they were on the road, she pulled the nanodrive through the tiny hole in the scrunchie and showed it to Beck.

"I'm hoping your computer system back at the B and B can read this, because I'm fairly certain it's our Rosetta stone. Or as close to it as we're likely to get."

"Is this what you were searching for in New Haven?"

"Sort of. I was actually looking for the hard copy. Which the Flock now has. But I put several pieces of information together about halfway through my interview with the FBI agent. The drive was slipped into this"—she held up the scrunchie—"by Shepherd when I was on Mars. Which means I had it with me all along."

"Just like the ruby slippers."

Claire nodded, even though she wasn't entirely sure of the reference aside from the slippers being from *The Wizard of Oz*. She'd learned from past experience that trying to untangle Beckisms could pull a conversation pretty far off-track, and she had a lot more to tell him.

"Anyway, this is what they were trying to get rid of by burning down my house. They took out two more buildings and killed two other people down in Virginia trying to cover up whatever is on this drive. Which basically means that our best hope of translating that manuscript survived only because I never got around to completely emptying out my daypack after I got back from Mars. Score one for procrastination, I guess."

She put the drive back inside the hair band. It was an incongruous carrying case but made the tiny thing a lot easier to locate in her bag.

"What exactly do you think is on the drive?" Beck asked.

"An alien children's book. Along with the translation. Something called *Tales from the Aveezi Forest*. And maybe the notebook that Tobias Shepherd used when he was learning the language as a kid." She had to laugh at Beck's stunned expression. "I had the same reaction. It's so hard to picture Shepherd actually helping to advance knowledge when he's spent so much time trying to stifle it."

As the car carried them north toward Ogunquit, she brought him up to speed on everything. When she reached the end, Beck was quiet for so long that she almost felt like she was in the car with Joe. To be fair, though, it *was* a lot to take in. The idea of advanced life on Mars in the distant past was pretty easy to swallow compared to the idea that there might be actual aliens on the Earth right now, hiding in plain sight.

"How much of Shepherd's memoir have you been able to verify?" he asked.

"I haven't caught him in any lies so far, if that's what you're asking. The basic information about Nathaniel Everett checked out. And Shepherd did receive the house from someone on his eighteenth birthday. I haven't yet had the chance to track down whether it was actually Shepherd, but he was the legal owner of the property prior to his death about seven years earlier. And VersaBio did hire a synthetic biologist that year who died shortly after leaving the company. Obviously, none of that even comes close to proving Shepherd's claims about aliens planning to destroy the Earth. The easiest way to sell a lie, after all, is to wrap it in a few layers of truth. And some parts of it also sync up with the transcript of a speech that Corbin Drexel gave at one of the Flock compounds."

"Which parts?"

"The part where Shepherd worries that Everett was just softening the blow when he told him that these Sentinels were benevolent. That they would save the Flock from being destroyed with the rest of us, as long as they made a good faith effort to curb the damage to the planet. Drexel seems equally convinced that the Sentinel's intentions are not good."

"What's your assessment of the memoir? Do you think Shepherd fabricated all of this, or does he believe it's the truth?"

"He believes it's true. And based on the evidence he lays out, I can see why."

"You're not telling me *you* believe it?"

"I don't really know." Claire said, bristling slightly at the incredulity in his voice. "I keep going back and forth. At this moment, I guess you could put me down as a solid maybe."

"Okay. Fair enough, I guess. Do you think Wyatt would be okay with me reading the memoir?"

"Sure. I already told him I needed to pull you and Joe into the loop, and that I'd explain why when I see him in New York. He needs to know about *our* find, too, since it all seems to be connected. And yes, he'll keep it quiet until we're ready to go public."

"I'm not worried about that."

"Okay. Hand me your phone then, so that I can transfer the file directly. I know you said that communications are secure at Bellamy House, but I can't imagine why the Flock would have left the same bible verse in New Haven as the one the cicadabot was chirping outside my house unless they knew I was coming today. I strongly suspect it was intercepted on Shepherd's end by KTI, since they monitor pretty much everything going on and off Mars, but I didn't tell Shepherd when or even if I was going to New Haven. It's possible they were already tracking the bogus email address I used to schedule the showing with the realtor, though, since I most likely set it up using the system at the *Post*. But Alice pointed out that someone could also have a signal scoop locked onto your place, which she said can be a little tricky to detect."

"Okay." He handed her his phone. "The guards said they were going to do a sweep for surveillance devices as part of securing the property. Not sure if that's one of the things they know how to spot, but if not, I'll get Wilson to send up a specialist."

"Isn't my mother going to object to him pulling more security personnel away from the lab?"

"Are you kidding? Kai has been so nervous about spies lately that we've got more comsec people than actual scientists. What about Alice?"

Claire shook her head, not quite following him. "If you're thinking she might be the leak, there's no way. She didn't know I was going to Allen House until I met her at the café this morning."

"No. I was just wondering if she's still in. Finding a dead body stashed in a closet must have been more than a little unnerving.

That's not a typical day for anyone but I'd imagine it goes double for your average academic."

"I'm not sure I would call Alice your average academic," Claire said, thinking back to how quickly her pistol had appeared when Devin's body tumbled out of the closet. "The experience rattled her, but she seems very resilient. And she's absolutely still in. In fact, I think she would be pounding down my door—once I actually have a door again—if I tried to cut her out. And she doesn't even know that I have this." She nodded down at the scrunchie in her bag.

"Good. I'm glad it didn't scare her off. Because Joe is right about turning the larger translation project over to her. All I can do is dabble. She's the expert. But I'm still very curious about the bigger picture. How—or even *if*—Shepherd and this … Everett guy fit into it. It just feels staged to me. Even more so when you add in Drexel. Like you said, it's easy to use a few facts to cover up a lie. And Shepherd's been doing that sort of thing for decades now."

Claire nodded. There was no sense arguing the point, especially when she still had doubts herself. But she couldn't help wondering if Beck would be quite so certain that Shepherd was a fraud after he read the memoir.

EIGHT

THEY STOPPED in Ogunquit and picked up their leaning tower of pizzas, garlic knots, and the sad little salad that Claire added at the last second in case Ro wanted to try to get something green into the kiddo. The guy who helped Beck carry everything out to the car eyed the tiny trunk warily, but they managed to get it all back to the B and B in one trip.

To Claire's surprise, a rickety looking metal gate now extended from one stretch of white fence to the next, blocking the path that led down to the house. The Jonas Labs security vehicle she'd seen at the airport was parked on the other side.

"That was fast work," she said, nodding toward the gate. "I wouldn't have thought that was something you could buy so quickly in a town this size."

"It's not. They rented it from a homeowner a few miles down the road. He was reportedly more than happy to keep his two horses in the other pasture for a couple of weeks in exchange for five hundred bucks. And he'll probably get quite a few drinks off the story down at whichever bar he frequents, speculating on exactly what the city folks renting out Bellamy House are up to. When we called to get Finn's pizza prefs, he told Mike—that's the guard who just checked out this car—that the local cops have already stopped in to chat with him."

"What did he tell them?"

"Corporate retreat. The downside is that the locals are probably going to start driving by hoping to see a bunch of middle-aged executives running around on the lawn in haptic suits and firing holoweapons at each other."

Once the gate was open and their car was inside, Beck got out and found the sausage and mushroom pizza the guard had requested. Then they continued down the gravel path to the house where the garage door was open. The other car was already on the pad, so Joe had beaten them home. As they were unloading the pizza, in fact, she spotted her brother on one of the private balconies on the second floor. He was talking on the phone—or more accurately, listening to someone else talk. She couldn't hear from that distance, but judging from Joe's expression, she had absolutely no doubt that Kai was on the other end of the call.

As Beck handed her a stack of boxes, he followed her gaze up to the balcony and sighed. "Yeah, that's the third time she's called him today. She's left me several messages as well, which I have resolutely refused to answer since I am officially on vacation. That may mean I end up with a pink slip when I get back to the lab."

"Yeah, right," Claire scoffed. "Not unless she wants Joe to leave, too."

"She has a bit more leverage there than you might think. If forced to choose between saving my job and losing his research, I'm pretty sure I'd be out. With a very generous severance package, to be sure, but…"

"Nope. Not buying it."

They carried the food in, then Beck went out to deliver one of the pizzas to the other guard. She heard Ro and Jemma upstairs and was about to join them, but Joe came around the corner.

"You okay?" he asked.

She gave him a weary smile and a hug. "I will admit that I've had better days."

"What the hell has Wyatt gotten you into, ClaireBear?"

"*Wyatt* hasn't gotten me into anything." She turned around and began getting plates out of the cabinet, hoping to conceal the fact that what she'd just told him was only a partial truth. Wyatt *was* the one who had given her Shepherd's memoir, after all, and he *had* asked her to help verify its authenticity. But Joe had his protective big brother face on. He'd met Wyatt a few times and they got along very well. Claire didn't want to say anything that might change that, especially when Wyatt had been doing his best to keep her at a distance from anything that smacked of danger.

"In fact," Claire added, "this is more a case of *me* getting Wyatt into trouble than the other way around. The Flock, despite their current crime spree, still has a low death count compared to the groups he usually investigates. I doubt he'd have gotten involved in the investigation at all if not for the fact that they nearly killed me on Mars."

"Yeah, but what were you doing down in New Haven today? A favor for him, right?"

"Not exactly. I was picking up our Rosetta stone. Or, at least, I hope so."

"But Beck said you told him the same message was on the wall of that house as…" He trailed off at the sound of footsteps, light and rapid, coming down the stairs. "Guess we'll have to finish this discussion after dinner."

A few seconds later, a whirlwind of dark curls came barreling into the kitchen. "Claire!"

"What?" Claire said in mock outrage. "No one told me that they allow cheeky monkeys in this place!"

"I'm not a cheeky monkey!"

Claire scooped her up for a tickle hug. "Did you have a good flight from Vancouver?"

"Yes. Did you know we had the whole plane all to ourselves?"

"Really? So…did your mommy fly it, or did you?"

"I *meant* except for the captain and the other worker. They even said I could walk around the plane when the air outside wasn't too bumpy." She looked out of the corner of her eye at Joe, who was piling slices of pizza from various boxes onto his plate, and then dropped her voice to a stage whisper. "I asked him about it, and he said he really *is* a giant. Only he *doesn't* eat kids. He's like the nice giant in that *BFG* book that we read."

"That's true," Claire said. "Joe stopped eating kids nearly a year ago. Except occasionally for breakfast. But you'll be fine as long as we have enough pizza. Probably."

Jemma rolled her eyes to indicate that she knew Claire was teasing her. *"He doesn't eat kids.* He said he never, ever ate kids."

"Never, ever," Joe agreed. "They give me heartburn. I prefer pizza."

"And how, pray tell, would you know that kids give you heartburn if you *never, ever*?" Claire asked.

He grinned. "Same way I knew your appendix would have to come out in college. *In silico* trials. Chalk it up as one of the many miracles of modern science."

Jemma was on tiptoe peeking into the pizza boxes on the counter. "Did you get one with only pepperonis? And is there really a beach near here? And will you go in the pool with me after dinner?"

"Yes to pepperoni, assuming that the Big Friendly Giant doesn't eat it all. Yes, the beach is only about a mile away. But you'll have to ask your mom about the after dinner swim. I have to do a bit of work tonight," she said, thinking about the data drive waiting in her bag. "But I'm sure I can carve out some time for the pool if she says yes."

Claire found the plates in the cabinet and had just seated Jemma at the table with a slice of pepperoni-only, a garlic knot, and some salad that would almost certainly go uneaten, when Ro joined them in the kitchen. Claire was fairly certain that she hadn't told Jemma about the fire yet, so she just gave her a weak smile.

Ro came around the kitchen island and squeezed her arm. "They're just *things,*" she said, echoing her earlier words. She was clearly playing nonchalant because she knew Claire felt awful about the situation and she didn't want to make it worse. "No point in thinking about any of it until we can actually do something about it. I'm just going to relax and enjoy my vacation."

"Are you sure you're okay with just you and Jemma hanging

out here on Tuesday and Wednesday? The guards will still be around, but I feel kind of bad leaving you alone."

"Being alone *here* is worlds better than being at my mom's house. And we'd have been alone at a hotel. Or at…" She winced, and Claire knew she'd been about to say *home*.

"Things, things, *things*," Ro repeated softly. "And things can be replaced."

"Yeah, but they're *your* things. And you hate to shop as much as I do."

"Will you feel better if I say you can hire a shopper for me?"

"Maybe a little."

"Then do it. And look at the bright side. We won't have to clean out the storage room now."

"Or the pantry," Claire said, deciding to just go with the bright-side flow and not mention that even *with* hired help it was going to be a lot more effort to sift through the wreckage and replace an entire household of goods than it would have been to clean out a few long-deferred closets.

They had both grabbed food and were just sitting down at the table with Jemma and Joe when Beck returned from outside. The other guard was behind him, and the two of them went into a room just off the living area. A few minutes later, Beck joined them in the kitchen. Claire introduced him to Rowan and Jemma, and Ro thanked him for offering to take them in for a few days.

"More than happy to help." Beck grabbed a plate and started toward the pizzas, but then he put it back down on the counter and shook his head. "At the risk of being an awful host, I think I need to pass on dinner in favor of a big glass of water and some painkillers. I don't know if it's just too much sun or if I'm coming down with something, but my head is pounding."

They all assured him that it was no problem. He did look pale, especially in contrast to the red patch on his cheek.

"Finn, the guard I just took back to the office, has comsec experience, so I've asked him to run a full diagnostic on the system, including the scramblers. It shouldn't take long, but…" Beck gave

Claire an apologetic look. "Do you mind if we wait and check out that drive in the morning?"

"Oh. Oh, sure. That'll be fine. I'm probably going to turn in early, too. *After* the pool," she added quickly to forestall any protest from Jemma. "Get some rest, okay?"

Once Beck was upstairs and the door closed behind him, Joe snickered and said, "*Oh, sure. That'll be fine.* Good thing Beck can't spot your lies as easily as I can."

"No kidding," Ro said. "It was like all of the air drained out of you."

"It *is* fine. He's not feeling well."

"What's on the drive?" Ro asked.

"That's kind of the problem. I know what I *hope* is on it, but I'm probably going to have a hard time sleeping until I know for sure. It's a long, very complicated story and I need to explain most of it to Joe, too, so maybe after the pool and after..." She tilted her head slightly toward Jemma, who was in the process of moving her salad from her own plate to her mother's one leaf at a time.

While she hadn't specifically cleared telling Ro with Wyatt, he'd said to use her discretion. And given the current security threat and the fact that everything Ro and Jemma owned had just gone up in flames, Claire felt it was only fair to at least tell her why.

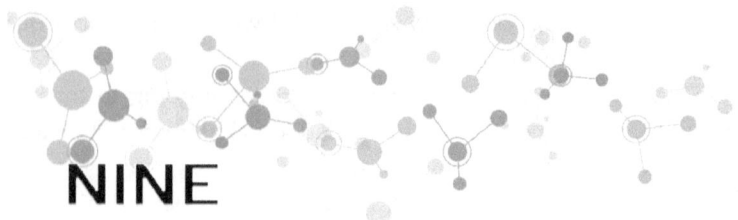

NINE

AFTER DINNER and the better part of an hour in the pool, Ro handled story time and tucked Jemma into bed while Claire and Joe put away the remaining pizza.

The guard stuck his head into the kitchen as they were finishing up to say that the system checked out, including the audio scramblers. "I cranked those up a bit, since Mr. Beckett said you were worried that someone might be using a signal scoop on this location, but otherwise, I think we're in good shape."

They thanked the guard and then headed back out to the patio. Once Ro joined them, Claire spent the next half hour bringing them both up to speed. When she finished, she couldn't decide which of the two looked more skeptical.

While Joe had seemed relaxed enough around Jemma, he'd barely said two words over dinner, so Claire was a little surprised that he was the one who spoke first. "So ... you think Shepherd actually *believes* this Everett guy was an alien?"

"And not just an alien," Ro added. "An *immortal* alien, which really takes it to the next level."

Joe and Claire exchanged a look, which Ro—being unaware of his stretch goals for Rejuvesce— completely misinterpreted.

"Okay," she said. "You're right. He wasn't *immortal*, since Shepherd admits the man killed himself. But *biologically immortal* is pretty darn close. The alien part, though ... that isn't exactly untrodden turf for cults. Aliens and motherships are pretty standard cult material, after all. Heaven's Gate, Scientology..."

"That group down in Florida in the 2030s," Joe said.

"And the Cochranites in Montana back in 2063," Ro added, "although I think that one may have been more cosplay than an actual cult. And I'm sure there are others. My point is that a lot of cults make extraterrestrial claims of some sort. Shepherd himself has been talking about these Sentinels for years. I wouldn't have assumed he *believed* it—it seemed like just another way of milking his followers for more cash— but I'm still not clear why the Flock would burn down our freaking house in an attempt to keep Shepherd's memoir a secret."

"They didn't," Joe said. "The point is that they did all of this to hide whatever is in the *other* manuscript. Or rather, to prevent it from being translated."

Ro frowned. "You mean the one hidden in the DNA sample? But, then ... same question. Why are they so determined to hide it?"

"We think it's a warning of some sort," Claire said.

"Or, to be more specific, *Claire and Beck* think it's a warning. Which is why they've both been kind of obsessed about translating it. Personally, I lean toward all of this being a massive hoax perpetrated by Shepherd."

Joe elaborated on this theory for a bit, saying that Shepherd must have gotten hold of the symbols inside the chamber from the video that Brodnik's team brought back from the first trip. Or maybe he'd bought the information from someone at KTI. Shepherd then created a language based on the symbols, and translated the folktales, which he had probably written years earlier, into the Martian script because he was looking for a gimmick to sell copies of his memoir.

"But that doesn't really explain how a manuscript in something very close to this language got into the *Deinococcus* sample," Claire said. "I *might* be able to buy your idea that Shepherd had someone plant the substance that I collected from inside the second chamber, if not for the fact that we also found the *same* manuscript inserted into samples that were collected from the surface. One of those samples was from several years earlier, long before anyone had even seen the symbols carved into those chambers."

"Unless…"

"Unless what, Joe? Unless the chambers were also fake? That would make all of this a vast conspiracy between Kolya, the mining companies, Tobias Shepherd, and the Flock. And we're talking about the *new* version of the group, because we have pictures of Stasia and her two assistants with Corbin Drexel. That would mean that Shepherd is working on this huge plot you're describing in partnership with the woman who ordered the drone attack that very nearly killed him onboard the *Ares Prime*. How does that make sense?"

Joe raised his hands in submission. "Okay. You have valid points. I'm not saying you shouldn't investigate it, but I'm sticking with my theory until we have more evidence. And on that note…" Joe pushed himself up from the patio chair. "What size is this drive?"

Claire shrugged and held up the tip of her pinky. "*This* size?"

"Oh, *that's* really helpful." Joe laughed, shaking his head. "Go get it. I probably have an adapter in my bag. If not, I'll break into Beck's room and get his. And yes, he's going to feel like we opened Christmas presents without him, but he'll survive."

"If it helps, you can tell him he wasn't the only one who missed the party," Ro said. "I'm going to check on Jemma and grab a shower."

Ten minutes later, Joe and Claire were back in the living room looking at the file directory on the wall screen. The files were numbered rather than named, but a few clicks revealed them to be exactly what Claire had hoped to find in physical form up in the nook at Allen House—*Tales from the Aveezi Forest* in the original script with illustrations, Everett's translation of the tales, and a surprisingly large cache of notes. A few hundred pages of notes in all, some in neat, narrow handwriting, a smaller number in a rather immature scrawl, and still others printed in a mixture of English and the same typeface as the original book.

Joe transferred the files to her device, then entered Beck's password—which he knew *because of course he did*—and sent her copies of the documents Beck shared with them the night before, including the alphabet and his own notes about the translation.

"I can't seem to transfer the program he used," Joe said. "Must have a lock on it."

"That's okay. I'll get it from him before I leave for New York."

He huffed. "Are you *sure* New York is a good idea?"

"Wyatt asked me pretty much the exact same thing. Did you guys plan this out in advance?"

"No. I suspect it comes with the territory when someone you care about seems to have a target on her back."

"Okay," she said, feeling bad now for having been so glib. "Fair enough. But no more complaining about Wyatt getting me into this mess. He didn't. And it's more the people *around* me who have targets on their back. I'm like a modern version of Typhoid Mary."

"It could also be that you've just been lucky, and they keep missing you. That was *your* house after all."

"Could be," she admitted. "But they knew I wasn't there. And whether going to New York is a *good* idea or not, it's a necessary one. Anton Kolya will be at the conference, and … he has to know more about all of this than he's letting on."

"You think he's behind the attacks?"

She considered it for a moment. "No. But he was married to Drexel for several years. He has to have some idea as to what is motivating her."

"Maybe. But personally, I wouldn't count on it. One of the reasons I wasn't interested in Jenelle was that she didn't seem … real … to me. Everything felt like an act. Maybe I'm wrong. I didn't spend that much time with her, and I doubt she'd have been able to sustain an act day in and day out with Kolya since she was with him for several years. But Claire … we've already *got* a security team investigating her."

She frowned. "You mean Jonas Labs?"

"Yes. Although it was Beck who actually got the ball rolling. He was planning to hire a private investigator on his own to pinpoint Drexel's location as soon as we saw her picture in the *Post.* I talked him into going through the company instead, mostly to keep it from being a distraction. He told me out on the boat today that he doesn't think we're putting enough resources into it. And he may be right. Mom still doesn't see the group as a major threat. She says they're just a *rogue element,* whatever the hell that means, but since Wilson came on board it's getting more attention. You know how he feels about the Flock. And these are *professional* investigators. They can probably find out more than you'd be able to by questioning Kolya." He waited for Claire to respond, then gave a rueful laugh. "But you're still going, aren't you?"

She nodded.

"Okay, then. Can I make a deal with you?"

"Maybe…"

"Travel down on Monday with Beck. I'll get one of the lab's copters to take both of you into the city. Stay at the apartment, not at a hotel."

"Um … *no.* Wyatt is meeting me there."

"So? He can stay, too."

Claire shuddered. "She could have cameras in the place."

"You have to be kidding me. Mom loans that apartment out to investors who are visiting New York. Do you think she'd risk any of them running a scan and finding recording equipment? Anyway, stay at the apartment. Go out only when you have to. And when you *do* go out, use the car we keep there."

"You've cleared this with Kai?"

"No. But I will. It's as much my place as it is hers. I'll make sure she doesn't go anywhere near it for the next few days. I'm *not* asking you to avoid risk entirely. I'm just trying to get you to minimize it. Can you at least do that much for me?"

"Okay. Deal."

He grinned. "Wow. You're losing your touch. You didn't even ask what *my* side of the deal is."

"I thought arranging the travel and clearing everything with Kai *was* your side of the deal."

"Nope. You and Beck want me to take more time off. And it *does* seem kind of rude to leave Rowan and Jemma alone with just the guards. So I'll take Tuesday and Wednesday off, too, and stay here until you get back. Maybe this will convince Beck that I *do* understand the moral tradeoffs of my research. I *know* what children are. I actually like them. And, no, not for breakfast. Because I have absolutely no doubt that's why he extended the invitation to Ro when he learned about the fire."

Claire decided not to mention that Beck had invited them even *before* he learned about the fire. "Okay. Then we definitely have a deal."

"Could you keep this between us for now, though? I'm not in the mood for his gloating and … I'm thinking maybe Beck actually *needs* the time off. I don't want him to feel like he has to come back to the lab until he's ready. Like I said before, I know I've been an ass about this and … well, I suspect it's about to be a moot point anyway."

"How so?"

He waved a hand. "Nothing. Just mama-drama."

She laughed. The phrase was Wilson's, whispered on many occasions when she was a kid. *Might want to make yourself scarce unless you're in the mood for mama-drama.*

"I don't suppose there's any chance I could add just one more condition?" Joe asked.

"No, you may not," she said, rolling her eyes at the classic Joe maneuver. "I just said we have a deal. That means the negotiations are over."

"I know, I know. It's just … I'd feel a lot better about this trip if you took a weapon. I'm sure the guards have something that—"

"No thanks. I've spent enough time in police stations lately."

"Oh, give me a break. You haven't been charged with anything. You're certified to carry. And you're fully insured. All you'd have to do is enter your info into the system and get clearance."

He was right. She'd had a handgun certification since just after her eighteenth birthday. Kai had initially insisted that she have a full-time bodyguard when she went off to college, stating that she would be too tempting as a kidnapping target, otherwise. Claire had told her that wasn't happening, and the gun had been the eventual compromise. Owning it meant that she had to live off-campus, but the whole dorm experience hadn't sounded all that appealing to her anyway. Wilson had trained her, and she was a decent shot. Her certification had lapsed at one point, but after the whole Southern Sons scare at the *Post*, Wyatt had convinced her to get it reinstated. She hated carrying the gun, though, and once Jemma was in the house it had gone into a lockbox on the top shelf of her closet. Now it was just one more thing destroyed by the fire.

"I'm serious, Claire. I can't see any reason that taking a gun would be a problem."

"Maybe not. But it won't *solve* any problems, either. I won't be able to take it into the UN, or wherever I end up meeting with Kolya. And I've already promised you that I won't go anywhere else. It's just another thing to worry about, and you know I don't like carrying a gun. So, no. We stick to the original deal. Do you want me to transfer these files to your device or should we look at them here?"

He sighed. "Neither. I'll leave all of that to you and Beck. As for me, I'm going to grab some cold pizza and then go to bed. You can stay up and play amateur detective to your heart's content."

Claire said good night, even though she chafed a bit at his indulgent, slightly condescending tone. And as she watched her brother head off toward the kitchen, Alice Dobroski's comment about Leffler popped into her head. *I hope I never reach a point in my life where my curiosity dies.*

That wasn't fair, of course. Joe's curiosity was alive and well. It was just laser-focused on a single goal. He'd always been that way. And once he achieved that goal, he moved to the next, even bigger challenge.

But that was going to become a problem fairly soon. What goal could possibly be a challenge after you tackled death itself?

FROM TALES FROM THE AVEEZI FOREST

TRANSLATION BY NATHANIEL EVERETT

THE STARSPRITE

AS EVEN THE smallest child knows, the Aveezi Forest is a place that you should never, ever go. Dark and wild, the forest teems with creatures that snap and snarl. They will happily gobble up any child so foolish as to enter.

But even in the Aveezi Forest, light and dark must find a balance. Deep, deep inside the forest—where, I must again caution, you should never, ever go—there is a wide glade called Alestria, where gloom and danger may not tread. Here, the trees hang lush with ripe babda and usimi fruits, the waters flow sweet and cool, and the wind hums a soothing song. Here, the suns shine brightly in the daytime, the sky shimmers emerald and violet as they set, and the creatures live (mostly) in harmony.

It is here in lovely Alestria, on a bright sunny morning, that we find Motz and Tibbo—the very best of best friends—out in search of the wessleberries that grow for only a short time each season near the swampy edges of the glade. Wessleberries are delicious, but they grow far too close to the forest for Tibbo's liking. Motz had, as usual, lumbered in farther than she should, seeking the fattest, reddest wessleberries, and her dark blue fur was now speckled with mud.

"You should come back now, Motz," said Tibbo, who was quite small and whose tummy was now rather full.

"I'm coming," said Motz, who was quite large and whose tummy was still rather rumbly. "Just a few more."

Tibbo said nothing, just paced nervously at the edge of the swamp. Even on his hungriest day, the reddest, plumpest berry would not have tempted Tibbo to venture that close to the forest. Vurgas sometimes built their webs in the woods near the wessleberry bog, and then watched and waited in the taller trees nearby. They hated the sunlight, preferring to hunt at night, but they'd been known to snatch an unwary creature who wandered into the shadowy regions near the forest. Vurgas wouldn't risk tangling with Motz, who could swat the nasty things out of the air with her giant paws, but tiny Tibbo was an entirely different matter. It was all too easy to imagine one of the monsters risking a bit of a scorching to soar out of the mossy treetops and snatch him up as a tasty snack.

"Aren't you getting sleepy, Motz? The grass is nice and warm, and perfect for a nap." Tibbo knew his friend well. Eating was her very favorite thing, but sleep was a close second. And sleep followed eating as surely as night followed day.

As much as he might have liked to leave the bog right this minute, Motz would need her nap first. Tibbo spent a rather large part of his day staring up at the sky or bouncing pebbles into the stream as he waited for his slumbering friend to wake up. He didn't mind really. In fact, he did his best thinking to the sound of Motz's gentle snore.

"Just a few more," she said. "And I promised to pick a few extra to take back to Ossa."

They had invited Ossa to come along, but he had laughed and said that mucking about in the bog was a pastime far better suited to younglings. "Just bring me a berry or two, if there are any left.

Don't forget to be back in time for chores, stay well away from the shadows, and never, ever go into the forest."

If Motz did bring back extras for Ossa, Tibbo resolved to hide them away. Otherwise, Motz would be likely to absentmindedly pop them into her mouth on the walk back to the village, and then she'd be sad that she hadn't been able to keep her promise.

Finally, Motz patted her belly contentedly and began making her way back toward drier ground, grabbing a berry here and there that she had missed, and singing a drowsy, rather tuneless song about wessleberry jam. Tibbo thought the song must be from the long ago, because there were never enough wessleberries to make jam. Not if Motz got to the bog first, and Motz *always* got to the bog first.

Tibbo began to relax as he watched his friend's progress, enjoying the warmth of the suns on his small orange face, the vurga all but forgotten. But then he saw something beyond Motz, right at the edge of the woods. Not a vurga, but a pulsing light, suspended in midair between the trees. He thought he heard something, too—a faint, plaintive hum—but it was hard to be sure over Motz's singing.

It couldn't be what Tibbo thought it was. Everyone had heard stories about the tiny, delicate creatures, but starsprites weren't real. Or if they *were* real, then they must be—like the song about wessleberry jam—from the long, long ago.

Tibbo was so focused on the flickering light that he barely noticed when Motz sat down next to him.

"What are you looking at, Tibbo?"

He pointed one claw toward the glow shining out of the shadows. "I am looking at *that*. It looks quite a bit like a starsprite to me. And I think it's caught in a vurga web."

Motz bent down closer to her friend's level and squinted. "It does look like a starsprite. It even sounds like a starsprite. But starsprites aren't real. They're just in stories and pictures. Make-believe."

"Perhaps. But I see it. And I hear it. You also see and hear it.

And if it *is* a starsprite, it's in danger. It's smaller even than I am. The vurga will gobble it up. We have to help!"

Motz shrugged and yawned, placing the three fat wessleberries she'd picked for Ossa on the grass next to her. "If the vurga doesn't eat it today, it will die tomorrow anyway. Don't you remember the poem? *If you see a starsprite, full of light and song, stop to watch and listen for they don't last long.*"

"That's no reason not to help!" Tibbo insisted, thinking that Motz had entirely missed the point of the poem.

But Motz's belly was full, and her eyelids were heavy. She yawned again and rolled over on the warm grass for a nap.

Tibbo moved the wessleberries to a safer spot where they wouldn't be crushed if Motz rolled in her sleep. As he sat back on the grass next to her, he found himself rather angry with his friend, even though Motz couldn't entirely help her nature. Eat, sleep, play. Eat, sleep, play. Maybe a bit of time for lessons in between. So it had always been and so it would likely be when they were as old as Ossa.

"Fine, then," he said. "I will go myself."

"No, you won't," Motz mumbled sleepily. "The forest is much too dangerous for you, Tibbo, and you are much too scared. If the light is still there when I wake up, I'll go and check. But it's probably just the sunlight ... reflecting back ... from the bog."

Soon, Motz was snoring. The sound almost, but not quite, drowned out the sad song of what Tibbo was now certain was a starsprite. Reflections, after all, do not hum.

Tibbo paced around for several minutes, trying to figure out the best way to rescue the creature. The quickest route was straight across the bog. From there, it would be just a few paces into the woods. Only that wasn't an option. Motz could make it and never have the swampy water go above her waist, but it was far too deep for Tibbo. He would have to go around the edge of the bog, walking a hundred paces or more in the shadow of the forest.

And what would he do when he reached the sprite? It was

barely above Motz's head. She could raise one paw and easily untangle its wings from the web. Tiny Tibbo would have no choice but to climb the tree to reach it. But his claws were strong enough for climbing, and his teeth, though small, were sharp enough to chew through the strands of the web.

So Tibbo headed off to rescue the starsprite, staying so close to the bog that he stumbled in on several occasions, once falling flat on his bottom in the mud. Slowly, Motz's snores grew fainter in the distance, and the gentle hum of the sprite grew louder. And yes, the forest was very dark, but not as dark as he had feared, with the glow of the starsprite as a beacon.

"I'm coming," he whispered, even though he was fairly certain that the sprite could neither hear nor understand him. But the light pulsed twice at his words, before continuing the steady glow, so perhaps he was wrong about that.

And he was very close now. Almost there.

Tibbo looked out over the bog. He was directly across from Motz, and for the first time, it occurred to him that while he had almost reached the starsprite, he wasn't even halfway done with his ordeal. He still had to climb the tree and free the sprite from the web. Assuming that the vurga didn't return and make a meal of them both. The starsprite had wings, so she could simply fly away. But Tibbo would then have to climb back down the tree, walk back toward the bog, and make his way slowly around to the other side.

Still, he had come this far. He certainly wasn't going to turn back now.

Tibbo turned to walk into the wood toward the starsprite, hardly daring to breathe. When he found the tree that held up one side of the vurga's black web, he began to climb. Drawing ever closer, he could now see the creature itself, instead of just that light that surrounded it. The luminous being at the center had four delicate, iridescent wings and eyes as bright as the suns. As small as Tibbo was, the starsprite could fit inside his palm.

Tibbo was amazed that something so tiny could emit so much light and sound. Even if the vurga was waiting nearby, it probably didn't consider the sprite worth the effort of flying over to check the … trap.

That thought sent a tiny shiver through Tibbo. Had the vurga ignored the starsprite, hoping that the light and the music might draw in a bigger, better meal?

Suddenly, that seemed like a very real possibility. The wisest move would be to back down the tree as quietly as he could and wait for Motz to wake up.

The music grew louder and more plaintive, again almost as if the sprite had read his mind.

And Tibbo knew that he couldn't go back now and leave this tiny marvel to its fate. So, he dug his claws into the tree and began, slowly and carefully, to gnaw at one of the silken threads.

Several minutes later, two threads hung loose. The sprite was now able to free its arm, and it began to pull at the other threads. Tibbo was surprised at its strength. Between the two of them, the creature's right wings were soon free, then its left wings, and finally it burst from the web. Its hum was joyous now, and it hovered next to Tibbo for a moment, its tiny wings a kaleidoscope of color as they fluttered in the light.

Tibbo and the starsprite heard the screech of the vurga at the same instant. Both of their heads jerked toward the noise and Tibbo braced for the talons that would surely snatch him from the tree.

Motz heard the vurga, too. Or maybe she heard Tibbo's cry for help. Either way, his lumbering friend was on her feet in an instant, flying across the bog.

Tibbo could already feel the wind from the vurga's wings, though. Motz would be too late to save him from certain death.

But then, the corona of light around the starsprite surged outward, brighter than anything Tibbo had ever seen. He squeezed his eyes tight and pressed his face into the rough bark of the tree, so he did not see the vurga swerve away from the light. The monster came close enough that he smelled its fetid stench, close enough that he felt the edge of one leathery wing against his neck, but the vurga's talons missed him.

Motz roared into the forest, yelling Tibbo's name. Soon, he was safely clutching the familiar blue fur of his friend's back as she stumbled back toward the safe side of the bog, barely able to see anything after the blinding light.

"Where is the starsprite?" he asked, once they were both on the warm grassy bank. "Did it get out of the woods safely?"

"It flew away!" Motz said. "You could have been vurga food, and all to save a tiny blip of nothing that very nearly blinded me when I came to rescue you. Why didn't you listen to me?"

"Because it was in danger," Tibbo said. "I couldn't do nothing."

Motz huffed in exasperation and flopped back onto the grass.

"Thank you for coming to get me," Tibbo said. "But ... you'd never have made it in time if the starsprite hadn't stunned the vurga with its light. I had already freed it from the web. It could simply have flown away right that minute, but it stayed behind to help."

Motz could be grumpy, but she was also honest. "That's true, Tibbo. But doesn't it also mean that the starsprite could have saved itself?"

"Maybe. But it couldn't have *freed* itself. It would have spent the rest of its life trapped in that web."

"A nasty couple of hours, true," Motz said. "But you should never, ever have gone into the forest. What if—"

"Shh," Tibbo said. And for once, Motz didn't argue. She just cocked her head to the side and in that moment of quiet, he picked up a faint melodic hum.

Tibbo followed the sound, and Motz followed Tibbo. His eyes were beginning to clear now, and he could make out a timid, flickering glow near the bush where he'd hidden the last of the wessleberries.

"See," Motz said. "What did I tell you? It's dying already."

"You don't *know* that," Tibbo protested. "It could just be tired. Or sick. We should take it to Ossa. He'll know what to do."

Motz sighed heavily and plucked a large leaf from a nearby usimi tree. Tibbo carefully nudged the tiny creature onto the leaf. Motz spotted the extra berries she'd picked, and very nearly popped them into her mouth until Tibbo reminded her that they were for Ossa. And so they headed back to the village, Motz carrying the berries and Tibbo carrying the tiny starsprite on its bright green bed.

By the time they reached Ossa's house, the sprite's glow was almost entirely gone. Tears shone in Tibbo's eyes as he held the leaf and its contents out for their teacher to inspect.

"Fascinating. No one has even *claimed* to see a starsprite since I was little more than a youngling myself." Ossa, who was nearly as tall as Motz, arched his long brown neck forward, peering down in amazement. "Although my own teacher often said that if you ever *were* to see one, it would likely be near the bog at the peak of wessleberry season."

"They eat wessleberries?" Motz asked, reluctantly handing two rather mushed berries over to Ossa. Tibbo was quite sure there had been three berries when they left the bog, which meant his friend had shown far more restraint than usual.

"No, no. The berries are far too large. But according to the legends…" Ossa chuckled softly, then popped one of the berries into his mouth. "Which I can no longer call mere legends, apparently. According to my teacher, starsprites like to collect the morning dew as it drips from the berries. Where did you find the creature?"

Tibbo told Ossa the story. "And now," he said when he reached the end, "its light is all but gone. Can you do anything to help it?"

Ossa shook his head sadly. "I'm afraid all that we can do is to make it—although I believe it would be more correct to say *her*—comfortable."

"That's what I told him," Motz said. "He risked his life for something that was going to die only a few hours later."

"Oh, no," Ossa said. "Given her size, I'd say that this is a rather young starsprite. She probably had a few *days* left, which is most of her lifetime. But they usually only glow softly while at rest, and you rarely hear their song. Light and song take energy, and they have a limited supply. She expended some of that energy calling for someone to free her from the web, and … far more of it, based on what you have told me, warding off the vurga."

As their teacher spoke, he dipped the last wessleberry into a glass of water. Then, he held the fruit near the sprite's mouth, but she was too weak to take the nourishment.

They stood around the leaf and watched as the starsprite's aura slowly faded. When it was all but gone, she gave one last shuddering breath and then vanished in a prism of light, leaving only the leaf behind.

Tibbo began to cry in earnest now. "She gave up the rest of her life to save me."

"Just as you risked the rest of your life to save *her*," Ossa said.

"And it was even more of a risk in Tibbo's case," Motz said. "Not just a few short days, but a long, long life. He should never, ever have gone into the forest."

"You're wrong," Tibbo said in a small but defiant voice. "A starsprite's life may be shorter, but *all* is *all*. She risked *all* that she had left."

Ossa was quiet for a moment, but then he shook his head. "Motz is right, Tibbo. You meant well, but you risked your life and Motz's safety for a tiny blip of light. And you broke the most important rule. I'm afraid you'll have to do extra chores this afternoon. And you should apologize to Motz. She was forced to break the rule as well by your own careless actions."

Tibbo hung his tiny head in shame. "Yes, Ossa. And I'm sorry, Motz."

"It's okay, Tib." Motz shrugged her big blue shoulders. "Everyone makes mistakes. You just need to be more careful."

So, Tibbo headed out to start his chores. He was still sad about the starsprite, but Ossa was right. He'd broken the most important rule.

From that day forward, Tibbo was very careful. He didn't go chasing starsprites and he never, ever again went into the Aveezi Forest.

TEN

RO PUSHED the door open and plopped down on the foot of the bed where Claire was reading. "Okay. I'm done. With the first one, that is, although I think it will also be the last one. That's a seriously messed up ending. And the big blue … gorilla thing. Why do they let her off the hook?"

"You mean Motz?" Claire asked. She'd been thinking of the character as more like a bear, although the illustrations left the question very much open to interpretation.

"Yes. Motz. She could have taken on that vampire bat, or flying spider, or whatever a vurga is supposed to be, with pretty much no risk from the sound of it. There was no reason she couldn't have gone in with Tibbo—I have no idea what kind of creature *he's* supposed to be—but anyway, Motz could have taken him into the forest and let him save Tinkerbell before taking her nap. And that *ending*. The teacher-creature comes *so* close to saying that every life is important, that the sprite's life was worth saving, but then he does almost a complete one-eighty and just says they should never go into the woods. Without even mentioning that Motz being a lazy blue coward was really what nearly got them killed and what forced Tinkerbell to sacrifice herself. No way would I read this thing to Jemma." She frowned, seeing that Claire was still looking down at her screen. "Are you actually reading the next one?"

"No," Claire said, even though she knew she'd probably read them eventually. "I'm just comparing the translation to the original. You're right about the ending, though. It almost feels like someone didn't like the way that the story wrapped up and decided to tack on an entirely different lesson at the last minute."

"Or maybe this Everett guy is just one of those writers who can't stick the landing."

"Maybe."

The Martian symbols from Shepherd's book weren't identical to the ones from the chamber and the DNA manuscript. Many of the characters were more rounded and there were even a few symbols in *Tales from the Aveezi Forest* that weren't in the alphabet that Beck had pieced together. While it went beyond the minor differences that you find between typefaces or between serif and sans-serif fonts, they were clearly the same language or at least in the same language family.

"Here's what I was checking," she said, sliding over toward Ro. "See this cluster? The two symbols together here … and here. They pop up regularly in the same order. The program Beck was using is reasonably confident that it's their version of the word *the*. Or some sort of definite article."

Ro was quiet for a moment, staring down at the symbols on the screen. Then she shook her head slowly. "The rational side of my brain very much prefers Joe's theory. It wouldn't be the first time a writer made up a language. That *Lord of the Rings* guy made up a bunch of them. And you used to be able to take college courses in Klingon. But … I'm getting the sense that you actually believe it. You think this is a book of *alien* folktales. That really seems *more* rational to you?"

"At this point? Yes. I actually think it's more likely that Shepherd is telling the truth than it is that hundreds of people with very different interests—*opposing* interests, in some cases—are all working together to keep this a secret. When has that ever happened?"

"Area 51. The Kennedy assassination. QAnon. Fendergate."

Claire arched an eyebrow at her. "None of which you believe. Are you having fun yanking my chain?"

Ro grinned. "A little. What does Wyatt think?"

"Don't really know, since he only has part of the information right now. He's supposed to call in about thirty minutes. I'll bring him up to speed as much as I can and then show him the rest when I see him in New York. But … he doesn't believe in conspiracy theories any more than you do. He once said that if large groups of people were *that* good at keeping secrets, he'd never have published a single article. Leaks are his bread and butter."

"True. And … I only said that the rational side of my brain *prefers* Joe's theory. Which it does. The weird ending of that story, on the other hand? That doesn't feel entirely human to me."

Claire thought back to the message Tobias Shepherd had sent to her. Something about how folktales were the ties that bound cultures together. Even though the words had almost certainly been chosen merely to remind her of the hair tie he'd handed back to her at Ehden, they were also true. Similar threads run through most folktales, but each culture and even each generation finds a way to put their own spin on the story, weaving the same threads into very different tapestries.

She had taken a course in her first semester at Stanford that examined the differences in a few classic fairy tales between countries and even between generations. *The Little Mermaid* had been one of the starkest examples. In all versions, the mermaid falls in love with the young man whose life she saved, and then searches for a way for them to be together. The version that she and Ro had grown up with, the one that Jemma had watched a few months back, ended with the two of them creating a fabulously successful community under the sea where humans and merpeople coexist and learn from each other. In the original, though, the sacrifice was entirely on the poor mermaid, with a harsh penalty for her decision to leave her ocean home—every step she took on land would feel like walking on knives. Claire suspected there would be a Martian version of the story a few decades out, with one member of the star-crossed couple born on Mars and unable to survive in Earth's higher gravity.

"Stories like this are … malleable," Claire said. "And while the ending doesn't feel *humane* to me, it does feel human, in a sense. I told you about that course on fairy tales, right?"

"You mean the one that you took specifically to piss off your mom?"

It was true. The class had fulfilled a general education requirement on comparative cultures, but if she was being honest, she'd mostly picked it knowing that it would totally exasperate Kai when she inevitably asked Claire how her semester was going over Christmas dinner.

"Yes. It was actually a good class, though. One of the things we did was try to imagine how the stories could be used to support different social structures and ideals. Cinderella, for example. She has a lousy family, a menial job, but she does her work happily and is kind and grateful even to those who exploit her. And it's because of those attributes that the fates intervene to lift her out of her misery."

"Her beauty, too," Ro says. "Can't forget that part. So Cinderella is a story to support a society that wants women to be beautiful, domestic doormats?"

"Pretty much. And this starsprite story … maybe it was written for children in a society with a rigid social structure. The lesson seems to be that it's good and noble for the lower class to risk their lives to save the upper class, but not the reverse."

"Which is why Tibbo is scolded for going into the forest and Motz is vindicated for being a lazy coward. So … you're planning to hand all of this over to the other linguistics expert when you go back down to New York?"

"Yeah. Beck has made some headway, but Joe wants the mystery to end so he can get his research partner back full time. And I think Beck is tired of arguing about it. On a related note, Joe has decided to stick around until Wednesday. Beck agreed to come back from vacation a day early for each day Joe takes off."

"Good. I suspect Jem is planning to live in that pool while we're here and it will be nice to have someone else for her to goof around with." She sighed. "I'm dreading telling her about the fire even more than I'm dreading clothes shopping."

"You said you'd let me hire a shopper."

"For house stuff, sure. Not for clothes. You know how picky I am. Really wish I hadn't packed so light."

"Same." Claire nodded toward her daypack. "I'm going to need to have a suit or something delivered to the apartment, because I didn't even pack anything for the conference."

"You could always wear your blue dress," Ro said, trying and failing to keep a straight face.

"Oh, sure. Because a plunging neckline and a skirt split to mid-thigh just *screams* professionalism. And … I got up with Paul Caruso a few minutes ago. Kolya has agreed to meet privately for breakfast just before the conference begins. Given our history, I should probably order a nun's habit for that meeting."

"He came on to you when you were wearing a *biosuit*, so I don't think that would help. But … you did *pack* the blue dress, right? Please tell me it wasn't in the house."

"I packed it," Claire said. "But I almost wish I hadn't. Having that dress go up in flames with the rest of my clothes might have been a blessing in disguise."

Ro widened her eyes in mock horror. "But then you and Wyatt would have to work out an entirely new mating ritual." She dropped her voice an octave, adopting the plummy tones of a British nature documentary. "And here we see the rare courtship dance of *Homo journalos* in all its complexity. Observe how the female of the species signals her willingness to mate by changing the color of her plumage."

Claire tossed one of the throw pillows at her. "Not fair. You do *not* get to tease me about my relationships when you refuse to even go on a date. I don't have any ammunition to fire back at you."

For the past year, Claire had been pushing gently, and occasionally not so gently, trying to get Ro to at least *think* about dating. But Ro had been so thoroughly disappointed by her brief marriage to Jemma's feckless dad that she wasn't inclined to roll the dice again. The guy had wanted kids. He'd actively pushed Ro to get pregnant, even though she was still in medical school. And then about eighteen months after Jemma was born, he suddenly decided that he really didn't want to be a dad after all. Or a husband, for that matter. He'd quit his job, taken a new position that involved constant travel, and now saw Jemma maybe twice a month.

"Just keep a running tally and you can get even later," Ro said. "Right now, I have no time, no patience, and even less energy. But the good news, thanks to your brother's research, is that I'm going to have about twenty years extra to play around with later on. My current plan is to just wait and have a very *interesting* retirement. And unlike *Aunty* Nina, the first thing I'll show prospective dates is pictures of my grandkids. If they can't handle that, they're not worth my time."

"I'll believe it when I see it. You'll just shift to claiming that you're too old and tired to party."

Even as the words left Claire's mouth, she realized that they weren't true. Ro's birthday was the day after Jemma's, and she'd always said there was no point in bothering with a separate cake. They just left Jemma's candles in place on whatever was left of the cake she'd requested—a chocolate cake this year, decorated *of course* with one of the WonderKitties—and then added twenty-six extra candles the next day for Ro's celebration.

If Joe's predictions for Rejuvesce panned out, the odds were good that Ro would *never* age beyond forty, no matter how many candles were on her cake. She could take time off to be a wild retiree, then come back and work for another twenty years or so. In fact, she'd almost certainly have to do that since her retirement funds wouldn't last forever. She could even switch careers entirely if she grew tired of medicine. And she might actually *need* to switch. The next generation would have fewer health problems since they wouldn't face any of the age-related conditions that made up nearly half of all medical expenses in the developed world. The fields of geriatric, pediatric, and obstetric medicine would inevitably shrink as people stopped aging and fewer children were born.

When Claire had first considered the ramifications of Joe's research, she'd naturally been thinking mostly of how it would impact her own life. Aside from having extra time, it really wouldn't change much, although she might have to speed up any plans for motherhood given Beck's prediction that governments would have to restrict population growth. Otherwise, though, almost nothing would change. Claire worked only because she wanted to. She had the luxury of knowing she could retire at any time. Going back to school, switching careers, or doing absolutely nothing had always been viable options for her.

But that wasn't true for the vast majority of people. This was going to radically alter their day-to-day lives, their relationships, their choices.

Claire had claimed neutrality in the argument between Joe and Beck, in part because she didn't want to get involved. But Beck had understood the full extent of Joe's stretch goals for months, if not longer. He'd had time to think about the wide-ranging impacts. No wonder he was pushing so hard for Joe to fight against Kai's pressure and move slowly. This was the most significant change in human history and there was really no predicting the ripple effects.

Only it wouldn't be ripples.

Ripples are what you get when you drop a pebble into the water, like she'd done at the lake inside the biodome.

But this? This was more like a massive meteor landing in the ocean.

It was going to launch a tsunami.

ELEVEN

AN AEROLYFT BRANDED with the Jonas Labs logo landed on the wide front lawn of Bellamy House at a little after eight on Monday morning. The original plan had been to leave in the late afternoon, but Beck's schedule had changed, and he told Joe that he needed to get an earlier start.

Claire waved through the window once she was strapped into her seat, but the only response was from Ro. Joe was still asleep, and Jemma, who had insisted on being awake to see the helicopter land, had already curled up on the steps with her head in her mother's lap by the time they were on board, clearly still worn out from the previous day's activities.

After a long discussion about which beach would be the safest option given their current security situation, they had decided to take the boat that Beck rented out to one of the small islands that he and Joe had visited the day before rather than risk the holiday crowds in Ogunquit. The island itself was little more than a glorified sandbar, but they'd spotted a pod of pilot whales off in the distance on the way over and Jemma had collected a small bag of shells, which had apparently been her key reason for wanting to go to the beach.

Claire was tired, too. After giving in to Jemma's entreaties to please, *please* come with them on the boat, she'd been relieved that the anti-nausea meds warded off the queasies, but she'd gone through the day in a bit of a fog. After popping a second pill for the return journey, she'd slept through most of the boat ride back and again on the couch after dinner ... which left her wide awake when she actually needed to fall asleep. She'd finally come down

a little before three a.m. in search of a sleep aid, and finding nothing, had settled for a glass of warm milk with a hefty shot of
whiskey.

Her plan had been to go into the living room and read for a
few minutes while she finished the drink, but then she spotted
Beck pacing around outside by the pool. Having opted out of the
boat trip in deference to his overexposure the previous day, he
had come down briefly to eat the Mexican food they picked up on
the way back from the marina and then vanished back into his
room, claiming he was still feeling a bit punk. Joe had mumbled
something under his breath, but simply shook his head when she
asked if anything was wrong.

She'd been tempted to stay downstairs until Beck finished his
conversation, because they still hadn't had a chance to talk about
the memoir or discuss the information on the nanodrive. But ten
minutes later, when her drink was gone and Beck was still out
there, she'd decided they could always chat on the flight to New
York.

"We're both going to be wiped out today," she said as the
AeroLyft ascended. "I saw you out by the pool when I came down
for something to help me sleep."

"Yeah. Dealing with some last minute arrangements. Sorry for
making you get such an early start."

"Not a problem. I can always nap at the apartment."

For the next few minutes, they engaged in small talk, although
it was stretching things to say that Beck *engaged* in the conversation. He answered a few questions about the reunion, confirmed
that he was feeling better when she asked, and then reached into
his bag and pulled out his earphones.

As he started to put them on, she placed a hand on his wrist.

"Are you mad at me about something? Or at Joe?"

"What?" Beck seemed genuinely puzzled. "No."

"Wait … you're not angry that he opened the files when you
weren't around, are you? Because if so, that's *totally* my fault. I'm
the one who didn't want to wait."

"No. I'm just … I've got a lot on my mind. Plus, I'm feeling better, but still not a hundred percent, and … as you noted, I only got a couple of hours of sleep."

"Sorry," Claire said. "I didn't mean to pry."

"It's okay. Really." He squeezed her arm and gave her his usual warm smile. "But I do think I'm going to try to catch a quick nap if you don't mind? I've got a hectic day ahead."

"Oh, sure. I may try to do the same. Before you go to sleep, though, I need to message Alice about Wednesday. What would be a good time for you?"

Beck frowned. "Wednesday?"

"Yes. You were going to meet with the two of us to go over your findings? Wyatt's probably going to join us, too."

"Oh, right, right." He thought for a moment. "To be honest, I'm not sure how much help I'll be now. I've barely even glanced at the files, but I'm guessing that Shepherd's notebook will be a lot more useful than what I discovered puttering around."

"You mentioned giving her some tips on the transcription program, though. I mean, she can't exactly contact the guy you bought it from if she has questions, right?"

"Yeah. I guess that's true. But I figured it out and she probably has far more experience with that sort of program than I do. I *might* be free after two, but I can't guarantee it. How about I just transfer the program over to you now? That way, the two of you can meet up earlier if you want."

"Sure. Sounds good. And I need to get your number. I realized the other day that I don't have it."

He transferred the program and gave her the password, along with his phone number. Then, he put in the earphones and closed his eyes.

Claire was now quite certain that whatever time they set for the meeting on Wednesday, Beck would be a no-show. He was acting as if he'd lost all interest in translating the manuscript. That wasn't so surprising on its own. He certainly had plenty of other things to occupy his time. But the change had been much too rapid to be credible and she couldn't shake the feeling that his disinterest was a ruse.

Maybe Joe's not-so-subtle pressure had finally gotten to him. Or Kai's, for that matter. Beck had said she'd been messaging him. Had she delivered some sort of ultimatum?

On the other hand, maybe he really *was* disappointed at knowing he wouldn't be the one to solve the mystery. Claire could understand that, at least. Hadn't she always hated it when Joe peered over her shoulder as she worked a sudoku puzzle and started giving her the answers? Still, it seemed kind of petty and out of character, especially if he still believed there was any chance that the manuscript might contain a warning.

She messaged Alice to see if she wanted to bump the meeting up to that afternoon and, after a short internal debate, asked if she had suggestions on the best apps to check for recording equipment at the apartment. Joe was *probably* right that Kai wouldn't risk hidden cameras, but she needed to be certain. Otherwise, she and Wyatt would most definitely be getting a hotel room.

Alice didn't answer. Of course, it was barely eight thirty in the morning, on a *holiday*. She was probably sleeping in. Which was what Claire knew she should also try to do. But she'd chugged two cups of coffee before leaving Bellamy House, so sleep wasn't going to happen anytime soon.

Instead, she opened another one of the folktales. This one was about Motz only, and vaguely reminiscent of the Aesop fable about the farmer who takes in the snake only to have the snake repay his kindness with a fatal bite. Unlike the farmer, Motz survives her encounter, but she is cautioned that you cannot expect a kind response from a creature whose nature is to act with violence and anger. As with the other story, it ended with the same warning that Motz should never, ever go into the Aveezi Forest. A quick scan of the document revealed that sentiment was at the end of all but a few of the tales, and occasionally at the beginning as well, suggesting that it was a rule that Motz and the other creatures broke on the regular.

Beck slept the entire time, waking only as the chopper slowed for its descent to the helipad on the roof of Kai's apartment building. Once they touched down, he gave the navigation system the address that he was heading to in the Bronx. It located the nearest landing pad, near Van Cortlandt Park, and informed him that there would be about a five minute wait for clearance to take off.

She retrieved her bag from behind the seat. "Enjoy the reunion."

"Thanks. I'm sure I will." That same hint of a shadow she'd noticed when she mentioned the reunion a few days before passed over Beck's face, but then it was gone.

"Enjoy the conference," he added.

"Thanks. I'm sure I *won't*. I just hope I can get some answers."

She started to get out, but Beck grabbed her arm.

"Will you do me a favor?"

"Sure…"

He reached into the console between their seats. "Would you please carry this?"

It was a handgun. Joe had again brought up the subject of taking one the day before when they were on the boat.

"Did Joe put you up to this? I already *told* him, it's not worth the hassle. I can't take it into the UN, and—"

"Joe didn't put me up to anything." Beck entered the password into the pad on the side of the weapon. "But yes, he did mention that he suggested it, and you said no. I remember the battle royale between you and Kai before you went off to school, so I know you don't like carrying. Neither do I. But I also saw how rattled you were the other day when you got off the hyperloop. Even if you can't take it everywhere, it's crazy not to keep it on you when you can. I've already registered it in the local database and listed you as an authorized user. You just need to input your fingerprints. Your brother and I will both feel much better if you have it. I'm guessing Wyatt will, too."

She sighed.

He held the gun out toward her, his eyes locked on hers. "Please?"

Claire started to repeat her refusal, but the genuine concern in his expression stopped her. It was the first time in the past few days that he'd seemed like ... well, like *Beck*.

"Okay, okay." She took the gun, shaking her head in resignation as she pressed first her right forefinger and then her left against the trigger. "I'll message Joe and let him know you win the prize for finally wearing me down."

TWELVE

CLAIRE HAD BEEN to the New York apartment at least a dozen times but had always traveled by ground from the hyperloop terminal, so it took a moment for her to find the entrance to the elevator. She entered the code and then waited for security to let her in. Joe was right that she'd be safer here than at a hotel. The building was designed with a single apartment on each of its eleven floors, remote monitoring of the corridors by the security team, and a thumbprint pad for entry into the apartment itself.

Still, she wasn't thrilled at the prospect of hanging out here alone for an entire day. Agreeing to travel down with Beck hadn't seemed like a big deal when he'd been planning to leave Maine in the late afternoon, but it wasn't even ten a.m. now and unless Alice was willing to bump up their meeting, she had absolutely nothing to do until her breakfast with Kolya the next morning. Going out when she didn't have to would violate the promise that she'd made to Joe about taking precautions where she could, and she'd probably be glancing over her shoulder the entire time anyway.

Unlike the house in Massachusetts, with its memories of childhood and her dad, this place held only *recent* memories—awkward Christmas dinners that Kai had catered, a few hours of stilted conversations, and the occasional argument. On the plus side, while the apartment didn't hold fond memories, there were also no traumatic ones, and it was far too impersonal a space for *any* of the memories to be especially vivid.

The apartment's elegant blandness was largely by design. It was technically owned by Jonas Labs and, as Joe had noted, Kai occasionally loaned it out to visiting investors or other people that she wanted to impress. The exterior was early twentieth-century construction, with an art deco vibe, but it had been thoroughly renovated a few years before Kai bought it. Inside, the furnishings were sleek and modern, the kitchen fully-equipped but never used, and it had the two most important amenities for any status-conscious property owner in New York—a convenient location and a stunning view.

Three boxes were waiting in the delivery nook next to the elevator when Claire reached the tenth floor. Two were packages with the clothes that Claire had ordered the day before, but the third appeared to be a box of long-stemmed roses. Not exactly Wyatt's style, but he was the only one who knew she'd be here. Any packages that made it upstairs would have gone through security screening before entering the building, so she scooped it up with the others.

Her phone buzzed several times with incoming messages as she was taking the packages into one of the bedrooms. They were all from Alice. The first said that she was happy to bump up the meeting and could be there within the hour. The other three were links to apps for finding hidden cameras and listening devices.

Claire sent her the address, then went app shopping. Ten minutes later, when she'd confirmed that Joe was indeed correct and the place was bug-free, she went back into the bedroom and opened the card attached to the flower box. She suspected that they were apology roses, and the card would say that Wyatt wasn't going to be able to make it to New York after all. But the message didn't sound like an apology.

And you say I never plan ahead.

She opened the box to find a single red rose, barely visible inside layer after layer of bubble wrap.

Laughing, she took a photo and sent it to him along with a question.

> How exactly did you explain this request to the florist?

She unwrapped the rose and was in the kitchen searching for something to serve as a vase when Wyatt responded with a video call.

He was sitting at the desk inside the bedroom of his tiny apartment a few blocks from the *Atlantic Post's* headquarters. The bedroom seemed even more cluttered than usual, with a pile of laundry—*probably* clean—piled next to the open suitcase on top of his bed.

"Believe it or not, the florist didn't even ask," he said. "She just told me it would be an extra twenty plus the cost of the bubble wrap. And judging from her tone, I seriously doubt that it was the oddest request she's received. I'm surprised it was there when you arrived, though. I didn't think you'd be getting into New York until late afternoon."

"Beck's plans changed. I moved my meeting with Alice up to today instead of Wednesday, but I still kind of feel like I've been grounded. Sure you can't get away early?"

"Positive. In fact, I probably won't even be there until tomorrow night. But ... I may have something you can help me with if you get bored. How do you feel about doing a stakeout?"

"Um ... remember the part where I said I feel like I'm grounded?"

"I do. But this is a *virtual* stakeout. Not exactly in real time, either. It's footage from a couple of surveillance cameras I had someone set up the other day. Remember the lead I told you about over dinner?"

"Not really."

"The anonymous tip on Corbin Drexel's whereabouts?"

"Oh. I ... *vaguely* remember you saying something about an

anonymous tip. You said it might be more important than you thought, but you never mentioned Drexel. I'd definitely have remembered that. Wait a minute. Is that why you didn't want me covering the conference? Because you think she's in New York?"

"It *may* have been a consideration. I wasn't convinced that the information was valid, but it seemed worth the trouble of planting the devices." He paused, clearly weighing his words. "But now … I'm thinking we should check the footage sooner rather than later, because I have it on good authority that facial recognition software picked someone up matching Drexel's description last night. She was leaving the hotel where we think Kolya is staying."

"Hotel Mir? At Beekman Place?"

"Yes…"

There was the slightest hint of a question in Wyatt's tone and Claire was tempted to simply leave it at that, given how adamantly he'd claimed not to be jealous. But if she wanted to end the games, it had to go both ways.

"Paul gave me the address. I'm supposed to meet Kolya there tomorrow for breakfast, since that was apparently the only spare moment on his schedule until Thursday. So … is this sighting of Drexel based on more hidden cameras? Or do you have another anonymous source?"

"Not anonymous. The same very *reliable* source who placed the hidden cameras I mentioned earlier also has access to top-of-the-line facial recognition programs, but *seriously* sucks at tailing. They somehow managed to lose Drexel right after she turned at First Avenue."

"You mean Kes?"

"No comment, given that placing the cameras I mentioned earlier may have involved illegal trespass. But knowing that Drexel had been spotted did get me to thinking back to that earlier *anonymous* tip, and I started going through the footage late last night. I've made it through the first eight hours or so, and I haven't seen any familiar faces. Not many faces at *all* to be honest. It's a very quiet, very upscale neighborhood. I've got about seventy-two hours of footage left to go, though, from two different cameras. You're better qualified to handle it than I am, anyway, since you've seen all of them in person ... and Erica needs my draft tonight and the final version bright and early tomorrow."

"So ... who would I be looking for aside from Drexel?"

"The tipster just said the people in my 'farm' video. Meaning the first video that Devin recorded at the Culpeper compound, I guess. The one I showed you right after you got back."

"The one with Stasia, Meadow, and Pax?"

"Yeah."

The farm video, which had been only a few seconds long, was taken shortly before Claire returned from Mars. From what Paul and Kolya had told her when she was in the hospital at Daedalus recovering from her injuries, Stasia had gotten off the planet, along with Meadow and Pax, before the final bomb at Icarus went off. They'd apparently hitched a ride on a cargo or worker transport that left Ares Station that afternoon, which should have made them fairly easy to apprehend, since it narrowed the list of possible ships to four.

Security had been waiting when each of those ships docked at Tranquility Base, but there was no sign of Stasia. When Claire asked Agent West, he said the working theory was that the ship they were on must have made a side trip to one of the smaller suborbital resorts and then booked passage into a country where security was less stringent. Claire found it hard to believe. Stasia had left Mars only a few days before the *Ares Prime*, and even though the worker transports were smaller and usually a bit faster, the video had been taken at Culpeper almost a week before Claire got back. That didn't leave much time for side trips and international travel, although she supposed Canada or Mexico were possibilities. She thought it far more likely that Stasia had simply bribed her way past the checkpoints.

Stasia had been easy for her to pick out in the video, due both to her height and the amount of time that Claire had spent with her on the *Ares Prime*. She'd spent a good bit of time with Pax and Meadow, as well, since they'd been assigned as her videographers for most of the *Simple Science* segments that she recorded on Mars. Pax was average height, average weight, and not very distinctive, but Claire had recognized the splash of color that Wyatt had thought was a scarf as Meadow's bright green braid.

"So, assuming this tipster is right," Wyatt continued, "it sounds like Drexel might be planning to blow something else up. Otherwise, why bring the bomb experts?"

Claire shook her head at the description. "I'm having a really hard time thinking of Pax and Meadow as *bomb experts*."

"You don't think they set the bombs?"

"No, I'm sure they set them, although I'm not entirely convinced that they wanted to. It's more like they felt they had no choice. They tried to discourage me from going over to the tunnel that morning. Brodnik's crew, as well. I think they accepted that there might be casualties, but they tried to minimize them."

"Didn't try very hard," Wyatt said. "Because there was a real easy way to accomplish that. Don't want to kill people? Don't plant a bomb."

"True. But ... the *expert* part feels off, too. If you'd worked with them, you'd understand why. They were both kind of ... I don't know. They didn't strike me as the sharpest tools in the shed when they were doing my recordings. Awkward, I guess. I wouldn't have thought that anyone that klutzy would survive long around explosives."

"Maybe they were only klutzy with the video setup. But see? That's what I'm talking about. That kind of observation is exactly why you're the better choice to go through the footage."

"*Sure*," she said. "I suppose it doesn't have anything at all to do with the fact that you have that deadline sign dangling over your head."

"Well, that's obviously part of it. But all I've got to go on is appearance alone, since I'm working with just photos and a few videos. You, on the other hand, have spent time with them. Maybe you'll pick up on mannerisms, so you'll be able to spot them even if they've changed their hair color or whatever. You can run it at quadruple speed or more, and then just slow it down when someone goes in or out of the place. But only if you're bored. I can always look at it after I'm done if—"

"Oh, give me a break." She laughed. "Just send me the access code. Even if I'm not bored, I'll be too curious not to watch. Which you knew perfectly well when you suggested it."

THIRTEEN

CLAIRE SWITCHED the video from fast-forward to standard speed when the white van appeared on the screen. It turned into the driveway, pulled up to the yellow line a few meters away from the black iron gate and waited. There was no logo, unlike the easily identifiable Amazon delivery vehicle that had come and gone a few hours earlier. Or rather, a few hours earlier for Claire. It had happened a little over a day ago in actuality, given that she'd been running the video at eight times normal speed.

She'd started a little before one, just after Alice left the apartment. Alice had clearly been anxious to get back home so that she could start playing around with her new treasure trove of data. She seemed pretty confident that she could figure out the transcription software, so they made a tentative agreement to meet again at three on Wednesday. If Beck could meet with them, fine. If not, they would have a cup of coffee and go over the findings, although given that Alice had classes to teach for the next few days, she wasn't expecting much.

Claire had, however, made quite a bit of progress working through Wyatt's surveillance footage. As he'd noted, the house was in a quiet neighborhood with little traffic of any sort. There were long, long stretches when absolutely nothing happened. Every half hour or so, when she got tired of staring at the gate and the brick wall on either side of it, she switched from the street cam to the one that offered a view of the house. And then, when she got tired of staring at the house, she went back to the surveillance footage from the street cam. This made for a rather boring stakeout, but on the plus side, it had also made it possible for her to zip through much more quickly. She'd finished maybe three quarters of the archive and was now watching video taken around five p.m. the previous day.

The white van had a New York license plate, like all three of the other vehicles that had entered the property thus far. She paused, zoomed in, and added the tag number to her list. Then she switched to the second feed to wait for the van to appear in front of the house.

This camera offered only a partial view thanks to an inconveniently located birch tree, but she could see enough that she knew without any doubt that her father would have called the place a McMansion. It was mind-numbingly symmetrical—Georgian-style, red brick construction with white dentil molding under the eaves. The main entrance was in the very center of the house, flanked by two tall, white-trimmed windows on either side. Its only distinctive characteristic was that there was no front lawn. The driveway ended at a courtyard that was the size of a small parking lot, spanning the area from the front door to the four-car garage. It was the same red brick as the house, arranged in a circular pattern that reminded Claire of a dartboard.

The audio had proven next to useless, due in part to the fact that the distance between the camera and the house was greater than the distance between the camera and what sounded like a much busier road off to the left. All that she'd picked up so far, aside from traffic noises, was a faint thump when the robotic arm on the Amazon van dropped two boxes into the delivery area near the garage. A middle-aged woman—thin and very tall, with dark hair and light brown skin—had come out to retrieve the packages a few hours later. She was one of three people Claire had seen so far, none of them familiar.

As the plain white van approached the house, however, she caught the sound of a doorbell, much louder than anything else that the cameras had recorded. She waited, thinking that the van must have triggered the bell automatically, until it occurred to her that the sound hadn't come from the speakers on the viewscreen but rather from the actual doorbell of the apartment she was in. Feeling a bit stupid, she paused the video and went to collect the takeout she'd ordered earlier.

She grabbed a fork from the kitchen and refilled her water bottle. Then, she parked herself once more in front of the screen in the living room. As she sat there, eating her noodles from the cardboard container and waiting for something to happen, she couldn't help feeling like she'd wandered into a really low-budget cop movie.

A few seconds later, the rear hatch of the van went up. The passenger doors opened at almost the same time. Two guys walked around to the back, pulled out a cart, and began loading it with catering trays. At least a dozen trays in all, along with several bakery boxes.

Someone was expecting company.

A dark-haired woman opened the door to let the men inside. Claire thought it might be the same woman who'd picked up the packages earlier, but she never stepped out of the shadows of the doorway, so it was hard to be sure.

Ten minutes later, the van rolled back down the drive. Claire switched to the street cam and watched as it exited the property and the gate closed behind it. She stayed in super fast-forward mode for the next fifteen minutes or so until the first guest arrived around seven. Four more straggled in after that, the first at around eight and the last just before midnight. All of them were carrying weekend bags. None of them looked familiar, but she was only able to get a clear view of two faces.

The one thing that struck her as a bit odd was that all five— three men and two women—were unusually tall. She hadn't noticed it until the last arrival, who had to duck slightly when he entered the house.

There was no real point of reference aside from the vehicles that dropped them off and the height of the front door, which appeared to be standard size for homes built in the first half of the century. But she'd watched her brother going in and out of enough doors that she was a pretty good judge. At six-seven, if there was more than the slightest heel on Joe's shoe, he had to duck.

She ran the video back to the section with the caterers. They appeared to be around average height next to the van and there was still plenty of clearance when they entered the house. So, yeah. Everyone at this party was taller than the norm, some by half a foot or more.

Nothing else happened overnight. Around ten a.m., however, another tall woman arrived. Two more cars pulled up a few minutes before noon, one after the other, both carrying tall thin men.

Not long after that, a blue sedan passed the gate, proceeded slowly to the end of the road and made a U-turn. Claire didn't think much about it. Even automated cars take wrong turns from time to time. When the same car did the same thing about an hour later, though, she zoomed in as close as possible, hoping to see who was inside. All she got was a reflection of the side of the road where Kes had placed the camera.

Twenty-five people arrived over the next three hours. Some came separately, and some came in groups of as many as five or six, streaming out of airport passenger vans. She could only see faces about half the time and the only thing she could say for certain was that all of them were well above average height, and all but two or three were unusually thin.

About once an hour, the blue car made its trip to the end of the road and back. On its eighth trip the sun dipped behind a cloud, and she caught a glimpse of a woman's profile through the window. She thought she spotted a second person in the car, as well, but they were leaning back into the seat, and she couldn't be sure.

The woman turned slightly toward the camera when they circled back around. And for the first time since she began watching, Claire felt a twinge of recognition.

She ran it again, and yes. The woman looked like Corbin Drexel.

A *lot* like Corbin Drexel.

The hair color was hard to judge through the tinted window, but the woman's eyes were the same. And her nose had the same upward tilt at the end. Hopefully, she'd get a better look the next time the car came by. Given that the sun was already going down, it was likely the only chance that she'd have before it was too dark to see anything at all.

Claire zipped forward again, waiting for the blue car. But about five minutes before she would have expected it to show up again, the video stopped suddenly. There was a slight shimmer on the screen, and then the picture resumed. After a second of confusion, she realized that the clock at the top of the screen now showed the current time. She'd reached the end of the archive, and it was ticking off the seconds at normal speed.

She continued watching in real time for the next few minutes. Her eyes were so focused on the edge of the screen where she thought the car was about to enter that she didn't realize that the driveway gate was moving until it was almost fully open. This time, however, there was a man instead of a car on the other side.

A tall thin man, which came as absolutely no surprise given how many she'd seen entering the place. He took a left when he reached the end of the driveway, walking away from the entrance to the neighborhood.

It was too dark to get a good look at the guy's face. But there was something very familiar about his walk as he came out of the shadows toward her.

FROM THE JOURNAL
OF EBERIN DAS

02.05.507

A word of advice to whoever may read this: should you ever find yourself planning to go against the core precepts of your civilization, tell *no one*.

For no matter how dear the friend, how close the confidant, they *will* betray you. They will do this without the slightest qualm, telling themselves that a true friend would not let you throw your life away and risk everything that everyone they know holds dear. Everything that you *yourself* once held dear.

Given the opportunity, they will justify this betrayal to your face, telling you that their actions were for your own good, in your own best interest. They were, after all, simply trying to save your life. Once you are again in your right mind, they will insist, you will understand why they had no choice but to do this.

And because you *are* already of sound mind, you will understand that they were, by objective standards, entirely right to act as they did.

That will not make their betrayal sting any less.

(Confidence interval: 91.6%)

FOURTEEN

"EXACTLY *WHERE* IS this house that I've been watching?" Claire asked once she got Wyatt on the phone.

There was a pause as he swallowed, so her call must have interrupted his dinner. "Um … Goodridge Avenue. I'd have to look up the house number, though. It's in the Bronx. Riverdale area."

"Is that near Cortlandt Park?"

"It's near *Van* Cortlandt Park. Why?"

"I don't know. Maybe nothing. I'll call you back."

Claire hung up and placed a second call, holding her breath as the phone on the other end began to ring.

The streetlight came on just as the man reached into his pocket. If she had waited a few seconds longer, she wouldn't have needed to call. When she zoomed in, she could even make out a slightly darker patch on his cheek where he'd gotten sunburned.

"Hey," Beck said. "What's up?"

She took a deep breath, trying to keep her voice from shaking. "Sorry. I meant to text you, but accidentally called instead. Um … does three o'clock work for you on Wednesday?"

"Yeah. That should work. I'll message and let you know if anything changes."

"Is everything going okay?"

"Sure. Going great." There was a hint of annoyance in his voice. He turned his head to the right just as the headlights of the oncoming car lit up that side of the screen. "Listen, I've gotta go. See you on Wednesday."

"Wait, no…"

But he was gone.

She tapped the button to call again.

His phone didn't ring this time. It went straight to voicemail.

As she listened to Beck's recorded message, two scenes played out inside Claire's head. In the first, the blue car accelerated, swerving onto the sidewalk and pinning Beck against the brick wall. In the second, the car slowed as it drove by, sending a spray of bullets into Beck and the wall behind him.

But neither of those things happened.

The car drove past the spot where he was standing. It was moving faster than it had on the previous trips, so Claire couldn't see inside at all on the first pass, but it didn't swerve onto the sidewalk. No bullets.

She had a better view after the car turned around at the end of the street and stopped near Beck. Now, she could make out silhouettes of two people in the passenger area—two women, she thought. But it was still too dark for her to tell anything more about who was inside.

The right door swung open abruptly as the car approached Beck and he took a quick step back from the curb. His hands shot up several inches, in a warding-off gesture, but then he lowered them slowly and got inside. A second later, the car took off again, heading away from the house and toward the main road.

Claire stared at the screen for a moment, trying to make sense of what she'd just seen. Then she called Wyatt back and asked him to pull up the live feed of the video.

"It's up now," he said a few moments later. "First time I've seen the gate left open."

"Go back about a minute. No. More like a minute and a half now."

"Okay. Got it. I still see an open gate, but there's also a guy under the streetlight talking to someone on his phone."

"Yeah. He's talking to *me*. That's Beck. Keep watching. Tell me when you see the—"

"The car?"

"Right. One of the passengers may be Drexel."

"How sure are you?"

"I don't know. Sixty … maybe seventy percent? The car has been driving back and forth in front of the house for the better part of the day, but the only glance I got before this was brief. Keep watching."

"Okay. The car is coming back around. Stopping now. And … and he's getting inside."

"I think they had a weapon."

"What makes you say that?"

"See his hands go up? And look at his expression."

"Maybe…" Wyatt sounded skeptical. "It looks to me more like he was worried that they were going to clip him with the car door. They came pretty close. But you could be right. What do you think Beck is doing there?"

"I don't know," she said. "Maybe he's investigating on his own? Joe told me that Jonas Labs hired a team to dig up more information on the Flock, but he said Beck wasn't happy with their progress. And … did I tell you who Drexel was interested in before Kolya?"

"Beck?"

"No. She was going after Joe, apparently with a bit of encouragement from my mother who wanted her as an investor. Anyway, when she realized that Joe was already in a committed relationship with his research, she moved on to Kolya. Beck called her a science groupie."

"Is that a thing?"

"That's exactly what I said." She ran the video back to the point where the car approached so that she could again watch Beck's reaction when the door opened.

"We should get the tag number."

"Already did, but I don't think it's going to be much help. It has *For Hire* at the bottom, like the others that came and went earlier today. I'll send you the list. But, Wyatt … I'm watching it again. Beck did *not* want to get into that car. Roll it back and see.

He doesn't raise his hands over his head, but they're at least halfway there. And … he's unarmed."

"How do you know?"

"He gave me his pistol. I think Joe put him up to it. He kept trying to get me to bring one, but…"

"Well, I'm glad *someone* managed to talk you into it." There was a pause, and then he said. "I don't know, babe. It looks to me like he's startled at first, because of the close call with the car door, but then he recognizes the person inside."

Claire watched it a fourth time. "It's possible," she said, still not convinced. "What information do you have on the house?"

"Not much. The last time it changed hands was back in the 2030s. Owned by a holding company based in Europe. They bought this place and also the empty lot next to it where the car turned around. Paid a little over twenty million. And they have a top notch security system, according to Kes."

So much for I can neither confirm nor deny, she thought as she ran the video back to watch again.

"I'll get someone on it, see if they can dredge up any record of police calls or anything of that nature."

"Sure," she said, only half listening now as she tried to figure out what to do.

"Claire? Gotta say I'm not liking the tone of your voice at the moment. You're thinking about going over there, aren't you?"

"I *was*," she admitted. "There are a lot of people in the place right now and I was thinking maybe I could just … gate-crash. Especially if the gate was still open."

"Very bad idea. Like I said before, Kes tested their security system. Their sentry would incapacitate you before you were halfway up the drive."

"I'd already decided it was a bad idea anyway. There's no way I'd be able to blend in."

"Why? Are they all men, or what?"

"No. It's nearly half women, as best I could tell. But I'm barely above average height and they're all … really tall. Beck's probably six-two and he'd have been one of the shorter people in that house. Several of them were even taller than Joe."

"Did Beck say what kind of reunion he was going to? Maybe he played basketball in college."

"Uh … no. I've seen him play against Joe. They have a hoop on the back door of the lab and let's just say I don't think he'd have made the team. He's good at ping-pong, but he kind of sucks at basketball. Also, what are the odds that his reunion just happened to be at the house that this anonymous source gave you?"

"I know. It's just that I don't think you're going to like the other possibility that this raises."

"He's *not* working with the Flock. That's … that's just not possible. And I still don't think he got into that car willingly."

"Okay, okay. Promise me that you are *not* going over there."

"I'm not going over there. But I *am* going over to Kolya's."

"Now? I thought you were meeting with him tomorrow morning."

"That was the plan before someone who may very well be a murderous maniac took off with Beck inside her car. If Kolya has any idea what Drexel is up to, I'm not waiting twelve hours to find out."

FIFTEEN

CLAIRE SPOTTED Beekman Place long before she arrived—both the top floors of the building itself and its shimmering reflection in the East River. Many of the structures in this area, including two of the United Nations Headquarters buildings, had suffered serious damage when Hurricane René wreaked havoc on the Eastern Seaboard during the early 2070s.

She remembered that storm clearly. Growing up in the Boston suburbs, she'd gotten plenty of days off from school due to winter storms, but that was the only time she could recall being out because of a hurricane. The UN had gotten a long-overdue complete remodel after the storm, as had many of the buildings nearby. That part she probably wouldn't have remembered if not for the fact that her father had complained that a bunch of architectural eyesores would soon replace most of the historical buildings in the area.

Martin Echols had never mentioned Beekman Place specifically. Claire wasn't even sure if it had been finished when he died. She was quite certain, however, that it would have been near the top of his list of atrocities. Kolya International, the parent company of KTI, had scooped up three square blocks along the East River, leveled what remained of the residences, and replaced them with the largest entertainment complex in New York. It was one of a dozen or more that the company operated on Earth, in addition to their suborbital resorts, the lunar resort at Tranquility Base, and Daedalus City on Mars.

While Beekman Place was the official name of the property, New Yorkers referred to it as Kolya's Palace, or more often simply the Palace, for reasons that were abundantly clear even to the casual observer. The façade resembled Mir Castle in Kolya's native Belarus, although it was almost certainly larger, and Claire doubted that the actual castle had lights that flashed like a fireworks display on acid. Unless, of course, Kolya had purchased Mir Castle too, in which case all bets were off.

The Palace was way over the top, even for Manhattan. But over the top was Kolya's stock-in-trade. Every plane that landed in New York offered passengers a glimpse of the glittering lights of the resort. While the Statue of Liberty and Central Park were still better known tourist attractions, the Palace was giving Times Square a real run for its money. The complex was now home to two of the most prestigious Broadway theaters and rumor had it that Kolya's people were currently lobbying to move the New Year's Eve countdown into its massive, climate-controlled courtyard where revelers wouldn't have to contend with the whims of nature. So far, tradition had won out, but Claire suspected that all it would take was another ill-timed blizzard or two before city leaders gave into the pressure.

Hotel Mir was the largest and most luxurious of the six hotels at Beekman Place. Kolya International's US headquarters occupied the lower level floors where the views weren't impressive enough to command premium prices from tourists. For Paul's sake, Claire hoped the atmosphere was less frenetic in the offices. She definitely wouldn't be able to work here. Between the traffic noise, the din from the casinos, and the flashing lights she'd be constantly fighting off a migraine.

Claire tucked Beck's pistol into the glove compartment as the car pulled up to the curb in front of the hotel. Otherwise, the detectors would go off when she entered, and she'd have to check the gun at the front desk. She told the car—a sleek black Aeris that cost more than the annual income of most families and was probably taken out of the garage only two or three times a year—to find a parking space nearby, but then changed her mind and ordered it to stay in motion within a three-minute recall. If Drexel had actually been here the day before, there were really only two possibilities. One was that Kolya's people hadn't spotted her. That seemed very unlikely. The Palace had top-notch private security, and their surveillance would be even more stringent right now given that Kolya was actually on the premises. The second possibility was that they had seen Drexel and let her leave *despite* the fact that they had to know she was wanted for questioning in connection with the bombings on Mars. Neither of those options made Claire feel especially secure, and it would be a lot more difficult for someone to tamper with her vehicle if it was on the street and in motion—or at least as close to *in motion* as Manhattan traffic would allow.

She headed toward the entrance, reaching for her phone to let Paul know she'd arrived. Before she could call, though, she saw him through the glass wall, sitting on one of the sofas near the middle of the lobby as he sipped something out of a copper mug.

"Well, *you* certainly look better than you did the last time I saw you," he said as she approached.

Claire really couldn't say the same. Paul seemed to have aged at least five years over the summer. He'd lost weight, too.

"I'm pretty sure that counts as a backhanded compliment," she said. "I was in a hospital bed the last time you saw me."

"You *still* looked gorgeous."

"And you are a lousy liar."

"I certainly hope not. *Ability to lie persuasively* is at the very top of my job description." He nodded toward the elevator. "Kolya's running late. He had to make a … side trip. Something related to the speech he's giving tomorrow. But he should be here within the hour. Have you eaten?"

"Yes."

"Well, I haven't. This is the first excuse I've had to take a break since I got out of bed. So you can have a drink and watch me eat while you tell me what it is that couldn't wait until tomorrow morning." There was a touch of reproof in his voice, which was fair. He'd already stuck his neck out to arrange the breakfast meeting, only to have her call back and insist on seeing his boss ASAP.

Three other people were waiting to enter the elevator along with them, so Claire just nodded and followed him inside. He pressed the button for the dining terrace, which had her worried that they were going to be staring out at bright flashy lights again. Sure enough, the terrace was lit up like a carnival, with about a dozen restaurants along the perimeter vying for customers. To her relief, however, Paul led her over to the interior section of one of the more dimly lit options.

"It will be quieter in here. And believe me, I *need* a bit of quiet. It's been a hellacious week." He took a sip out of the copper mug as they slipped into the booth. "Actually, make that the entire summer."

Claire smiled in sympathy. "So … I take it that Ayman's silver lining count is high this month?"

It was a running joke that Paul's partner Ayman, who had traveled with them on the *Ares Prime*, was tasked with reminding Paul of all of the things he loved about his job each time he complained about Kolya.

"Last month's tally was astronomical," he said. "This month doesn't really count, though. For one thing, we're only four days in. And Ayman has only been getting the daily digest version when we chat each night. He left on Friday for Nebraska. Did you know that people actually *live* there?"

She chuckled. "I had heard rumors to that effect, yes. What's he doing in Nebraska?"

"Attending his sister's wedding. Which I was supposed to attend *with* him, but then Kolya got a wild hair a few weeks back and decided that his big announcement needs to happen at the ACon dinner rather than at the end of the stage six lockdown as we had been planning for well over a year."

"Why the rush?"

"A couple of things. Lots of investors at ACon, for one, but it also helped secure a partnership that he thinks is important going forward. So I'm here instead of Nebraska."

"Guessing Ayman's not happy about you having to cancel?"

He shrugged. "No, but he didn't complain. If he wasn't so flexible about this sort of thing, I'd have to find other work. Although, I think we're inching closer to the point where he's going to stop counting the silver linings and start pushing me to just get the hell away from the thundercloud. Life was a lot easier as Stasia's right hand than it is as Kolya's."

"I can imagine. You look tired. And you've lost weight."

"You sound like Ayman. Personally, I think I needed to lose a few. Maybe not this much, though, so point taken." He tapped the button to pull up the menu. "I'll order the fries with my burger instead of the salad."

"In *addition* to the salad," Claire suggested.

"Even better. Like I said earlier, I'm on the run all day with no time to eat. I don't know if it's because Stasia was a lot better at juggling a thousand different things at once or if it's just that the situation really is more hectic now. Maybe it's a combination. But … enough about me. I'm going to go out on a limb and guess that this urgent need to meet with Kolya has something to do with your message that I forwarded to Shepherd the other day. The one with a request for information for your *colleague*?" One eyebrow arched up with the last word and before Claire could respond he went on. "A colleague I'm pretty sure is Wyatt Garcia—who, I might add, is becoming a colossal pain in my backside. What do you want to drink?"

"A whiskey sour, please. And … it is *loosely* connected to the message," she said, choosing to ignore the part about Wyatt. She waited until Paul finished ordering and then continued. "How much trouble have you guys had with the Flock since we got back from Mars?"

Paul was quiet for a moment, probably thinking that she was trying to change the subject. "Macek can give you a better answer on security issues than I can. But I do know that the Flock ramped up their protests with the launch of stage six. About a week after Kolya did the live reveal we had a few dozen of the nutjobs show up right here at Beekman. They had two giant inflatables, one of Earth and the other of Mars, and they doused everything—including a couple of tourists—with neon green paint to mimic the way that the *Azospira oryzae* spread over the planet. Those inflatables could have fit in someone's pocket before they were blown up, but I have no clue how they sneaked *paint* past Beekman Place security."

"Wow. I'm surprised I didn't see that online. The media has certainly paid enough attention to the protests at Jonas Labs."

"You didn't see it online because Kolya spent an ungodly amount of money, and I spent an ungodly amount of time keeping the whole thing under wraps. Your mother needs better people in charge of her PR."

"Maybe," she said, feeling odd that she was about to defend her mother even if it was indirectly. "But that kind of ... cleanup work ... is more of a necessity in your industry. Jonas Labs doesn't have thousands of tourists coming through the property each day. And they're marketing a *tangible,* high-demand product without any sort of competition at the moment. But here? People have options. No matter how fabulous the setting, they generally avoid spending their time and money at resorts—whether on Earth or off—where they run a risk of physical harm."

"I wouldn't really call it physical harm. It was just paint. The Flock didn't even target the tourists directly—a wrong place, wrong time sort of thing—and no one was actually hurt."

"That wasn't true at Icarus Camp, though. Or at Millex."

Paul's eyes widened for an instant and then his face relaxed. "Oh. You mean the bombing during the labor negotiations."

Claire was tempted to press the point, since that brief look of panic almost certainly meant that Paul knew something about the containment breach at Millex. Maybe even that he suspected it hadn't been an accident. There was no way he was going to tell her anything, though, and if she pounced on his little slip, it would likely confirm his suspicion that she was at ACon, at least in part, as Wyatt's spy.

"Yes," she said. "The Flock was implicated in the bombings at *both* mining camps, right?"

"Right, although I think Macek still has some doubts about the one at Millex. I just meant the Flock hasn't actually hurt anyone on *Earth*. They've made a number of threats recently, but so far—"

"Except they *have* hurt people here on Earth. Even killed a few."

Claire went on to tell him about the deaths of Leffler, Devin, and the couple in Virginia, and ended with the firebombing of her house. She stuck to the basic facts without going into the information encoded in the Martian samples or the Flock's assumed motives.

"And now," she said, "they appear to have kidnapped Joe's research partner, John Beckett. Although, I guess *abducted* is a better word, since I'm not aware of any demand for ransom."

Paul remained silent as she recounted all of this, but his face was easy to read. He hadn't known any of what she'd just told him. "So … this Beckett guy. He's just missing, at this point, right? You only *assume* he's been abducted."

"No. I saw video of him being forced into a car."

Admittedly, she wasn't certain about the *forced* part. There was also the possibility that a ransom had been requested, because any demand would probably have gone either directly to Jonas Labs or to Joe. Claire had toyed with the idea of contacting Joe on the ride from the apartment to Beekman Place, but ultimately decided to wait until after she spoke with Kolya. There was nothing Joe could do to help if it was an actual abduction, and on the off chance that Wyatt was right and Beck had gotten into that car willingly, Claire wanted more information about why he'd done it before she broke that sort of cataclysmic news to her brother.

"And you think Kolya can help?" Paul asked.

"I don't know. But I'm fairly certain that one of the people inside that car was his ex-wife. And I have it on good authority that she was here yesterday."

Claire watched Paul's face carefully as she spoke. He hadn't shown any surprise when she said that Drexel had been at Beekman Place, but he seemed to be debating whether to admit it. Ayman probably *should* start pushing him to find another job. Paul's comment earlier about lying being at the top of his job description had been intended as a joke, but this position almost certainly required him to lie frequently and convincingly. Stasia clearly possessed that ability, otherwise someone would have realized what she was up to on Mars. Paul, on the other hand, was a bit more of an open book.

"Yeah," he said. "I know she was here. I was over at UN HQ dealing with some logistical issues at the time, but ... I heard Macek and Kolya arguing about it last night." Paul glanced around and lowered his voice before continuing. "If I'd been here, I swear to God I'd have called the cops, even if it cost me this job. The real cops, I mean, even though they probably wouldn't have shown up. Beekman is policed entirely by our own security unless there's a body, which hasn't happened yet. I just..." He clenched his teeth and took in a long breath. "Jenelle brainwashed Stasia. It's the only thing that makes sense. I worked beside that woman for four years. Every single day. Stasia is not a murderer. I'll admit that I didn't know Meadow and Pax all that well, but ... come on. Did they strike you as cold-blooded killers?"

"They didn't," Claire admitted. "But we *know* that they planted the bomb at Icarus. And Pax punched you. He locked you and Ayman up in an equipment shed overnight."

"That's exactly my point, though. Both of them kept saying that they were trying to keep us out of harm's way. You said yourself that they tried to discourage you and Brodnik's team from going over there until later in the afternoon. There was also evidence that they tried to minimize casualties at the other camp. I'm *not* saying they're innocent, Stasia included. But ... none of us can understand how she changed that quickly. It's like someone flipped a switch. Even Macek agrees. Stasia may not have had Macek's personal history with Kolya—those two have known each other their entire lives—and you know Macek and Stasia didn't always get along. But even he says he would have sworn that she was one hundred percent behind Kolya's work. Not just the terraforming, but his long-term plan. His goals, his vision."

Paul's words reminded her of something Kolya had told her a few months earlier.

"During that dinner at Della Luna," she said, "when Kolya was trying to convince me to moderate the debate, he told me that his goals and Shepherd's are essentially the same—the long term survival of the human race. He said their only difference was in how to achieve that goal. Maybe something convinced Stasia that the Flock's tactics—the new, more aggressive ones—have a better chance of success?"

"No. Not buying it. Again, it's just too quick of a change. She would have agreed with them that we've wrecked the planet, agreed that it may well be too late to roll back the damage entirely. But—as Kolya said at the debate—we need practical, long term solutions. Shepherd deals in fairy tales. Going back to some sort of agrarian existence *isn't* going to happen and there's no mother-ship coming to save us. We have to save ourselves and..." He trailed off. "And I should shut up because you're going to hear all of this tomorrow night anyway."

"What's tomorrow night?"

"The keynote speech?" He frowned at her confused look. "The big announcement I mentioned, remember? Dinner in the Mir Ballroom?"

She shook her head. "Dinner isn't on the agenda included in the materials I received from the UN Press Office. I assumed Kolya's big speech would be tomorrow morning at the plenary session. And I was hoping maybe it would include pictures of Dr. Monroe's little lemur dog so I can finally show them to Jemma?"

"Nope. He's not showing pictures of Fenris. And I can't *believe* the dinner isn't on your agenda. Hold on." He pulled out his phone and expanded the screen, staring furiously at it as he typed. Once he'd fired off whatever message he composed, he slumped back into the booth, shaking his head. "I clearly told them that we wanted to *maximize* press coverage for the event. That's the entire reason that we moved the dinner here instead of the smaller venue we'd planned earlier. I need to go over the list again when I get upstairs and see how badly they've fumbled the ball."

"It could just be me. I did sign up late, after all."

"I hope you're right. Anyway, you can be my plus-one since Ayman is in cow and corn country. Because you *absolutely* have to be there." A tiny smile lifted the corner of his mouth. "For *several* reasons, none of which I can go into detail about at the moment. But I can promise you it will be newsworthy. We'll be recording the speeches, of course, but you might want to get at least a bit of background footage. Oh, and it's formal. Wear something gorgeous."

SIXTEEN

PAUL RECEIVED a notification that Kolya's AeroLyft was on the roof just as he was finishing up his burger. He shoved the last few fries into his mouth and tipped back his drink.

"He's back a bit sooner than I thought. Must be losing his touch. I have to double check with the kitchen about staffing for tomorrow night. Then, we'll head up to the penthouse."

Claire had no idea what the *losing his touch* comment was about and wasn't at all sure that she wanted to know. Her phone had vibrated twice while she was talking to Paul, so she took advantage of the few minutes alone to check her messages. She'd hoped that one of them might be from Beck, but no luck. The first one was Wyatt, so she sent back a confirmation that she was at Beekman Place and promised to let him know when she was on her way back to the apartment. The second message was from Alice, wondering if Claire could meet her at the Data Sciences Institute.

She asked if that meant tonight and got an immediate reply.

> Yes. I know you weren't planning to go out, but this translation program requires a bit more processing power than you're likely to have at your apartment. And you really are going to want to see this.

Claire debated telling her about the situation with Beck but decided to just keep it vague.

> I ended up going out after all. And I guess I could stop by on my way back to the apartment. It will be at least an hour before I can get there, though. Maybe longer.

> Not a problem. I was planning to work for a few more hours anyway. Buzz me when you're on campus and I'll come down and let you in. They lock up early on holidays so you can't even get into the lobby without a faculty member.

Paul returned to the table a few minutes later, looking even more frazzled. "The person I need to talk to is at one of our other hotels. I'll take you up to the penthouse and then see if I can track her down."

They navigated around the sightseers and diners on the crowded terrace, heading toward one of the twin turrets that towered at least thirty stories overhead. Two glass elevators on each turret carried passengers to the upper levels.

"You okay with this?" Paul asked, his finger hovering over the *up* arrow.

Claire frowned, momentarily confused. Then she spotted the teasing look in his eyes and realized he was referring to her reaction to the open maglev platform they'd had to take in order to reach the mining tunnels at Icarus Camp. Those tunnels had been about a kilometer up from the floor of Clark crater, and she'd clutched the bar for dear life each time she had to go up or down.

"This?" She laughed. "I'll be fine. This is an actual *elevator*, in a place where they require regular inspections. That thing was a death trap on a planet with no safety regulations at all."

"True." He lowered his voice to a conspiratorial whisper. "New York inspectors are notoriously easy to bribe, though. Sure you don't want to take the stairs?"

Claire was glad to see that stress hadn't entirely doused his sense of humor. "All the way to the top? I think I'll risk it."

When they reached the penthouse, she was surprised at how

much it reminded her of Kolya's apartment at Red Dahlia. It was another massive, torus-shaped area with living quarters at the center and transparent outer walls designed to showcase the three-hundred-sixty degree view. She suspected it was the work of the same architect. An architect with a limited repertoire, apparently. Or maybe both apartments were built to match his client's tastes.

They found Kolya behind the bar, pouring a hefty shot of amber liquid into a tumbler. He glanced at Claire and held the bottle up wordlessly, a question in his eyes.

"Yes. Thank you." She didn't especially want or need another drink after the whiskey sour. But she was fairly certain she recognized the liquor. Showing the proper appreciation for Kolya's precious krambambula might make him less annoyed at having his schedule disrupted and more inclined to answer her questions. And it was actually good.

"Just a little, though," she cautioned. "I didn't get much sleep last night."

Paul shook his head when Kolya tipped the bottle toward him, saying that he needed to double check that they had enough temporary staff for the keynote dinner.

Kolya arched one dark eyebrow. "Isn't that something that should have been nailed down weeks ago?"

"It *was* nailed down weeks ago," Paul said, a tight smile fixed on his face. "But then you added over twenty new people to the guest list last week. And we may be adding a few more since it looks like the UN Press Office has dropped the ball on at least some of the attending journalists. Claire said that the dinner wasn't on the itinerary in her press packet." He held up a hand. "Don't worry. I've got someone looking into it as we speak. Claire, if I'm not back up here before you leave, I'll see you tomorrow."

Kolya sighed and shook his head at Paul's retreating back. Once he was in the elevator, he said, "I miss Stasia. She had a knack for anticipating problems like this *before* they happened. Paul is doing his best, but…"

"*But* unlike Stasia, he's loyal. And he's not a terrorist." The words were a bit harsh, given that she knew Stasia's betrayal had wounded Kolya deeply. But she didn't like how dismissive he was of Paul's efforts.

He chuckled and handed her the drink. "Fair enough. That's definitely a point in his favor."

"I'd say it's far more than a single point. And let me guess. You simply moved him up to Stasia's job and never hired anyone to fill his old position, didn't you? So your entire personal staff is now *two* people—Paul and Macek—instead of the three you had before."

"Correct. Stasia's treachery didn't exactly improve my trust issues. I still don't like pulling new people into my inner circle. So I doubt that I'll be taking a page from your mother's book and hiring a gaggle of assistants any time soon. *Please* tell me you didn't come here to critique my staffing arrangements?"

"No. But if you don't want to be down to a *single* assistant, you might want to consider hiring Paul some help. I was thinking when I saw him in the lobby that he's aged five years over the summer."

As she said the words, Claire realized that the same was true of Kolya. He was still disturbingly handsome, but the lines around his blue eyes had deepened and there was a faint purple tinge beneath.

"Stasia's abrupt departure made for a difficult transition. But the good news is that I've just made a deal that should lighten Paul's load a bit. You, on the other hand, look much, much better than the last time I saw you. Has your leg fully healed?"

She shrugged. "It still twinges a bit. And they can't do anything about the scar for a few more months. But it has come in handy on more than one occasion when people claim that the chambers were VR or some other sort of hoax you're playing on the public. I'm sure it doesn't change their mind in the slightest, but one look at the scar and they stop giving me grief about it."

He handed her the drink and gestured toward one of the sofas that faced out toward the East River. "Unless you'd prefer the city view?"

She shook her head. "I've always liked the reflections in the water more than the lights themselves."

"Agreed. So … as delighted as I am to see you again, your timing could be better. I have to make a few last minute adjustments to my speech for tomorrow night. Because if anything I say or do is remembered by future generations, I think it will be this."

"Really? I would have laid bets on it being your unveiling of stage six. That was a jaw-dropping bit of showmanship."

He grinned. "It *was*, wasn't it? I was afraid that the timing would be off and had several minutes of filler planned if needed, but Davy swore that it would sync up. And, as usual, she was right."

The visual had definitely been impressive when Claire watched it in the lab with Joe and Beck, even though she'd already seen it on a smaller scale inside the tiny test dome at Fenris and had a good idea what was about to happen when she saw the speck of green appear in the upper corner of the screen. KTI's lead synthetic biologist, Davina Monroe—Davy to Kolya, and a few other close friends—had explained how they'd tweaked the reproductive genes of the perchlorate-eating bacteria in order to speed up multiplication, in addition to adding the vivid green color Kolya wanted for demonstration purposes. While normal *Azospira oryzae* spread through binary fission, splitting into two daughter cells, the modified version split into five identical copies. After releasing the compound inside the dome, Claire had watched for several minutes as the bacteria spread to cover about a quarter of the ground, and then only a second or so later, the entire surface had been carpeted in dayglo green.

Kolya had timed his speech officially launching stage six of the terraforming to coincide with the last few spurts of exponential growth from the bacteria samples that KTI had released at about five thousand locations across Mars. For nearly a month afterward, Mars hadn't exactly lived up to its nickname as the Red

Planet. Instead, it had looked a bit like a tennis ball, before fading to a grayish-green, a grayish-red, and eventually back to its usual tawny hue as the bacteria consumed the last of the perchlorates and died off. KTI had begun the second half of stage six immediately thereafter, peppering the surface of the planet with a variety of what Dr. Monroe called AE (advanced evolution) biobots, which were designed to mimic the process of natural evolution within a dramatically accelerated timeframe. By switching key genes on or off, the biobots would "evolve" into an array of flora uniquely adapted to each individual region of Mars. In later stages of the terraforming project, a different collection of these biobots would do the same for animals, although Monroe had stressed that fauna was a luxury that she was adding at Kolya's insistence rather than out of necessity.

The stage six lockdown still had several months to go, since the second step with the biobots was more complicated and would take more time to complete than the perchlorate remediation. Dr. Monroe had explained the dangers that the *Azospira* posed if humans were accidentally exposed, but Claire was now wondering whether the biobots were similarly hazardous during their evolutionary phase.

Which, of course, brought her mind back to the containment breach at Millex. She would probably have yielded to temptation and asked Kolya about it directly if their meeting had taken place over breakfast the next morning as originally planned. But she held her tongue. Any questions on that front would almost certainly piss him off and she needed to focus on information that would help her find out what had happened to Beck.

SEVENTEEN

"I HAVE to admit I was a bit surprised to hear that you were attending ACon," Kolya said. "Not just because of our ... miscommunication ... on Mars, but also because the conference tilts far more toward investment issues than scientific breakthroughs. As I believe I mentioned on our trip to Nepenthes, the Ares Consortium is really more of a commercial adjunct. You may have to hunt around to find sessions that will be of interest to your *Simple Science* subscribers."

"My editor has been pushing me to do a few episodes that focus more on applied science," she lied. "This seems like a good choice, since the background features about stage six brought in a lot of new followers."

"Okay. Just remember that you were warned when you find yourself bored to tears. At any rate, I *am* glad that you'll be there for my speech tomorrow night. In fact, you were on the list of journalists that I asked Paul to contact on Friday with an invitation to the dinner. When he said that you were already attending, I'll admit that I wondered if you might not have gotten a tip off from an internal source about my plans."

"From...? Oh," she said, realizing he meant Paul. Not only was Kolya overworking the poor guy, he still didn't fully trust him. "No. Paul absolutely did *not* leak your big secret. When I messaged him Thursday night, it was the first time we'd corresponded since a few weeks after our return from Mars."

He frowned for a second, then seemed to shrug off whatever question was lurking below the surface. "Well, again, it's good that you're here. And, at the risk of sounding like the raging egomaniac that my PR team likes to project, you should probably tell your editor to reserve a few column inches on Wednesday's front page."

"I'll let him know." She decided not to point out that while the *Atlantic Post* still printed a physical edition on Sundays, they hadn't published weekday print editions since around the time she was born. "I'm guessing this is about stage seven? An exclusive is apparently out of the question now, since you've invited all these other journalists, but maybe you could give me a hint in advance?"

He smiled and shook his head. "Sorry. I'm not giving *any* hints or exclusives this time. The only thing I'm willing to say before tomorrow night is that recent developments in the scientific world have convinced me to shift certain projects on my long-term agenda to the forefront. Now ... perhaps we should get to whatever it is that was so urgent you couldn't wait until our previously scheduled breakfast meeting?"

"Yes. When I contacted Paul initially to see if you could meet with me, I wanted to find out whether the Flock is targeting KTI the same way they're targeting me. They've killed four individuals, two of them people I was in direct contact with, burned my house in Maryland to the ground, and sent a fake FBI agent to interrogate me. All within the past few days." She held up a hand before Kolya could express his surprise—a reaction that looked sincere—and continued. "But all of that receded into the background earlier tonight when I watched my brother's research partner, John Beckett, being forced into a car with your ex-wife. Beck isn't just Joe's partner. He's my friend, and I'm worried."

"Where did this happen?"

"In Riverdale. Over in the Bronx. He was attending a college reunion."

"Well, I doubt that it's a ransom situation. Otherwise, Kai would have ... I mean, they would have probably contacted her security team immediately. And she'd have told your brother, right?"

"It's possible that they *have* contacted her. I haven't told her or Joe about this yet."

"You came straight to *me*?" He shook his head in bemusement. "Okay. How can I help?"

Again, his expression seemed sincere, but it didn't escape Claire's notice that he hadn't volunteered the very pertinent information that she already knew.

"Why did Corbin Drexel visit you yesterday? And before you jump to conclusions, that information did *not* come from anyone in your organization."

"Well, that's good to know, I guess." He took a deep breath. "But you can't seriously believe that I had anything to do with your friend's abduction. Or with any of what you've just told me. The Flock is targeting us, too, Claire. And … surely you don't think there's any chance that I would wish you *harm*?"

"I actually don't."

It was true. But would she have written it off so completely an hour ago? The possibility that she was taking a risk had certainly crossed her mind more than once. That tiny quiver of unease in her stomach as the elevator zipped up the side of the turret hadn't simply been the sight of the city far below, but also because she didn't entirely trust the man waiting at the top.

It had taken only a few minutes in his company, however, for her to slide into an easy banter, chiding him about his treatment of Paul and trying to cajole him into an exclusive. And that was the key problem with Anton Kolya. He had an uncanny knack for putting her at ease. It was probably true for everyone in his orbit, and undoubtedly at least part of the reason he was so successful.

"But," she added, "I *do* think you have information that I need in order to protect myself and the people I care about. You were married to Drexel, and you worked side by side with Stasia for nearly a decade. From everything I've heard, both of those women were strong supporters of scientific progress until suddenly they *weren't*. I'm trying to understand what could have driven them not just to *join* the Flock, but to take it over and turn it into some sort of anti-science hit squad."

"I've given that question a considerable amount of thought over the past couple of months." He hesitated, then said, "Anything I tell you about Jenelle has to be off-the-record. *All* of it. I will only talk to you about this if you give me your word that nothing I tell you about her will appear in the *Post*."

"Done. I'm trying to locate Beck and protect myself and those around me, not researching a story."

"I'd also appreciate it if you would avoid sharing any of this with Kai, at least for the time being."

"That's not a problem, either. It's only September. I won't see her until Christmas. And even then, I can't imagine bringing you up during the hour or two of forced pleasantries over our holiday dinner. I usually try to stick to safe topics that won't set her off, like politics or religion."

One corner of his mouth twerked upward. "Fine. Yesterday was the *second* time Jenelle dropped in unannounced. She and I hadn't spoken for nearly two years, and then the day before we left for Mars, she showed up out of the blue at our headquarters in Minsk. Macek said she was looking for Stasia, but she and Paul had departed for Tranquility Base that morning. So Jenelle asked to speak to me, instead. She didn't say anything at that time about joining the Flock or that she was involved in ousting Shepherd. Nothing about her name change, either. She just asked me to cancel stage six. No, that's not right. She *begged* me to cancel it, almost in tears. Kept saying that we were about to cross the Rubicon and if we didn't stop now, it would be too late to turn back."

"So … what did you tell her?"

"What do you think I told her? That I wouldn't do it. *Couldn't* do it. I kind of lost my temper, to be honest. The only reason I could think of that she would approach me with a request like that was if Westmoreland or some of the other mine owners who were opposing the mandatory lockdown had gotten to her. She knew several of them from her time at Daedalus, and I thought maybe they'd bribed her to try and influence me. Or that they had some other sort of leverage over her. She swore it wasn't true, but I mean, it would have at least explained why she was acting so strangely. Because … Jenelle doesn't beg. Certainly not to the point of tears. If you'd asked me when we were married, I'd have told you she was fearless. It was one of the things that attracted me to her. But the woman who showed up in Minsk, the woman who was here yesterday? She's a different person. I mean, she *looks* the same. She has one of those faces that doesn't seem to age, but in terms of personality? It's almost night and day."

"Would a bribe have worked? I thought she was rich *before* she met you. Someone told me that Kai courted her as an investor in Jonas Labs."

Kolya gave her a wry smile. "There's rich, and then there's *rich*. Jenelle has expensive tastes." He shook his head. "Or at least she did. That's a trait that her Corbin Drexel persona doesn't appear to share. She showed up here yesterday in one of those T-shirts with the garish EWA logo. Although maybe that was intentional, since it meant security spotted her instantly. They contacted Macek, who wasn't entirely happy that I asked him not to call the FBI."

"I don't blame him. Why *didn't* you call them?"

"Because I think she needs help—*psychiatric* help—more than she needs a jail cell. The American justice system isn't exactly known for its progressiveness in that regard. And I actually got her to agree to see someone. I've got a friend with connections to a clinic in Sweden. I'm going to take her to see a doctor there on my way back to Minsk on Friday. She didn't promise to check herself in for treatment, but she finally agreed to talk to them. And, to be clear, Jenelle is adamant that she did *not* order the bombings or the attack on Shepherd. I received a message from her shortly after the news broke about the attack at Icarus stating in no uncertain terms that she wasn't behind it. She stressed that point again when she was here yesterday."

"And you *believe* her?"

He shrugged. "I don't know. She seemed sincere. Crazy, yes. But sincere."

"Kolya, there are *photographs*—videos, even—of her meeting Stasia, Pax, and Meadow at a Flock compound right after they returned from Mars."

"Yes," he said dryly. "I'm all too familiar with Wyatt Garcia's investigation into the Flock. Among other things. Your *colleague's* name seems to be popping up everywhere these days."

She noted his sardonic emphasis on the word *colleague*. Was Kolya saying that he knew her relationship with Wyatt went beyond the fact that they both worked at the *Post*? That he knew she was at ACon at least in part because Wyatt had been banned? Or maybe he was aware of the subterfuge in the messages she'd exchanged with Shepherd about needing information for a colleague. It could be any or all of the three, so she decided to just ignore his snark and direct him back to the main reason she'd asked for the meeting.

"We know that Stasia and the others were behind the attacks on Mars and onboard the *Ares Prime*," she said. "We know that the Flock, under Drexel's leadership, took them in when they returned to Earth and that they are apparently keeping them hidden from the FBI. I have no clue whether this is a radical departure from her usual behavior, since my only face-to-face encounter with the woman was when she dropped a listening device into my bag. So, you'll have to forgive me if I'm far more skeptical than you are about her innocence."

"I didn't *say* I think she's innocent. I said that I think she's lost her mind. Jenelle is a brilliant woman. Brilliant, and charismatic. We weren't a good match in terms of temperament, but I admired her greatly. And yesterday…" He ran one hand through his dark hair and pulled in a deep breath. "I thought she was at a low point when I saw her in Minsk, but she's deteriorated even more over the past few months. Seeing her in her current state is heart-breaking. Knowing that she's pulled Stasia into this fantasy world just makes it that much worse. They've been close since university, but Stasia is much more levelheaded and practical. I can't fathom how she could be taken in by all of this. The first time she dropped in, Jenelle— and her name *is* Jenelle. This Drexel thing is part of her delusion. The first time, she just begged me to stop the terraforming. That was odd enough, but yesterday…"

"What did she say?" Claire prodded when he fell silent.

"Jenelle claims that when Stasia targeted Shepherd with the nanodrone, she was acting on orders from these alien Sentinels that Shepherd is always raving about. Except, she called them some other name, saying that *sentinel* was a botched translation. She says that she is—or rather, that she *was*—a member of that group. That she's an *alien*. Stasia is apparently an alien, too. And they must be long-lived aliens, since she claims they arrived on earth in the late 1950s."

"The 1950s?" Claire felt a sinking sensation in the pit of her stomach, even though she knew it wasn't rational. There was a perfectly logical explanation for these elements in Drexel's story syncing up so closely with the ones in Shepherd's memoir. The woman could have read the book herself, and simply adopted Shepherd's delusions as her own. And it was still more comforting to at least *think* of his memoir as a delusion, even if she couldn't entirely convince herself of the fact.

"Yes. She said they arrived a few years after the launch of Sputnik." Kolya gave her a weak smile. "Although, given your brother's research, I guess her extreme longevity claim isn't as odd as it would have seemed to me a while back. Anyway, Jenelle says she and Stasia both believed their assignment was to monitor Earth's scientific progress. Maybe even encourage it a bit here and there. Only now, she's discovered that the actual plan is to *destroy* the Earth. The leaders of the group seem to have determined that we're some sort of existential threat to the greater galactic good or whatever."

"That's … the same thing Tobias Shepherd believes."

"Uh…no." Kolya shook his head firmly. "I've had several *long* conversations with the man. Shepherd believes his Sentinels are benevolent gods who will whisk all of the faithful ecowarriors off to some sort of EcoValhalla when science and progress inevitably render the planet unlivable."

"Yes, that's mostly true. I guess I should have said that it's the same thing that Shepherd *fears*. He hopes the Sentinels are benevolent, but he *fears* that they are not."

"He told you that?"

"Indirectly, yes. You'll understand in a few days when…" She frowned, realizing that Shepherd's memoir probably wouldn't be coming out in a few days after all, unless the couple that ran Greenleaf Books had posted digital copies before the Flock burned their place down. "I got an advance draft of his memoir. His publishers were two of the victims I mentioned earlier."

Kolya was quiet for a moment, then shook his head again. "But *why*? I truly cannot imagine Jenelle or Stasia resorting to this kind of violence. Why target Shepherd if they apparently are working toward the same cause? Why target you?" His eyes, which had been fixed on Claire's face as he spoke, narrowed slightly and he tilted his head to the right. "And … you have a *theory* about that, don't you?"

Apparently, Paul wasn't the only one whose expressions were easy to read.

"I do," she said. "I'll tell you more when I have some concrete evidence to support it. But, to get back to Stasia and … *Jenelle*." She emphasized the name, since he seemed rather touchy about using the new one. "You said you can't imagine either of them being violent. Would that still be true if they considered it *protective* violence?"

"You mean self-defense?"

"In part. But I think it's more protecting others. I read the transcript of a speech that Jenelle gave at one of the EWA compounds. She told them that Shepherd was a good man, but he wasn't willing to go far enough now that the situation was much graver than he was willing to admit. She said they were at war and warned them that there would be casualties. And while any loss of life was regrettable and it would weigh on their consciences, she knew they were capable of doing what had to be done because they're not a flock of sheep, as others claim, but rather a flock of geese."

"See what I mean? She's completely lost it." He laughed humorlessly. "*Geese*."

"No, that part makes sense. Geese don't generally run away from a fight. They'll attack creatures that are much larger than themselves to protect their young. To protect their flock, too. You can even put a goose in with a flock of chickens and it will attempt to scare off predators."

"You know quite a lot about geese for a city girl. Did Kai take you and your brother to petting zoos when you were small?"

"Hardly. That sort of outing was always with my father." She paused, perfectly willing to let him be uncomfortable for a moment. "I simply looked up protective behavior in geese after I read the transcript of her speech. And she's right."

He gave her a point-taken look. "Okay. Maybe the analogy isn't quite as strange as it sounded at first blush. But the rest of it? Again, Jenelle says that she and Stasia are *aliens*."

"I told you before I agreed to moderate your debate with Shepherd that I was agnostic on the whole question of extraterrestrial life. And while your position that we are *alone in the universe*"— she said these words in the same ominous tone he'd used in the debate—"might have swayed me back then, recent events have me leaning much more toward Shepherd's position. Not necessarily his broader claims about the Sentinels. I still have major reservations on that point. But we now know that *two* planets have generated intelligent life, which doubles the previous count. Why is it so much of a stretch to think that there could be others?"

"Except we *don't* actually know that. Life on Earth could very easily have evolved from the same thing that triggered it on Mars. It could have traveled here on a meteorite. But, fine. Let's assume that we now have two planets. We still know of only one *solar system* with advanced technological life. We've been scanning for signs of other civilizations for well over a century. And we were sending signals out into the universe for nearly a century before that."

"That's still only about two centuries," Claire countered. "In the galactic scheme of things, that's not much more than the blink of an eye. And as for sending out signals ... do you respond to every call you receive? Because I don't. Maybe they picked up one of those early beacons that we sent out into the universe. And maybe they decided to investigate first so they could decide whether we're worth talking to."

EIGHTEEN

CLAIRE WAS HAVING major second thoughts about the meeting with Alice by the time the car arrived. It was just after ten-thirty, and between the bright lights of Beekman Place, staring at the viewscreen half the day for the virtual stakeout, and the four hours of sleep she'd gotten the previous night, going back to the apartment and crawling into bed seemed like a far more appealing option.

But curiosity won out over exhaustion, and she headed for the campus. As the car inched northward along FDR Drive, she messaged Wyatt to let him know where she was going and why, even though she was fairly sure he was going to try to talk her out of it. He didn't respond, however, and she realized he was probably talking to Erica about the draft of his article. When she tried calling Beck, it once again went straight to voicemail. She considered calling to find out if he'd spoken to Joe, but Joe would wonder why she needed to get up with Beck at this hour. And she still didn't *know* anything. Everything she'd stated as fact with Kolya was based on a few seconds of video that Wyatt had interpreted differently. While her gut instinct told her that the woman in the car was Drexel, she couldn't even be certain on that front and there was no way she could justify worrying Joe until she knew more.

As the car approached the Data Sciences building, she messaged Alice, who said that she would meet her at the ground floor entrance on 120th. The Aeris navigated into the only empty spot on the block, about ten meters away from the door, and she repeated her earlier instructions for the car to keep circling until further notice.

She started to get out, but hesitated when she spotted two people outside the entrance. They were dressed in matching dark clothes. Uniforms, maybe, but she couldn't see any insignia. One of them was entering a password or maybe trying to get the system to read his fingerprint. Whatever they were doing, it didn't appear to be working. Probably *not* campus security, then.

One of them turned and glanced at Claire's car, hand over his face to block the glare from her headlights. He nudged the one who was hunched over the security pad and Claire got a brief but crystal clear look at that person's face. She had thought both of them were men, due to their height, but she instantly recognized the tiny fringe of hair across the forehead of the one trying to open the door.

The bogus FBI agent with the wispy baby bangs was staring straight at her. Emily Wheeler, although she strongly doubted that was her actual name. Claire held her breath and stayed perfectly still, even though she knew there was no way the woman could see anything inside the car thanks to the headlights.

She tapped her phone. "Call Alice Dobroski."

Alice picked up instantly. "I'm coming, I'm coming. Stepping into the elevator right now."

"No! Stay there." As Claire spoke, whatever Agent Baby Bangs was attempting with the door finally worked. "Two people just broke into your building. One of them is the fake FBI agent I told you about. They may be wearing security uniforms, so I suspect they're armed. Is there somewhere safe on your floor?"

"Yes."

"Good. I'll call 911."

"No need," Alice said. "Campus security will be notified when I pull the lockdown alarm. And there's no point in both of us dealing with them. Just describe what you saw and go."

Claire gave her a quick description of the woman. She heard noises on the other end as she spoke, like something being dragged across the floor. "I didn't get a good look at the guy's face, though. I actually thought it was two men at first because they were both so ... tall."

Exceptionally tall, now that she thought about it. And after spending her afternoon watching dozens of *exceptionally tall* people going into that house in the Bronx, it was a bit too much of a coincidence for her liking.

"Got it," Alice said. "I'll call you back in a few."

"Wait. Are you in the safe room yet?" Claire asked as the alarm began ringing inside the building.

"No. But I've got time. They're either waiting on the elevator that I just propped open with Holly's office chair, or they're climbing five flights of stairs to the door that I just locked. But in case they somehow get through, they're *not* getting our data."

"The data isn't worth risking your life," Claire said.

"Do you think this manuscript is ancient Martian crime fiction?"

"What? Uh ... no. I can't see why anyone would go to that much trouble to preserve a novel."

"Then, it's worth a small amount of risk to be sure that we have the data, and they don't. I'm almost done anyway. Seriously, get out of here."

Alice ended the call. Claire had a sinking feeling, remembering the lengths to which these people had gone in order to destroy the data they thought was tucked inside a scrunchie at her house. But it would take a massive number of armed bugbots to take down a building this size, and surely a swarm that large wouldn't go undetected in the middle of the city.

She was about to move the car a bit farther down the block, but then the street level door of the Data Sciences Institute flew open, and the two exceptionally tall people she'd just watched break into the building spilled out onto the sidewalk. Heads down, they bolted across 120th, prompting a horn blast from one vehicle, and piled into a car parked on the opposite side.

"Aeris, follow the silver car now pulling out. I think it's a Neon Pulsar."

"Yes," the AI replied in the same crisp British male accent that Kai used for all of her vehicles. "It is a 2082 Neon Pulsar SE. But I cannot follow the vehicle."

"Why not?"

"Following a vehicle in city traffic would require an unacceptable level of risk. Please provide a physical address."

"I don't *have* an address. I'll risk the fine. Just *follow* the car."

The Aeris again gave her the same polite refusal and repeated its request for her destination.

"Can you at least zoom in so that I can make out the tag number?"

The image on the dash screen switched to a close up view of a New York license plate. She could almost make out the first digit —it was a *P* or maybe a *B*. But the tag had been splattered with a thick coat of mud—odd, given the otherwise clean car and dry weather—making it impossible to tell anything else.

At the end of the block, the Pulsar turned right and disappeared.

While Claire didn't know for certain where the car was headed, she could take a guess. It was entirely possible, even probable, that she was wrong. There were plenty of exceptionally tall people in New York. But…

"Take a right on Amsterdam and then head toward the Bronx. As fast as possible. I'll give you the address in a moment." The car's AI might not be programmed to follow another vehicle, but she knew her mother well enough to be certain that she'd paid for the upgrade that allowed it to exceed the speed limit.

"Proceeding to the Bronx at the fastest *safe* speed," the AI replied in a voice heavily tinged with disapproval. Apparently, Kai's upgrades allowed you to bypass the speed limit, but not the judgmental tone.

As the car pulled out of the parking space, she called Alice.

"The lockdown alarm must have scared them off. They're in a

silver Pulsar heading north on Amsterdam, but I couldn't get the tag. I think I know where they're going, though."

"You're following them?"

"Yeah. Just to see if my hunch is right. You want to meet over breakfast? It's not the end of the world if I miss the opening session at ACon."

"Okay. But not here. I'll get back to you with the address."

They agreed to meet at seven, and then Claire turned her attention back to traffic, scanning for a glimpse of the silver car.

"Aeris, I can't remember the street name, but it starts with the letters g-o-o-d."

"Your options within those parameters are Goodwin Street and Goodridge Avenue," the Aeris replied as the car pulled out of the parking space.

"It's Goodridge Avenue. I don't know the number, but it's a house with a large black iron gate near a dead end."

It was probably a waste of time. Baby Bangs and her companion had just broken into a university building, so Claire found it highly unlikely that they were sticklers about following traffic rules. Which meant they would get there before she did. She'd arrive to find the gate closed, and she'd have no clue whether a silver Pulsar had entered or…

"Is this the correct house?"

As the image of the gate appeared on the dashboard screen, Claire had a strong urge to smack her forehead with the palm of her hand. The picture was taken from a slightly different angle, but it was still close enough to what she'd been looking at all day that it finally jarred her sleep-deprived brain enough for her to realize what should have been obvious.

"Cancel the previous instructions and take me back to the apartment."

"Proceeding to Park Vista. May I resume normal speed?"

"Sure." There was no point in rushing when she could rewind and see anything she'd missed.

Wyatt returned her call just after she arrived at the apartment.

"And you're sure it was the same woman?" he asked after she told him about the break-in.

"Positive."

"Do you think they knew you were meeting Alice there?"

"It's possible," she said. "But it could also just have been a lucky break that I showed up when I did. Alice said she didn't think anyone else was there. The building was closed early due to the holiday, so she was coming downstairs to meet me at the street entrance. Maybe the burglars decided it was a good time to go after the data in Leffler's office."

"Or maybe they know that Alice now has a copy of the *other* manuscript?"

"Maybe." Claire didn't even want to think about how they might have gotten that information, and Wyatt must have known that since he didn't mention Beck. "Alice has managed to translate at least some of it, and something she'd found seems to have her worried. I'm going to stop by her place in the morning before ACon since my breakfast calendar is now free. Which reminds me. You can take your time getting here tomorrow. A *formal* dinner has been added to my agenda—which is probably good since I'm guessing that tongues will be a lot looser once the alcohol starts flowing than they'll be at the conference."

She settled onto the couch and pulled up the surveillance footage of the entrance to the house on Goodridge Avenue, winding back about ten minutes and watching at quadruple speed. The lights were on downstairs, and a shadow flitted by the tall window on the right side of the door.

"While we watch and wait, I need to tell you about my visit with Kolya, but ... I promised him that anything he told me about Drexel would not show up in print. Obviously, you already knew she was at Beekman Place, so there's no reason you can't publish that. But the rest of it has to be off the record, okay?"

"Sure."

Claire could tell from both Wyatt's tone and his expression that he wasn't happy with the agreement, but she knew he'd keep his word. So she spent the next few minutes telling him about Kolya's two visits from Drexel.

"You're telling me he just let her *walk out* of the place? Knowing that at a bare minimum, she's been giving shelter to the people responsible for damn near getting you killed? Not to mention the people who died in that tunnel. I mean, I'm in agreement that the whole I'm-actually-an-alien story suggests that she needs psychiatric help. I can't even argue his point that she's likely to get better treatment abroad. But that doesn't mean he should have just let her leave. There are plenty of private hospitals if you've got his kind of money, and—"

"Hold on," she said as a flash of headlights appeared on the screen. Glancing at the clock, she saw that this had happened about three minutes earlier. She slowed the video to normal speed as a car entered the brick courtyard. One of the garage doors went up and the silver Neon Pulsar rolled inside.

"I was right," she said. "Now I just need to figure out what to do about it."

"Call it in. You saw two people trying to break into a building. And you have their vehicle information and their address. The university probably has security footage of them fleeing the scene after Alice pulled the alarm. And since it was an anonymous tip that pointed me toward the place, you can pay it forward and send one to the NYPD. Or the university, if campus security has a tip line."

It was a good idea, and she intended to follow through on it as soon as they ended the call. If nothing else, maybe a bit of official scrutiny would put some sand in their gears.

"Damn it," she said. "I just wish I knew why Beck was there. And where he is now. And, for that matter, who the people inside that house are."

"I don't know about Beck," Wyatt said. "Maybe you're right. Maybe he was trying to investigate on his own. But on the other question—we know there were two different groups vying for control after they pushed Shepherd out. My best guess is that this house belongs to that other faction."

It was definitely the most logical, rational answer. But as Claire watched the two exceptionally tall would-be burglars emerge from the garage and cross the courtyard toward the house, she found herself leaning toward a different conclusion, one that would undoubtedly have Wyatt and Kolya and everyone else who knew her thinking that she should join Corbin Drexel in that padded room.

NINETEEN

CLAIRE LEANED back into her chair in Alice's tiny apartment, which rivaled Wyatt's place in terms of chaos, and stared at the two samples of untranslated script on the viewscreen.

"The one on the left is *Tales from the Aveezi Forest*. Right?"

Alice nodded. "And the one on the right is the beginning of the manuscript from the DNA sample. I'm guessing you're as tired of calling it that as I am, so the good news is that we now have a working title." She highlighted the very first line and clicked. The translation was now visible just below the symbols.

The [Journal] of Eberin Das.

"The last two words are obviously approximations, based on the phonetic list in Shepherd's notebook, and it might be closer to Eberin Tas or Thas."

"Those symbols—the two that you're translating as *Das*—are the ones I recognized when we first saw the manuscript. They're the same ones carved into the door of the outer chamber. Brodnik said it was probably the name of whoever was buried there, so I guess it would make sense that we'd find his journal inside. Still not sure why it was scattered in other locations, but ... anyway. Why is the word *journal* in brackets?"

"Because it's a guess, but I think it's a good one. As you noted before, the characters in the section breaks correspond fairly closely to the list of numbers in Shepherd's notes. I could also have translated it as *diary*, but the bits and pieces I've gotten so far seem pretty ... introspective ... and there seem to be gaps in time between entries. It could also be an epistolary novel—plenty of fiction here on Earth is written in diary form. But I have to agree with what you said last night. This seems like much more effort than even the most aggressive of self-promoting novelists would put forward to get someone to read their book. Another point against it being a novel is that the word *Tales* that you see on the left doesn't appear to have changed much at all between the two languages."

"Wait ... you're saying these are *different* languages?"

Alice gave the little half nod, half shake that Claire had seen her use on several occasions when she was trying to explain something complicated. "They're the same basic script, although there are a few additional letters, as you mentioned the other day, and several of the ones that are shared are altered. And, yes, I would class them as different languages, but only in the strictest sense. Did you read Chaucer's *Canterbury Tales* in school? You know ... *whan that Aprill with his shoures soote?"*

"I recognize the title, but I don't think I've ever read it. And if that last part was supposed to be English, I didn't follow it at all."

"You might follow a bit more of it if you *see* the words." Alice grabbed a napkin to brush the powdered sugar from her fingers and then pulled up a quote.

Here bygynneth the Book of the tales of Caunterbury.
Whan that Aprille with his shoures soote,
The droghte of March hath perced to the roote,
And bathed every veyne in swich licóur
Of which vertú engendred is the flour;

"This is Middle English," she said. "Not exactly how it would have looked when it was printed back in the day, but it's close. Middle English is *technically* a separate language from both Old English and our current version. Go ahead and read the first few lines and then tell me what you think it means."

Claire groaned. "You didn't tell me there would be a pop quiz. After two nights of crappy sleep, I need more coffee for that."

"Tell me about it. I didn't fall asleep until after two. I'm glad the lockdown alarm scared off your fake FBI agent and her buddy, but I think campus security would have taken me more seriously if they'd stuck around." She nodded toward her door, which had a total of six locks, ranging from a complicated electronic system to a simple latch and padlock. "And even with all of this, it still took me a while to fall asleep. I guess you can see now why my mom calls it Fort Knox."

Alice had messaged her a little before one a.m. from her office where she was waiting for the campus police to escort her home. They'd found no physical signs of tampering when they examined the keypad and, at first, seemed to think that Alice had over-reacted. Then they checked the logs and discovered that the most recent print entered into the system, at 10:52 p.m., had belonged to Dr. Holly Leffler. When Alice pointed out that Leffler was dead, they decided that it might be worth the trouble of going through the security cam footage. It showed two people—neither of them Holly Leffler—entering the lobby at 10:53. One of the guards noted that the woman's right hand looked a bit darker in the video, so their working theory was that she'd been using one of the nanopolymer gloves that can be programmed to hack into less sophisticated systems.

"I was thinking on the way over here … maybe they got Leffler's fingerprints while she was collapsed on the sidewalk after the drone attack. Several people gathered around to check on her before the EMTs arrived. They might be able to compare that footage with the camera at the CVS to see if either of the two who broke in were there. I don't think it could be the woman, because I'd just viewed that footage before the NYPD took me to the precinct office and I'd have recognized her hairstyle when she came in to get my statement. It could have been the guy, though."

"Maybe?" Alice said. "But they could just as easily have tapped into the university's system that stores the fingerprints and retrieved the data that way. Something similar happened a few years back. "

"Well, hopefully the NYPD will check their anonymous tip line in a timely fashion. I added that I thought it was the same woman I'd seen near campus wearing an FBI badge a few days ago. I'm sure they've gotten flak from the *actual* FBI about not checking her credentials more thoroughly, so maybe they'll follow through."

"I'm guessing you haven't heard anything from your friend?"

Claire shook her head. "I called Beck again this morning and got kicked straight to voicemail. I'm going to give it until tomorrow at three, which is when we're supposed to meet. If he doesn't show, I'll contact my brother and see if he's heard from him." She took another long sip of her coffee and a bite of her donut, being careful to avoid getting crumbs on her one and only suit. Then, she turned her attention back to the lines on the screen.

"Okay. Test time. The first line is easy. *Here begins the book of the tales of Canterbury*. After that, I'm only picking up a few words. We have *March* and *April* in the mix, and something that looks like *showers* and *drought* and *root*. I'm going to guess that it's something about April showers piercing the drought of March and bathing the roots of the flowers in … I don't know. Sweet liqueur?"

"Close enough. My point is that even though these lines were written in the late Middle Ages, you can still get the gist more than seven centuries later. That's because some kinds of words don't change much over time." She switched back to the two Martian samples. "That's true here, as well, and there are enough differences that I *do* think you'd have to call these separate languages. The etchings in the two chambers found on Mars and *The Journal of Eberin Das* are the same. Both were written in what I'm labeling *AM* for the time being—for *Ancient Martian*. The book of folktales is *NM*, or *New Martian*."

"How *much* newer?"

She made a hesitant sound. "I wouldn't even want to try to

estimate that because it hinges on so many different factors. We can assume this is an advanced technological society, which probably means high literacy levels and more standardization in the written language, unless there were a lot of languages competing for supremacy. Most of the changes to modern English over the past few centuries have been cases where we add new words and others fade out. We've pulled in a lot of words and phrases from other languages and dialects. We've also added new words—and dropped old ones—as culture and technology changed. Words that deal with the natural world or the basic human condition haven't changed much, though. *Bread, water, beer, apple, sun, hand, love, heart, blood*—you could probably pick all of those and more out in a sample not just of Middle English, like Chaucer's work, but of *Old* English, which is closer to German in many ways. If this civilization was similar to our own in that regard, with thousands of languages and many more dialects, then their language would have morphed from one version to the next far more rapidly than if there were only a handful. And in the case where there was only one language? It might barely change at all over many centuries or..." She shrugged. "Even millennia, I suppose. This is all highly speculative, of course."

"Of course. Okay … my brother's theory about all of this is that Shepherd wrote *Tales from the Aveezi Forest* himself and maybe had it stashed in a desk drawer for a few decades. Then after someone leaked the images of the symbols inside that first chamber to him, he decided that it would be a cool gimmick for his memoir if he created a language based on those symbols and then translated this book into it. Any chance that he's right?"

Alice laughed. "I mean, sure, Shepherd could have taken the symbols, fed them into a computer, and had the AI spit out a basic vocabulary, syntax rules, and grammatical structures fairly quickly. But there's just too much consistency here between the two languages. Unless the chambers themselves are a hoax and the Eberin Das journal was faked by this same person … who purposefully created two different languages, one of which evolved from the other. Even if Shepherd had access to the journal in advance from Dr. Kimura or some other source, he wouldn't have had any way to translate it and I don't think we'd see this sort of internal consistency between the two. It seems like a really convoluted way to sell his memoir. My professional opinion is that it's far more likely that what we have here are two related languages that evolved on Mars. The real question, at least to me, is whether Shepherd's story about how he got the book is true. Oh, and as you were saying last night, I'd also love to know what was so important about the DNA manuscript that someone on Mars would go to such lengths to preserve it."

"And why someone here on Earth seems to be willing to kill in order to destroy it," Claire added. "Which leads me to my next question. Why did you ask if I thought this might be an Ancient Martian crime novel?"

"Because death and murder are also core elements that persist throughout human history. Those words haven't changed much in English, and they apparently didn't change much for this civilization, either." She highlighted a word. "We already know from the translation of the *Aveezi Forest* manuscript that this word means *death*. This phrase seems to mean *by my hand*. So…"

She clicked a button near the top and the paragraph in Ancient Martian on the right was now shown in English:

And I wouldn't do that. That is why my [?] who after his second drink is giving all his [knowledge? research?] to me, would have to die later that night. And unless he chokes on dinner or has a heart [attack?], his death will be by my hands. There is no other choice.

Sitting at the table, I tried to remember the philosopher's name as the man kept talking, but he knew I ignored the [? from context: conversation or maybe lecture] because he smiled [?].

(Confidence interval: 52.2%)

"That confidence score goes way down if you take out the words the program is fairly certain about. Two of those are the words for *death* and *die*, because they're completely unchanged between the samples. It's still really rough, but…"

"It's a whole lot more than we had this time yesterday."

Alice nodded. "The next step is to begin entering in data from the notes. I've only skimmed them so far, but I can already tell that will take me a good bit longer. I'll probably have to go through and pick out the individual words and phrases, because two of the three sets of notes are mostly handwritten, and the program really isn't set up to handle that."

"*Three* sets of notes?"

"Yes. Two are from Shepherd's files, related to the New Martian script used in the *Aveezi Forest* book, and then there's the other set of notes about the journal. I'm guessing that was Beck's work. His notes were actually the main reason I wanted you to stop by last night. They're kind of confusing."

"That's why I asked him to meet with us on Wednesday. We haven't really discussed them in much detail beyond him nailing down a few common words like *the* based on things like frequency and word order. I don't think I'll be much help."

"He's nailed down a lot more than a few words, Claire. And one of them in particular has me confused. See the word *philosopher*, in the second paragraph? It was one of the words in brackets when I first ran it through, using just the *Aveezi Forest* translation and the basic tools that compare structure and so forth. The confidence interval was around twenty percent at that point. As I was skimming through Beck's notes, however, I saw the word translated as *philosopher*. I thought maybe there was an error at first, that the word was actually somewhere in the *Aveezi Forest* translation. But I ran a search, and the word isn't *anywhere* in the book. I can't find it in Professor Everett's notes, or in Shepherd's either. There are others, too. Single words and a couple of phrases. There was even one idiom—*the abeeda has a sweeter peel,* which he translated as a cloud having a silver lining. Idioms can be *really* hard to translate, even between closely related languages, let alone something from a different planet. So, I was wondering if maybe there was another set of notes from Everett that you forgot to include when you transferred the files?"

"No," Claire said. "That was everything I had. The *Aveezi Forest* book, with the translation. And the notebook, which was partly Everett's and partly Shepherd's notes from what I could tell."

"Well, damn," Alice said. "I was hoping there was another treasure trove of data out there. Beck must have found some things in those handwritten notes that I missed on my first pass."

Claire nodded and forced a smile. Once again, she knew that was the most rational explanation. But Beck had told her on the flight from Maine that he'd barely looked at the documents on the nanodrive. "Can you do me a favor and make going back through those notes your first priority? I mean, aside from your classes, obviously."

Alice shrugged. "There's not a whole lot of work for the first week of classes. I've taught these courses before, except for a graduate seminar I'm covering for Holly. I'll be done today by lunch time, and I can spend the rest of the day on it." She was quiet for a moment, and then added, "Do you think Beck's work on translating the journal is connected to his disappearance?"

"I don't know. But given everything else that's been happening, it seems likely. Be extra careful, okay?"

FROM THE ATLANTIC POST

(SEPTEMBER 4, 2084)

TURMOIL AT JONAS LABS

~ Bryce Avery

(Washington, DC) As Jonas Labs prepares for its first annual meeting since the launch of its groundbreaking longevity drug, Rejuvesce, there are widespread rumors of discontent among shareholders—including some employees—over CEO Kai Jonas's controversial decision to release the patent after only two years. The move, which has been applauded by the World Health Organization, paves the way for more rapid distribution of the drug, and has helped to quell some of the complaints from nations in distribution Tiers Two through Six. It will also decrease the waiting time for those who are beyond the current cutoff age of sixty-nine.

One shareholder, who requested anonymity, told the *Post*, "I get it. People want the drug now. But the drug wouldn't exist at all without the money that we put into this company, and this decision seriously undercuts our return on investment. She's basically giving away four entire years of exclusive worldwide sales. We were blindsided by this move, and yes—we are evaluating *all* options, including legal remedies, to protect our interests."

He went on to note that the proposed lawsuit, which could have far-reaching implications for the pharmaceutical industry, would challenge the decision on the grounds that the company's board of directors breached their fiduciary duties to stockholders.

These developments will be closely watched by industry analysts and investors alike, as they could signal a shift in how pharmaceutical companies balance profit-making with their broader societal roles, particularly in matters of global health access.

A source inside Jonas Labs said the complaints from shareholders were premature, noting that potential new applications of the drug were in the wings. Under current patent law, that could trigger a reinstatement of the exclusivity period for the new formulation.

TWENTY

TEN MINUTES into the first panel of the conference, Claire was already convinced that Kolya's warning the night before had been dead on. The session was listed simply as "Stage Seven Forecast," and she'd hoped it would talk about whether the next stage would include the launch of biobots to create specialized animal life on the planet. She didn't know whether that was actually on tap for stage seven—Kolya, Paul, and Davina Monroe had all been rather closemouthed about what would take place in each stage—but this panel had seemed like a better bet than "Proposed Taxation and Regulatory Structures." As she stared at yet another chart of economic data compiled from the past decade, however, she wasn't so sure.

The second panel on materials science was drier than the Martian regolith. And while the final panel of the morning sessions on transportation advances had some interesting visuals, it must have been designed for prospective investors who had yet to visit the planet. She'd either seen or actually traveled in every vehicle they displayed while she was on Mars, and several of them had even been in the various bits of video that she'd used in the *Simple Science* segments she'd filmed during the trip.

There wasn't even much chance of another academic controversy like the one at the ACon a few years back when Kimura claimed that the *Deinococcus* samples had been altered, since the current panels were very light on academics. Most of the presenters worked either with KTI or with the other companies currently operating on Mars.

To be fair to the speakers, though, it would have been really hard for anything to hold her attention after what she'd just learned from Alice. As the Aeris fought its way through the morning traffic to UN Headquarters, Claire had skimmed through the notebook entries by Shepherd and Everett. She'd kept her tablet open during the panels, as well, returning to the notebook as soon as her interest waned—in other words, pretty much immediately—and she was becoming convinced that Alice was right. The word *philosopher* wasn't in either set of notes. Nor could she find any idiom about bitter fruit.

So between her lack of interest and her lack of attention, when the conference broke for lunch, Claire still didn't have anything she could use in a segment that wouldn't risk half of her viewers unsubscribing. Hopefully, Kolya wasn't grandstanding about the newsworthiness of his keynote speech. Otherwise, there was a decent chance she'd be going back to Bernard empty-handed.

She grabbed a sandwich from one of the trays in the dining area and then scanned the room to see if Paul was around. She'd spotted him between the first and second sessions, and even got a brief glimpse of Kolya and Macek in the middle of a small crowd before they entered the elevator. None of them were anywhere to be found now and she thought it highly likely that Kolya had opted to go out for lunch instead of settling for chicken salad on soggy croissants.

After she finished eating, she checked her messages. Ro had sent a couple of pictures of Jemma horsing around with Joe in the pool the day before and said that they were planning to go back out on the boat that afternoon. Claire was about to forward them to Beck along with a note saying that his devious plan was working. She was thinking it might jar him into a response, but realized at the last second what a profoundly stupid idea that would be if Beck—and his phone—were being held by Drexel.

And what if Wyatt was right? What if Beck had gotten into that car voluntarily? Not that she thought for a moment that he was a danger to her or anyone else, but … Kolya claimed the same thing about Jenelle and Stasia. And what Paul had said about

Stasia— *it's like someone flipped a switch*—wasn't all that different from what she'd been thinking about Beck's behavior over the past few days, aside from those last few minutes in the AeroLyft when he urged her to take the gun.

She tossed the rest of the sandwich into the trash. The afternoon torture sessions were about to begin, and she'd lost what little appetite she had. Having utterly failed at her cover story for attending, she needed to tackle the more important task of getting information about the Millex containment breach for Wyatt.

Scanning the agenda, she decided that the most likely candidate would be the panel on economic forecasts for the mining industry and was surprised to spot a familiar face heading into that room. Kolya had said her name was Elizabeth, and she was one of the two mining executives whose conversation Claire had eavesdropped on at the Red Dahlia during the MFL negotiations. Since the woman had already shown herself inclined to engage in a bit of gossip with her fellow mining executives, Claire followed her into the room and took a seat in the row behind her.

After a brief exchange of pleasantries with the man on her left, however, Elizabeth listened quietly for the entire session, occasionally nodding her perfectly coiffed head of silver hair or jotting something down on her tablet. At the end of the panel, she told the man that she was going to head back to her hotel but would see him at the dinner.

Claire quickly leaned down when the two of them stood up, pretending to look for something in her daypack so that her face was hidden.

"I just hope the food is better than what we had at lunch," the man said.

"Oh, it will be," Elizabeth assured him. "Everything on the UN campus has to go through the onsite catering staff, but the dinner is on Kolya's turf. And he'll be pulling out *all* the stops given how amped up the man is over this big announcement."

"Any idea what it's about?" he asked as they made their way toward the aisle.

"I tried to get him onto that topic this morning. All he would say is that it's a stellar opportunity for forward-thinking investors. So your guess is as good as mine."

The man lowered his voice. "Maybe he's going to announce that KTI has upgraded their contractors' biocontainment systems."

Elizabeth chuckled darkly. "Too damn little and too damn late."

The two parted ways at the door. Claire followed Elizabeth, but she was clearly headed toward the exit. When she turned back to see if she could find the man, he was nowhere in sight.

After a quick glance at the remaining panels on the agenda, she decided to just page the car to come and rescue her. None of the subjects dealt with mining or anything else likely to be useful, and they all sounded deadly dull. If she was going to fall asleep, she'd much rather do it in the nice comfy bed back at the apartment than in a conference chair.

About twenty minutes later, as the car was pulling out into traffic, a message came in. It was Kolya, not Beck.

> I hate to say I told you so, but … I absolutely did.

She felt a twinge of annoyance. Neither Kolya nor Paul had been in the hallway when she left the conference. Had he assigned someone to keep an eye on her?

> On the contrary. In fact, the panels were so invigorating that I find myself in need of a few hours to unwind before tonight's festivities. Also, my new shoes hurt.

The last bit was actually true. As soon as she got back to the apartment, she headed straight for the sofa and peeled the shoes from her aching feet. If she set an alarm for four-fifteen, that would give her time to shower, dress, and make it to Beekman

Place in time for the pre-dinner cocktail hour, so she grabbed a glass of water from the kitchen and went into the bedroom.

To her surprise, she found Wyatt on the bed, shirtless and snoring softly. He must have been too wired to sleep after finishing the article and decided to come straight to New York.

If she'd seen his face before she spotted his very familiar body, she might not have recognized him. He was clean-shaven, and his normally shaggy hair was cut well above his ears. Wyatt strongly preferred a beard trimmer over a razor and the last time she'd seen his hair this short was during their senior year at Stanford. He'd been about to leave for Christmas at his grandparents' house and told her that he was testing a theory that the amount of cash in his Christmas card was negatively correlated with the length of his hair.

A faint whoosh of traffic came from behind her. At first, she thought it must be from the street below. But cars didn't *whoosh* on Fifth Avenue in the middle of the day and the window was across the room. When she turned, she saw that the viewscreen was on and Wyatt had fallen asleep watching the courtyard of the house in Riverdale. All was quiet at the moment, aside from the distant road noise. No cars in the courtyard, no shadows on the window.

Claire quietly slipped out of her jacket and skirt, leaving on the camisole she'd worn underneath. When she opened the closet to hang up the suit, she found the reason for Wyatt's makeover hanging on the back of the door—a crisp white shirt, black pants and a bowtie, along with a burgundy vest bearing the gold castle logo of Beekman Place. She tugged on a bit of plastic sticking out of the vest pocket and found a restaurant union ID with a recent picture of Wyatt's new clean-cut persona.

The bed creaked behind her. "You're back early," Wyatt said around a yawn. "C'mere."

She went over to the bed and tossed the ID onto the mattress next to him. "I don't believe we've been properly introduced, sir."

He grinned. "Kelvin Reed, RWU Local 122, at your service, ma'am."

"Hmm." She sat down on the bed next to him. "You don't really *look* like a Kelvin to me. That would make you an absolute zero and even *without* the beard you're at least an eight."

"A *science* joke?" He groaned. "You spent too long at the conference, babe. They broke you."

"Hey, that joke would have been the highlight of the panels I sat in on today." She nodded her head toward the screen. "Any action in the Bronx?"

"Not unless something happened in the past few hours. I fast-forwarded through the buffer from both cameras before I fell asleep. Did you learn anything at the conference?"

"Not really. But I did overhear one of the mining executives I met at Daedalus City chatting with a friend. He joked that maybe Kolya's big announcement was that KTI was upgrading their biocontainment system. To which she replied too little, too late."

"Interesting. Did you catch anything else?"

"No, but the woman said that she'd see him at dinner. And I encountered her in Daedalus City. She seems to get chatty after a drink or two."

"Good to know. I definitely need to leave a recorder at her table."

"They're going to scan you for recording devices when you go in."

"Oh, I'm counting on it. They won't find anything." He leaned over the side of the bed, pulled a pair of glasses out of his bag, and handed them to her.

She was about to ask what she was looking for, but then she noticed four tiny, raised dots on the inside of the arm. Four more were on the other side, as well. They were a slightly darker color than the frame, but it definitely wasn't something you'd notice at first glance.

"Okay," she said, still confused at how he could possibly think this was going to work. "But they'll emit a signal, right? And the *signal* is what the scanners will be looking for."

"And again, they won't find anything. Not until about ten

minutes after six, when Kes activates them. By that time, I'll be long past the security check, and these will all be in place. Plus, by that time, you and all of the other members of the press who *aren't* on their blacklist will be there with your cameras, so they're going to be picking up signals anyway. They're not going to notice a few more."

"Between sneaking in cameras and the fact that you've never waited tables in your life, you're going to get this Kelvin Reed person kicked out of his union."

Wyatt shook his head. "According to the guy who got me the ID, Reed passed his bar exam earlier this year. I don't think he's going to be waiting tables again. And there will apparently be several dozen temp workers there tonight, so I'm sure I won't be the only one who's a bit on the clueless side. If they want experience, they shouldn't rely on temps."

"I don't think they had a choice. Kolya added a bunch of guests to the list this week. He's running Paul ragged."

"Paul should join a union. Although I'm not sure they have one for the henchmen of egomaniacal trillionaires. Wait … am I still allowed to make fun of him?"

"No. Paul's a nice guy."

"I didn't mean Paul and you know it."

"Nice try, but I'm still not ready to talk about the Kolya thing."

"No problem. I can think of many, many things I'd rather do than talk about Anton Kolya." He pulled her down on top of him, leaving no doubt about the nature of those many, many things he'd rather do. "But first, will you answer a question for me?"

"Maybe…?"

"It's *not* about Kolya. Just…" He closed his eyes, took a deep breath, and then locked her gaze with his own, "The other day, when you called me from New Haven. I'm talking about the second call, right after you finished talking to the police?"

Claire nodded and her stomach tightened into a knot. She knew where this was going.

"Pretty sure I was talking to dead air there at the end. You want to tell me why you hung up so fast?"

All of her earlier determination drained away. Maybe continuing with the games they'd been playing wasn't such a bad idea after all. If there was a chance that the alternative was losing him, then...

"Sorry about that," she said, keeping her tone light. "It was just a really emotional day. And it's not like you didn't already know how important you are to me." Claire gave him a teasing smile and ran her fingernail softly along his bare chest. "Less talk, more action, mister."

"So impatient." He grinned and flipped the two of them over so that he was on top. And then his expression grew serious. "I'm more than willing to save the talk for later, except for this. *I love you, too.* That's what you'd have heard me say if you'd stayed on the line."

TWENTY-ONE

LATER, as they lay side by side listening to the traffic sounds, Wyatt brushed a strand of hair from her face. "For people who make a living explaining complicated things, we both kind of suck at communicating. Although, in my defense, I thought we were on pretty solid ground since you got back from Mars."

"I did, too, at first. But then it felt like we were sliding back into our old patterns. I mean, you asked if I was packing the blue dress ... which I'm very glad I did because otherwise I'd have had to shop for something to wear tonight. And then at the restaurant, when you suggested that we take a rain check on the rest of the evening, I was almost certain you were going to tell me that you'd met this incredible woman when you were in Ohio."

He sighed. "I very nearly did. And there's a decent chance that I would have if you hadn't pointed out that what's happening now is a different situation. Before, as much as I hated being dishonest with you, I kept thinking that if I gave you a little incentive, you'd find someone ... safer. You'd still be in my life, we'd still be friends—or at least I hoped we would—and I wouldn't have to worry that the job I'm good at, a very necessary job that has saved lives, might get you killed. But you didn't take the bait and I was getting more and more to the point where I didn't want you to. And now ... like you said, it's not my job that's putting you at risk."

She pressed her lips into the hollow of his shoulder. "Did it ever occur to you that maybe, just *maybe*, you should let me decide about the risks and rewards of being with you based on *full* information?"

"Occasionally. But then I'd remember the message I found in my box at the *Post* just before the Idaho militia trial."

"The Boise Bois?" The Idaho militia's name had made it hard for anyone to take the group seriously at first, but several months after she started at the *Post*, they'd sent almost every woman journalist—and a few of the men—a letter. It was simple and effective—just a copy of the picture the *Post* placed next to their byline, only with crosshairs over their faces. "I got that message too, remember? We *all* had a security detail following us around until the trial was over."

"Yeah. Well, there were *two* pictures in my letter—probably not a surprise since I was the one covering the story. The first picture was the same one everyone else got. But they added a shot of the two of us together, taken on the slopes up at Seven Springs. Same MO, with the crosshairs over your face. The message was pretty damn clear."

"So, two weeks later, you started dating someone you met in ... I'm thinking it was the one in Vegas? Evie?"

"Sort of. I had dinner with a group of reporters in Vegas, one of whom was a very nice woman named Evie. After dinner, she went back home to her husband and kids. Everything else I told you was drawn from my fertile imagination. Then shortly after that, you moved in with Ro and Jemma, and ... I got close to them, too. Which made me even *more* nervous. And, if I'm being completely honest, it still does. For the most part, I focused on work when I was away. I didn't want you in danger, but I also didn't want to risk anyone else ending up as a target."

"Okay, since we're dropping truth bombs—"

"You don't have to tell me about Kolya."

"I've actually told you pretty much everything about that. It was a flirtation. Nothing more. And any possibility that it might have *led* to something more went out the window when I learned about him and my mom. This is about Beck ... no, not like *that*. It's just that I'm less certain than I was before about him being forced into the car."

"What changed your mind?"

"He's been acting strange for the past few days. I thought it was just that Joe and Kai were pushing him to get back into the lab rather than taking time off. Despite the fact that Rejuvesce is going to make them an incredible amount of money, Jonas Labs shareholders are apparently furious that she gave in to Joe's demand that they release the patent early in order to increase supply more quickly. He and Beck are working on something else —something that's going to boost the company's profit margin significantly in the long term—and she wants to be able to make her big announcement before the annual meeting, which is coming up in a few weeks. Joe wants to wait until they're at least done with the next stage of testing."

"How about Beck?"

"He wants to hold off even longer. But thinking back, Beck seemed to be dealing with all of that pretty well until Saturday night, which is when I told him about Shepherd's memoir and the book of folktales. And…" She glanced at the time on the screen and saw it was after three. "Wait. Did you need to sleep? Because this is going to take a while. We could always wait and go over all of it after we get back from the dinner."

He shook his head. "I got four or five hours before you arrived. I'll be okay. And unlike the invited guests at this bash, who just have to show up and look pretty, I have to be at the Palace early for training. In about ninety minutes, in fact. I'll be taking the subway in order to keep up my cover and I haven't eaten since breakfast, so I need to grab food on the way. Which means I have maybe twenty minutes before I need to hit the shower."

"All right, then." She took a deep breath. "To be honest, I was kind of hoping you'd opt for the nap. Because I'm still trying to work through all of this."

She spent the next few minutes filling him in on what Alice had told her.

"And you're *sure* those words aren't in the notes from Shepherd?"

"If they are, I couldn't find them. Neither could Alice. Admittedly, a few of the handwritten sections are barely legible. She's going back through the notes again this afternoon and said she'd let me know if she comes up with anything. What we do know for certain, though, is that those words are not in the *Aveezi Forest* book, because she was able to search that digitally. And all of the other notes I saw were about vocabulary from that book. I guess there *might* have been some other reason that Everett taught Shepherd the word for *philosopher*, but … Beck said he barely had time to look at the files. He may not have meant that literally, but I don't see how he could have just stumbled upon something that Alice and I both spent hours searching for specifically and never found."

"I know you don't want to hear this, but the most obvious answer is that Beck is working with Drexel. Or with someone else in the Flock who had access to Shepherd's notes from where he created the language. It could even be the person who was working with Devin."

"No. Beck would *not* be working with the Flock if they're connected to any of these attacks. Especially the ones aimed at me. I mean, he left his gun with me and … Again, as much as my angsty teenage self may have fantasized about the guy, there's nothing between us. But he's like a brother to Joe. I know he cares about me, too. And yes, I know it seems like the most logical answer to all of this, but I do not think Shepherd *created* that language."

"Okay, sure. I don't mean he created it entirely from scratch. He obviously used the symbols from the chamber as a starting point. You said yourself that someone could have sent him the images from inside the chamber several months before you left for Mars, either someone on Brodnik's team or one of Kolya's people. I mean, how long would it take to—"

"To create two different but closely linked languages? And

leaving all of that aside, I just can't believe they're killing people to hide a marketing scheme for his memoir. Even Joe had to admit —" Her mouth fell open and for a moment she just sat in stunned silence.

"What?" Wyatt prompted.

"With everything else going on, I didn't even think about this until just now, when I remembered Joe transferring Beck's notes to my device on Saturday night, along with the Eberin Das journal and the files he'd just extracted from Shepherd's nanodrive. Those notes are from Beck's work on the translation *before* we went up to Maine, using just the software. He told us that he'd made out a few other words, but ... not entire phrases. I can't see how frequency analysis or whatever else that software does could come up with a word like *philosopher*."

"So ... he lied, or at the very least, left out some important information."

"Some very important information. His notes are the main reason Alice has actually made progress on the translation."

"Does he know you have those notes?"

"I'm not sure. But it's not like he was being secretive about it. By the time we left Maine, he seemed eager to turn over everything he'd done on the project to Alice, so that he could get his mind back on his work with Joe."

"Okay." He frowned. "So you're saying you think this *Aveezi* book is real? That those are actual folktales from ancient Mars?"

"I actually *don't* think they're from Mars. But I also don't think they're from Earth."

He stared at her for a long time, eyes wide, and then sank his head back into the pillow. "So you believe that this Nathaniel Everett really was one of these Sentinels. That the story in Shepherd's memoir is true. But ... all of it? Even the warning just before the old guy killed himself?"

"Maybe. One minute I believe it and the next I'm telling myself that I've lost my mind."

He didn't say anything for several minutes. She didn't interrupt, because she'd seen him deep in thought before and could pinpoint the microexpressions that flitted across his face as he considered the various points and counterpoints.

Finally, he shrugged. "For the most part, it seems … implausible. But I keep coming back around to this. If someone *was* part of an alien organization tasked with deciding whether or not to destroy the planet, that might be the kind of secret they'd be willing to blow up buildings and even kill in order to hide. So where do you think Corbin Drexel fits into this? Or Beck for that matter?"

"I'm not sure."

It was true. She wasn't *sure*. But the possible explanations were narrowing rapidly.

Somehow, Beck had been able to translate a few words from this ancient language, just as she had been able to pick out bits and pieces of the *Canterbury Tales*. There were only two explanations for this fact that she could think of at the moment. Either Beck was working *with* people who had helped him translate portions of the journal, or he himself was fluent in a similar language.

As she'd told Kolya the night before, she was now far less inclined to accept his premise that humans were the only intelligent life. She was almost to the point where she could wrap her head around the idea that Nathaniel Everett and Corbin Drexel were aliens. Maybe even Stasia.

But *Beck*? Someone she'd known for half her life?

Her brain needed much more time to process that possibility and time was short at the moment.

"You need to get in the shower," she told Wyatt. "Otherwise, you're going to be late."

He pulled her over for a kiss. "You could join me…"

"I could. But based on our history in that regard, that would make it even more likely that you're late. There's half a container of shrimp chow fun in the fridge from last night. Do you want me to heat it up for you?"

"Sure…" His resigned tone was clearly more about her declining the shower invite than the leftover noodles she'd offered. He stuck his head around the door a few seconds later. "Before I forget though, what was the name of the mining executive you mentioned? The gossipy one?"

"Elizabeth, but I don't have a last name. Silver hair, probably in her late sixties or early seventies. Attractive, dresses very posh. Husky voice. Actually, if you have any more of your teeny-tiny cameras, I'll just place it for you."

"Well, look at you," he said with a grin. "Taking a walk on the wild side."

"More like the dark side. Congrats. You've corrupted me."

She lay in bed for a moment after the door closed behind Wyatt, debating whether to take a quick nap after he left for Beekman Place. But she'd only have about an hour and there was no way her mind was going to slow down enough to let her sleep. Better to chug some coffee and power through.

She went into the kitchen and put a pot on to brew, then searched around until she located a skillet. It looked brand new, and since she had no idea how long it had been sitting in the cabinet, she gave it a quick rinse before heading over to the fridge to grab the noodles.

Her hand froze a few inches from the container as the unmistakable sound of gunfire came from the bedroom.

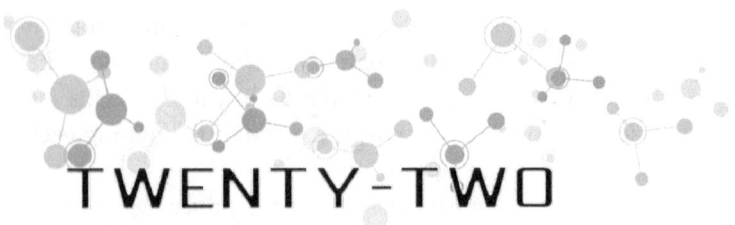

TWENTY-TWO

BECK'S PISTOL was in her daypack. But where the hell had she put the pack?

Then, she remembered the shoes. She'd sat down on the sofa to take them off, and ... it must be under the coffee table.

"Claire! Are you okay?" Wyatt yelled just as her hand closed around the daypack.

Twin waves of relief flooded through her. First and foremost, he was alive. And second, his voice was *loud*—much louder than the gunfire coming from the bedroom.

"I'm fine. Something must be going on downstairs."

"No. Something's going on in *Riverdale*."

When Claire reached the bedroom, she found Wyatt crouched next to the bed, naked and still wet from the shower, searching through the tangled sheets for something. On the screen, a body was sprawled face down at the center of the courtyard as a pool of red several shades darker than the brick spread out around his head.

"Have you seen my phone?" Wyatt asked.

"On the floor. By the other nightstand."

He retrieved the phone, skipped the recording on the screen back a few minutes, and hit play. A second or two later, the screen went dark. It wasn't a uniform shade of black, however. A puffy diagonal line ran from one edge to the other. She could hear breathing, too. The diagonal line moved slightly in time with each breath, and she realized it was a wrinkle on the shirt of someone standing in front of the camera.

"Okay," a man whispered. "On three." There was a trace of an accent that Claire couldn't place. He must have counted off on his fingers because nothing else was said, but about three seconds later, the blackness on the screen began to move.

Wyatt zoomed out and she could now see that there were three men and one woman, all moving toward the house, clad in body armor and carrying rifles. Five black drones that looked like dinner plates traveled a few meters in front of them. The drones paused just inside the tree line and spread out around the perimeter of the courtyard.

"Maybe the cops are following up on my anonymous tip," Claire whispered.

"I don't know. This seems like overkill, though, even if they do think someone in there was posing as FBI." Wyatt was whispering too, even though they were alone in the apartment. He must have realized that was ridiculous at the same time she did, because he added in a normal voice, "And those drones? They're top of the line. Same for the weapons and body armor. No way those are local government, not even in a city as big as New York."

"Whoever it is, they need to invest in better helmets," Claire said with a gulp, thinking of the man who was about to be shot.

At some apparently prearranged signal, the group on the screen picked up their pace. One of the four was slightly ahead of the rest, something Claire suspected he would soon regret. She scanned the windows of the house for movement or any sign of weapons and steeled herself for the gunfire.

A moment later, the shots began. She couldn't pinpoint exactly where they were coming from, but the man jerked forward almost instantly and collapsed onto the bricks. The woman and one of the other men were a few steps behind him. A bullet, or maybe several of them, caught her, but the man yanked her back. At the same time, he began shouting for the guy behind them to retreat. He could have saved his breath, though, because their rear guard was already barreling toward the camera.

The other two were also headed back now, with the man Claire was pretty sure must be the leader half carrying the injured woman. He was a big guy, so she didn't seem to be slowing him down much.

Behind them, the black drones pivoted toward the camera. Claire caught a flash of red light, and a second later, they fired a volley of rounds into the trees. For an instant, the screen filled with a spray of white shards as one of the bullets clipped the birch tree nearby.

She pulled in a sharp breath. The camera had been zoomed in on the house. Yes, they'd only seen one body. But there could easily be three more in the woods.

Blood was streaming down one side of the woman's face. "Those are *our* drones!"

"Not anymore." The words were barely out of the man's mouth when one of the bullets caught him in the shoulder. Both of them nearly went down, but he regained his balance and kept moving, spewing a stream of curses.

A very *familiar* stream of curses, including a few that weren't in English. The words triggered a flashback to crawling through the rubble of the chamber at Icarus Camp and listening to that same voice through her helmet as she tried to hold the pieces of Laura's ripped biosuit together.

"Go back! Just a few seconds. Zoom in on the man's face."

"Sure," Wyatt said. "Hold on."

Once he had it back to the right spot, she told him to stop. The face shield on the man's helmet wasn't completely transparent, but she could see enough to confirm what she already knew from the voice.

"Okay, you can start again."

After the two figures moved past the camera, Wyatt said, "You recognized him?"

She nodded.

"It's not … Beck, is it?"

"No. It's Macek. Kolya's head of security. And I have something in common with that woman, since he's probably the only reason both of us are alive. Assuming those drones don't start firing again..." She stared at the screen. "Wait. Where are the drones?"

"Someone disabled them." He backed the video up again. "You must have missed it while you were trying to figure out if you knew him."

Macek and the woman were once more at the forefront of the screen, but this time, Claire focused on what was behind them. Only two drones were visible, but both of them dropped to the ground, much like the bugbots that she'd been zapping in her cul-de-sac. The other three must have been taken out the same way, because once Macek moved beyond the camera, the view on the screen was exactly what Claire had seen when she came into the room—the house, the brick courtyard, and the dead member of Macek's team.

Her eyes remained fixed on the screen. "If these people have got equipment that can hack expensive drones that quickly, I'm guessing their security system doesn't just incapacitate. We're lucky that Kes didn't get any closer to the house."

"That wasn't luck. I asked why the camera was so far out when I first started going through the footage. According to Kes, that's as close as you can get without tripping the security system. It begins just beyond the tree that got shot up. I think your buddy Macek might want to start prioritizing brains over brawn for his team. But yeah, you're right about them probably having a fully armed system, and I don't even think the incapacitate-only variety is legal here. Not sure how they're going to explain that or the body when the cops arrive."

"Or the armed drones. I'm glad Macek seems to have gotten away, but ... those things have me wondering exactly who the bad guys are here."

"My money is on both. Bad guys fight bad guys all the time." He ran one hand over his scalp. "I need to get back in the shower. I've still got soap in my hair."

"Okay. I'll keep watching."

"Not for long, you won't. Those two cameras are about to go bye-bye."

"Literally?"

"Literally. They're triggered remotely like the ones on that pair of glasses, and they're biodegradable. There's a catalyst inside and when they get the signal to release it, they dissolve within a minute or two. Usually. Which is why we also need to wipe the archive, just in case it doesn't work. I doubt anyone could trace it back to us, but it's not worth the risk."

CLAIRE ARRIVED UNFASHIONABLY early for the cocktail hour, about ten minutes before the doors officially opened at six. There was nothing she could learn at the apartment and watching the attack on Macek's team had left her on edge. She wasn't about to approach Macek with what she'd seen, but she *was* curious as to whether his injury would be enough to sideline him.

When she arrived at the ballroom on the twentieth floor, she handed the young woman at the kiosk her *Atlantic Post* press pass. It had a standard-issue camera at the top, easily five times the size of the one Wyatt had given her, which was attached to a small plastic card and tucked away with her phone in the pocket of her dress.

The girl tapped the press pass against her tablet to register it, and then handed it back to Claire, along with a black magnetic name tag. A gold sticker with the number 1 had been pasted at the bottom. Claire stepped over to the mirror and attached both the badge and the press pass to the silk strap of her dress. It was clunky, but there wasn't much she could do about it.

"Your table number is on the badge," the girl told her. "There's still a little over an hour before we'll begin seating in the main ballroom, but the bar in the galleria will be open shortly. Have a lovely evening."

Claire thanked her and went inside. The bronze glass exterior wall of the galleria overlooked the river, bulging outward from the side of the building like a massive porthole. The galleria itself was separated from the main ballroom by a curved wall of the same glass, forming a long crescent, with the bar that the girl had mentioned near the center. Shadows shifted behind the top and bottom thirds of the inner wall, but the glass was too opaque for her to tell whether Wyatt was among the workers moving around inside the larger room.

The center third of the wall functioned as a viewscreen showing a variety of photos and videos taken on Mars. Some were essentially commercials for Kolya's interests on the planet, highlighting Daedalus City and the various tourist attractions, including his flagship resort, Red Dahlia. Others showed the progress of the terraforming project from the beginning through the current stage, with the highlight being Kolya's carefully timed shot of the neon green *Azospira oryzae* spreading across the dunes of Terra Sabaea. Still other screens highlighted the various investment opportunities, including an opal mine and a new housing development similar to the ones she'd seen at Elysia.

Claire was so immersed in the visual display that she very nearly forgot where she was until a man cleared his throat behind her, jolting her mind back to the present. She turned, expecting to see Wyatt or possibly Paul. To her surprise, however, it was Bryce Avery.

She didn't even bother to fake a smile. Any pretense of collegiality had gone out the window when he lied about being sick in order to avoid a meeting with Devin Shepherd, triggering the course of events that led to the man being killed. It had also led to Wyatt acquiring most of the information they had on Corbin Drexel and the Flock, but Claire had no qualms about focusing only on the bad where Avery was concerned.

Did he know about Devin? For that matter, did he even know that Devin was Wyatt's source inside the Flock? They'd shared a byline on one story about Drexel, but she'd gotten the sense from Wyatt that Avery had just provided some background information. Still, it might be best not to mention Devin unless he did.

"Bryce. What are you doing here?"

"I'm here for the keynote speech. Obviously. Bernard got the invite a few days ago and gave me the assignment. And, if my sources are correct, it should dovetail quite nicely with the *other* story I've been following. But I'm sure you wouldn't know anything about that."

He delivered the last words with a strong verbal eyeroll. It was almost certainly a reference to Devin's murder, but since she wasn't sure, she ignored him and began scanning the room for Wyatt.

"I was actually under the impression that you were covering the conference, too," he continued when she didn't take the bait. "But I stopped in this afternoon and didn't see you."

"How odd. I didn't see *you* there, either."

Avery's eyes traveled downward, and for a moment, Claire thought that she'd have to add lechery to the man's extensive list of negative personality traits. But his gaze halted at her name tag.

"*Table number one.*" He snorted. "Kolya's table, obviously, which means it will be front and center. I should have known you'd leverage your personal relationships to get a better seat. Have you already submitted your story to Bernard? Or are you planning to wait and hit send as soon as the speech ends to at least maintain the *illusion* that you're playing fair?"

Claire sighed, glancing down at the number 16 on the man's badge. "I don't know anything more about this announcement than you do."

That earned her another snort. "*Right.* Well, here's a tip, then. It's *obviously* about stage seven, and the smart money says if stage six is flora, stage seven is fauna. My guess is that he's planning to give us a sneak peek at some of the animal life they've been cooking up over on the Island of Doctor Monroe."

It wasn't the first time that Claire had heard that term used for Davina Monroe's work at Nepenthes. Both Kimura and Chelsea Friesen had dismissed the research of KTI's lead biologist as weird science. The nickname had apparently been Kim's little twist on the title of the H. G. Wells novel, coined after they got an accidental peek at the domes that contained animal life specially designed to thrive in the Martian environment, like Fenris the lemur dog. Claire wondered briefly if Avery had known Kim, or maybe Chelsea, and then decided she really didn't care.

"Everything that woman does would be highly illegal here on Earth," Avery continued, "but KTI is obviously a law unto itself on Mars."

"*Obviously*," Claire repeated, thinking that if the man used that word again, she was going to punch him. "But as I said before, I have no clue. He's being very secretive."

"Ah. So you *have* spoken with Kolya."

"Briefly, yes. But, hey … we'll both know the answers to all of your burning questions in a few hours, right? There's not much point in speculating. I'm going to go grab a drink."

She fully intended it as a dismissal, but Avery said that a drink sounded like a very good idea and followed her over to the bar. Great. The last thing she needed was him tagging along behind her like a … well, she was going to say *like a puppy*, but no puppy could be that obnoxious.

The bartender took her order first, which was *obviously* one more thing Avery would hold against her. Claire glanced around the room as she waited for her drink, both looking for a way to shake her toxic shadow and trying to find Wyatt, so she could give him a heads up to avoid table sixteen. He had a better working relationship with Avery than she did, but she was pretty sure that the undercover shenanigans, especially the surveillance cameras, were strictly Wyatt's idea and not something his editor had approved. His general tactic with Erica leaned less toward asking permission beforehand than begging forgiveness after. And Avery would absolutely rat Wyatt out if he thought it would get under Claire's skin.

But Wyatt didn't appear to be on the cocktail hour side of the ballroom. She did locate Elizabeth LastNameUnknown, however, standing at the far end of the bar with the man she'd sat next to at the panel and another guy who looked vaguely familiar. Claire thought he might have been one of the other men who'd been in the elevator with her and Kolya during the MFL negotiations.

Avery was now grumbling about his expense account, saying that he was trying to decide whether to stay in a fleabag hotel or take the 'loop back to DC after dinner. Claire waited until she had her drink in hand and Avery had given his order to the bartender, then flashed him a split-second smile.

"I just spotted someone from one of the panels this morning and need to ask her a follow-up question or two. I'll catch up with you later."

It might only buy her a couple of minutes. Hopefully, she could at least get close enough to check the table number on the woman's badge so that she'd know where to plant the recording device.

Several of the servers were now circulating the room with an assortment of canapés. One of them stopped near Elizabeth and her companions and offered a tray of tiny sandwiches. They didn't seem to meet with Elizabeth's approval, but she turned away from the bar just long enough for Claire to find out that her last name was Schwick, and she would be sitting at table one. The man who had been talking to her at the panel was named Johnston, also table one, but the last guy grabbed a sandwich from the tray and turned back around before she got a look at his badge. He was definitely one of the mining executives she'd seen at the negotiations, though.

The table assignment was a stroke of rotten luck. As soon as they realized Claire was sitting with them, there would be nothing but polite chitchat. If she was going to get any information at all, it would have to be here and now.

She moved to the very end of the bar, putting a two-person buffer between herself and the trio. Hopefully, that would be enough to keep one of them from spotting her. The good news was that the two people sitting between them were either strangers or so bored with each other's company that they were glued to their devices instead of talking. The bad news was that the room was filling up rapidly. There were well over a hundred people on this side of the barrier now, and her three primary targets all had deep voices that didn't carry well over the din of the crowd. From the few words she could make out, it sounded like they were talking about something that happened at a previous ACon meeting. She listened a bit longer, picking up pieces of the conversation here and there until she finally heard a word that was potentially of interest—*Nepenthes*.

It probably wouldn't have anything to do with Millex, since the mine was located in Cerberus Fossae, about 700 kilometers away. Ehden, on the other hand, was adjacent to Nepenthes Station, so they could be talking about Shepherd's transplanted flock. Davina Monroe's lab was there, as well, and she was an even more likely subject, given the current speculation that her work was connected to Kolya's big announcement.

Curiosity got the better of her, so she popped in her earphones and pretended to check her messages. Instead, she opened the amplifier app that she'd used at Ehden when she listened in on Kolya's meeting with Shepherd. It was almost certainly illegal in New York, but as Wyatt had noted she was already walking on the wild side. Might as well add one more potential crime to her list.

It took a couple of minutes to isolate Elizabeth's voice from the others and dial down the background chatter in the room. By that time, they had moved on to talking about someone who'd recently inherited control of one of the larger thorium mines and was, they all agreed, running things pretty much the same way his father had.

It didn't seem like an especially useful conversation for her purposes, especially when one of the men launched into an anecdote about some disagreement that he'd gotten into with the son, who'd been annoyed that he kept referring to him as Junior. The man had a very circuitous conversation style, and after several minutes of following the twists and turns in the story, she was about ready to switch over and actually check her messages, or maybe scan a few other conversations in the room to see if she could find anything more interesting.

But then the other man chimed in, apparently trying to push his companion to finally reach the point. "Yeah, well, I think we can all agree that kid is going to flame out fast given the pace at which he's been pissing people off."

"Right? That's the same thing Dex Miller told me. Although he added that the kid is ten times worse than his daddy."

Miller. Could be one of the two brothers who owned Millex, so maybe they were going to give her something useful after all.

"Oh, I doubt he's worse," Elizabeth said. "And yeah, I've heard the same rumors you have. We've all heard them. But, come on, Val. We already know there's bad blood there."

"I'm telling you, Dex swears he didn't okay anyone leaving the dome. Claims it was sabotage by Wes's people, just like the bombing in the spring."

Wes. Now they had Claire's full attention. The kid who inherited must be the son of Westmoreland, one of the men who had died in a plane crash while she was on Mars. Claire still wasn't entirely convinced that it had been an accident, especially since she'd seen Westmoreland get into a physical confrontation with Macek the day of the MFL negotiations.

"Thought they pinned that on the Flock," Johnston said. "That Ljubic woman who used to work with Kolya."

"Oh, come on!" Val said. "Dex tells Wes he's planning to agree to the three-quarters deal on the bonuses and … kaboom. The very next day, too. It don't take a genius to make that connection."

"On that point," Elizabeth said, "I'm inclined to agree with you. Someone had to have paid Stasia Ljubic very well to convince her to turn on Kolya. And then Wes shows up dead right after? All of it seems a bit *too* coincidental."

"So you think it was murder, too," Val said. "Question is, who did it?"

She snorted. "All I know is that I wouldn't want to be the person trying to work through the list of suspects. It could have been pretty much anybody on Mars."

Val snorted loudly. "Or, for that matter, anybody he did business with in *Texas*, back in the day. Did I ever tell you about the time that—"

"Exactly," Elizabeth cut in, probably trying to keep him from sailing off into another story. "It could be *anybody*. Wes's baby boy might be ranting about justice, but I can promise you he's the only one. Everyone else thinks justice was served. I think a toast is in order. To Wes. May he rot in hell."

One of the men laughed softly and asked something Claire didn't catch, aside from the last word—*investigation*.

"They're sticking with the sinkhole story," Val said. "I mean, they can't afford to do anything else, right? But Dex told me he's got proof someone released a canister of that green gunk into the ventilation system. I don't know if the can was marked *KTI*, but it don't really need to be for it to cause problems for Kolya. Half the world either watched that stuff spread across the planet live or caught the show in their feeds later. Dex also says they confiscated videos some of those workers took when they started getting sick. Said snot in that same shade of neon green was pouring outta every orifice. Outta their pores, even."

"God," Elizabeth said. "Thanks so much for that visual, Val."

"You're welcome. They got video of the guy who did it, too, but he was in one of them puffsuits. Well, I say *he*, but coulda been a girl inside. You know how them things are. Anyways, they can't see nothin. And then there's a complete communications black-out. Two, maybe three minutes. Not all that unusual in the..." It sounded like he said *CF*. A few other garbled words followed, and then, "... convenient, you know? To have it happen just at the time they need camera feeds to figure out where the killer vanished to?"

"So KTI came up with the sinkhole story?" Johnston asked.

"Dex didn't *say* that, but again, it don't take a genius, right? Kolya's not gonna want it connected to his labs when he's trying to hype everyone up for stage seven. And that goes double if there's any suggestion that the Flock was involved ... from what I hear, all you have to do these days is whisper the name *Corbin* and

Kolya is halfway back to Mars before the word *Drexel* is out of your mouth. I've heard some vengeful ex stories, but—"

A piercing whine filled Claire's ears. She clawed at the earbuds, and in her frantic attempt to remove them, knocked her drink off the bar with her elbow. The liquid sloshed onto her shoes, soaking the carpet around them, and everyone at that end of the bar turned in her direction.

Her ears were still ringing to the point that she could barely hear the voices around her. What could have caused that level of feedback?

The answer to that question came a second later when she bent down to retrieve the glass and saw a pair of dark shoes marching straight toward her.

Even before she looked up, she knew it was Macek.

TWENTY-FOUR

"OH, don't bother with that, Ms. Echols. We'll have one of the staff take care of it."

Even with her ears still ringing from the noise, there was no mistaking the amusement in Macek's voice. Intensely aware of the audience she'd attracted, Claire thanked him and got to her feet.

Macek barked a few words to a man behind the bar and then turned his attention back to her. "All right, then. Let's get you cleaned up so that you can enjoy the rest of the evening."

"That's okay, really. I'll just go to the ladies' room and—"

"No, no. I *insist*." He took her arm with his left hand, ostensibly to pull her back from the server coming around the bar with a whisk broom, but he also took the opportunity to tighten his grip just enough that she knew she wasn't getting away without answering his questions.

Claire followed him around the partition, getting her first glimpse at the rest of the ballroom. Kolya had gone all out. The entire room—walls, ceiling, and even the floor— displayed a video of deep space, creating the illusion that the stage and tables were floating among the stars. The only thing that marred the effect were the exit signs over the doors.

Macek motioned for her to take a seat at one of the back tables, wincing at the movement. That must have been the shoulder that was hit, but it apparently hadn't been anything serious.

"I'm going to get someone to bring a damp towel. *Don't move*." He walked off across the dark sky toward a woman who was lighting the last few candles at the center of the tables.

On the far side of the ballroom, a man burst through a side

door and hurried toward the stage. Claire couldn't see him clearly, but she recognized him as Paul from his walk. Hopefully she'd get a chance to speak to him before she was kicked out.

When Macek returned to the table, he flipped one of the other chairs around and sat facing her, no longer bothering to hide his grin.

She answered it with a sarcastic slow clap. "What a hilarious prank. My ears are still ringing."

"I'll admit it was an amusing spectacle, but it wasn't intentional. When I picked up the signal and realized what you were doing, my plan was to cut in and tell you to stop spying on our guests, but you had the volume up and..." He shrugged.

"So glad that I could give you a chuckle."

"It's been a lousy day, so it was appreciated. Anyway, I'm less concerned with you spying on Liz than I am about the teeny-tiny recorder you have hidden somewhere on your person. It's emitting the same signal as this one." He reached into his pocket and pulled out one of Wyatt's little black dots.

She gave him a faint smile. "Guess I didn't hide that one very well."

"Guess *you* didn't hide it at all. One of my team noticed that your accomplice kept taking his glasses on and off. When she rolled back through the security footage, she spotted him placing several of these little gems at the tables."

"Where is he?"

"No clue. I had a guard escort him to the exit about ten minutes ago. And that's exactly what I *should* do with you. Unfortunately, Kolya seems to be looking forward to your reaction to his speech tonight."

The server showed up with two towels, one wet and one dry, and Claire began cleaning up.

"So, perhaps you'd like to tell me exactly what the two of you are doing?" Macek said.

"Our jobs, same as you."

"Your tools of the trade are of … questionable legality."

"I believe that's something we have in common," she said, thinking of the drones he'd had with him earlier. "But this is also personal for me. I'm still not satisfied with the answers I've gotten for who was really behind me getting *this*." She swiped the wet cloth against her calf with the last word, removing part of the concealer she'd used to cover the scar. "Or for killing Brodnik and Kim. If not for your efforts, it would likely have been me as well. I never got the chance to thank you for that when we were on Mars, so … thanks."

She half expected him to echo her earlier comment and say he was just doing his job, but he simply nodded and said she was welcome. He fell silent for a moment, letting his eyes wander around the ballroom.

"I was about to send one of my people around to collect the rest of Garcia's hidden cameras, but … maybe we can help each other. I'll let those recorders stay in place under one condition—anything you find out has to be cleared with me before going to print. I seriously doubt you're going to pick up anything that my own surveillance team misses, but believe it or not, I want to find out who was behind the explosion at Icarus—and why they did it—every bit as much as you do."

She thought about his offer for a moment while she finished her cleanup. Whatever answer she gave him was effectively tying Wyatt's hands as well as her own. "We can *share* the information with you," she said finally as she placed the towels back on the tray. "We can also agree to let you know before anything goes to print and give you an opportunity to respond. But I can't see my partner agreeing to prior restraint."

Macek didn't look especially happy with her counteroffer, but after a moment, he nodded. "Fine, with one addendum. Tell me about the conversation you were listening to. I caught the last few seconds when I was about to cut in, so I know they were talking about what happened at Millex last month. Liz will give me a report later, but she's been known to be somewhat … selective in the information she chooses to provide."

"She works for you?"

"Not in the formal sense. Let's just say that she finds it in her *best interest* to share information with us from time to time."

Claire had only had a few conversations with Macek. The man's appearance—his build, his scowl, and his general demeanor—made it easy to dismiss him as hired muscle. But he wasn't just Kolya's chief of security. He was also his general counsel. And, apparently, his spymaster, too.

"I can tell you what they were talking about," she said. "But again, I can't guarantee it won't be printed, in part because their conversation confirmed some things we had already learned from more reliable sources." It was actually only one source, as far as she knew, and it was a lie to suggest that the woman was *her* source and not just Wyatt's. But Macek didn't need to know that.

He nodded, and Claire spent the next couple of minutes filling him in on the conversation about Westmoreland's son, leaving out her own personal questions about Macek's role in the father's death. Then she told him what the guy they called Val had said about the contagion in the barracks and the attempt to cover it up.

When she finished, he remained silent for a moment, clearly weighing the pros and cons of whatever he was about to say. "Okay, this is on background. Do not mention my name, or KTI, or even say that the information came from an anonymous source in the company. Are we clear?"

"Yes." Her phone was vibrating in her pocket, but it would have to wait.

"The sinkhole story was Miller's idea. I think he panicked. If he had simply said there was an explosion and a fire, that would likely have been the end of it. But I will give him this. His quick decision to *burn* that building probably saved the lives of everyone else inside the dome. Those workers were already dead or would have been within a matter of hours. There was nothing he could have done to save them, and the fire killed the bacteria and stopped the spread. But yeah. I saw the videos the victims sent out and Valmer's description is fairly accurate."

"So no one is looking into what happened?"

"They're in the middle of a planet-wide lockdown. Once stage six is over and I'm actually on the planet and can investigate…" He shrugged. "It may change. Or it may not. Millex is a contractor of KTI, but they don't operate under the exact same laws that we do at Daedalus."

"So how do *you* think the bacteria got inside? Are the Miller brothers still claiming it was sabotage?"

"It's actually just Dex. His brother came back to Earth years ago. And we don't know how it got into the barracks. All we have is the information the Millex security team has chosen to share. My guess is that Miller sent a work team out as a trial run, maybe because he was being pressured by Westmoreland's people to speed up fulfillment of their new contract. Most likely, a worker got careless and tracked something back in. But I also wouldn't be surprised to learn that the Westmoreland kid engaged in a bit of sabotage. Especially if he learned his business ethics at his father's knee."

She had to bite her tongue to keep from asking about Macek's altercation with the man. He was actually being helpful, and that question would almost certainly end their little détente.

"So you're saying KTI wasn't part of the coverup?"

"No comment. Except, I don't think it's necessarily a bad thing that these rumors about the breach are circulating. If nothing else, it seems to have dissuaded the others who were pushing to get their workers back out there before the official all-clear. Maybe it will save more lives in the long run and make the sacrifice of those who were killed a little less pointless."

His jaw clenched on the last word and Claire was sure he was thinking more about what had happened in Riverdale a few hours ago than about what had happened on Mars a few weeks ago. There was something very vulnerable about his expression, and even though she knew there was a chance she'd regret it, she decided to dig a bit deeper.

"This isn't the only place in the city that we have—or at least *had*—cameras. I'm sorry about your team member and glad to see you weren't seriously injured." She glanced at his shoulder. "Is the woman who was hit okay, as well?"

He stared at her, clearly stunned. There was also some anger in that look, and she found herself very glad that there were several dozen people in the room and a few hundred more on the other side of the glass panel.

"We weren't spying on *you*," she added. "We also want to know what the hell is going on at that house. I don't know how much Kolya told you, but that's where my brother's research partner was abducted. And no, we weren't spying on Beck either. Wyatt just got a tip last week that Drexel was going to be in town and—"

"My other team members are fine. And I got the same tip. We've been sharing information dealing with the Flock for about a month. But this wasn't the first time your people had sighted her without any action, so I'll admit I didn't give it much credence until she showed up here. I called for backup when she left Kolya's apartment. Two of the Beekman Place security guards followed her, and they traced her back to that same address. Listen, though. Kolya doesn't know anything about what happened this afternoon. I was planning to tell him after the speech. He's ... um ... let's just say he's not going to be pleased. He didn't even know I was going over there to investigate."

Claire wasn't sure *investigate* was the right word for showing up with armed commandos and military caliber drones. But she ignored it in order to focus on two things he'd said just before that. The first was about exchanging information *back and forth*. Wyatt's anonymous tipster apparently wasn't as concerned about keeping their identity secret from Macek as they were about keeping it secret from the press.

"I won't mention anything to Kolya," she said. "But a moment ago ... you said you'd shared information before. With whom?"

He raised an eyebrow. "Like I said. *Your* people. The new head of security at Jonas Labs. Guy by the name of Wilson. Do you know him?"

"Very well."

"What are the chances he set me up today?"

"Zero. He gave that same information to us. I've known Wilson most of my life. He's a good man, and even though the tip we got was anonymous, I'm guessing he was the one who sent it to us based on what you've said. I can't imagine him setting *anyone* up to walk into that sort of danger, but there's no way he'd be working with someone who nearly got me killed. But … did the team who tracked Drexel back to that house tell you that she went inside?"

"Yeah. There's a black iron gate on the drive out front. They said the gate opened when the car drove up. After the car went through and disappeared, they parked within sight of the gate and took turns watching the place until this afternoon. No one else went in or out during that time."

"Were either of those people on the team you took out there today?"

"No. Those were *my* people, the guards who travel with us. Like I said, the two who watched the house were Beekman Place security."

"Is one of them a tall woman with a little fringe of bangs on her forehead?"

His eyes widened. "Yes. How did you know?"

"Because I think you're going to find they don't actually work for Beekman Place."

TWENTY-FIVE

BY THE TIME Claire finished with Macek, it was ten minutes until they were supposed to begin seating for dinner, so instead of going back out to the galleria, she found her seat at table one. This would give her a few minutes to check her messages and hopefully get in touch with Wyatt or Kes to see if there was any chance that the archived surveillance video had survived. Macek seemed to believe what she'd told him about the security guards, especially when she added that she had written down the tag numbers of most of the cars that had gone in and out during a time when they'd assured him that there was no activity. Still, he'd clearly have been happier if she had some actual video to back it up.

She couldn't entirely blame him on that front. There was, after all, still a kernel of doubt in her mind as to whether he'd actually told her the truth about letting Wyatt go. It was all too easy to imagine the man locking Wyatt in an interrogation room for a few hours to make him sweat it out. She wouldn't even entirely discount the possibility of someone roughing him up a bit.

After a brief search through her pockets, she realized that she'd lost one of her earphones in the frantic attempt to stop the noise. No way was she going back out there to look for it, though. She switched to mono, stuck the other one in her ear and opened her messages. One was a text from Wyatt, saying simply to call him back. The other was a voice message from an unknown number.

She called Wyatt first. "You got busted," she said when he answered.

"Yeaaahh … and I'm guessing you did, too, if you've already figured that out."

"I did. But I've got some very good information. Some of it is strictly on background, but it's solid. First, though, tell Kes not to send the self-destruct to the cameras you planted here. And if there's any chance that the video archive from the Riverdale house survived, it might come in handy."

"I think that train has already left the station, but I'll check. And I was still debating whether to tell Kes to zap the ones in the ballroom. Kolya's people already know I was the one who planted them. They'll probably bitch to the *Post,* and a lack of physical evidence would be a plus there … but it's also possible that they missed one or two. Why do you think I should leave them?"

"Because we now have an information sharing arrangement with Macek."

"What exactly does that mean?"

Paul was in the ballroom now, talking to a group of servers at the back tables, so she probably didn't have much time.

"It's complicated," she said. "I'll explain more when we're back at the apartment. Are you heading there now?"

"No. I needed food. I'm at that Mexican place on Lexington. I may just work at the bar for a bit afterward and we can go back together when you're done."

"I'm surprised you made it that far before stopping. I saw that the noodles were still on the counter after you left."

"Yeah, I forgot to grab them and there was no time to get anything on the way. And I *would* have stopped someplace closer to the hotel, but I was given a security escort all the way to the edge of the Palace grounds."

Claire pulled in a sharp breath. "Security. That's the other thing I have to tell you before I go."

She filled him in on the fact that the anonymous tip came from Wilson and explained how Macek's team had been set up. "He thought Drexel was inside the house."

"Was he planning to kill her?"

"I didn't ask. But I don't think so. That's not something that Kolya would have forgiven and ... Macek seems very loyal. Anyway, if Kes hasn't deleted that archive, he would be very interested in seeing footage of that gate over the past few days. Can you text me and let me know?"

"Sure."

"As for waiting on me, I'm probably going to be late. You know how these things can drag on."

"How about we play it by ear? Message me when you're done. I'll either be here, or I'll be at the apartment getting the bubble wrap ready."

She laughed. "I need to go. Paul's heading this way."

"Okay. I love you."

"I love you, too."

Paul arrived just in time to catch the last few words. "Well, *that's* new."

"Maybe. Or maybe *not*. I could have been talking to my brother for all you know. Or my cat."

"Well, I certainly *hope* not given the expression on your face a few seconds ago. But hey, that's fine. Keep your little secrets. Love the dress, by the way." He dropped into the seat next to her and drained about half of the water from his goblet. "Speaking of secrets, what were you and Macek in a huddle about when I came through earlier?"

She didn't want to lie to him, especially when she had no way of knowing how much Macek would share with him later. Probably best to go with truthful but vague. "He *may* have caught me eavesdropping on a guest. But we worked it out."

"Are you sure about that? I just saw him in the hallway, and he looked like someone gut punched him. Come to think of it, though, he looked that way earlier. Fingers crossed that he's not coming down with something because I'll end up with it. My immune system is weaker than a newborn kitten when I'm exhausted. Fingers crossed for both our sakes actually." He nodded to the seat on her other side, where the place card read *Jaromir Macek*.

"So the man *does* have a first name."

"It's a *silent* first name. You do see it in print from time to time, but I've never once heard it spoken."

"Well, at least the rush is almost over though, right? You can sleep tonight. And you should tell Kolya you're taking tomorrow off."

"Oh, you sweet summer child. I'm going to be fielding *so many* press inquiries tomorrow." A server was now approaching their table with four people in her wake—Elizabeth, Johnston, and a middle-aged couple Claire didn't recognize.

Paul popped up from his chair like a toaster pastry, causing Claire to wonder whether he was on stimulants or had just downed way too much coffee. She rose as well, and Paul began the introductions.

"Macek should be here shortly," he said once they were all seated, "but we'll have a bit of extra elbow room, since Kolya has decided to take dinner in his apartment with the other person who will be speaking tonight."

"And who might that speaker be?" asked the female half of the married couple, with a slightly petulant glance at the empty chair next to her. Someone had clearly been looking forward to her dinner next to the brilliant Anton Kolya.

Paul shook his head. "Oh, no, no, no. Kolya will have my head on a spike if I spoil his surprise. But you're all invited to the after-party. And I can promise you he'll be much better company when he's not nervous about his speech."

Afterparty. She groaned inwardly, thinking she'd have to message Wyatt soon to let him know there was no point waiting around for her.

A serving cart arrived with a selection of amuse-bouche. Once they were served, Elizabeth—who had taken the seat on the other side of Macek's vacant chair—reached a hand across the table.

Claire's missing and now badly mangled earphone was in the woman's palm.

"I believe you may have dropped this out in the galleria, dear. Unfortunately, it appears to have landed under someone's *foot*."

Even in the dim light, Claire could see the little glint in Elizabeth's eye, and had no doubt that the foot under which it had landed was the woman's own.

The male half of the married couple, whose names she'd already forgotten, asked Claire if she was there as a journalist or a potential investor. "I'm sure you're looking for ways to put the windfall from Rejuvesce into action," he added with a little chuckle.

Johnston sniffed. "Less of a windfall than some of us expected. I'd never have pegged your mother as such an *altruist*." Judging from his expression, that last word left a foul aftertaste.

"That makes two of us," Claire said. She'd very nearly told him that it wasn't Kai, before deciding she was perfectly okay letting her mother take the credit—or blame—if it kept Joe out of the limelight.

Macek arrived at the table shortly after the salads were served, apologizing profusely for being late. He clearly knew the other four people at the table even better than Paul did, and the conversation shifted over to a discussion of Daedalus City, terraforming, and the suborbital resort in which the married couple owned a part interest. Claire joined in occasionally, but mostly focused on her food, which was every bit as good as Elizabeth had predicted earlier in the day.

Her phone buzzed twice while she was eating, so while the entrée plates were being cleared, she excused herself and headed for the restroom. The first message was from Wyatt saying that the archive had been deleted, but Kes might be able to resurrect some of the footage. The second an email from Genni Chatterjee.

She was about to shove the phone back into her pocket but clicked on it out of curiosity.

Claire — I meant to send this before I left for the holiday weekend, but completely forgot, and I took today off, as well, so I'm just getting back to my emails. Hope your colleague's article hasn't already gone to print. The picture is from a VersaBio newsletter in March of 2049. Noah O'Brian is the third guy on the left. And wow—someone should ask John Beckett if he was cloned. 😏

She wanted to close the message without scrolling down to see the photo, but her fingers seemed to be acting of their own accord. Genni was right. Take away the slightly receding hairline and the glasses, the man in the photo could be Beck.

Was Beck.

Claire typed out a quick message—*Should I call you Noah or Anak?*—and attached the picture. Then she sent it to Beck's number.

Might as well let him know the ruse was up.

TWENTY-SIX

"MANY OF THE assumptions that scientists have made about the existence of intelligent life in the universe are problematic, to say the least. In order for such life to develop, every element in the equation—the galaxy, the star, the alignment and size of the planet, a stable orbit, an atmosphere, and so on—needs to line up perfectly. Not too near, not too far. Not too big, not too small. Not too wet, not too dry. If even one of those elements is outside the parameters, you're no longer in that Goldilocks Zone that can create a potential cradle for civilization."

Claire took another bite of her orange mousse cake, trying to keep her mind on what Kolya was saying. Given that most of his talk so far had been recycled from the debate onboard the *Ares Prime*, it would have been difficult for her to focus even under the best of circumstances. But now? Her mind kept going back to that image of a slightly older looking Beck, taken more than three decades ago. Her skepticism had been hanging on by a thread, and that picture had completely severed it. And now Kolya was up there on stage, going on and on about there being no evidence for advanced extraterrestrial life. She was sorely tempted to stand up and ask how much he was willing to bet.

"And even on planets where those elements fall into place," Kolya continued, "life isn't a given. We now know of well over a thousand exoplanets in this galaxy alone that could, conceivably, support advanced life ... and at least a hundred that could, with a bit of work, even support *human* life. But we've seen no evidence that any of them *do*. Worlds capable of supporting life are scarce, but not extraordinarily so. The rare ingredient is the seed that generates life." Three screens appeared on the backdrop behind the stage. "And we now *have* those seeds."

A video of Daedalus City, taken from the spaceport, filled the center screen. The smaller dome housing the chamber was visible, as well. This was the same view that Claire had seen that first day on Mars, the same view that anyone in the ballroom who had traveled to Daedalus would have seen as they approached the resort.

The area inside the domes was unchanged. Dome Three was still barren aside from the black metal crypt in the center. The larger dome was still a lush, artificial fantasyland—Daedalus Disney, as Davina Monroe had called it.

Outside, however, was an entirely different story. Before, there had been nothing but a vast expanse of reddish-brown sand and rock. Now, the area looked much more like the inside of the test dome at Canillo, where Claire had gotten a preview of what would happen in the second half of stage six, after the AE biobots were launched and began to differentiate. The grass here was the same deep green hue, almost the color of spinach, unlike the bright green grass of Daedalus City that would never be viable outside of a dome. This was *Martian* grass. It wasn't quite as high as the field she'd seen inside Canillo and there were a few spotty patches here and there, but it hadn't had quite as much time to grow. Other plants were scattered about, too, including a patch of bamboo off in the distance and something similar to the odd palm-like tree she'd seen in the one section of Daedalus City with plants that—while not *native* to Mars—were still far better suited to the current level of terraforming outside the domes.

"This middle screen is a live shot of Daedalus City—well, as close as you can get to live, given the lag time. On the left, we see very different vegetation at Argyre Planitia—the seedlings you see here will eventually be something similar to a balsam poplar. On the right, we have a bamboo forest north of Nepenthes. You could almost see this species of bamboo growing in real time before stage six, and it should fare even better as the oxygen levels increase."

Kolya paused for a moment and grinned. "This is probably boring the areophiles in our audience who have been tracking the progress of stage six via the cameras we posted at various locations on the planet. What you *haven't* seen, however, are any examples of what we'll be introducing in a later stage of terraforming. Not the *next* stage—this is still a few years down the pike—but I'm going to give you a sneak peek this evening. The following three clips are from a domed crater near Nepenthes Station that's officially named Moghbeli. I've heard that some people have taken to calling it the Island of Dr. Monroe, however, so we may petition to have the name changed."

"Ha! I win the bet," Johnston whispered to Elizabeth.

The three screens blinked out briefly, then the center screen lit up with a video of a herd of creatures that looked a bit like two-humped camels. A few seconds later, the left screen displayed a closeup of a relatively normal looking rabbit, aside from its larger, slightly more protuberant eyes. The rabbit suddenly leapt up and out of the range of the camera, prompting a startled laugh from the audience.

"Wait for it…" Kolya said. "*There.*" The rabbit appeared again in the upper right corner of the screen, still airborne but now little more than a blip. "That's about ten meters, although I've been told they can do better than that when they're startled, thanks to the lower gravity on the planet. And if you look over here at the screen on the right *these* little guys are designed to help keep the bamboo forests clear of debris that might lead to wildfires."

The video on the right-hand screen now showed a bamboo grove. Several lemur dogs were wandering around in the background. One of the creatures that was a bit closer to the camera stared off into the distance, contentedly munching on a bamboo leaf.

Claire dug an elbow into Paul's side. "You're such a liar."

"Thank you," he whispered back. "But am I really? I said

Fenris wasn't in it, and he isn't. Also … this is *not* the big announcement."

"You may have noticed that these animals aren't all that different from their counterparts here on Earth," Kolya continued. "That's because we want colonists to be comfortable with them. We'll also have some varieties of fish and birds. We've had to avoid birds inside the domes, since they wanted to just keep flying. Sometimes, they damaged the tridygel panels and, even more often, the tridygel panels damaged *them*. But once we start introducing species outside the domes, we're looking forward to Martian varieties of chickens, ducks, *geese*…" He gave Claire a slightly condescending smile at this point, clearly thinking of their conversation about Drexel. "Perhaps even some songbirds. And bees, of course. The kind that don't sting but still make honey. All of these species will be lab grown and introduced gradually according to a set schedule. And the best news for those doing business on Mars? There will be no need for a second lockdown." He laughed at the smattering of applause. "I *thought* that might make a few of you smile. But before we move on to my *main* announcement and our guest speaker…"

Elizabeth chuckled and whispered something to Johnston. Claire couldn't make it out, but she was pretty sure he'd just been informed that he had not won their bet. There were similar rustles at the other tables, and she wondered whether Kolya's pause here had been intentional.

"Before we move on," he repeated, "I want to stress that we *could* have introduced animal life to the planet in the same way we did plant life. While the species that I've shown you and dozens more were created within our labs, they were designed specifically to thrive in the environments into which they'll be released. We *could* have simply peppered the surface with the AE biobots, and they would, over the course of about a year, have created lifeforms adapted to the conditions where they landed. This has been done in several dozen terraformed domes scattered across the planet, so we know that it works. And that's precisely what we *would* have done, if not for the desire to avoid either a longer lockdown or a second iteration. We had to take the more complicated path because Mars is not currently a blank slate."

He paused, looking around the room, as the video screens behind him faded into the earlier space backdrop. "Simply put, terraforming is much easier when you start with an uninhabited, unclaimed planet. Which brings us back to my earlier point. There are thousands of barren exoplanets in this galaxy alone where the conditions are amenable to life. Using the most recent models of nanocraft, we can now reach these planets more quickly than the Starshot program did in the 2040s—and instead of merely sending monitors to observe these dark little worlds, we can send the seeds of life that will make them potential homes for future generations of explorers."

As he spoke, pinpoint beams of light shot across the starfield from different locations around the ballroom, sending a cloud of tiny dots off into the ether. "To be clear, that was simulated. We're not there … yet. But we *could* be within a matter of years."

Macek's shoulder bumped into hers as he reached up to tap behind his ear. He listened for a moment, frowning. Then he pushed his seat back and hurried toward the exit.

Kolya glanced his way briefly, then crossed to the edge of the stage where a glass of water was waiting. From Claire's vantage-point, she could see the outlines of the clear table upon which it sat, but it probably appeared to be floating in midair from a few tables back. Maybe Avery had gotten the better seat after all.

After taking a sip from the glass, Kolya sat it back on the table and continued. "I believe we are now on the cusp of the single most important moment in human history. As in other milestone eras—including the Industrial Revolution, the space race, the early years of the internet, and the rise of artificial intelligence—it is not a single advance that catapults us into the future, but rather a matter of synergy. Change becomes exponential, as one advance builds upon the other. And the Flock is right about one thing. Change can be scary. *Progress* can be scary, and when people are scared, they do not tend to act rationally. Therefore, if we are to avoid societal upheaval, we will need to move carefully and with great forethought. We must plan for the future that we want ... and not just for ourselves. Not just for the next generation or the one after that. When societies reach this sort of inflection point, they have to look at the bigger picture. They have to consider all the generations to come. The future of humankind."

Claire's phone emitted the little stutter buzz that signaled an incoming voice call. An unknown number again. Scrolling through, she saw that it was the same unknown number that had left a message earlier. It could be Beck. In fact, she thought that was fairly likely. But after several days of waiting for him to answer, she decided he could damn well wait another half hour until she could get out of the hotel and check her messages.

Kolya walked along the edge of the stage, looking down at several of the tables in the front row. "If I were sitting out there like you with my dessert and coffee, I'd be thinking, *sure ... all of this sounds interesting. But where's the profit and when can I expect to see it?*" He paused. "Those are both fair questions. It will take a decade or more for our little biobots to reach even the nearest potentially habitable exoplanets. For potential colonists to reach those planets would take the better part of a century, barring some major advances in transportation technology—which could easily happen, but I wouldn't want to count on it. So, the answer to the payoff question is definitely not within the next decade. Probably not within the next century.

"And I see several of you out there looking around for the nearest exit. Terrified that I'm about to appeal to those elusive higher angels that *occasionally* overpower your economic good sense. You believe I'm about to say this is the moment to think of your legacy or of the future of your great-great-grandchildren. You'll applaud politely as I walk off the stage, then finish your dessert and walk out of here thinking that you've wasted an evening. But at least the food was good and the liquor plentiful, right? You'll chuckle to yourselves on the way out about Kolya's folly. That may still happen, in which case I'll fund the program myself. Because I could. What I am proposing is not a high-cost venture. I can afford to do it on my own. I *will* do it on my own, if it comes to that. But I'd rather not. For one thing, I like you … well, *most* of you. I like to see my friends succeed. And I think we can agree that it's always better to spend *other* people's money."

Paul was now up, too, moving toward the same exit that Macek had taken. Kolya frowned in his direction but kept going.

"But whether you choose to invest or not, this is a change that we *must* make. I'm sure you're thinking what's the rush? Barring a meteor strike—which is always possible—we have time. We even have a safety valve—an entire planet ready to colonize. Still, I truly believe that if we are to avoid chaos and catastrophe, we must start now. I stand by my statement that there will be no return on your investment in the next decade or perhaps even century. But … I think that will be far less of a negative consideration after you've heard from our guest speaker. Her name is not included on the program because I wasn't entirely sure she was going to accept my invitation until yesterday. It took a trip to Boston and all of my considerable powers of persuasion, but I managed to convince her that our work is far more complementary than competitive."

TWENTY-SEVEN

CLAIRE STARED open-mouthed at the stage, praying that Kolya meant someone else. But those were almost the exact same words that he'd used when he gave her the samples that she brought back to Joe. And ... he'd said a trip to *Boston*.

There was no way her brother would have agreed with Kai making this announcement so soon. As annoyed as he was at Beck for what he perceived as slow-walking, Joe had always been adamantly opposed to revealing any of their research until they had solid results in hand.

And what other reason could Kai have for being here?

Kolya was well into his introduction now, and as he enumerated her mother's achievements, she typed out a quick message to Joe.

> Kai is Kolya's guest speaker at ACon dinner. Did you know?

After a brief hesitation, she added Beck to the message. Whatever else was going on, whatever else he *was*, it was Beck's research, too. Joe would undoubtedly pull him into the conversation anyway, and this really wasn't the time or the place for the Beck-is-an-alien conversation she would soon need to have with her brother.

Claire then fired off a message to Wyatt with the info about Kai, adding at the end that Beck's origins had been confirmed. Then she turned the phone face down in her lap to wait for Joe's response. She was almost certain that this was being done behind his back. And if it was, she needed to find a way to shut it down.

Kai crossed the stage to Kolya and extended her hand. Everyone was applauding now, so she joined in. Several of her fellow diners had already been shooting her annoyed looks for breaching table etiquette with her fevered messaging and she didn't want to give them anything else to talk about.

After thanking Kolya for the introduction, Kai turned to face the audience. The fact that her eyes didn't go anywhere near table one confirmed to Claire that her mother knew exactly where she was sitting.

"Thank you so much. I want to begin by picking up on a point that Anton made a moment ago. We *are* at an inflection point. Events over the next few years will determine the future of the human race. We've been at similar junctures before, and we rarely navigate them well. Consider, for example, how long global leaders delayed meaningful action on climate change. Why did it take so long? The answer is obviously complex, but no one can deny that a major element was the impact that it would have on our economy and the potential ire of investors in the energy sector. Those of us who were alive in the 2040s remember all too well the upheaval when major governments—including our own —finally accepted the reality that prompt and drastic action was the only way to avert a global disaster. Better planning might not have *entirely* prevented that upheaval, but it would certainly have lessened it."

A murmur of dissent came from the table behind her. Claire couldn't pick up the words, but she had a pretty good idea what they were grumbling about. Most of the early colonists on Mars were in the extractives industry, many of them from states like Texas that had flirted with secession. When the state officially returned to the Union, quite a few of them decided they'd rather do business somewhere with less oppressive laws and Mars was, as Paul had put it, the Wild Freakin' West.

"As most of you are probably aware," Kai continued, "Jonas

Labs has been in the middle of a similar furor during the past few months after our launch of Rejuvesce. Much of the anger out there revolves around problems of supply and demand, which will work themselves out in time. Some of it is coming from our own investors who are disgruntled at the company's decision to release the patent after only two years—a decision that was unavoidable, due in part to our reliance on government contracts. I raise this issue because I will soon be asking our investors the same question that I am about to pose to you—how long might you be willing to wait for a return on investment if you knew your lifespan was potentially *unlimited*?"

Claire cursed silently. She'd been hoping her mother would wade in slowly. What if you had a hundred extra years? Even two. But no. The woman just jumped straight off the deep end. Her hand was on the phone, ready to fire off another message to Joe when it double buzzed again. Same unknown number. She started to let it go to voicemail, but instead put in her one good earphone and clicked to answer.

It was Beck. "I *know* you can't talk," he said. "I just need you to listen. You were right, okay? It's a warning. And if you've already listened to the other message, you don't need to worry. I just talked to Joe. He stayed in Maine a few extra days. He's fine. Ro and Jemma are fine. Wilson is increasing their security. I'm trying to save the biodome but ... I think I'm out of time, Claire. I'm sorry. You're safe where you are. Beekman Place is *not* on the list, but I suspect you're about to be—"

Whatever he said next was drowned out by a screech almost as loud as the one that Macek sent through her earphones earlier. The starfield encircling the ballroom went black, leaving the tiny candles in the centerpieces of the tables as the room's only light. Even the exit signs over the doors had gone dark. When she looked back up at the stage, she could make out faint shadows moving as Kolya led Kai down the steps.

Beck was still talking. There were several words she couldn't make out, and then "...be at my quiet place. But I ... whether—"

This time the sound that cut him off wasn't from the ballroom, but rather from Beck's end of the call.

"Beck!" Claire screamed, hoping to be heard over the noise and the screech of chairs as people began moving toward the exits. "Where are you? What *list* are you talking about?"

But the connection was broken.

As she tried to call back, the whining noise faded, and a woman's voice filled the room.

"Please do not panic."

"Well, *that* was definitely the wrong thing to say," Elizabeth muttered.

She was right. Several people were already banging on the doors, which were apparently locked.

"Again, there is no need to panic. Your lives are *not* at risk. You are here to bear witness."

The woman's voice was familiar. Claire's mind immediately went to Drexel, but no. It wasn't her. It was Stasia.

Six pictures of buildings were now visible on the screen behind the stage. The images were off center, and those on the top row were distorted because while the lower three-quarters was displayed on the wall, the top quarter was on the ceiling. Still, Claire had no trouble making out the building on the top right and her breath caught in her throat.

"Three of these facilities are owned by Jonas Labs. Three are owned by Kolya International. The security teams at these buildings were given fifteen minutes' notice. If they acted in a timely fashion, the number of casualties will be minimal. We are not so naïve as to assume that there will be *no* deaths, but we've reached the point where sacrifices are required for the greater good."

Most of the people in the room were now pushing toward the doors, including the couple that had been at Claire's table. Elizabeth and Johnston were still in their seats, although Johnston looked ready to bolt at any second.

Claire's eyes remained locked on the screen. She'd thought at first that they were still photos, but then two of the buildings on the top row shook and collapsed inward. The building on the bottom left went next, followed by the bottom right and center, almost in unison. Jonas Labs was the last to go.

"We are the Flock," Stasia said. "With these acts, we have bought you some time. This choice came at considerable cost to us. *Please use it wisely.*"

A single video now covered the entire ballroom, just as the starfield had while Kolya was speaking. It was a lake at sunset, the sky striped with orange, pink and crimson that reflected back in small patches on the brown lake below.

Once again, Claire heard a squawking noise. But this wasn't an electronic squawk like before. This was more natural, mixed with what sounded almost like applause as a massive flock of birds took wing, rising up from the lake into the clouds.

Thousands upon thousands of birds.

Thousands upon thousands of *geese*.

DARK LITTLE WORLDS

ICARUS CODE BOOK III

AUTHOR'S NOTE

Thank you for reading *First Watch of Night*. I'll keep this brief, since I've left you with a bit of a cliffhanger and time spent on the afterword is time that I could spend working on the final book, *Dark Little Worlds*. If you go to the preorder page, you'll see a date that's early next year, but that's just a placeholder. My current plan is to have the book finished by late summer.

Readers of my previous series know that my academic background is history and political science rather than hard science. I pulled in several readers with a strong background in science for the early stages as I mapped out the project and I've endeavored to get the details as close to feasible for the 2080s as possible. That said, this series isn't "hard" scifi. My interest has always been far more in what science fiction tells us about humanity than in the technical aspects. Where necessary to develop the story and characters, I have once again employed the most versatile and indispensable element in any science fiction writer's toolkit—*handwavium*.

Not every name that follows was involved in the current project, but they've all helped along the way: Peter Walniuk, Teri Suzuki, Oleg Lysyj, Steve Buck, Chris Fried, Theresa Kay, Cale Madewell, Karen Stansbury, Ian Walniuk, Mary Freeman, Meg A. Watt, Aletia Meyers, Alexa Huggins, Alexis Young, Allie B. Holycross, Amelia Elisa Diaz, Angela Careful, Angela Fossett, Ann Davis, Antigone Trowbridge, Becca Levite, Bianca Najjar, Billy Thomas, Brandi Reyna, Chantelle Michelle Kieser, Chaz Martin, Chelsea Hawk, Cheyenne Chambers, Chris Fried, Chris Schraff Morton, Christina Kmetz, Claudia Gonzaga-Jauregui, Cody Jones,

Dan Wilson, Dawn Lovelly, Devi Reynolds, Donna Harrison Green, Dori Gray, Emiliy Marino, Erin Flynn, Fred Douglis, Hailey Mulconrey Theile, Heather Jones, Hope Bates, Jen Gonzales, Jen Wesner, Jennifer Kile, Jenny Griffin, Jenny Lawrence, Jenny MacRunnel, Jessica Wolfsohn, John Scafidi, Karen Benson, Katie Lynn Stripling, Kristin Ashenfelter, Kristin Rydstedt, Kyla Michelle Lacey Waits, Laura-Dawn Francesca MacGregor-Portlock, Lindsay Nichole Leckner, Margarida Azevedo Veloz, Mark Chappell, Meg Griffin, Meredith Winters Patten, Mikka McClain, Nguyen Quynh Trang, Nooce Miller, Pham Hai Yen, Roseann Calabritto, Sarada Spivey, Sarah Ann Diaz, Sarah Kate Fisher, Shari Hearn, Shell Bryce, Sigrun Murr, Stefanie Diegel, Stephanie Kmetz, Stephanie Johns-Bragg, Summer Nettleman, Susan Helliesen, Tina Kennedy, Tracy Denison Johnson, Trisha Davis Perry, Valerie Arlene Alcaraz, and the person (or, possibly, persons) I've forgotten.

And as always, a huge thanks to my family—immediate, extended, and chosen.

In Tobias Shepherd's memoir, he says that he decided to choose hope, and I've done the same in writing the dedication to this book. Those who know me in person or online probably know that Griffin has been my canine writing buddy for the past eight years—a whopping ninety pounds of red fur who has kept my feet warm in the winter and reminded me to get up and take exercise breaks when I'm hunkered down in the Writing Cave. As this goes to print, he's in the hospital recovering from lung surgery, so he's missing the usual celebration … but I'm choosing hope. Griffin *is* going to be here for the next one and hopefully, for at least four or five more after that.

THE DELPHI EFFECT

BOOK ONE OF THE DELPHI TRILOGY

It's never wise to talk to strangers...and that goes double when they're dead. Unfortunately, seventeen-year-old Anna Morgan has no choice. Resting on a park bench, touching the turnstile at the Metro station—she never knows where she'll encounter a ghost. These mental hitchhikers are the reason Anna has been tossed from one foster home and psychiatric institution to the next for most of her life.

When a chance touch leads her to pick up the insistent spirit of a girl who was brutally murdered, Anna is pulled headlong into a deadly conspiracy that extends to the highest levels of government. Facing the forces behind her new hitcher's death will challenge the barriers, both good and bad, that Anna has erected over the years and shed light on her power's origins. And when the covert organization seeking to recruit her crosses the line by kidnapping her friend, it will discover just how far Anna is willing to go to bring it down.

MORE FROM RYSA WALKER

IMPROBABLE

Improbable

Slipstream

Split Infinities

The Icarus Code

The Cold Light of Stars

First Watch of Night

Dark Little Worlds

On Alien Skies

The CHRONOS Files

Timebound

Time's Edge

Time's Divide

CHRONOS Origins

Now, Then, and Everywhen

Red, White, and the Blues

Bell, Book, and Key

The Delphi Trilogy

The Delphi Effect

The Delphi Resistance

The Delphi Revolution

Enter Haddonwood (with Caleb Amsel)

As the Crow Flies

When the Cat's Away

Where Wolves Fear to Prey

Novellas

Time's Echo (A CHRONOS Novella)

Time's Mirror (A CHRONOS Novella)

Simon Says (A CHRONOS Novella)

The Abandoned (A Delphi Novella)

Graphic Novels

Time Trial (The CHRONOS Files)

Short Stories

"The Gambit" in *The Time Travel Chronicles*

"Whack Job" in *Alt. History 102*

"2092" in *Dark Beyond the Stars*

"Splinter" in *CLONES: The Anthology*

"The Circle That Whines" in *Tails of Dystopia*

"Full Circle" in *OCEANS: The Anthology*

Time's Vault: A CHRONOS Anthology

AS C. RYSA WALKER

Thistlewood Star Mysteries

Baskerville for the Bear (novella)

A Murder in Helvetica Bold

Palatino for the Painter

A Seance in Franklin Gothic

Courier to the Stars

Comic Sans for the Ex

Coastal Playhouse Mysteries

The Phantom of the Opal (novella)

Curtains for Romeo

Arsenic and Olé

Offed Off-Broadway

Exes! Stage Right

———

ABOUT THE AUTHOR

RYSA WALKER is the award-winning author of many books, including the best-selling CHRONOS Files. *Timebound*, the first book in that series, was a Grand Prize winner in the Amazon Breakthrough Novel Awards. *The Delphi Effect* was an Amazon Editors' Pick and a finalist in the ITW Thriller Awards. Rysa's books have sold nearly a million copies worldwide and have been translated into fourteen languages.

In addition to speculative fiction, Rysa writes mysteries as C. Rysa Walker. She currently resides in North Carolina.

Check out rysa.com for the latest news or to order signed copies.